SONS OF MACHA

By the same author

Shadowmagic
Prince of Hazel and Oak

SONS OF MACHA

JOHN LENAHAN

The Friday Project
An imprint of HarperCollins*Publishers*
77–85 Fulham Palace Road,
Hammersmith, London W6 8JB

www.harpercollins.co.uk

This edition published by The Friday Project 2013
1

A catalogue record for this book is
available from the British Library

ISBN: 978-0-00-745674-1

Typeset in Adobe Garamond by
G&M Designs Limited, Raunds, Northamptonshire

Printed and bound in Great Britain by Clays Ltd, St Ives plc

MIX
Paper from
responsible sources
FSC www.fsc.org **FSC C007454**

FSC™ is a non-profit international organisation established to promote
the responsible management of the world's forests. Products carrying the
FSC label are independently certified to assure consumers that they come
from forests that are managed to meet the social, economic and
ecological needs of present and future generations,
and other controlled sources.

Find out more about HarperCollins and the environment at
www.harpercollins.co.uk/green

For Tim and Sarah (Mel) Lenahan.
The only ones I still show off for.

Chapter One
Special Agent Murano

He wasn't a Scranton cop. I could tell that as soon as he walked in. The pressed suit and the newly cut hair made me suspicious but the Italian shoes were a dead giveaway.

'Conor O'Neil?' he said in a low voice that made me think he had been practising it in a mirror.

'Hay-na,' I replied using the local vernacular. His confused look confirmed that he was an out-of-towner. Not that I minded; the local police had been none too gentle with me. Understandable, considering they were certain that I killed my father, bombed their police station, hospitalised about two dozen of their fellow officers and kidnapped their favourite detective. So when a Scranton cop elbowed me in the ribs when no one was looking it was forgivable but not pleasant. This new guy was a relief. He looked like he played by the book – hell, he looked like he wrote the book.

'My name is Special Agent Andrew Murano.'

'You're a Fed?'

He flashed his identification card emblazoned with a big 'FBI' across it.

'Wow, what did I do to deserve the Eliot Ness treatment?'

'Kidnapping is a federal crime.'

'Well then you can go home, I didn't kidnap anybody.'

'That's not what Detective Fallon tells us,' the FBI man said, opening a folder on the table between us.

'Well Detective Fallon can kiss my …'

'You claim,' Murano interrupted, 'that you accidentally took Detective Fallon to a magical land where you rode dragons together.'

I winced. 'Well, when you say it like that, it sounds a *bit* far fetched.'

'No, not at all, Mr O'Neil. Do go on.'

I really didn't want to. Telling a story as crazy as mine is kind of fun the first time around but after a while it loses its appeal. I've often heard that women hate it when men mentally undress them with their eyes – well, I had the opposite problem. Everyone I told my story to mentally dressed me *in* a straitjacket. But I recounted my tale once again, 'cause Brendan told me to tell the truth.

Brendan and I had arrived from Tir na Nog into the Real World not far from Brendan's house. The portal connecting The Land to the Real World deposited us inside a small patch of trees exactly at the spot where Brendan's mother said mystical ley-lines converged. Brendan had always considered that just another one of his mother's hippy-trippy crazy ideas, but he was learning that many of her crazy ideas were turning out to be true. Detective Fallon and I were the only ones who made the trip. Essa was supposed to join us but she was still mad at me for the Graysea thing.

Brendan's mother Nora was one of those older women who looked great even into her seventies. You could see by her face that she had all of her marbles (and then some) and her physique showed that she was still strong. Good thing too, 'cause the shock that Brendan and I gave her when we showed up to the front door on horseback would probably have killed a lesser senior citizen.

When his mother asked him where he had been, Brendan started by saying, 'You're not going to believe this.' But only a couple of minutes into the story it was plain to see that she did. She had believed in Filis and Faeries and Brownies and Tir na Nog all of her life and tears came to her eyes as Brendan told her that the Queen of the Druids recognised him as one of their own.

Brendan's daughter Ruby was at school. He wanted to go and get her but Nora convinced him that that was a bad idea. He was apparently a very famous missing person. There had even been a TV show recreating Mom and Nieve's attack on the police station and Brendan's picture had been on every TV, newspaper and Internet screen in the country. Showing up in a third-grade class-room, we decided, might cause a bit of a commotion.

We were sitting down to a nice cup of tea in the kitchen when Brendan saw something outside the window and said, 'Oh my gods.' He jumped up and took a big carving knife out of a wooden block on the counter and said 'Take it!'

I did.

'Now drop it.'

I didn't have a clue what was going on. 'What?'

'I said drop it.'

He was so frantic I did what I was told.

Then he said, 'Tell the truth – it'll keep you out of a serious jail until I can figure things out.'

Before I even had time to say, 'Huh?' a zillion screaming cops barrelled in the front and back doors with guns drawn. Brendan hit me in the stomach, spun me around and dropped me to the ground with my arm twisted behind my back. 'I've got him,' he shouted. 'He's disarmed!'

I was cuffed, dragged to my feet by my hair, slammed against the wall and then tossed head first into a police wagon. All the while I kept hearing cops asking Brendan how *he* was. I saw

Brendan's mother on her porch as they were closing the doors of the van.

'It was very nice to meet you, Mrs Fallon,' I said.

Brendan was right. Telling the truth got me a room in a secure mental hospital where my daily interrogators alternated between cops who wanted to kill me and shrinks who wanted to understand me. I couldn't decide which I liked better. Special Agent Murano was my first change in a couple of days.

I took a deep breath and told the story of how my dad was not dead. That he was alive and well in Tir na Nog, the mythical Irish Land of Eternal Youth, where I assisted him regaining the throne by helping him attach his missing hand and then chopping off my uncle's hand.

Then I narrated the story of how, when I got back home, Detective Fallon arrested me for my father's murder and how my mother and aunt busted me out of jail and how they took me back to The Land and how Detective Fallon got transported with us by accident and then we had to search all over The Land and had to fight a battle and ride a dragon so I could use its blood to save my father's life. And now we are back again so Brendan can see his daughter and tell his mother that he is a Druid. I left out the mermaid stuff 'cause that just sounded kooky.

When I finished I had a long hard look at Special Agent Murano to see if I could figure out which group he was going to join. The group that thought I was crazy or the group that thought I was pretending to be crazy. Agent Andy was difficult to read. He clicked off his tape recorder and tilted his head towards the armed guard that was standing by the door.

'Would you object, Conor, if we had a little conversation in private?'

'Why?'

Agent Murano leaned in so close I could smell his heavy cologne. 'I have a lot of experience with unusual events,' he said in a conspiratorial whisper. 'Let's just say I would prefer to talk about your situation without prying eyes.' Then he winked at me.

'What, are you like an X-File guy?'

He smiled. 'When we are alone.'

'OK,' I said.

The FBI man dismissed the guard and then lowered the Venetian blinds that were in front of what I assumed was a two-way mirror.

I started to get excited. When you tell a story as crazy as mine, to as many people as I had and none of them believe you – you start to doubt your sanity. Could it be that I had finally met some-one who truly believed me?

'Have you met people from The Land before?'

The agent shushed me, took off his jacket and covered the secu-rity camera that was mounted on the corner of the wall.

'So you have a file on Tir na Nog, right?'

Once again he raised his finger in front of his lips, picked the intercom off the table and unplugged it. Then after looking around to see that no one or nothing could overhear us, he covertly gestured for me to come close. I stood and looked around myself. It was very cloak and dagger. I just got within striking distance of him when – that is exactly what he did – he struck. He slammed the intercom into my stomach just below my ribs. Whether he had been trained or had lots of practice in using office equipment to cause pain, I don't know, but he was certainly good at it. Every molecule of air flew out of my body and the agonising spasms in my solar plexus made it so I was having a hard time replacing any of them. I was on the ground, doing a convincing impression of a fish out of water, when he bent down and slammed the intercom into my right shin.

I once heard that the only good thing about pain is that you can only experience it in one place – let me tell you now: that's not true. Getting slammed in the shin just meant that I hurt from my chest to my toes. Then he slammed the damn thing into my head and I hurt all over. I tried to ask why but my breathing still wasn't working and then I had a thought that terrified me so much I didn't even care about the pain.

'Did Cialtie send you?' I said as loud as I could.

Apparently it wasn't very loud at all because Agent Murano leaned over and said: 'What did you say?'

'Were you sent by my Uncle Cialtie to kill me?'

He grabbed me by my hair and dragged me back into a chair where he handcuffed my hands behind my back.

'Still with the Faerieland stories. Do you want me to kick the crap out of you again?'

'No,' I answered honestly.

'Then enough with the dragons and the Pixies.'

'There are no Pixies in Tir na Nog.'

That line earned me a backhand across the face that made my vision swim for a second. 'What do you want?'

'I want you to knock it off with the insanity talk. The last four federal crimes I have investigated in this state have all gotten off with insanity pleas. My nickname in the office is The Shrink. I refuse to lose another case to the nuthouse.'

Relief washed over me; he was not an assassin hired by my uncle, he was a plain old ordinary Real World jerk. I smiled.

'What, O'Neil, is so funny?'

'The Shrink,' I said laughing.

Murano flew into a rage, he re-hit me in the stomach and over-turned the chair I was cuffed to, my head bounced off the floor and I thought I was going to throw up. I really didn't want to get hit again but I couldn't help it, I was still laughing.

'OK, OK,' I said, my face pressed against the linoleum. 'What do you want me to do?'

The agent picked me off the floor – the cuffs cut in to my wrists. He put his face inches from mine. For a horrible second I thought he was going to kiss me. 'You are going to confess to being a terrorist.'

'What?'

'You're going to admit that you are a terrorist. You don't have to name names. You can claim that you never met your masters but you kidnapped Detective Fallon because you hate your country.'

'You're crazy.'

'Maybe I am,' Murano said, 'but I'm going to make sure you are *not* crazy.'

'So let me get this straight – you are punching a man who is tied to a chair and I'm the terrorist?'

The crazy G-man tipped my chair over once again. This time I think I did black out for a short time. The next thing I remember there was drool on the floor and I finally had a pain in my head that hurt enough to block out all of the other pains in my body.

'OK, OK, I said, 'I'll say anything you want. Let's just try and keep my grey matter inside my skull.'

You know all that talk about how advanced interrogation techniques are no good because a tortured prisoner will tell you anything? Well, it's all true. I talked about how Tir na Nog was really a code word for a bunch of anarchists that wanted to overthrow the United States of America and then the world. When I started to get too outlandish, Agent Murano shook his head until eventually I just let him write my confession. We started getting along so well I even persuaded him to get me a burger and a shake. Don't get me wrong, I still loathed the man. Anyone who would use their power to beat a shackled insane person (I know I'm not really insane but he didn't know that) is just below snakes – and that's giving snakes a bad name. I was slurping at the last of my shake when Murano came in holding my 'confession'.

I hesitated before signing. I had been called a lot of nasty things in my day. Once I had even been called 'unfunny' (can you believe that?). But 'terrorist' was not something I wanted people saying about me. I imagined that in prison hierarchy, a terrorist would be just a tiny step above a guy who cooks puppies for supper.

'I don't think I can sign this,' I said.

'You want we go through all this again, O'Neil?' Agent Murano said, rubbing his knuckles.

'Well the way I figure it, either I get a beating from you today or I get one every day from my white supremacist flag-loving cellmate. Sorry, Andy, but I'm sticking with the fire-breathing dragon story.'

'Sign it,' the FBI man said as he stepped menacingly towards me.

'No.'

'SIGN IT!'

'Sign what?' Brendan said as he entered the room. The so-called kidnap victim was flanked by a local cop in uniform and an old, grey-haired lady that I at first thought was his mother. Brendan picked up my confession and scanned it. I kept staring at the wrinkled face of the old lady – something about her intrigued me.

'So you're a terrorist now?' Brendan said to me.

'Special Agent Murano thinks so.'

'Did he coerce you?'

'I'd say he counselled me,' I replied. 'Agent Andy is like a shrink.'

Murano bristled and pulled Fallon into the corner. I'm sure the special agent meant to whisper but he was worked up and not doing it very well. I could hear every word.

'What do you care if I rough him up a bit? According to the report he had you locked up in a closet for a couple of months.'

'It wasn't that bad.'

'Come on,' Murano said, 'you probably want to take a few pops yourself.'

'I'm not sure his attorney would approve,' Fallon said, pointing to the old woman.

'No,' the grey-haired woman said, 'I'd be fine with that.'

At the sound of her voice all the hairs on the back of my neck stood straight out.

'No you are not,' Fallon said to her. 'You were about to tell your client not to sign anything.'

'My what?'

'Your client, Mr O'Neil?' Brendan said pointing to me. 'You were about to tell him not to say or sign anything.'

'Oh yes, I was.' A look of confusion crossed her face – it was maddeningly familiar. 'Yes, what Brendan said – do. Or don't do.'

The old woman tilted her head down and with inordinate interest began inspecting the bulb on the desk lamp.

'She was also about to say that she would like some time alone with her client.' Brendan stared at the woman again. 'Wasn't she?'

The woman straightened up and hurriedly said, 'Yes, I'd like to be alone with Master On-el.'

'O'Neil,' Brendan corrected.

'Yes, Prin— Mr O'Neil.'

Agent Murano finally took notice of the woman. 'Can I see some identification please?'

'Some what?'

'Identification.'

The old woman looked like she didn't know what he was talking about. She looked over to Brendan and said, 'Can we get on with this?'

'Yeah,' Brendan said with a sigh, 'go for it.'

The woman reached up to her ears and pulled off the marble-sized gold earrings that were hanging from her lobes. She held the two shiny spheres in her palm and incanted under her breath. The gold balls glowed then rose from her palm and encircled each other like tiny binary stars.

The uniformed cop stepped in to get a better look but Murano backed up and said, 'What the—' He didn't get to finish before the two balls shot through the air and exploded into the chests of the two officers. They were thrown against the wall in a shower of light. When I could see again it looked like they weren't getting up any time soon.

Brendan went through the FBI man's pockets for the handcuff key while the old woman checked on the health of the cop.

''Bout time you got here,' I said to Brendan. 'That Fed is a nutcase. It was only a matter of time before he dropped a starving rodent down my trousers.'

I stood up and went over to where the old woman was holding the policeman's head. I leaned in and took a close-up look at the old woman.

'Essa?'

She smiled – it wrinkled up her whole face. 'Miss me?'

Chapter Two
Ruby

'Essa, you're so …'
    'I'm so what?' she said in a tone that sent warning bells exploding in my brain. 'How do I look, Conor? Tell me.'
    'Well, you look …'
    'If you say "wrinkled" I'm going to chain you back to that chair. For you, I got off my horse and set foot on the ground in the Real World. Because you and Brendan don't know how to hide, I am what an eighty-year-old woman looks like in this gods forsaken land. So once again, how do I look?'
    'I was just about to say that you don't look a day over seventy.'
    'Can we get out of here please,' Brendan said, 'I've just assaulted a federal agent. I'd like to be gone before that appears on my permanent record.'
    Essa opened her briefcase and took out a jar of Vaseline.
    'Are we going to slide out of here?'
    Essa didn't even bother with a dirty look.
    'Oak tree sap,' Brendan said. 'It was my mother's idea to put it in a Vaseline jar to get it past security.'
    Essa smeared the sap in a circle on the windowless wall. Then she placed her hand on the sticky circle and incanted. When she removed her hand a gold handprint glowed in the brown circle. She straightened up, groaned and rubbed her back.

'Ready to leave?'

'I sure am, grandma.' That got me a dirty look.

She shouted a single word that sounded like a sneeze and the circle silently blew out of the wall. Daylight poured in among the dust and I could see parked cars through what moments earlier had been a wall.

Brendan crouched down and pointed. 'We have to get past that gate. My car is parked on the other side.'

I walked over to the unconscious Agent Murano. He was starting to come round and if I was honest, I'd have to admit that I was toying with the idea of kicking him in the ribs so he would have something to remember me by. That's when I saw it. Brendan had emptied the FBI man's pockets looking for the handcuff key. In a pile on the floor, was scattered change and car keys attached to a keychain that said Porsche.

'I've got a better idea.'

In the parking lot I pressed the fob attached to the keychain and lights on Agent Andy's white sports car blinked. It was almost like his car was saying 'Steal me.' The car, like the special agent's shoes, was meticulously cleaned and waxed. It wasn't new but he tried to make it look like it was – right up to the new-car smell air freshener. It was obvious that my torturer loved this vehicle and I was looking forward to smashing it through the front gate. I didn't get a chance. Brendan wouldn't let me behind the wheel. He pointed out that he'd been trained in high-speed driving and I had only been driving for a year. I wouldn't have gotten to smash it into the gate anyway because it was open. We zoomed past a surprised (and soon-to-be unemployed) guard without even a scratch.

It was a tight fit in the car. I got stuffed in to the back and we broke all Pennsylvania speeding laws. After my incarceration I needed some air, so I reached into the front and pulled the latch for the convertible top. The wind took the roof and ripped it right off the car.

'Oops,' I said with a smile worthy of Fergal.

'Yeeha!' Essa whooped.

I laughed and shouted over the sound of the rushing wind, 'Where did you learn to do that?'

'Isn't that what you and Fergal used to do when you were excited?' Essa said, her grey hair swirling around the car.

'It is – well remembered.'

Brendan was tearing around the back country road at an alarming speed. I would have thought that Essa would be terrified but she loved it.

'This is like being on dragon-back,' she shouted. 'Can everybody go around in contraptions like this?'

'If they go this fast they get in trouble from the police,' Brendan answered.

'But it's OK because you are police – right?'

'Not any more,' Brendan said, 'I handed in my badge the instant the FBI man hit the wall.'

Brendan slowed a little bit as we turned onto the narrow roads that led to his house. At last we skidded around a corner and saw Brendan's mother and daughter waiting for us at the exact place where Brendan and I had arrived from Tir na Nog a week earlier.

It was the first time I had ever seen Brendan's daughter. She stood there in a purple tie-dye tee-shirt, a small pack on her back, a white stick in her hand and classic full-sized Ray-Ban sunglasses that took over her whole face.

Essa quickly busied herself opening the portal. Brendan's mother, Nora, said, 'It is very nice to see you again, Conor. Are you OK?'

'I'm fine, Mrs Fallon.'

I crouched down and addressed Ruby. 'And you must be Brendan's little Gem?'

Ruby straightened up and said, 'Only Daddy can call me Gem.'

'Oh, sorry. It is very nice to meet you, Miss Fallon.'

She shot her hand straight out in front of her. 'It is nice to meet you, Mr O'Neil.'

We shook. 'Call me Conor, Mr O'Neil is my dad. Can I call you Ruby?'

'You can call me Miss Fallon.'

'That's my Gem,' Brendan said smiling.

'Well, Miss Fallon, I like your shades.'

Ruby adjusted the huge sunglasses. 'If they're good enough for Ray Charles,' she said, 'then they're good enough for me.'

'Indubitably,' I agreed.

The sound of distant sirens pulled my attention away from the undersized child in the oversized sunglasses. Essa had started the portal to Tir na Nog – there was an outline hanging in the air but it didn't look like anything I wanted to step into.

'Pick up the pace, old lady,' I said. 'We'll soon have company.'

'You want to do this, Duir Boy?' she grumbled. 'Stepping through an unstable portal is almost as dangerous as calling me "old lady".'

'Seriously,' Brendan said. There was concern in his voice. 'How long?'

'It could be soon if you would allow me to concentrate.'

Brendan and I left her alone. The noise of the approaching sirens meant the cops were almost there.

'We've got a problem,' Brendan said.

'You think?'

'Essa wields our only non-lethal weapon and she's busy opening the magic thingy.'

'You missing your bow and arrows?'

'If the cops get here before she finishes they'll shoot you.'

'Me?' I said. 'What about you? How about when they get here, I tell them that this is all your fault, 'cause now that I think about it – it is.'

'I've got an idea of how to slow them down,' Brendan said, 'if Ruby is game.'

For the record I thought it was a dreadful idea. And it certainly made it so I can never return to the Real World. When the two cop cars screeched to a halt in the gravel road, Brendan and his mother stood in front of me frantically waving their hands. Three policemen and Special Agent Murano all got out – guns drawn.

'Don't shoot,' Brendan shouted. 'He's got my daughter.'

What the cops saw was me holding a knife to little Ruby's throat. Actually it was the nail file from Brendan's Swiss army knife but hopefully none of the cops' eyesight was good enough to notice that.

'Stand back coppers,' I said in my best Jimmy Cagney voice, 'or I'll let the girl have it.'

That was Ruby's cue to let loose what her father called one of her 'migraine screams'. Despite the name, I was unprepared for the ear bleeding, high-pitched volume of the screech. I almost dropped the knife and I'm sure that every dog in a five-mile radius ran underneath a sofa.

'Ow,' I said.

Brendan turned around and whispered, 'Told you so.'

'Take it easy, O'Neil,' one of the policemen shouted.

'I don't want to talk to you. I want to talk to The Shrink.'

'OK, O'Neil, we'll get you a psychologist,' the cop replied. 'It's just going to take a little time.'

'I don't want to talk to a psychologist, I want to talk to THE SHRINK aka Agent Andy. Didn't you guys know? That's what they call him at FBI central.'

'Don't hurt the girl, O'Neil,' Murano shouted.

Ruby let loose another one of her sonic screams that made us all tilt our head a bit until it was over. I was surprised that the lenses in her Ray-Bans didn't shatter.

'This is your fault, Shrink,' I shouted. 'I was a mild-mannered fantasist before you tied me to a chair and tortured me. You turned me into a child killer.' I gave Ruby a shake for effect and she bit my arm. It really hurt. I lowered the knife and I saw the cops levelling their guns.

Brendan stepped in front fast and said, 'Don't shoot,' while I repositioned the nail file. I whispered to Ruby, 'What you bite me for?'

She whispered, 'I'm trying to make it look good.'

'Well, ow,' I said and then got back to work on the FBI man. 'So is attacking a shackled man in the FBI interrogation book?'

'I never …'

'Don't make me do it,' I shouted. 'You know what you did. You tortured me and wrote out a fake confession.'

I was stalling for time but I also wanted Murano to feel a little bit guilty about all this. I'm sure in his mind he now felt exonerated about how he treated me. After all, I wasn't being very chivalrous – I had a knife to the throat of a young blind girl – but I hoped that someone would investigate his actions and get him busted to airport bathroom security.

'Almost there,' Essa shouted.

'Thank the gods,' I said.

'O'Neil,' Murano said, 'what is the old woman doing?'

The familiar ring of an active portal reached my ears as Essa said, 'Who you calling old?'

Mom, Dad and Nieve burst through the portal on horseback. Mom threw two of her Shadowmagic exploding light bombs at the two cops on the left and Dad and Nieve threw what looked like small knives at the other cop and the FBI man. The knives swerved directly into the chests of the cop and Agent Murano.

While Mom's victims were blown off their feet, the cop and the FBI man just looked at the knives sticking out of their chests and fell over backwards.

'Hi, son,' Dad said casually as he rode over to Murano.

'You didn't have to kill them!' Brendan shouted as he ran to the FBI man and reached for the knife sticking out of his chest.

Dad stopped him. 'It's not a knife.'

'I can … I can't move,' the Fed said.

'It's a knife handle but no blade,' Dad explained, 'instead of a blade it has one of Nieve's paralysing pins in it. Pull it out.' Brendan pulled the knife blade out of the FBI man's chest and looked at the gold pin.

'Cool,' Brendan said and handed it to me.

Murano sat up and felt his chest. 'I can mo—'

I stuck the pin/knife back in his chest and he fell over like a stuffed teddy bear.

Nieve rode over and while hanging dangerously low to the side of her saddle, gave Brendan a long kiss. When it seemed like it would never stop, Brendan's mother gave a discreet cough. Brendan looked up to see his mother staring at him with her arms crossed.

'Oh yeah. Um, Mom, Gem, this is my … friend, Nieve. Nieve, this is my mother Nora and my daughter Ruby.'

Nieve replied, 'It is very nice to meet you, I've heard so much about you both.'

'We'll have plenty of time for niceties once we are back in The Land,' Mom said, riding by. 'Let us leave this place.'

Brendan turned to his mother and daughter. 'Are you sure you want to do this? You might not ever get to come back.'

'We have already discussed this,' Nora said. 'What you did today was right and I am proud of you but your actions mean you can no longer stay here.'

'We want to be with you, Daddy,' Ruby said taking her father's hand. His mother took the other and the three of them walked through the portal.

Mom was next. I asked her to relay a message to Tuan for me when she got back to Tir na Nog then I cuffed the cop with his own handcuffs and hog-tied the FBI man with his belt. I took back the paralysing throwing pins and made sure that Murano could see both the portal and his car. The Fed was obviously very shook up and when he finally could find his voice he asked, 'Who are you people?'

'We're Faeries from Pixieland and you, Agent Andy, are a jerk, but you were right about one thing – I'm not crazy. I really did ride a dragon and to prove it to you …' I grabbed his hair and turned his head towards the portal. Tuan in all of his dragon splendour popped his head through and Agent Andy gasped.

'I was thinking about having him eat you,' I said as I walked over and gave Tuan a rub on the snout, 'but then I had a better idea.'

I whispered into Tuan's earhole and stepped back. He gave a shrug that meant, 'If that's what you want', and puffed a perfect little ball of fire directly at Agent Murano's precious Porsche. The car exploded and as the radiator ruptured it gave out a little squeal like a dying mouse. The look on Murano's face almost made this whole debacle seem worthwhile.

Chapter Three

Macha

Ruby stood in the centre of the Hall of Spells. She tilted her head and spun, dragging her stick on the tiles that represented all of the major runes. 'We're not in Scranton any more.'

'How can you tell that?' I asked.

'I'm blind, not stupid.'

'Ruby!' her father and grandmother shouted simultaneously.

The young girl shrugged, turned to me and said sorry, but it didn't seem like her heart was in it. I laughed.

'Don't encourage her,' Brendan said. 'We are working on Ruby's rudeness.'

'Well,' I said, 'it sounds like frankness to me. If I need an honest opinion I will know who to ask.'

'See?' Ruby said to her father.

'Ruby's opinions tend to be too honest.'

I looked up to see Mom and Dad standing waiting for our discussion to end. I cleared my throat and pointed to Brendan's mother and daughter.

'Nora and Ruby, may I present to you Lord Oisin of Duir and Princess Deirdre of Cull – my mom and dad.'

Nora bowed then whispered to Ruby who bowed too. As she did, Ruby's huge sunglasses dropped from her face. Her eyes were dark blue and seemingly unharmed but scars were still visible high on her cheeks where the shards of glass had entered her face and ruined her optic nerve.

Mom stepped up and took Brendan's mother by the shoulders. 'It is I who should be bowing to you,' she said with a nod of the head. 'You risked your lives today in aid of my son.'

'I would hardly say our lives were at risk, Your Highness,' Nora said.

'You went toe to toe with the FBI and the Scranton cops,' Dad piped in, 'I'd say you were risking something. Welcome to Castle Duir. This is our home and for as long as we live here, it is your home as well.'

I leaned in to Nora and whispered, 'And people live a long time around here.'

'Daddy promised me a huge bedroom,' Ruby announced. 'I'd like to see it now.'

'Ruby,' Nora and Brendan again admonished in unison, but Mom, Dad and Nieve just laughed.

'Of course,' Mom said. 'You must be tired. Let me show you to your rooms.'

As Mom and Nieve escorted the Fallons to the west wing, I looked about for Essa and Tuan but they had left.

'I think she is off with Tuan getting a dragon blood youth tonic,' Dad said.

'Who?' I said nonchalantly.

'Who?' Dad scoffed. 'Essa, the princess that you are looking for.'

'Who said I was looking for Essa?'

'Oh, my mistake,' Dad said sarcastically, 'maybe you were looking for Graysea? By the way, how are the princess and the mermaid getting along?'

'You're enjoying this, aren't you Dad?'

'Oh yes,' Dad said over his shoulder as he ran to catch up with Mom.

Dad came into my room as I was practising my knife throwing. He gingerly pulled the dagger from the wall and inspected the woodwork. 'Don't do that.'

'Mom and Aein told me that you used to do it.'

'Yes and I got in trouble with my father for it too. I'll get you a dart board or something. Just go easy on the walls. It probably took an elf fifty years to carve this little section.'

'OK,' I said, 'sorry.'

Dad laid the knife across his palm, feeling its balance. 'You're not using one of Dahy's gold-tipped specials?'

'No, it's too easy. Also I don't like seeing the way the knife swerves in the air. It … it reminds me of how Spideog died.'

'Oh, of course,' he said, handing me back the knife, 'I was sorry to hear about that. You really liked him, didn't you?'

'Yeah, I did. You didn't though, did you?'

'Oh, I wouldn't say I didn't like Spideog, it was just … well, now that I think about it, I really didn't know him very well. You have to realise that I was Dahy's student from a young age so I just took my master's side. I never really knew what those two guys were feuding over until you told me. It makes sense now. Dad never talked about my mother much. Most of the things I know about her are from what Dahy told me.'

'Don't you remember Macha at all?'

'Oh, I have a memory of smiling eyes, but maybe it's just a false memory that my child mind conjured up while looking at her portrait.'

'Is there a picture of her in the castle?'

'Sure – in the north wing.'

'Can we go see it?'

'Now?'

'Why not?'

We walked through the castle together. Jeez, I thought the bowing and scraping was bad with me but for Dad it was just short of grovelling. He didn't try to discourage it. It was the way I was dealing with it too. You just can't spend all day saying 'Stop that.'

Even though Dad looked like my fraternal twin he was starting to regain the grown-up manner that I remembered. When he first regained his youth by drinking Tuan's dragon blood he acted exactly as he looked – like a teenager. He still drags Mom giggling into private corners of the castle but he doesn't do it *all* the time and he has stopped challenging me to wrestling matches.

'So how's the kinging going?' I asked as we walked.

'To be honest, it's a lot of paperwork,' he said. 'All of the king-doms are kicking up a fuss about the volatility in Duir and espe-cially how unreliable the gold stipends have been. Mom's been a huge help. She has been holding them off while I was ... resting – but now everybody is looking for stability. I'd like a little stability myself but I think pretty soon my brother is going to do some serious destabilising.'

'He told me he wants the throne.'

'Not surprising. Once a guy like Cialtie gets a taste of power – it's hard to let it go.'

'I don't think it's that,' I said. 'I mean it's not just that. He told me that if he became king he would be safe.'

'I wonder where he got that idea.'

'Ona's book.'

That stopped Dad in his tracks. 'What book?'

'Cialtie showed me a book that he found in Ona's bedroom the day he killed her.'

'He told you that?'

'Yeah, but he wasn't bragging. He really believes that he can do nothing except what she wrote in that book.'

Dad started walking again. 'And she wrote that he would be safe if he was king?' When he spoke it was more like it was to himself than me. 'If he had just told me that, maybe I would have renounced the throne … but I did renounce the throne. He had the throne. Why did he insist on trying to blow things up?'

'He told me that he wanted to free The Land of Ona's prophetic chains.'

Dad snorted with derision. 'Freeing The Land by destroying it – typical Cialtie.'

We rounded a corner and entered the north wing's portrait gallery. Pictures lined the walls stretching into what seemed like infinity. That's the funky thing about living in a huge castle. You think you have explored every nook and cranny and then you come across an amazing place you have never seen before.

'Wow,' I said, 'Who are all these people?'

'These are portraits of all of the major and minor rune holders in The Land, and all holders of a yew wand.' Dad pointed far into the distance. 'Your grandmother is over here with the House of Nuin.'

As we walked I asked, 'Can I get one of these?'

'I'd love to have a picture of you if you would ever hold still long enough to sit for one, but I can't hang it in the north hall until you have taken your choosing. I don't have a portrait yet either. Tell you what, after your choosing we should get our pictures painted together.'

'OK,' I said, but didn't relish the idea of having to have to sit still for hours while Dad bestowed his pearls of wisdom.

I spotted the portrait of Macha before Dad pointed it out to me. She had amber hair like Nieve and Dad's long face but her eyes weren't dark like her children's. Her eyes were clear blue – like mine. She was portrayed sitting astride a black horse holding the reins with one hand and her yew wand in the other. Behind her was a hawthorn in full bloom.

'She's definitely your mother,' I said.

'Yes,' he said dreamily like he was lost in the picture.

'You once told me she went on a sorceress's quest and never returned.'

'That is what my father told me but I had a talk with Dahy recently and he says one day – she just vanished.'

'You talked to Dahy about her?'

'How could I not? That's all he wants to speak about since you came back from Mount Cas with that knife.'

I smiled at the memory of the helpful message that had been hidden inside the gold-tipped knife and thrown at us on that mountain pass. 'He thinks Macha is up there with the Oracle?'

'He does,' Dad said.

'But you don't?'

'Actually I'm starting to think that Dahy and Spideog are right. Well, maybe not right but that knife of yours and the message you found with it raises enough doubts in my head to make me think we should find out for sure.'

'Wait,' I said, 'we're gonna storm the Oracle's Yew House?'

He didn't answer at first. He just kept looking at the picture of his mother and then, as if he was making the decision right there on the spot, he said, 'Yes.'

'How? That guy is seriously bad ass. He took out Spideog with a flick of the wrist. And I have no doubt he could drop half of that mountain on your head if he wanted to.'

'Dahy thinks it can be done. There is planning to do. I'll keep you posted.'

Dad ruffled my hair in a way that he knew really annoyed me and rushed off for a meeting with some runelord who I'm sure had a good reason why he needed more gold in his stipend. I was left alone under the dark stare of yet another grandparent I never knew. As much as I didn't want to face the Oracle guy on Mount Cas again – I sure wanted to meet my grandmother. Well, if anybody could come up with a working plan of attack, it was Dahy.

I arrived back in my chamber to find Ruby waiting for me. She sat almost swallowed by an overstuffed chair, her feet sticking straight out, her stick folded across her lap. I don't know if it's the huge sunglasses or just her general demeanour but every time I saw this kid I got the distinct feeling that I was in trouble.

'Where have you been?'

I was a bit shocked by the abruptness of the question and when I didn't answer right away, Ruby said, 'You were probably smooching with your mermaid girlfriend.'

'I was not,' I said and sounded to myself like I was ten years old. 'I was in a meeting with the king.' I thought that sounded better than 'I was with my daddy.'

She seemed to find that acceptable.

'How do you know about Graysea?'

'My father brought her to me to have a look at my eyes. She cooed and ooed and cried and kissed me. She's not very clever, is she?'

'Graysea has other talents,' I said.

'Yeah right. Well, she said she couldn't fix my eyes. That I had waited too long.'

'Oh, I'm … I'm sorry.'

'It's nothing I haven't heard before,' Ruby said dismissively as she stood. 'Now, I would like my pony.'

'I beg your pardon?'

'My pony. Father said I would have a pony when I came to Tir na Nog. When I asked him about it he said he had to talk to you. Since he hasn't yet, I am. I'd like my pony please.'

'I … I don't know where I'd get a pony at this time of day.'

'I would assume,' Ruby said as she opened the door for me, 'that we will find one in the stables.' She motioned me out of my room like it was hers. I started to protest but then just decided that getting her a pony was probably the path of least resistance.

'I feel sorry for your future husband,' I said.

'Funny, that's what Father says.'

Ruby grabbed my arm and then swung her stick back and forth as she walked so fast I thought we were going to break into a jog.

'You know, Ruby,' I said, 'I'm not sure if I can get you a pony.'

'Why not?' she asked without slowing down in the slightest.

'I don't think they're just going to give me one.'

'Your father is the king – right?'

'Yes but …'

'And you are a prince?'

'Well, yeah.'

'So just ask for a pony. What is your problem?'

The stable master saw us coming and greeted me at the entrance. He was an old one. It had gotten to the point where I could spot one from a mile away. 'I am Pilib,' he said without bowing or even offering to shake my hand.

'Hi, I'm Conor.'

'I know,' he said. 'You have your grandmother's eyes.'

'Oh, did you know Macha?'

'Of course, she held the Capall yew wand. She had the supremacy over horses. When she lived in Duir she was only ever truly happy when she was here.'

As he spoke Pilib's eyes glossed over lost in the memory. I remembered Spideog telling me that my grandmother loved him and Dahy at the same time. I wondered if I should add the stable master to that list.

Ruby hit me in the shin with her stick. 'Ask him.'

'Ah … Master Pilib, I was wondering if I could have a pony.'

'Certainly. Am I safe to assume that it is for this little lady?'

'I'm not a lady, I'm a young girl.'

I looked down at Ruby, astonished. 'You speak Ancient Gaelic?'

'Grandma taught me some words.'

'OK,' I said turning back to Pilib. 'Can we get this young girl a young-girl-sized pony?'

'Right this way, Prince Conor.'

The stables were quite an operation here at Castle Duir. He led us past what must have been a hundred stalls and then outside to a paddock that contained four ponies.

'Spirited or docile?' Pilib asked.

I toyed with the idea of answering, 'Super spirited.' That would teach her a lesson for putting me through this but I had to remember that no matter how bossy she was – the kid was blind. 'Docile please.'

Pilib placed his fingers in his mouth and emitted a series of whistles. The ponies looked up and then at each other as if saying, 'Who, me?' The smallest of the ponies slowly walked over to us. She was glossy black, just like Ruby's sunglasses. I picked Ruby up and placed her feet on the bottom wooden rail of the corral so she could reach over. The stable master whistled again, this time quietly without the fingers in the mouth and then pointed to the young girl. The pony walked slowly up to Ruby as I guided her hand to the animal's snout.

'This is Feochadán,' Pilib said.

I remembered a story my father used to tell me when I was young about a sheep that got covered with *feochadán*. As Ruby tentatively stroked her pony's nose I said, 'It means thistle.'

A huge smile crossed Ruby's face. It was the first smile I had ever seen on that face and it changed her from a bossy tyrant to the young girl that she was. 'Thistle, that's a lovely name for a pony. Hello Thistle.'

That pony looked up and I could have sworn it recognised its new name. A stable hand showed up with a saddle.

'Oh no, I'm not teaching her to ride.'

'On the day a young girl receives her first pony,' Pilib said, 'surely she must ride it. I wouldn't worry, Feochadán is very easy to ride. Shall I get Acorn for you, Your Highness?'

Acorn, I thought, I did so want to see Acorn and it was a beautiful spring day. Well, I could see no harm in having a quick wander around Castle Duir.

Ruby allowed herself to be hoisted onto Thistle without any of her usual *I can do it myself* fuss. Acorn was brought to me and even though he tried to hide it, I could tell he was pleased to see me. I mounted up and we left through the stable exit. True to Pilib's word, Thistle was the calmest mount I had ever seen. Ruby showed no signs of being scared. She sat on her pony like she had been doing it all of her life.

Outside the castle walls the sun from a cloudless sky stopped the cool spring breeze from being too cold.

'I would like to talk to a tree,' Ruby said.

'You want to talk to a tree?'

'Yes, now. Father said I would have a big bedroom, a pony and I would get to talk to a tree. I'd like to talk to a tree now.'

'Wouldn't you like to just ride for a bit and save some of the other stuff for later?'

'No.'

The best tree to have a conversation with is, of course, Mother Oak but Glen Duir is almost a day away at a hard ride. With Thistle it would probably take a month. Well, Duir doesn't mean oak for nothing. Castle Duir was certainly surrounded by oaks – so I just started for the nearest treeline.

When I got to the edge of the oak forest I had some misgivings. These trees didn't have the same welcoming feel that Mother Oak has – but then what tree does? I dismounted and walked up to a huge snarly barked oak and wrapped my arms around it. Instantly I knew I was in big trouble.

Chapter Four

The Oak

This was different from any tree I had ever communicated with. When I touched it I knew instantly that I wouldn't be able to let go until it released me. The world disappeared. All of my senses were lost except for the touch of where I was held to the bark. This tree didn't talk, it probed my mind. What it found it brought to the fore and what it found was stuff that I had buried for a reason.

I was in grade school and all of the kids were bullying Jimmy Murphy. Jimmy was overweight and crap at sports. I just stood there. I should have done something but I just stood there. I liked Jimmy but I just couldn't be seen being his friend. Then the memory I had long tried to forget. He came to me for help and I pushed him over. Aw Jimmy, I'm so sorry.

Then my mind conjured up the image of a Banshee growing up with his family. I saw his entire life, right up to the moment when I stabbed him at the edge of the Reedlands. He was the first man I had ever killed. As my sword pierced his chest I could see everyone he had ever known and loved watching me with eyes filled with hate. I tried to protest, I tried to say that I didn't mean to kill him. That he was trying to kill me. But the words wouldn't come. My mind was not my own. I felt a pain rise in my chest.

That Banshee was replaced by another. This one I knew. This one I loved. I was lying on my sleeping roll the night before we snuck into Castle Duir. Don't make me watch this, I tried to scream. I tried to pull away but my hands, like they were latched onto a high-voltage wire, wouldn't let go. I remember that night. He came to talk to me but I was too tired and I sent him away, but as this memory progressed, instead of sending him away, I sat up and said, 'What's on your mind, cuz?'

He told me about his plans to kill Cialtie. I told him he was nuts and talked him out of it. After Cialtie was kicked out of Castle Duir – Fergal lived. We talked and drank. He met a lovely girl and I was his best man at the wedding. At the wedding reception he stood and tapped his wineglass with a spoon. He turned to me and said, 'I'd like to propose a toast to the man who saved my life …' The memories abruptly ran in reverse and then the scene in the camp played as it really happened. I fobbed Fergal off and then I watched as the next day Cialtie humiliated and killed him. Then I saw it again … and again … and again. The pain in my chest intensified. My head felt like it was going to explode. I watched again as the sword pierced his chest. I watched but this time the man who was wielding the sword – was me.

I screamed.

I was lost. Down so dark a well that I couldn't see the top. The walls of the well weren't made of stone or dirt, they were made of … me. I was lost deep in my own mind. Deeper even than after the shock of killing the Banshee at the edge of the Fililands. But it was safe down there. Up there was The Tree. The Tree that grew its roots into my memories and plucked out of them everything I had ever regretted and feared. I was safe down here. I had to shut down; I couldn't let him into the brain cells that contained the faces of the scores of Banshees and Brownies I had killed during the battle of the Hall of Knowledge. I wouldn't survive that. Protests, like *I had no choice* and *We were at war*, cut no mustard with the oak. I couldn't let him in there – I was safe in my well. I wasn't ever coming up. I was safe in my well I was never coming up. I was …

The walls of my well, the walls of my self, my refuge, started to shake. A far-off voice called my name but they would never find me. I was deep, deep in my …

The voice became louder but still it was tiny, tinny, miles away. I could never be harmed … would never let him …

The walls of my sub-subconscious shook more. The voice … I heard the voice. It was … it was … Ruby. I laughed. You'll never find me down here, Ruby. I'm safe. Safe from the forest of trees … I'm safe. But then I heard her scream. It was that high-pitched piercing scream that she does. The one her father calls The Migraine Scream. I forced myself to think. Where are you, Ruby? It doesn't matter I am here and I … I am safe. But where are you Ruby? You were with me. I took you riding. You are alone and blind in the Forest of Duir. But I'm safe here. But little Ruby you are not. I must … safe. Safe here. Safe. No. Save. Save her. I must save her.

I reached to the walls of the well. No. I forced myself to think. Not a well – the walls of my mind. I placed my back against a corner of my brain and I climbed. I climbed. I climbed to the sound of that scream. I still couldn't see anything but the further I went, the closer the sound became. It got so loud it hurt.

I opened my eyes to see Ruby taking another big breath in preparation for another scream. I reached up to stop her but my arm was blocked by a white bed sheet. As she screamed again I freed my hand and caught her by the arm.

'Ruby,' I said.

She stopped, smiled and then started hopping around. 'You see,' she almost sang, 'it worked. It worked. I told you it would work.'

I was very confused. I was indoors and in a clean bed. All around me people were rushing into the room. Presumably to see what all the screaming was about. I looked to my left and saw Dad chuckling.

'Dad? What happened?'

'I've been waiting three days to ask *you* that,' he answered.

'Why was Ruby screaming?'

'I have no idea,' he said. 'She has been waiting by your side for most of the three days that you've been in this coma. Just a minute ago she said to me, "Can I try something?" I said yes and she started screaming.'

'And it worked!' Ruby said returning to my bed and bouncing her arms off the mattress. 'Daddy always said my scream could wake the dead and it can. It can, it can. It can. I'm going to tell Daddy.' And she was off.

'Where am I?'

'You're in one of Fand's healing rooms.'

'How did I get here?'

Dad pulled up a chair. 'That's an interesting story. Three days ago, the sergeant at arms was shocked to find a seven-year-old blind girl screaming at the Great Gates of Duir. She told him that you were in trouble and he sent a detail out to investigate. They found you curled up on the ground at the edge of the oak perimeter. Ruby says you went out there to talk to a tree – but you're not that stupid – are you?'

'Well,' I said, 'Ruby wanted to talk to a tree. I, of course, would have liked to have introduced her to Mother Oak but she was too far away …'

'So you just went out and wrapped your arms around any old oak?' Dad was almost shouting. 'What is wrong with you?'

'What's wrong with me? What's wrong with that tree? It was like it grew roots into my head.'

'Didn't anybody ever tell you about the Oaks of Duir?'

'No. No one did and whose fault is that – do you think?'

That stopped Dad's anger, 'Oh, well, I guess I should have told you.'

'You think?'

'Yeah, sorry. '

'So what did that tree do to me?'

'Oaks are dangerous trees, son. If you even brush past one it can snare you. We seem to have no defence against them. They can access our memories and then manipulate our emotions. That's one of the things that makes Mother Oak so wonderful. She searches out the best in people and reminds you that you are a good person but not all oaks are so affirmative. In fact, almost none are. For the most part, oaks are nasty pieces of wood. I liked to think of them as the junkyard dogs of Castle Duir.'

'Gosh, and I thought yews were the dangerous ones.'

'Yews can snare you without touching them but yews aren't nasty. Yews are the judges of The Land – oaks are the criminals.'

'But yews can kill you, right?' I asked.

'True,' said Dad, 'but oaks can drive you mad. Speaking of which – are you OK?'

'I think so, the worst part was …'

'You don't have to tell me. I assure you that whatever the oak stirred up in your mind is nowhere near as bad as he made it seem.'

'Yeah, it was awful, all of the stuff that filled my head but the oak was right about one thing. I did let Fergal down.'

'We all dropped the ball on that one, son. We should have seen it coming but never forget – the one who stuck the sword in Fergal was Cialtie.'

Fand entered and told us that there was a host of people wanting to visit with me. Dad picked up a vial from the bedside table.

'Your mother told me to give you this as soon as you awoke and seemed OK.'

'I'm fine Dad, I don't need any medicine.'

'So you want me to go back to your mother and say that you are defying her?'

I looked at him and frowned. 'You wouldn't do that – would you?'

'Hey, this is your mother we're talking about. You're on your own here, pal.'

I took the vial of liquid. 'OK, I'll take it,' I said, 'but I would really like to …' That's the thing about medicines in Tir na Nog – you don't have to wonder if they are working. There was no possible way I could have even finished that sentence and whatever I thought I wanted to do was instantly of no concern to me. I was back down in my well but this time it was only about six inches deep and lined with satin. Dad said I passed out with a huge smile on my face.

I woke to a question. 'Are you nuts?'

'No, I'm OK; the oak tree didn't drive me mad,' I said before I opened my eyes.

'Oh, that's a huge relief,' the voice said with an uncaring tone that I didn't like. I opened my eyes to see a very angry Brendan looming over me. I instantly sat up and backed into the headboard – he looked like he was going to hit me. 'What were you thinking?'

'I … I …'

'Nora and I didn't know where Ruby was and then you plop her on a horse and take her out to the most dangerous forest in The Land – where you abandon her – on a horse.'

Second most dangerous forest, and it was a pony, I said – to myself, because I knew if I said that to Brendan, there would have been some police brutality.

'You're right, I'm sorry,' I said, 'I wasn't thinking.'

'You're damn right you weren't thinking. She could have been killed, or driven insane. What possessed you to do it?'

'Ruby showed up in my room and said that you promised her a pony but were being slow about it.'

'So you just went and got her a pony?'

'Well,' I shrugged, 'she's kinda hard to say no to.'

Brendan relaxed and sat down. 'Yeah, I can't argue with that, but you've got to remember that even though she acts like she's forty-two she's only twelve.'

'I know, and I'm really sorry. I promise it won't happen again and I won't take her anywhere without you knowing about it.'

He patted me on the head like I was a schoolboy. 'You are forgiven, Mr O'Neil. So,' he said, changing the subject, 'how are you?'

'I'm fine. Dad said I was out of it for three days.'

'The oak roughed you up a bit, eh?'

'The specifics of what happened are fading now. All I remember is that he made me remember every bad thing I had ever done and I couldn't stop it. It was horrible.'

'As bad as being arrested for your dad's murder?'

'I don't want to bruise your ego, Detective Fallon, but compared to the oak – you're a pushover.'

A commotion outside the door made us both turn. A woman was screaming and guards were shouting.

'O gods,' Brendan said, 'I might be a pushover but my mother is not. If she gets in here she's going to tear your head off.'

The door opened and a very fierce looking Nora stomped towards me in a way that reminded me of an attacking Banshee. I looked to my left and saw there was a vial of that medicine on my bedside table. I grabbed it and downed it in one. Nora started screaming. I heard it but really didn't care as I snuggled blissfully down into the satin bed of my unconsciousness.

When you take one of Mom/Fand's potions you really do go out. No dreams, no visions, no nothing. I had no idea how long I had been asleep. It could have been days or minutes. When I woke up I opened one eye and had a look around. Sitting at my bedside, reading a book, was Essa.

She was back to her beautiful young-looking self. I just watched as she brushed a wisp of hair away from her forehead with a gesture that I knew oh so well.

'Hey, old lady,' I said and then braced myself. Essa had been plenty mad at me for so much of the time that I knew her that I was never sure if our meeting was going to be pleasant or not. But then she smiled and my body relaxed and my heart pounded.

'Hi, I … was worried about you.'

I looked around the room to see if anybody else was there. 'You talkin' to me?'

She laughed. 'Yes I am. Are you OK?'

I sat up. 'I am now.' There was an awkward silence where we just stared at each, other until I broke it with, 'You look good without the wrinkles and the grey hair.'

'Why, thank you,' she said with a nod of her head.

'What's it like drinking Tuan's blood?'

'Gross but kind of – wonderful. I haven't felt this good in years. I have tons of energy.'

'Maybe I should order a green dragon cocktail for myself?'

'Maybe we should get my father to whip up some Tuan blood wine?'

36

We both laughed. It was nice – normal. Could it be that I was forgiven? I wondered. Could Essa and I ever be – normal?

The question was cut short by the sound of bare feet slapping against the stone floor. I was smothered in kisses even before I could see whose lips were administering them. Not that I had to look, there's only one mermaid in all of The Land that greets me like that.

'Oh Conor,' *kiss, kiss*, 'I have been so worried about you,' *kiss, kiss, kiss*.

'Hi Graysea,' I garbled between smooches, 'have you met Essa?'

The introduction had the desired effect of getting Graysea to let up on my face.

'I remember Essa,' Graysea said in a tone I had never heard from her before. 'The first time I saw her she hit you in the head with a stick.'

I expected Essa to storm off, hopefully without hitting me in the head, but instead she stood her ground. 'What are you still doing here?'

Oh my, I thought to myself, this has the potential to turn into a serious cat fight – or a cat and fish fight and they usually don't turn out very well for the fish. I know it was cowardly of me – I reached for the bedside table but, damn it, there wasn't any of that knock-out medicine there.

'Where else should I be but by my beloved Conor's side?'

To be perfectly honest I wasn't the only reason she was still here – Graysea had nowhere else to go. When the Mertain King found out that she had stolen his dragon's blood to give to me, he banished her.

Essa was close to snarling when she said, 'I can think of several places I would rather you to be.'

'Essa,' I said as gingerly as I could, 'Graysea helped me escape from a very difficult situation.'

'Oh, did she?' the Princess said. 'And what other situations did she help you in or out of?'

'I don't understand you,' my mermaid said with her usual tilt of the head. 'Why are you here? Shouldn't you be mourning the loss of your fiancé?'

I instantly popped up on my knees on the mattress between them. Essa had stepped back in what I recognised as a preparation to spring. I really didn't want to be in the middle of this and suspected that any second I was going to get the worst of it.

'Everyone out,' came a command from the doorway. Dad was standing there in his drill suit. He wore that kingly face that made the two women snap to attention and then quickly leave. Neither said goodbye to me as they never really took their eyes off each other for the entire exit.

'Thank you,' I said when the Princess and the mermaid were out of earshot.

'Don't thank me too soon,' Dad said, throwing me the clothes that he had been carrying. 'Your mother and Fand have given you a clean bill of health, so come with me – it's time for some training.'

'Training for what?'

'We're going to launch an assault on the Oracle of Mount Cas.'

I thought about the prospect of going into battle again and then thought about the skirmish that Dad had just saved me from. War didn't seem that bad at all.

Chapter Five

Graysea and Essa

I was back in Dahy's boot camp. This time it was worse than the
first time. The first time I knew I didn't know anything. This
time I thought I knew everything and Dahy proved to me that I
once again knew nothing. We were learning a new technique. The
master didn't have a name for it so I called it ninja school – 'cause
that's what it felt like. None of us were allowed to execute any of
our showy spins or flip manoeuvres. Every movement had to be
minimal. All over the armoury, where we practised, were wooden
dowels balanced upright with feathers perched on top. Every time
one of us disturbed a feather, or worse, knocked over a dowel,
Dahy would shoot us in the legs with a crossbow bolt that had a
woollen ball stuck on the end. If you think that doesn't sound like
it would hurt – then think again.

Araf was really good at it. It wasn't until I saw him in a room
full of feathers did I realise just how economical a fighting style he
had. Except for his figure of eight propeller-like stick move, Araf
hardly had to change his technique at all. Essa was lucky she didn't
have to learn this stuff. Without all of her flipping and twirling she
would have been very unhappy. And when Essa is unhappy –
everyone is unhappy.

Gerard, Essa's father, forbade her to go into the Oracle's house.
She wasn't about to let her father boss her around like that but

when Gerard threatened to withdraw all of Castle Duir's wine shipments – Oisin took Essa off active duty. She was furious and Dad had to remind her that he was, like, a king. She stormed off kicking anything, and anyone, in her path. In short, Essa was to be avoided, but I was doing that already.

Even though our practice was deadly serious it was also fun. Dad joined us and so did Mom and Aunt Nieve. The ladies had a hard time casting spells without all of that dramatic wicked-witch arm waving. Dad, who already had, like, a hundred years' worth of Dahy tutelage, just seemed to do whatever the master told him to do without any effort at all. One time I pushed Dad over, just to see if Dahy would shoot the king with his crossbow. He didn't, he shot me.

Brendan trained with us but he wasn't going either. He wanted to come, just like he wanted to ask the yew trees if he could use Spideog's bow, but he had a responsibility to his daughter Ruby not to put himself in harm's way.

'And actually,' he confided to me one day at lunch, 'I'm in no hurry to see that Oracle guy again. If I recall he kicked our butts good with just a flick of the wrist.'

I pointed that out to Dahy but he said he had a plan. So by day we continued to practise our non-feather-disturbing fighting techniques and by night I rubbed healing salve into the black and blue bruises on my legs that Dahy gave me with his crossbow.

The banging on my bedroom door would have busted any Real World door off its hinges but Duir doors are made of hardy stuff.

'Conor,' the voice on the other side bellowed, 'I want to talk to you.' I knew who it was right away – everyone in the castle was talking about it. New wine is news around here but when it's delivered by the master winemaker himself – that's big news.

I opened the door and there stood the largest of all of the larger-than-life characters in Tir na Nog. Gerard stepped into the doorway, blocking out all of the light beyond. In his hand he held a metal bucket with a piece of cloth over the top – it didn't look like a weapon but I kept my eye on it.

He strode further into the room, forcing me to back up, and said, 'If I didn't know better I would think that you have been hiding from me.'

'I … maybe I have been,' I confessed.

'Why would you do that?'

'I guess you haven't spoken to Essa yet?'

Gerard frowned and placed his bucket on the floor. 'Oh, I have spoken to my daughter all right. She is mighty mad at you and this – what did she call her – "fishy floozy" of yours.'

'That's why I've been avoiding you,' I said.

'Let me get this straight, you think that because my daughter is angry with you, that I will be too.'

'Aren't you?'

He came at me with his arms outstretched. I had a brief flashback of the bear attack in the Pookalands. He wrapped his arms around me and gave me one of his laughing hugs that lifted me off the ground. 'Oh my boy,' he said, and I relaxed even though my ribs were threatening to crack. 'If Essa is mad at you, then you already have more enemies than any one man can stand.' He let go of me and I tested my diaphragm to see if I could still breathe. 'Good gods and monsters, if I had to be angry at everyone that my *little darling* was irritated with – I would not have any friends or customers at all.'

'So you're not here to give me the "don't you dare hurt my daughter" speech?'

Gerard laughed, picked up his bucket and moved over to the table on the other side of the room. 'Oh, I don't give that speech. I usually just try to discourage Essa's beaus for their own safety.'

We laughed at that as he whipped the cloth off his bucket like a TV magician. 'I've brought you a gift.' Buried deep in snow, with only their necks sticking out, were four bottles. I grabbed one, releasing it from its icy bed.

'Beer!' I shouted.

'I remembered that last time you were in Castle Muhn you said you wanted beer that is "lighter, fizzier and colder" – well, try this.' He reached over and placed his hand on the neck of the bottle and mumbled. The cork began to spin and then rise until it shot out of the bottle with a satisfying pop.

I took a quick gulp to catch the foam from overflowing onto the floor. Gerard scrutinised my face for any hint of criticism. 'Well?' he asked as I wiped my mouth with my sleeve.

'I think you should give up on this wine stuff and become a full-time brewer.'

Gerard beamed like a child who had just received a stick-on star on his homework.

'Did I hear someone shouting beer?' It was Brendan at the door.

'Brendan,' I said. 'Come in and meet Essa's father, Lord Gerard of Muhn.'

'Oh,' Brendan said, a bit surprised while improvising a bow. 'How do you do? I'm a big fan of your wine.'

'Well, come in and try my beer,' Gerard said without standing.

Brendan hesitated and said, 'Actually I was just passing with my mother.' Brendan reached into the hallway and took his mother's hand and guided her into the room. 'Lord Gerard, may I introduce Nora Fallon.'

I hadn't seen Brendan's mother since she arrived in the Hall of Spells. She was dressed in a green felt-ish tunic with gold embroidery and leather trousers – pretty much what everyone around here wears and it suited her to a T.

Gerard jumped to his feet, and bowed. 'Of course I have heard about both of you. Welcome home, Druids. Please join us in a drink.'

Nora bowed. 'Thank you, my lord, but no. I have to tend to my granddaughter.' Brendan started to go with her when Nora said to her son, 'No, please stay. I know how much you are missing beer.' She bowed once again to us and left.

'Your mother,' Gerard said after seating Brendan and uncorking a beer for him, 'is … old.'

'Yes, try not to point that out to her when you meet her next. She's getting a bit tired of that.'

'But according to my daughter a couple of drops of blood from that remarkable Pooka friend of yours would change that – would it not?'

'Tuan has offered my mother some dragon blood but she says she feels great and likes herself the way she is.'

'Well, it sounds as if your mother knows her own mind. I like that in a woman.' Gerard slapped Brendan on the shoulder, changing the subject. 'My daughter speaks highly of you, Druid.'

'Well, she hasn't hit me yet,' the cop said.

Gerard laughed, 'It's a shame you are not going on our little expedition but I understand about parental responsibilities.'

'Wait,' I said. 'Are you coming?'

'Oh yes,' Gerard said, 'Oisin has summoned me – I am an integral part of the plan.'

'Look it's a three and a half day ride to the base of Mount Cas,' I said. 'There is no reason to leave at dawn. We can leave at, like, ten and still be there way before it's dark on the fourth day.'

'Son, we leave at dawn – that's how it is.'

'Who says? Where is it etched in stone that all expeditions must leave at dawn?'

Finally Dad gave me one of his patented withering stares that, although he looked like my annoying younger cousin, still worked.

'Yes sir. See you in the morning.'

'Before the morning,' he called after me.

So here I was, yawning while dragging my pack on the ground behind me, trying to get some kind of enthusiasm for the adventure ahead.

Believe it or not, I was early. The only ones in the stable before me were Gerard and four brawny soldiers. I watched and yawned as they hoisted a huge wine barrel on to Gerard's cart.

'Are we planning to get sloshed on this trip?'

'I wish,' Gerard said. 'There is no wine in that barrel.'

'What's in there?'

'Salt water.'

I was about to ask why we needed a barrel of salt water when I was blinded by a pair of hands covering my eyes from behind. 'Guess who?' said the unmistakable voice.

'Is it a person or a fish?' I asked.

'Both.'

I turned to see the ever bubbly Graysea standing behind me. She kissed me on both cheeks and said, 'Good morning.'

'Good morning to you too – how nice of you to see me off.'

'Oh, I'm not seeing you off. I'm going with you.'

'Graysea, this is a very dangerous mission. I really don't think you should come.'

'Think again, son,' Dad said while arriving around the corner with his mount.

I walked Dad out of earshot. 'Why is Graysea coming with us?'

'Because we are going up against a tough customer and I want a healer with us, and I have never seen anything like that Mertain healing power of hers.'

'Yes, Dad, but she's …' I tried to remember what matron had said about Graysea. 'She's a sensitive fishy.'

'I think you underestimate your mermaid, son. Graysea saved your butt out there in the ocean and defied her king. She can handle a three-day hike.'

'Don't you want me with you?' Graysea asked when I got back to her.

'No, I … I'm just worried about you.'

'It'll be fun.'

'Graysea, we are going into battle.'

She put on her serious face but then smiled that room-lighting smile of hers. 'Well, it will be fun until we get there.'

I just couldn't resist the infectious joy of that girl's smile. 'You're right,' I agreed, 'welcome along.'

Who knew what we were going into? At least until then I would have some pleasant company along the way. And luckily Essa wasn't coming so I wouldn't be caught in the middle of a week-long oestrogen nightmare.

Araf showed up and I grunted at him – I've discovered that wordless communication is best with the taciturn Imp. Mom, Nieve and Dahy all dramatically feigned surprise at me being ready before them. I saddled up Acorn (I was tempted to take Cloud but she was Brendan's horse now) and then helped Gerard hitch up the wagon to his monsta-horses.

Actually it was nice being early and not having everybody scowling at me to hurry. I was mounted up, waking up and starting to feel good about this expedition when my spirits were dashed by the arrival of the last two of the party – Tuan and Essa.

I cantered Acorn over to Dad. 'I thought you forbade Essa from coming?' I said in a harsh whisper.

'Gerard had forbidden her to enter the Oracle's house on Mount Cas so she and Tuan are performing a different task.'

'You did this on purpose.'

'What, son, do you accuse me of doing on purpose?'

'You know perfectly well what you did. You invited Graysea and Essa on this trip so you could watch me suffer.'

Dad, who had been wearing the slightest of smirks, became gravely serious. 'Essa is a very important part of Dahy's plan and as I said before, Graysea is the finest healer I have ever seen. The world does not revolve around you, son. I would never ask anyone to join an undertaking as perilous as this just to annoy you.' He kicked his horse away but as he did he said, 'That's just an added bonus.'

We took the main road out and travelled three abreast. On my left was Graysea and on my right was Essa. No one said a word. I was even afraid to shift in my saddle lest the noise break the agonisingly painful silence. Dad looked around and didn't even try to stifle his chuckle. This was going to be a long, long trip. I thought, maybe if I'm lucky I'll die a horrible death on Mount Cas. At least then I'll be saved from a trip home with these two.

Chapter Six

The Yew House

We travelled like that for a day and a half. No one said a word. Anybody who knows me understands that I'm uneasy with uncomfortable silences. This was pure torment. I thought my head was going to explode. On the first night I ate and went straight to bed. I was hoping I could get to sleep quickly so I would have someone in dreamland to talk to, but sleep wouldn't come. I was sharing a tent with Araf and still wasn't asleep by the time he came to bed. I was so desperate for conversation I said, 'Say something.'

'What would you like me to say?' he answered, without the puzzlement in his voice that he should have had.

'I don't care – anything. You can tell me about crop rotation if you want.'

'Really?' he said, with more excitement than I have ever heard from him before.

'Yes, anything.'

So off he went babbling on about plants and seeds and hoeing and dirt and bugs. He was so wrapped up in his subject I'm sure he didn't notice me nodding off with a smile on my face. Anything was better than the silence I had been enduring sandwiched between the icy glares of those two women.

I got a reprieve the next day when Essa dropped back to have a planning chat with Tuan.

Graysea startled me when she spoke. 'Do you still care for her?'

'Who?' I said lamely.

'Conor, I'm stupid but not that stupid.'

'You're not stupid,' I said, 'you're the cleverest mermaid I know.'

'And how many mermaids do you know?'

'Well, that's not the point.'

'No it's not,' she said. 'The point, which you seem to be avoiding, is whether or not you still have feelings for Essa.'

'Well, that's complicated.'

'And you think I am too stupid to understand. Is that it?'

'No,' I said looking around hoping that a pack of wolves would attack and get me out of this conversation. 'Essa and I have a history.'

'You still haven't answered the question,' she said and then mercifully continued so I didn't have to. 'I just don't understand. When you were on the island with me she was engaged to that Turlow fella – right?'

'Yes.'

'So she is mad at you for being with me when she was engaged to somebody else. That doesn't seem fair.'

'Well, ah …'

'And she hits you all the time.'

'Well, I don't know about all the time … but often.'

'And is it true that last summer she tried to kill you?'

'She … she didn't try to kill me,' I stammered, 'she was just part of a plot to have me killed.'

Graysea shook her head and sighed. 'And people think I'm stupid.' She kicked her horse and sped ahead.

Gosh, I thought, when you add it all up like that she had a point. Araf had silently sidled up next to me. I turned to him and said, 'What do you think, big guy?'

'About what?'

'About my women problems?'

'I think,' the Imp said, 'I was more comfortable with questions about crop rotation.'

I got another reprieve that night when they both ignored me. Essa finally came up to me after dinner. A firefly sat on her shoulder illuminating one side of her face.

'Your little mackerel is lounging in her barrel.'

'She is not a mackerel, she's a Mertain. She is a healer from the Grotto of Health on the Mertain islands. And she is not lounging. She is recharging – preparing herself so she can help any of us in case we are injured.'

Essa was taken aback by my tone. She stood.

'Maybe you would prefer to join her in her bath tub.'

'Maybe I would. At least she's not mad at me all the time and she never hits me with sticks.'

Essa looked at me like she had never seen me before. I stood and faced her. 'Anyway, I haven't seen you for an hour or so – are you sure you haven't gotten engaged to someone in that time?'

Essa looked like she had been slapped. 'You promised you would never mention that.'

'No I didn't. *You* told me not to mention it. I never got a chance to promise. Well, maybe I'm tired of being bossed around by you.'

It didn't take long for the surprised Essa to kick back. 'Fine,' she hissed. 'I hope you and your fish will be happy together.' She stomped away, leaving her firefly to flutter around confused, and then she turned. I took a step back expecting a blow. 'Now that I think of it, you and your fish are perfect together – because you're an eel.'

I tried riding with Araf the next day but he insisted on continuing his dissertation on agriculture so I dropped to the rear to have a long overdue catch-up with Tuan. Araf didn't even notice I was gone.

'Councillor Tuan,' I said, 'I'm surprised you're still in Duir. Don't get me wrong, it's great having you around, but shouldn't you be in the Pinelands impressing girls with your super-Pooka act?'

'Girls,' Tuan sighed, 'are the reason I am here.'

'Oh?' I said with my inflection going up.

'My mother wants me to marry.'

'Oh,' I said with my tone going down.

'Yes, Mother wants me to marry a mousy woman from the council.'

'When you say mousy, Tuan, do you mean she's small or that she changes into a mouse?'

'Both.'

'And you're not into rodents?'

'It's not that …'

'What is it then?'

Tuan looked around to make sure no one could overhear. 'There's this girl in Castle Duir.'

'Oh, do tell.'

'This mustn't get back to my mother.'

'I'll be as quiet as the mouse you're cheating on.'

Tuan snarled at me then straightened up in his saddle and said, 'Never mind.'

'No, no, I'm sorry T. I promise I won't make jokes. Who is she?'

'I better not say.'

'Aw come on, what's the big secret?'

'She is an Imp.'

'Oh, and Mom's not into mixed marriages?'

'Mother thinks that Pooka power as strong as mine shouldn't be diluted.'

'So she's hooking you up with a mouse?'

Tuan shrugged.

'Why don't you just tell your mother to get stuffed?' I said. 'You do realise you're a dragon?'

Tuan laughed. 'Being one of the most powerful creatures in The Land has little sway with my mother.'

'Yeah, big guy,' I said, nodding. 'I guess I can relate to that.'

We made good time and got to the base of Mount Cas on the evening of the third day. As we set up a base camp, I expected Dad to make some comment like, 'Aren't you glad we left at dawn?' but all he gave me was that look that said it all. Where do parents learn that all-encompassing look? Is there some sort of instructional video you get when you have your first kid? Does it come with a mirror to practise in?

Gerard brought out a couple of bottles of dark red wine. It was fabulous. I wasn't worried about the upcoming confrontation until I tasted it. When Gerard brings out the special stuff then you know there's going to be hard times ahead.

That night I dreamt about the Oracle. He leaned forward into the light. As his wispy grey hair blew in a breeze, his wrinkled eyes smiled at me. Then with the tiniest flick of the wrist, he sent me sailing off the side of Mount Cas. I screamed all the way down until the moment I hit the ground. I sat bolt upright in my tent and stared into the darkness, willing my breath to calm and my heartbeat to return to normal. Was that just a nightmare, I wondered – or a prophecy?

We set out long before dawn. Every campaign seemed to be getting earlier and earlier. Soon we would be leaving before we even went to bed. Essa, Tuan, Gerard and Graysea stayed behind in base camp. The last time I climbed Mount Cas it took us three days but that was in the winter. This day was dry and sunny and we set a ridiculous pace. We hiked way into the cold night and found a place to camp on the opposite side of the mountain from where the Yew House stood. We didn't know if the Oracle had enough power over the mountain to cause avalanches, but didn't want to chance it.

Mom sat next to me over what was laughingly called dinner. 'Are you OK?' she asked.

'Other than the fact that my legs feel like jelly after that climb and I have to sleep on cold hard stone on the edge of a cliff the night before I re-tangle with the nastiest sorcerer I have ever seen – yeah, I'm fine.'

'I was talking about your girlfriend problems.'

'Oh, well I don't think I have a problem any more 'cause after this trip I probably won't have any girlfriends.'

'Well, that would suit me fine. Then I would have you all to myself.'

She put her arm around me and gave me a hug that made me feel like I was five. I placed my head on her shoulder and closed my eyes. I was awfully tired. I don't know if it was Shadowmagic or just Mom magic but the next thing I noticed I was in my sleeping roll and Dahy was shaking me awake and offering me a cup of breakfast tea.

If yesterday my legs felt like jelly, today they felt like lead. Dad, in front, set a stride that some would call a sprint. We only slowed down on the parts of the trail that were visible from the Yew House above, then we would press against the rock face and slink along in single file so as not to be seen.

It was nightfall when we reached the wide shelf where, months before, Araf and I had almost fallen off the side when caught in an ice slide. If we had been spotted during our ascent, we figured that the Brownie guards would be there to meet us as they had done the last time. Since they didn't, we decided to camp the night there and meet the Oracle guy in the morning. We didn't risk a fire but Nieve got some water hot using gold wire she incanted over and then dropped into the kettle. Dad hadn't spoken all day and looked kinda off. I made him a cup of tea and then pointed to the stone wall next to him. 'Excuse me sir, is this seat taken?' I asked.

He was lost in thought but then finally said, 'No,' without even noticing any irony in the question.

'You OK, Dad?'

He noticed me then and said, 'Yeah, yeah, I'm fine.'

'You know I'm old enough that you don't have to play Strong Dad for me. You're obviously distracted. What's on your mind?'

'It's nothing. I'm just mulling over tomorrow.'

'Or maybe you're nervous about meeting a mother that you hardly even remember?'

Dad looked shocked – then smiled. 'How did you get so smart?'

'I actually have experience in meeting a mother for the first time in adulthood, remember?'

'Yeah, I guess you do. Any advice?'

'Yes, I do,' I said, sipping my tea. 'Get some rest, 'cause it's nothing you can prepare for.'

The next morning as we walked to the front porch of the Yew House, Dahy threw something off the side of the mountain. There was no one outside the house so we opened the door and let ourselves in. We obviously caught everyone napping. A Brownie saw us in the hallway and yelped like a puppy that had accidentally been trodden on. He scurried away and it wasn't long before there was a wall of armed Brownies between us and the end of the hallway.

I recognised the tall Brownie in front as the one that, months earlier, I had pinned to a wall by the neck. I knew that these guys weren't as tough as they looked.

'You are not welcome here,' tall guy said.

'We are not looking for a welcome. We are looking for Macha,' Dahy said.

They all flinched in surprise at the mention of her name. If I had any doubts that my grandmother was there they left me then.

Tall guy repeated himself. 'You are not welcome here.' This time he emphasised his words by levelling a crossbow at us. Or I should say started to level a crossbow at us, because he never got it even close to level. As soon as the weapon started to rise, Mom and Nieve performed some kind of magic. There was a flash of light and the Brownies went down like bowling pins.

'Strike,' I said, and Dad gave me a smile.

We walked the length of that dark stone cold corridor until we reached the yew door with the Eioho Rune carved into the finish.

'Ready?' Dahy asked and in response we fanned out into our rehearsed positions.

The room beyond was exactly as it had been the last time I was there. Light shining from round discs set into the ceiling refused to bounce off the pitch-black floors. On a dais in the centre of the room, bathed in shadows, sat the Oracle on his Yew Throne. You couldn't see his face, only the outline of his hair and robe as both fluttered in the wind that whistled through the room.

We stepped through the doorway, spread out and awaited Dahy's command.

I stood at the back and tried to be as inconspicuous as possible. I wasn't interested in having my conversation with him pick up where it had last left off.

'Where is Macha?' Dahy demanded.

Oracle guy leaned in, letting the light hit his face for the first time. It was as effective as any lighting trick done in a Hollywood horror movie and I'm sure he did it for its impact. The next time I had to scare the crap out of someone I decided I would hire this guy to do my special effects.

'The last time I spoke to a Lord of Duir, he had manners,' he said, looking at Dahy, but then he turned to my father and said, 'and the last time I spoke to a Lord of Duir, he spoke for himself.'

'I have had reports of the reception you offered my son at his last visit,' Dad said, 'the time for manners was then.'

The Oracle cast an eye in my direction. *I wish you'd leave me out of this, Dad*, I thought to myself.

'As for my general's question,' Dad continued, 'I shall repeat it. Where is my mother?'

The Oracle started to smile and then sat back into the shadows and laughed. One of those bad-guy laughs that irritates everyone except the laugher. We waited.

'I never thought I would see the day when the Lord of Duir would climb up my mountain only to say, 'I want my mommy.' He laughed again. I'm glad it was dark in there 'cause I smiled too.

'Conor, welcome back,' he said, wiping the smile from my face, 'I see you have brought your Imp with you. But where are the archer and the Druid? Oh dear, did I kill them?'

'No,' I said trying hard not to let my voice wobble. 'Not that you didn't try.'

'Impudent as ever,' he said in a tone that almost had some warmth in it. 'Someday that will get you killed.'

'I would advise you not to threaten my son.' Dad obviously had heard something different in his tone than I had.

'Or what? Your Shadowwitch will cover me with sap?' Oracle looked to Mom and Nieve. 'Which one of you is the Daughter of Hazel that practises the forbidden lore?'

Mom stepped forward but didn't say a word.

'So who are you?' the Oracle asked pointing to Nieve.

'I am Nieve of Duir and I too want my mommy.'

That should have been funny, but the way my aunt said it made it sound menacing. Saying that, Oracle guy laughed – apparently he doesn't menace easily.

'Well, now that we are all introduced,' the Oracle said rising, 'it is time for you to go. Apologise to my Brownies on your way out.'

Dahy is not the kind of guy who lets emotions get in the way of his tactics but on this day, the arrogance of the Oracle and the anticipation of seeing Macha again got the best of him and he jumped the gun. He raised his *banta* and stepped towards the dais. All I remember of the next ten seconds was: G-forces, wind and pain. By the time I came back to my senses I saw that I, like everyone in my party, was pinned to the wall by a force of wind that made our faces scrunch up like astronauts during take-off. When I finally could force my head to move, I saw I was three feet off the ground.

Oracle guy was standing in front of his dais with his arms outstretched as dust and leaves swirled around him under the light from the ceiling discs. If before I thought that this plan was maybe a mistake, now, seeing Oracle guy looking so all-powerful, I wondered if this was actually a fatal mistake.

'What arrogance,' he said; his voice, carried on the wind, was so loud it made my head vibrate against the stone. 'To imagine that sticks and swords – and even Shadowmagic are enough to defeat ME!'

Chapter Seven

Diddo

I tried to speak and then yell but the wind seemed to push my
words back in to my head. I wasn't party to the entire plan for
this campaign but I was pretty sure that getting pinned to a wall
wasn't part of it. I could only hope that we got back on schedule
before Oracle guy killed us.

The pressure of the wind was so intense that I was starting
to have trouble breathing. Now that would be one for the
books – being suffocated because of too much air. I looked to
my left. Not because I wanted to, it was just that I could no
longer keep my head straight. As my cheek pressed painfully
against the stone wall I saw Mom moving her hand into her
pouch. I don't know how she did it, I couldn't move a thing.
Her hand came out with one of those gold and amber balls that
she had invented. It was a hybrid weapon made from Real and
Shadowmagic. I had never seen it fail to kick the crap out of
anybody she had lobbed it at. Ever so slowly she brought her
hand to her lips and incanted directly onto the ball. The gold
and amber glowed and then despite the force of the wind it
started towards the Oracle – but not for long. I heard him
laugh through the howl as Mom's bomb came back at her and
silently exploded as it reached her chest. Normally I would
have had to turn my head or cover my face at the brightness of

it but all I could do was close my eyes. When the flash blindness finally receded to small black dots I saw that Mom was out cold. At least, I hoped she was just unconscious. For all I could tell she might have been dead.

The horror of that thought hit me at the same time as all the noise stopped. Blessed quiet filled the room as the wind and pressure ceased and I slid down the wall onto my feet. Mom crumpled to the ground. As I ran to her I heard Dahy's voice shouting the word that I had taught him, 'Ninja!' My training kicked in and I slowed to a crawl. Mom looked like she was still breathing so I slowly turned to see that the rest of my team had already gently flowed into action. Oracle guy looked very confused. He waved his arms and flicked his wrists but in the windless chamber he seemed powerless.

I breathed a small sigh of relief, making sure I created no air current. We had all been working on the assumption that Oracle guy's powers came from wind. It seemed not to be such a stretch after seeing how the Mertain harvested power from ocean currents. Days before, Tuan in the form of a crow had carried a parcel of stuff that Mom, Essa, Nieve and Fand had come up with. I know it sounds silly but it was like magic expanding cavity filler. As a test they had set off a teaspoon of it in Castle Duir. It filled the room with an amber coloured substance with the consistency of light pumice. It kept going into the hallway and for a minute Mom was worried that it was going to take over the entire floor. There were people back at the castle who were still trying to dig out the room.

Tuan had reconnoitred the mountain and discovered two large holes at about the height of the Yew Throne Room. We figured that if we plugged those holes, the wind in the chamber would stop and Oracle guy would be powerless. The Shadowmagic baton Dahy threw off the mountain just before we entered the Yew House was Essa's signal to ride Dragon Tuan up to the summit, detonate the parcels and draught-proof the throne room. If Dahy hadn't jumped the gun maybe we could have done all this without so much pain.

Once the wind stopped, subduing Oracle guy was easier than any of us expected. He was still trying to figure out what had happened to his powers when Nieve came up behind him and pinned him with one of her paralysing specials. As soon as he was incapacitated Dad and Nieve went to Mom. Nieve placed her hands on both sides of Mom's head. She was like that for a long time before she said, 'I think she will be fine, but I would like to get her to your mermaid as quickly as we can.' I didn't like hearing Nieve using words like 'I think'. I sat and held Mom's hand, not knowing what else to do.

Dahy made us all jump when he shouted into the darkness, 'MACHA.' Just the sound of that one word spoke the decades of loss the old warrior felt. Dad rose and stood beside him.

A form in a black hooded cloak seemed to appear out of the darkness as it stepped into the light. It made the hairs stand up on the back of my neck. I was half expecting the hood to drop back to reveal the face of The Grim Reaper. As if we were still in our ninja mode none of us even breathed. The reaper raised her hands and pushed back the hood. Amber hair, just like Nieve's, fell across her face. As she pushed it away I saw her eyes. They weren't dark brown like Dad's and his sister's but pale blue – like mine. Then I remembered something that Spideog had said to me: 'You have your grandmother's eyes, you know.'

No one said a word. Like a bunch of zombies, we all stood and stared at each other until I just couldn't stand it any more.

'Are you my grandmother?' I asked.

She smiled at me then. It was strange. Not the grandmotherly smile that I had ever imagined. She was far too young looking and beautiful for that. 'Yes, I am,' she said. 'I see you received my message.' She looked to my father.

Dad stood stock still as she walked up to him, placed her hands on both sides of his face and tenderly kissed him on the forehead. 'I thought, my son, I had lost you to the Real World and when I heard Conor's tale of your strange illness, I thought I had lost you again. But here you are and looking fit and well.'

Dad was at a loss for words. They stared at each other and as every agonisingly long second passed, my father seemed to lose a year. When he finally spoke he sounded like a five-year-old. 'Where have you been?'

Tears welled up in Macha's eyes. 'Here my son, locked in this dreadful place.'

Nieve stepped into the light and quietly said, 'Hello Mother.'

Macha looked to her daughter and then took her hand. 'You have become a proper sorceress, my child.'

Nieve could only nod yes.

Macha hugged her and then turned to Dahy. 'General, can you take me away from here?'

'I can, my Queen,' Dahy said dropping to one knee.

My grandmother walked over to him, knelt down and placed her hand on his cheek. 'Not your queen, Diddo, only me, Macha.'

'Did you just call Dahy Diddo?' I blurted.

Dahy stood and gave me a look that made me think he was going to snap me in half. And considering that Dahy *can* snap me in half, it was a pretty scary look.

'Hey,' I said, raising my hands in a gesture of surrender, 'I'm sorry to break this tearful reunion, but we have an injured Shadowwitch here and I for one would sorely like to get the hell off this mountain. What do you say, guys?'

Dahy kicked into leader mode, with a little more chest-puffing gusto than normal. If I didn't know better, I would have said he was showing off. 'How many others are in the house?' he asked Macha.

'There are seven Brownies that live here,' she replied, 'but I think one is away from the mountain.'

'Well, we took out six on the way in. Conor and Nieve, go see if the ones in the hallway are still down.'

Nieve and I opened the door and peeped around the corner. The pile of Brownies were still there but they were moaning and moving. Nieve dashed up and quickly poked all of them in the butt with one of her pins while I picked up the weapons.

The tall Brownie opened his eyes fully and then a look of panic crossed his face. 'I cannot move my legs! What have you done to me?'

'Relax,' I said, trying to pat him on the shoulder but he took a swipe at me when I got close. 'Seriously, chill. You just got pinned by one of my aunt's specials. You'll be fine in a couple of hours.' He sat up and then pushed himself along the floor until he had his back to the wall. I felt sorry for him.

'Where is Lugh?'

'Lugh?'

'Yes, the master of this house is Lugh. Lord of All. Where is he?'

As if to answer the Brownie's question my party came into the hallway. Dad was carrying Mom and Araf had 'The Lord of All' hoisted over his shoulder like a bag of manure. Most of the Brownies, now conscious, watched with open mouths as their master was carried to the front door.

'Did you kill him?' the tall Brownie asked.

'No,' I said, 'but we are taking him back to Castle Duir. You're free now. Go back to the Brownielands, he no longer has a hold on you.'

He smiled at me then. One of those smiles that lets you know that the smile-ee knows something you don't. 'As long as he lives,' he said, 'we will never be free. We will await Lord Lugh's return. It will not be long.'

I left them with a canteen of water and they left me with a feeling of ... doom.

Outside, Dragon Tuan began to ferry all of us off the mountain. Early on in his dragon life, Tuan made it perfectly clear that he was not going to be an air taxi service for the House of Duir so this was a favour I really appreciated. I had no desire to ever see this mountain again and getting off it as fast as I could was a top priority.

Dad and the unconscious Mom went first, then Araf and the unconscious Lugh, followed by Dahy and Nieve. As my grandmother and I waited for Tuan to return she said, 'I worried about you trying to get blood from a fire worm, I worried that I led you on an impossible task – never in my life did I imagine that you could enslave a dragon.'

As I started to reply, Dragon Tuan flapped up onto the shelf. We had to cover our faces to protect our eyes from the swirling dust. 'Oh, I wish he was my slave,' I shouted over the noise, 'then I wouldn't have to walk as much as I do.'

I took Macha by the arm and led her over to the green lizard. 'Grandma, I would like you to meet my friend, Councillor Tuan.' Tuan rocked his head back and blew a puff of fire that finished with a perfect smoke ring.

Macha bravely walked right up to him and patted him on the snout like he was a horse. Tuan dropped to one knee and lowered his head as Grandma said, 'I am honoured to meet you, Councillor.'

The flight down was the scariest ride I had ever had with a dragon – and that included when Dragon Red tried to kill me. Tuan was so tired from all the upping and downing that he pretty much just dive-bombed off the mountain. I screamed like a little girl all the way down but Grandma didn't make a peep even during the G-force-inducing last second level-out. When Tuan became Tuan again I promised I would punch him for that – immediately after I threw up.

I was expecting Macha to be open-mouthed like everyone else who witnesses Tuan's transformation for the first time but when I looked at her, she had her eyes closed and her arms outstretched. I heard a snort from Acorn – looking not like the bold stallion that often gives me a hard time but more like a colt approaching his mother. That's when I noticed that all the horses were doing the same thing. They slowly approached Macha with their heads down and then shivered with delight as my grandmother caressed each one of them. It was remarkable to watch. It was like she was part of them but also above them, like a horse god. Macha the Horse Enchantress – the yews had given her the power over horses, and there in front of us was the proof. She hugged each horse in turn. The look on her face was like a mother returning to her children after a long time away.

Mom was awake, sitting with her back against a rock, with a blanket on her lap and drinking willow tea when I found her. She gave me one of those forced smiles that let me know she was OK.

'Hey Mom, it's good to see you with your eyes open. You gave me a scare. How do you feel?'

'Good, considering. Your Graysea is a remarkable healer. I'm starting to see what you see in her. I don't think she is as witless as she would have us believe.'

'That depends on which side of her brain she is using.'

'Seriously?'

I nodded and she laughed but stopped right away and held her chest in pain.

'I think you need another session. I'll see if she's up for it.'

I found Graysea and asked her if she could gill-up for Mom again. She said she was on her way to do just that now that she had seen that everyone else was OK. Out of the corner of my eye I saw Gerard's big fist hand me a glass.

'Is that wine?'

'It's something a bit stronger,' the big man replied.

'Good,' I said, knocking whatever it was back in one. The whole world wobbled like I was about to do a flashback on a bad sitcom.

When I could risk moving again without falling over, Gerard said, 'More?'

'Yes please,' I replied holding out my glass.

'You wouldn't have any of your wine with you, Gerard?' Macha asked, coming over to the fire. Behind her stood all of the horses, like groupies awaiting the beckon of a prima donna rock star.

'You know I do.' Gerard poured her a glass and she took a sip with her eyes closed like it was a chalice filled with the elixir of youth.

'Oh, it has been so long,' she sighed.

'It has indeed,' Gerard said. 'You look good for a dead woman.'

Macha smiled at him but he didn't return it. 'I'm surprised to find you here, winemaker. Thank you for coming to save me.'

'Spend no thanks on me, my Queen, I came because of Dahy. I would follow that man to the gates of hell if he wished it and I will defend him from all harm.'

'Well then let us both make sure no harm befalls him,' Macha said, still smiling but not as much.

'Let's,' Gerard said. 'More wine?'

'No,' she said, placing her hand over the top of her glass. 'I have been long away from your wine for too long. Like your company, too much of it would be overly intoxicating, but thank you.' She handed me her empty glass and walked away.

'So you two have met?' I asked Gerard.

'Oh yes,' he replied. 'We have met.'

Tuan offered to fly Mom home. She must have still felt pretty banged up 'cause she accepted. Oracle guy was given something that put him into a coma, and then stuffed in the barrel that just yesterday had held Graysea's saltwater bath. For good measure he also had a paralysing pin stuck in his neck. I wanted to feel sorry for him but I once had travelled on a wagon in a barrel and I'm sure that it was much more comfortable to do it unconscious. Still I made sure he had a few pillows in there with him.

As Gerard hammered the barrel lid closed I said, 'Well, Lugh is lugh-ed up tight.'

'What did you say?' Dad asked, and I also noticed that everyone else had stopped in their tracks.

'It was a joke. You know, locked up tight?'

'But what did you call him?'

'Lugh, the Brownies said Oracle guy's name is Lugh.'

Gerard stepped back like the barrel was about to bite him. All eyes shot to Macha.

'Is this true?' Dad asked.

She looked surprised. 'I thought you knew.'

Nieve stepped up to Macha. She had a look on her face I'm pretty sure I had never seen before. She looked – frightened. 'Are you saying that the one who had kept you prisoner for all of these years is Lugh of the Samildanack?'

'Yes,' Macha replied.

Gerard actually stumbled into me when he heard this. I steadied him and said, 'What does this mean?'

'It means,' he said, looking at the mallet in his hand, 'that in that barrel, I have just sealed – a god.'

Chapter Eight
Lugh

Macha rode in front on the way home. Not because she was a queen, but because we quickly figured out that if she wasn't in front then all of the horses would keep trying to look around to see where she was. Dahy rode with her and the two of them chatted the entire time like teenagers on the telephone. Dad and Nieve rode wordlessly behind. If Macha had any guilt in leaving them motherless for so long, she showed no sign of now trying to make up for it. I couldn't see their faces but their body language in the saddle made them look like unhappy children forced to ride a pony at a birthday party.

I was behind them with Araf – tantamount to riding alone – and behind me rode my girls, Essa and Graysea. I didn't hear them share even one syllable and I wasn't about to turn around to see if they were OK. The tension permeated the entire group to the point where Gerard, riding in the cart at the rear, was singing dirges as opposed to his usual ditties.

It wasn't just the imminent outbreak of a cat fight that was upsetting the group, it was like the whole party was spooked. And the thing that was spooking everybody was the guy locked in the barrel on Gerard's cart. I needed more details on this 'Lugh being a god' thing but Mom and Nieve were not in a talkative mood and Gerard didn't like talking to me when Essa was around, in case she thought he was taking sides. (Even a father can be afraid of a child like Essa.) And I could never get Dahy away from Macha.

At night I tried to entice Grandma into talking about Lugh and her imprisonment but she said that it was far too horrid to speak of. She went to bed early every night with a horse standing guard outside her tent.

I was reduced to spending my days staring at the scenery – not a bad thing. Spring had fully sprung and summer was once again upon The Land. The vibrancy, the … aliveness permeated everything, and – if they were like me – everyone. The feeling – no, not the feeling – the knowledge that you can live for ever came from days like these.

News of Queen Macha's return preceded us. An hour before our arrival at Castle Duir a rumble and a cloud of dust could be seen in the distance. Dahy and Dad sped to the front and were about to throw us all into battle stations when Macha said, 'There is no need for concern. It is just my children.'

Sensing the Horse Enchantress's approach, the horses in Castle Duir's stables had become anxious. The master of the stables, having heard that Macha was soon to arrive, left open all the stable doors and let the horses run to meet their mistress.

Macha dismounted and walked ahead of us as the sound of thundering hooves intensified. What a scary and magnificent sight: Macha standing alone in an open field, her hands held out as a stampede of galloping horses came directly at her. As they got nearer they squeezed together so as to be close to the Horse Enchantress as they passed. I thought for sure they were going to trample her but at the last second they parted. They swarmed past her like a flock of birds – her hands brushing the charging beasts. They swung around for another pass. They did this three times and I'm sure they would have done it all day if Macha hadn't put a stop to it. She raised her yew wand and the horses swung in front of her and then stopped as if at attention. From the middle of the herd came a huge silver stallion. I recognised him. The stable master had told me that his name was Echo because he was the spitting image of the horse that sired him – King Finn's horse. When I once asked if I could ride him I was told that he was wild – unrideable. Yet here he was, head down, offering himself to the Horse Enchantress. Macha patted him on the snout and Echo quivered. Then, fast as a tree monkey, she mounted him and galloped towards Castle Duir. The herd whinnied and followed – leaving us behind.

We didn't even have to kick our horses to catch up; Acorn leapt to join the herd whether I liked it or not. I galloped up next to Dad and Nieve. 'I'll say this about Grandma,' I shouted into the dust-filled air, 'she knows how to make an entrance.'

Mom had not been idle with the days that travelling dragon-back had given her. She had prepared a special airtight cell and had a Leprechaun smith make a pair of silver gloves/handcuffs that would hopefully render Lugh unable to whip up a breeze or any magic. While Dad and Nieve secured the prisoner, I went in search of answers.

I found Fand in the Shadowmagic laboratory she set up with Mom. She was stirring something in a small pot.

'If that's a super delicate Shadowpotion you're working on,' I said, 'I can come back later.'

'It's tea,' Fand replied reaching under the counter and producing two cups. 'Would you like some?'

'Oh, yes, thank you.'

She stirred the pot with a gold stick and when she removed it all of the used tea leaves had stuck to it. She mumbled something and the leaves all fell into a rubbish bin. Then she poured us both a cup.

'What brings you down here, Prince Conor?'

'I want to know who Lugh is.'

That query made Fand lean back and sigh. She took a sip of tea before she answered. 'Maybe that is the wrong question,' she said. 'Maybe you should be asking: what is Lugh? A question that many have been asking for a long time. Or maybe the most important question is: who is the man we have locked up in the windless cell? I'm not certain he is Lugh.'

'Gerard said he was a god.'

'A god. One man's god is another man's false idol. What is a god?'

'I don't want to interrupt you mid-flow, Fand, but do you think maybe you could answer one of my questions with something other than another question?'

Fand laughed; it was not something I had ever heard her do before. It was sweet. 'Sorry Conor, it is just that this appearance of Lugh, or whoever he is, has raised many questions.'

'OK,' I said, 'let's forget about this Oracle guy we have locked up. What are the old stories about Lugh?'

'Well, that depends on who you are talking to. Among most of the houses of Tir na Nog, Lugh is thought of simply as Banbha's consort.'

Banbha, there was that name again. Whenever there are dark tales of the early days of The Land, Banbha is the name that usually comes up. 'Banbha was one of the three original sisters that founded Tir na Nog right?'

Fand nodded.

'So Lugh was Banbha's husband.'

'This was long before customs such as marriage came about but that is essentially the idea.'

'So why did Gerard call him a god?'

'Well, as you know, many in The Land worship one or all of the sisters as gods. Leprechauns pray to Ériu for gold and most Imps venerate Fódla.'

'I've seen Araf make a blessing gesture when hears Fódla's name.'

'Yes, I imagine he does,' she said. 'But others in The Land revere Lugh as much more than a consort. There are many, especially the Brownies, who look at him as a deity.'

'Why?'

'Most in The Land believe that the first land of Tir na Nog was Duir – the Oaklands – and this was found or created by Ériu who then sent for her sisters who in turn created other lands.'

'I know this much,' I said. 'Fódla created Ur – the Heatherlands – and Banbha created Iodhadh – the Yewlands.'

'That is what the Faeries believe, but lore reads differently. Most Brownies believe that the Yewlands were first and that Lugh was already there when Banbha found it. They say Banbha was the first sister and that Ériu and Fódla betrayed and banished her. What happened to Banbha no one knows but when she vanished – so did Lugh.'

'Yeah, but the Brownies will believe anything if it gets them closer to Duir's gold.'

'It is not only the Brownies that believe that Lugh was The First – my mother believed it too.'

Fand's mother was Maeve. As the inventor of Shadowmagic, she had decimated a forest to steal sap, the blood of trees, to fuel a war against my grandfather and the House of Duir. At almost her moment of triumph she blew herself up along with many of the Fili, with a giant Shadowspell that went terribly wrong.

'No offence, Fand, but your mother had a lot of wrong ideas.'

'I will not argue with you on that point, Conor, but she once told me that she learned these tales from an Elf.'

'So the Elves are in the Lugh-is-a-god camp too?'

'Who can tell what the Elves think. I've never had a conversation with an Elf that was not about trees or wine. They do know the yews though. They are the only ones that can pass through the Yewlands unmolested by the trees.'

'I've been to this Oracle guy's house. You know it's made from yew wood.'

Fand thought and then poured us both some more tea. 'As I said, Conor, this man raises many more questions than he answers.'

When I got back to my room Ruby was waiting for me. She was sitting in my big leather chair.

'How did you get in here?'

It was like a scene from a spy movie.

'I walked in. I'm blind, not lame.'

'Well, you can walk right out again. Last time you came here I almost got killed by a tree and then again by your father and now that I think of it, I'm pretty sure your grandmother wants to kill me too.'

'Yeah,' she said with no intention of leaving, 'sorry about that.'

'Are you?'

'Of course I am. It was very nice of you to take me riding and I'm sorry you got hurt and I'm sorry you got in trouble.'

I took a hard look at her with her huge sunglasses and her feet sticking straight out from my chair and I reminded myself that even though she acted like she was forty-two, she was still only twelve. 'OK,' I said, 'and I'm sorry you had to fend for yourself outside the wall. Let's not do that again. OK?'

'Deal,' she said, sticking her hand out, not quite towards me, to shake.

'Deal,' I said, shaking. 'So what are you doing in my room?'

'I need something Daddy and Grandma can't give me.'

'Hold on, isn't this how we got into trouble last time?

'Relax, O'Neil,' she said, and I had to laugh. She sounded so much like her father. 'I just need some advice.'

'About what?'

'I want to be a sorceress. How do I do it?'

'Oh, I don't really know.'

'Who does?'

'Well, my mother is a sorceress.'

'OK,' she said, sliding off the chair and striding to the door. I just stood there befuddled until she turned around and said, 'Are you coming or what?'

Now I promised myself the last time Ruby got me into trouble that I wouldn't allow myself to be bossed around by someone a third of my weight, but I had planned to check in on Mom later anyway, and I really wouldn't mind knowing how she had become a sorceress myself.

'Fine,' I said, taking her by the hand. 'We'll see if she's busy.'

While Dad was ill, Mom had set up the room next to the master bedroom as her queenly office. As we drew closer I saw that the door was ajar and stuck my nose through the crack.

Mom was down on all fours behind her desk, I could only see her feet sticking out. I heard what sounded like hammering and then wood splintering.

I walked over and said, 'Are we doing a little remodelling?' It wasn't Mom. Macha popped up so quick that I jumped and almost fell over Ruby.

'Ow,' Ruby squealed. 'Watch it. There's a blind kid here you know.'

Macha initially looked like I had just caught her with a hand in the cookie jar, but when she noticed Ruby she became very interested. She walked around the desk, took Ruby's sunglasses off, then placed her hands on both sides of her head and tilted her face up so she could look closely into Ruby's sightless eyes.

'Hey, who are you?' Ruby demanded.

I wasn't quite sure what to do. Macha was being awfully rough with Ruby, but then she was my grandmother and what do I know about how to treat kids? Still, it was plain to see that Ruby didn't like it. When I saw Ruby cock her blind stick back ready for a strike, I grabbed her wrist and got between the two of them. I never saw Ruby hit anybody with her stick but I'd bet money that she was good at it. Macha looked angrily at me.

'Sorry Macha,' I said trying to explain myself, 'but she can't see, you know.'

'I do know,' Macha said. 'I have been waiting for you, little girl.'

'Is my mother here?' I asked.

'No,' Macha answered absently, never taking her eyes off Ruby. 'Are you waiting for her?'

Macha didn't even answer that. I walked over and looked behind the desk. There was a dagger on the floor and the skirting board had been prised away from the wall.

'What were you doing behind the desk?' When she didn't answer me I said, 'Does Deirdre know you are here?'

That seemed to get her attention. She started to answer then looked to Ruby then back to me like she was trying to make up her mind about something. 'Oh well,' she said reaching into a fold on the side of her dress. 'I was hoping that I could be around for longer but it seems that now is the time.' Out of a pocket she produced a lace fan that she snapped open like a Spanish lady at the opera. With a flick of her wrist the door to Mom's room slammed closed in a way that looked a lot like the magic that Oracle guy used on the mountain. I started to ask her how she had done that but I only got as far as, 'How …' before her fan flicked in my direction and I sailed across the room and into the wall. By the time I came to my senses she was sitting on my chest painfully holding my nose. I opened my mouth to gasp for air and when I did I felt and tasted some kind of liquid hitting the back of my throat. She then pushed my mouth closed and jumped on my chest – it was swallow or drown. It tasted awful and I coughed and rolled onto my side as Macha jumped off me.

Ruby let loose one of her migraine-inducing screams. Macha was on her in an instant, covering her mouth, snatching her stick and throwing it across the room. I got up to help her but Macha shouted at me, 'Stay where you are!' And I did. Unlike one of my aunt's paralysing pins it wasn't like I couldn't move, it was like my body just didn't want to move.

'What have you done to me?' I said, desperately trying to move my legs.

'That fluid I placed in your mouth was horse … well you are better off not knowing what part of a horse it was but now that you have ingested it, I have control of your body. Sit,' she commanded and I dropped hard on my butt. 'See?'

'What do you want?'

Ruby squirmed and then Macha pulled her hand away in pain. Ruby had obviously bitten her. As she started to scream again Macha gave her a hard slap. Shock and then tears came to the poor kid's face. She went instantly from the woman-child that bosses me around to an all-too-fragile twelve-year old.

'What I want,' Macha said, looking at her bitten hand, 'is this child to be silent.' She reached into her pocket and produced a handkerchief. 'Come over here, Conor, and gag her.'

I almost laughed. There was no way I was going to do that but even as the smirk hit my face my body stood up, took the handkerchief from my puppet-master grandmother and pulled it across the child's mouth.

Macha said, 'Make sure it's tight,' and, despite every cell in my brain telling me to stop, I pulled it tighter before I tied it in the back. A muffled cry of pain came from Ruby and the only thing I could do was say 'Sorry.'

Macha went back down onto the floor and recommenced ripping up the skirting boards. I looked to the door and felt that with Macha's attention elsewhere I could pick up Ruby and make a break for the door, but when I tried Macha said, 'Don't even think about leaving.'

'What are you doing?' I tried to ask and was surprised to find I could.

Macha didn't stand up but from the floor said, 'Do you know whose room this is?'

'Yes, it's my mother's.'

'Do you know whose room this was before your mother?'

'No.'

There was another sound of splintering and wrenching of wood. I heard Macha exclaim, 'Ah ha,' followed by the sound of scraping. Macha then reappeared from behind the desk in a plume of dust and loudly dropped on it – a leather-bound manuscript. 'This room was once Ona's lair.'

Holy cow, I said to myself. A manuscript chock full of Ona's predictions. As if her prophecies hadn't caused enough problems – here were a stack more.

'Where are they keeping Lord Lugh?'

I didn't want to answer her but found myself saying, 'The guest chambers, one floor down.'

'Come. Bring the girl and make sure you are not seen.'

My possession was the strangest thing. I was still able to do ordinary things as long as they didn't seem to contradict the will of Macha. Before we left the room I picked up Ruby's sunglasses and put them on her face. I pushed her hair back and told her everything would be OK just before I gruffly dragged her by the arm. I stuck my head through a crack in the door and saw a guard on his usual patrol. I tried to shout to him but instead I unwillingly ducked back inside the room and waited for him to pass. When he had gone I led us past my room and down the servants' staircase.

The floor had been cleared of all guests except Lugh. There were two guards posted outside the door and another two walking a patrol. Macha waited for one of the patrol guards to come past and blew him hard into the wall with her fan. I was surprised his head didn't crack open.

Macha pointed to the unconscious guard and said, 'Take his sword and kill the other one.'

'No,' I said. I was proud of myself when that came out. All the way down the steps I had been incanting a Fili meditation chant and was beginning to think I was getting control again.

Macha spun on me, 'I said … take his sword and kill the other guard.'

I felt a strange nauseous pressure building in my stomach and chest. 'I … I will not … not kill one of my … my own guards.'

'Kneel, Conor,' Macha commanded and I dropped to my knees. 'You will …'

With all of my will power I struck at her. I wanted to get her in the head and hopefully knock her out against the wall but she hissed, 'Stop,' just as I began to move and I only succeeded in slapping Ona's manuscript out of her hand.

'You cannot breathe,' she said to me and instantly the breath that I had been taking at that second stopped in my throat. My lungs and diaphragm seemed to still be working but nothing could get past my throat. She rolled me on my back and said, 'You will kill that guard or I will have you strangle the little girl. Do you understand?'

I nodded, clutching my throat, I couldn't even gasp. Tears flooded from under Ruby's Ray-Bans as she whimpered, lost in this confusing darkness.

'Good,' Macha said, 'then breathe.'

Precious air filled my lungs as I propped myself up on all fours.

'Now hand me the manuscript and kill that guard.'

I did as she commanded and handed her Ona's book from the floor, then went to the fallen guard. As I reached for his sword I said, 'Please Grandma, don't make me do this.'

'Fine,' she said, 'take the stick. Just get it done.'

I walked the length of the hall past the two guards at the door and met the second patrolling guard around the corner. He was an Imp and was surprised to see me.

'Prince Conor,' he said, 'I … I don't think you are supposed to be here.'

'Relax, I'm the Prince of Hazel and Oak,' I said and then pointed behind him saying, 'and he's the King of Duir.'

The guard looked around and I clocked him high in the neck with the banta. I caught him before his head hit the stone floor. I wished I had a willow tea bag to put in his pocket for when he woke up.

I was just about to walk back to the guest room/cell when the two guards sailed past me in the air and smashed into the wall in front of me. Two more victims of my grandmother's hurricane fan. Since Macha was out of vision I felt I could make a run for it but just as I took my first steps to leave Macha said, 'Conor,' and I could do nothing but follow that voice. Macha was at the door holding Ruby in front of her by both shoulders.

'Search the guards for keys,' she said and I obeyed.

I tried not to give the keys to her but was unsuccessful in operating my hand. I did manage to get a question out. 'Why are you doing this?'

'Why am I following Lugh's plan? Because dear boy, he is a god and not to would be a sin.'

'But you also helped Cialtie, didn't you? Why help him?'

Macha turned the key in the lock. We walked in and then opened the inner doors that had been newly constructed to prevent any wind from entering the room when the outer door was opened. Lugh was chained to the bed. A muslin cloth across his mouth stopped him from even whistling and his hands were shackled in silver gloves. Macha pointed to him.

'I did not want to take sides when it came to my children,' Macha said, 'but Lugh insisted on helping – his son.'

Chapter Nine

Ona's Book

Cialtie is not Finn's son, he's Lugh's son. He's Dad's half-brother. I imagine news like that would shock some people but as soon she said it I thought, *that makes sense*. Sure Dad and Uncle Cialtie looked alike, but I could never get over how differently their minds worked. Now that I had met Lugh and then heard this news – it all started to make sense.

Lugh, still under the influence of one of my mother's specials, was awake but looked pretty out of it. Grandma ordered me to unlock his custom-made silver gloves and chains. Macha then stood over him and fanned his face like a trainer between rounds in a boxing match. The more the wind hit his face the clearer his eyes became until he reached out and grabbed her fan. Macha backed away as Lugh ripped the sheets from the bed. In one hand he fluttered the fan towards his chest. Even to me, uneducated in the ways of wind magic, it looked like he was building up energy. In his other hand he swirled the sheet around his head. He then turned to the window that only days before had been bricked up and let loose a scream. A blast of air blew the bricks and the window right out into the night.

'Open the doors,' Lugh commanded.

Macha looked to me and said, 'Well? Open them.'

I opened the inner and outer doors and a breeze flew through the room. Lugh stood on the bed feeding on the air. The colour returned to his cheeks and lips; it almost looked like he grew muscles and a couple of inches. He took in a huge gasp of air, then turned and vomited out of the blown-out window. He turned back to us, wiping his mouth on his sleeve and smiling.

'Excuse me, my love, I had to purge the poisons that that Shadowwitch had filled my body with.'

Macha let go of Ruby and ran into Lugh's arms. As they embraced, Ruby made a pitiful attempt to find her way out of the room. Macha saw her as Lugh's embrace spun her around. 'Stop her,' she said and I did.

'I'm sorry Ruby,' I whispered, 'she has control of me but I'll find a way to get us out of this. I promise.' She buried her face in my stomach and hugged me. I hugged her back, glad that I could at least do that but desperately wishing I could do more.

I looked up to see Macha kissing Lugh. If there was any part of me that wasn't sure that these two were in love and in league with each other, it was dispelled then. Anybody that kisses someone immediately after seeing him puke … well … that's true love.

'How long have I been here?' Lugh asked.

'Not even a day, my love.'

'And so soon you have found the girl, Ona's writings and the bows?'

'The girl came to me as I was searching for the book. As for the bows – they are in the armoury. Not far from here in the north wing.'

'What do you want with Ruby?' I said.

Lugh looked shocked and turned to Macha. 'I thought you had him under your control.'

'His body and will are mine, my love, but that impudent tongue is harder to subdue.'

Lugh laughed. 'Well, he is your grandson. Would you prefer if I killed him?'

I felt Ruby's shoulders begin to shake, or maybe it was me.

'There is no need, my lord, he knows no more than they will deduce when we are gone.'

'He is a loose end and you know how I hate loose ends, but I understand your sentimentality, I will do it.'

'No,' she said, and for a moment I thought she was about to fight for me until she said, 'Let me. Sleep.'

I felt my knees buckle but then I heard her speak again and my body stopped its race to unconsciousness just long enough to hear my own grandmother say, 'Sleep and *never* awaken.'

Sleep and never awaken. That refrain followed me down into the well of unconsciousness. *Sleep and never awaken.* Unlike the well of despair the oak tree had dragged me into, this well had no sides, no bottom, no top. No nothing. Calling it a well was wrong. I wasn't falling, because falling would imply I fell from somewhere and there was no longer a somewhere to fall from. As I existed in a void so lacking anything, my mind tried to grasp onto thoughts. Thoughts of a world where senses actually sensed things. Things, tangibles, objects began to be impossible for me to even imagine. As I fell … no, drifted … even words to represent anything were slipping away from me. I forced myself to at least remember where I was.

I remembered going to an old cemetery once when I was a kid and seeing names on gravestones where underneath it said 'Sleeping', and I remembered thinking, *they're not sleeping – they're dead.* But now I was doomed to an eternal sleep and I thought maybe those stonemasons got it right. But I didn't think that for long because my thoughts were fleeting. Or maybe my thoughts were long thoughts and just seemed fleeting because I had thought them for a long, long time. Never is a long time to not awaken. What is time when the last hour on the clock – is for ever?

It was only a matter of time in that un-land of timelessness before I would go mad. Either that or sail into nothingness. *Madness or nothingness, here's a choice you don't get every day*, said the man existing in a realm with no days.

Vivid memories filled my thoughts. I was a child. I was sick. My mother sang to me in a language so old I couldn't understand it but I felt it healing me. My mother placed a cool compress on my brow. I could feel her smile but not see it. Then it came to me that this couldn't be a memory. My mother was never there when I was a child. These memories were false and I was losing it. I was slipping into a world made only of my own making. Madness – that's what my mind had chosen – an eternity of madness. I wanted to shout and wondered if I could. I almost felt my lungs expand, I …

I shot up in bed and screamed, 'NO!' The cold compress fell onto my lap. Mom had her arms around me in a second.

'It's all right, Conor,' my mother said, patting my hair. 'You're safe, you're with me, it's Deirdre.'

I reached up and felt her hand – the first sensation I had actually felt in … I don't know how long. I looked and she was there. I touched her face and she felt real.

'Mother?' I asked and was surprised at the sound of my own voice. It was deep. I felt my chin and the stubble there brought me forward in time – I was not a boy – I was a man. 'Where am I?'

'You're safe, my son, you're with me in your own room.'

I looked around and saw the knife-marked wood panelling and said, 'In Duir?'

'Yes.'

I pushed myself higher in the bed. The world around me solidified as the dream world I had been lost in receded. 'How long have I been gone?'

'You have been asleep for two days. We could not wake you.'

'Two days?'

'Yes I have been worried about you. How do you feel?'

'Only two days? I feel like I have been gone for … ever.' I smiled then as that blessed relief hit me. The relief that comes with the realisation that the nightmare was only a dream and its burdens were only an illusion. But as the problems of the dream realm faded into smoke, the waking world crashed down on me. 'Ruby!' I swung my legs out of the bed. 'Where is she?'

'Easy, Conor,' Mom said placing her hand on my shoulders, 'She's missing. We have scoured the castle and the grounds but she is gone.'

'They have her.'

'Who?'

'Macha and Lugh.'

I dropped back into bed and for the first time looked in to my mother's eyes. She had that haggard look that moms get when their children are sick. I never saw it when I was young but it was instantly recognisable now. I reached up and touched the side of her face. 'I'm OK, Mom. I think. Macha forced some sort of essence of horse down my throat and I was like a zombie.' When she looked confused I said, 'It was like she had control over me and I had to do what she told me to do. The last thing she commanded me to do was, "Sleep and never awaken." I thought she had killed me.'

Mom thought for a bit. 'That would make sense. Her power over you only lasted for as long as the horse essence was in your system.'

'You're saying the reason I woke up was that … I, like, sobered up from the spell?'

'Basically.'

So I filled Mom in on how I caught Macha searching her room and finding Ona's book of prophecies and then how they said they wanted the book, the girl and the bows.

'The bows on the wall of the armoury – the ones left by the dead Fili – are they the bows they were talking about?'

'Yes,' she said, 'they are gone.'

'All of them?'

She nodded.

The door opened and when Brendan stuck his face in the room and saw me awake, he ran up to the bed.

'Where is she?'

He had the same look on his face that I had seen on my mother's just moments before, except he looked a lot worse. Brendan wore the frantic face of a parent who had lost a child and I could tell just by looking at him that he had been playing worst-case scenarios over and over in his head for the last two days. 'I don't know where she is. Macha and Lugh took her.'

'Why?'

'I don't know,' I said. 'I do know that it was not a whim. From the way they were talking, it seemed that kidnapping Ruby and stealing the yew bows was part of a plan.'

Brendan sat on the bed and hung his head. 'But it doesn't make sense.'

'I know,' I said, placing my hand on his shoulder, but he shook it off. This was Detective Fallon and he wasn't looking for sympathy.

'Taking my Ruby makes no sense, but taking the bows makes no sense either. I once asked Master Spideog if I could use his bow and he said I could not. I thought he meant I wasn't allowed but he said I couldn't because I wouldn't be strong enough to pull the string back. I scoffed, so he handed over his bow with that all knowing look on his face and – he was right. I couldn't even bend the bow an inch. Spideog explained to me that a yew bow changes its tension in tune with the archer that owns it. The wood is flexible when the string is drawn back and then stiffens when the arrow is being released. Only the person who has been judged by a yew, and given that piece of wood, can operate that bow. Those bows should be useless to all except their owners.'

'Lugh has proved himself to be a master of yew wood so who knows what his plans for the bows are,' Mom said. 'One thing is clear: it seems that we have all been unwitting players in Macha and Lugh's puppet play. And we have lost an important clue – the book of Ona's writings that Macha found in my office.'

A memory flashed in my mind. A memory of something that seemed like years ago but as I smiled, I knew it was just from a couple of days earlier. I reached for my pocket and then realised I was in bedclothes. 'Where are my clothes?'

Mom pointed to a chair in the corner of the room. I ran to them and found in a pocket what I was looking for.

'When I was under Macha's control I had a moment when I almost broke free. I slapped Ona's book from her hand, but then she regained control and made me pick it up for her.' I held out a small ripped piece of paper. 'But as I was giving it back, I ripped a corner from a page.'

Mom removed an amber stone that was clipped onto the collar of her robe. It was one of her Shadowmagic book clips. She attached it to the sliver of paper I had given her and almost instantly a ghost of a book appeared in her hand. It was a shimmering translucent replica of the one I had seen Macha remove from under Mom's desk.

'Is that a book full of predictions from that prophet Ona you guys keep talking about?' Brendan asked.

'Yes,' Mom said, 'I believe it is.'

'So with this maybe we can learn why they took my little girl?'

'Perhaps,' Mom said, holding the Shadowbook like it was about to explode, 'but are you sure you wish to learn whatever else this contains?'

'I don't care. I want my daughter back.'

John Lenahan

'As do I, Brendan,' Mom said, but learning one's future is not a soothing thing. It has sent many over the brink of madness. In others, like Cialtie, foreknowledge is the fruit that eventually distils into evil.

'I will read it,' said a woman as she entered through the door. She was beautiful, tall with a huge mane of dark brown hair tied back into a ponytail; her cheekbones were high and rosy with youth. She stormed in like she owned the place but I had never seen her before.

'I had thought my future was already written and almost ended,' she said in a voice so pure that I almost wanted to hear her sing. 'I now have a new lease of life and I shall use it for the sole purpose of saving Ruby. The only fear I have of that book is that it will not tell me where the child is.'

Brendan stood up and faced the woman, then crouched down a bit to look directly in her eyes and said, 'Mom?'

Chapter Ten

Nora

Later in the council room it was decided that Fand should read Macha's manuscript. Everyone agreed that knowledge of the future was a dangerous thing. Fand would tell us if she found anything relevant that could help us find Ruby and then, using her Fili mind juju, she would forget the rest.

'You can do that?' I asked

'No problem-o,' she replied using the phrase I had taught her.

'Wow, can you teach me? I've done a couple of stupid things in my day that I'd like to forget.' Fand smiled but never took her eyes from the book.

'Only a couple?' Essa piped in.

Dad held his hands up and shot both Essa and me a look that said, *not now kids.* 'Let's keep focused people. If Fand can find out why my mother took the girl then maybe we can figure out where she is. Deirdre, could you perform a Shadowcasting?'

'I will try,' Mom said, 'but Shadowcasting is not a reliable locator. It is good at predicting events but as a tracking spell it is often lacking.'

'Surely she is either on Mount Cas or in the Reedlands,' Nora said. It still unnerved me a bit when Brendan's mother spoke. Her voice was completely different and she was so young looking.

When Nora heard that her granddaughter had been kidnapped she immediately went to Tuan and took him up on his offer of dragon's blood to make her young again. She said she needed to be strong if she was going to fight to get her Ruby back. It was going to take me a while before I got used to equating the wise deliberate old lady, whom I had originally met, with this jumpy, young and, I'm a bit embarrassed to say, fanciable woman before me.

'The Reedlands is not a place to enter blindly,' Dahy said.

'I can vouch for that,' I said. 'I almost died the two times I went there and you know what they say: the third time's the charm.'

'And I believe,' Dahy continued, 'that our assault on Mount Cas was easy because it was part of Lugh's plan. If he were to oppose us he could defend his Yew House easily – with disastrous results for us.'

'We can't just sit here!' Nora banged the table then closed her eyes to compose herself. 'I apologise, with this body comes the hormones of the young.'

'No apologies are necessary,' Dad said. 'Deirdre, how long will it take to set up a Shadowcasting?'

'Two days,' she said, reaching across and taking Nora's hand. 'That is the very soonest I could be ready.'

'Then I'm going to the Yewlands,' Brendan said.

'What?' was pretty much the reply from everyone there.

'If we are going to war, I want a bow. A yew bow. Spideog said I could have his if the yews allowed it. I'm going to ask the yews for his bow.'

'Brendan, love,' Nieve said, 'it takes decades of study to prepare for a judgement by a yew.'

Brendan stood. 'I have studied with the greatest archer in The Land. He has deemed me worthy and my quest is to save my daughter. I dare them to find me unworthy.'

I expected someone to object but that statement shut everyone up.

'I'll take you,' I said.

'Conor,' Mom said, 'you cannot enter Ioho. The yews will kill you.'

'Oh, don't worry, Mom. I ain't going in there again. I'll just take him to the edge and wait. I know the way.'

'I will accompany them,' Araf said, and as usual everybody jumped a bit.

'Great,' I said, 'I'll have somebody to talk to while I wait.'

'I'm going too,' Nora said. Before anybody could say that that was a bad idea she explained: 'This new body has too much energy for me to be sitting at home and waiting. I'll travel with my son.'

Later that night I stuck my nose into Dad's study. He was busy doing kingy stuff: allotting the stipends to all of the different kingdoms. He looked up and said, 'Do you want me to give more gold to the Vinelands and maybe Essa will start talking to you again?'

'I don't think you have that kind of money, Dad.'

'You looking for advice on your love life?'

'You got any?'

'Sure,' he said. 'Go ask your mother.'

He dropped his pen and got serious. 'Do you think Brendan's mother will be OK with you outside of the castle walls?'

'Well, back in the Real World when, like, a thousand cops invaded her home, she hardly even batted an eyelid. She's coping with all of the turmoil around here pretty well and Brendan says she's a good rider. So I think she'll be fine. And anyway, if she is anything like her son – she'll come whether I let her or not.'

'All right then. I've had scouts patrolling for quite a while now and it's been library-quiet out that way but still – be careful, OK?'

'Hey Dad, it's me. What kind of trouble can I get into?'

The look from Dad said it all.

'Dad? I want to tell you something but I don't know how to, other than to just say it.'

'Shoot.'

'Before Macha left she told me that Lugh was Cialtie's father.'

Dad leaned forward and did that thing he always did when he was deep in thought. He reached up with his left hand and attempted to take off his reading glasses, except he didn't have glasses on. Since his dragon blood rebirth he didn't need them any more. He smiled self-consciously then covered his mouth with his hand. That's the other thing he does when he's deliberating or stressed. It's like he's stopping himself from saying anything stupid before he has thoroughly thought things out. Finally he leaned back and said, 'Good.'

'Good?'

'Conor, it is an awful thing to hate one's brother. Now I only have to hate half of him.'

We left at, you guessed it, dawn. Even when my parents weren't going on the trip, I had to get up before the sun. I didn't try to talk Brendan into leaving later. He was not in the kind of mood where you could joke. Not that I blamed him. The way my luck with women is going these days I will probably never have kids, but I imagine having your child kidnapped is enough to literally drive you crazy. I was impressed with how well Brendan was holding up. He was acting with a swift and deliberate purpose that was hard to keep up with but on the whole he was pretty together. Saying that, he reminded me of the cartoon character that after falling off a cliff only needs one pebble to hit him in the head before he crumbles into tiny pieces. I didn't want to be that pebble.

Nora I could no longer read. She seemed to be all over the place. She was a good rider. The stable master hearing that she was new to The Land gave her a gentle mare that she instantly returned like he was a used-car dealer who had tried to sell her a lemon. He shrugged and gave her a frisky stallion named Blackberry. Nora handled him but it took some time. Periodically Blackberry would try it on with his novice rider and bolt or try to rear onto his hind legs, but Nora was up to the challenge and finally got him to calm down. When I felt it was safe enough I rode next to her.

'You've got your hands full with that one,' I said, pointing to her horse.

'I've raised a son,' she said with a nod towards Brendan. 'You just have to set some boundaries and then they're OK.'

'Yes, but baby Brendan couldn't throw you and break your neck.'

'You would be surprised as to what kind of trouble baby Brendan could get into,' Nora replied looking over to her son, who smiled with the forced smile of a man who just couldn't come up with a real one. We slowed a bit to leave him with his thoughts.

'I wish there was more I could do to assure him … and you … that Ruby will be all right.'

'You can't assure that, Conor,' Nora said, 'that's the problem.'

'No, I guess I can't. But she just has to be.'

'Amen to that.'

Blackberry snorted then threw his head back while almost side-stepping into me. Nora tightened the reins and pulled him back into line like an old pro.

'How are you doing?' I asked.

'Ol' Blackberry and I will be OK,' she said patting his neck, 'we just need to get to know each other.'

'No I mean how are *you* doing?'

She laughed a sad laugh. 'Well my body is raging with hormones and wild energy – it's like I went through puberty in a day. And then there is the anger – they took my little Ruby. I want to kill them with a baseball bat – you know?'

I nodded yes – 'cause I did too.

'And then there's this place. Just because I believed in Tir na Nog all of my life doesn't mean I *always* believed it. When you have faith in things that everyone else thinks are crazy, you often have doubts. But here I am. And it's more than just seeing Tir na Nog or smelling it or touching it … I feel it … inside. I feel …'

I waited for her to find the word. When she failed I offered it to her. 'Immortal?'

'Yes,' she said.

We rode in silence for a while. This route was almost identical to the first trip I had ever taken in The Land, except that this time there was no one firing arrows at the back of my head. This was the same place where I first felt what Nora was feeling now. This was where I first learned that beech trees were gossipy and where I caught my first sight of the white plumes of the mountain ash. Riding, with my mother behind me, this was where the vitalising energy of The Land transformed me. It was here where I, too, learned how it felt to live for ever.

We followed the path. It was mid-morning when we came to water.

'River Lugar,' Araf said as he dismounted and then washed his face in the water in a way that seemed more like an ablution.

'Lugar?' Nora said. 'That sounds too much like Lugh for my liking.'

'I was taught that the river was named after him,' Araf said.

'If only the man were as easy to find as the river,' Brendan said.

We followed the river path until we came to the Duir boat-house. Inside were half a dozen small riverboats. Dad said we could take the royal barge with its gold-plated rudder that would propel us if we incanted to it in Ogham. Back at the castle I made Araf learn the mumbo jumbo. Having Dad teach me words in an ancient language was too much like my schooldays.

Just because we were being propelled by magic didn't mean that we were breaking any speedboat records. The ride was less like a high-speed chase from a spy movie and more like that old science experiment where you put a sliver of soap on the back of a bit of balsa wood. But as the old saying goes, beggars who don't want to row can't be choosers – or something like that.

There was plenty of light left in the day but we had been warned by everyone that if you have to disturb a yew, then it should be done in the morning. I wanted to know why. 'Do they get grumpy in the afternoons?' – No one was sure but as a matter of statistics more people survived a yew judging in the morning than in the afternoon. If I were a yew it would probably be the other way around. Gerard had told me that there was one of his luxury camping huts just before the last bend in the river before the Yewlands. I pointed it out to Araf and he beached the barge. After wrapping the rope from the boat around the base of a holly bush we all filed past and touched the tree to say thanks. Nora watched us and then did the same. A small squeal came out of her that at first I thought was a cry of pain but then I saw her face – she was elated.

'You OK?' I asked.

'That tree just said, "You're welcome."'

'Not all of them are so nice,' I warned. 'Trust me on that.'

Dinner was a stew prepared by the chef from Castle Duir that we only had to heat in the fireplace of Gerard's hut. It was the closest thing The Land has to compare with a TV dinner. Actually if any of the Real World's TV dinners were this good there wouldn't be any restaurants. Nora ate like she had never seen food before. I worried that she might just eat her spoon.

She caught us all staring and apologised. 'I haven't had an appetite like this in fifty years.' And then continued eating like there was no tomorrow.

Brendan was outside and the only one of us not chowing down.

'You nervous, Detective?' I asked.

'I'd be lying if I said no.'

'Are you ready for this?'

'I'd better be.'

'No,' I said, 'I mean, have you prepared?'

'Spideog, and others, told me that a judgement for an archer is different than for a sorceress. Sorceresses must prepare for their specialty but an archer need only be a good archer and Clathandian.'

'Clathandian? What does that mean?'

'There is no good English word for it. Even Nieve's gold ear thingy doesn't come up with a translation. The best I could get would be pure of spirit.'

'And is your spirit pure?'

'I once asked Spideog how I could tell if I was in the state of Clathandian and he said, "That is for the yew to decide."'

'That's a drag. It would be nice if you could have, like, a breathalyser test before you risked your neck in there.'

Brendan laughed, the first laugh I had heard from him since Ruby was taken. 'There's a project for your mother – a Clathandian breathalyser. She'd make a fortune.'

But Brendan's good humour didn't last long and his attention drifted away to his daughter and his task ahead. Before I left him alone I said, 'Try and eat something, my friend. I think you might need your strength tomorrow.'

Back inside, Nora, who had eaten probably half of the stew, was asking Araf if she could finish off his leftovers.

'Your nice new body is going to get a bit big around the middle if you keep that up,' I said.

'You know, Conor, I have been given a new life and I think this time around, I'm not going to care.' She smiled the same smile I saw on an older version of the same woman when she saw her son return to her; but then a shadow crossed the face. The smile vanished, replaced by a look of guilt – guilt for even allowing a smile. 'First we find Ruby,' she said.

'You mentioned before that you had believed in Tir na Nog. How did you even know about it? How did you know you were Hawathiee?'

'Hawathiee? What does that mean?'

Oh sorry, Hawathiee means … of The Land. It's like in the Real World when we say human.'

'Oh, my father told me that his father and his father's father, going back to before there were calendars or even letters to write on them, told him that we came from a race that was banished from paradise for going against the laws of nature. He, and my mother too, believed that my ancestors arrived in the Real World in a barbarous age when Ireland was a vast forest. The newly banished arrivals were humbled by their experience and chose not to subjugate the barbarians of that island. Instead they chose to teach them.'

'Druids,' I said.

'That is what my parents called themselves and their most important rule for me was to keep the faith. Their grandparents had come over to America during the Irish Famine. Keeping the faith was hard in the new world but just as I was about to lose mine to the modern world, I found a man whose parents had handed down to him the same family lore. We were made for each other. I had a friend who once said that rooms were brighter when we were in one together. He was my soulmate.'

'Brendan's father?'

'Yes,' she said with a sigh, 'I lost him to war. He didn't want to leave me but back then they made young men go to war. I was left alone to raise a son on my own. We did well until Brendan became a teen. Then he started to think that what I believed was crazy. I didn't have his father to help me and I feared that I was going to be the first in all of that time to break the chain. To have a son who lost the faith.' She looked out the doorway to her son pacing in the twilight. 'But here I am. If not for you and all of the chaos you have inflicted on my son and my family – my heritage would have been lost.' She reached across and placed her hand on my cheek.

'You're welcome,' I said.

She gave me another one of those forced little laughs. The only kind of laugh I was going to get until Ruby was found.

I heard Araf douse the fire. I shouted out the door. 'Hey copper, you sleepin' tonight?'

'Yeah, I'll be in in a little while,' Brendan called back.

I curled up in one of Gerard's bunks – oh so much better than sleeping on hard ground – and was asleep before I heard him come in.

I awoke feeling great. I made another mental note in the imaginary book *Things to Do When Life Calms Down Around Here*. I promised myself that I would get a map from Essa's dad and take a trip where I only slept in Gerard huts every night. Then I wondered if things ever did calm down around here. I washed in the River Lugar and shared a breakfast with Araf. The other two were too nervous to eat. Brendan sat waiting in the boat, his legs jittering, while Araf and I closed up the hut.

The river bent ahead and if I remembered rightly, as soon as we took it, we would be in view of the two guardian yews that stood on top of the boulders on either side of the river.

The yews were as scary and magnificent as I remembered. A cold sweat dripped down my back as I recalled the first time I had been here, as part of a desperate escape from my uncle's dungeon. Then we travelled silently through the Yewlands hoping the deadly trees would take no notice. And they didn't. I had no desire or intention of repeating that gambit and I worried for my friend who would soon be entering that forest and asking one of those trees to judge his worth – knowing that the price of failure was death.

I saw a small sandy bank on the left and told Araf to steer to it. He was just about to turn the rudder when I saw him bring his hand up fast to his neck like he was swatting a mosquito. He then stared at me wide eyed and fell over the side of the boat.

I was so shocked I didn't do anything for a second, but when I saw him bobbing face down in the water I started to take off the Lawnmower – the Sword of Duir – and dive in after him. As I was fiddling with the buckle, a sharp pain in my neck made me turn. That's when every muscle in my body turned to jelly. I crumpled into the bottom of the barge, but before the world went black I had a chance to see in what direction the boat was heading. It was sailing straight and true into – the Yewlands.

Chapter Eleven

Judgement

The stinging in my neck was the first thing I noticed when I awoke. I reached to the source of the pain and removed a gold dart that I only had a couple of seconds to inspect before it dissolved into smoke and ash between my fingers. I was alone in the barge. I knew where I was. The green light filtering through the canopy confirmed I was deep in the Yewlands. I popped my nose up over the side of the barge like a soldier sticking his head out from a foxhole. My travelling companions were nowhere to be seen. Where were they? What had happened? What should I do? I definitely should get out of the Yewlands but what about Brendan and Nora? And Araf? If he fell face down in the water with the same thing that got me in the neck then … he must have drowned. What the hell happened?

Think, Conor. I had to assume that the barge wasn't too far into the Yewlands so if I could get it turned around without disturbing the yews, then I could get back and find Araf, or at least his body. If Brendan and Nora survived then that's the only place I could think that they would know to go.

I crawled to the stern of the barge and then kicked myself, remembering that I hadn't paid attention when my father was teaching Araf the magic words in Ogham that made the rudder propel the boat. Dad had said I should learn the ancient vocabulary too, but as usual I didn't listen. Gods I hate it when he's right.

I could see the entrance to the Yewlands off in the distance. I maybe could have swum that far if the current was with me, but against it I didn't think I could make it. I knew instinctively I couldn't walk along the banks of the river without the yews noticing me. I was literally up you-know-what creek without a paddle. My only other option was to push the barge back into the river and hope the current would eventually take me through the Yewlands without notice. What I would do on the other side was something I would have to deal with when, and if, I got there. This was the least worst of all my options. I hated the thought of abandoning my friends but I really had no way of getting to them even if I had a clue where they were – which I didn't.

All my deliberations were for naught, 'cause when I placed one foot on land to push off the barge, every muscle in my body froze up. No, that's not right, my muscles were fine, I could feel them trying to work. It was my bones. I felt like I was being pushed and pulled from the inside. I tried to yell but as soon as noise began to fly out of my mouth my jaw slammed shut making an audible clack of my molars, which thankfully didn't crack. With one leg still in the barge and the other on the shore, I stiffened up like a guy in a body-cast from some old black and white comedy movie. I stood like this for a minute, only able to grunt and move my eyeballs and then was mercifully released. I instantly tried to push the barge out but as soon as I tried I was turned into a human board again. Whatever was holding me made me wait for several minutes before I was once again released. This time I dove into the river. My thinking (I admit there really wasn't much thinking) was that if I could get some distance between me and whoever my puppet master was, I could get away. What happened was that I froze up again – this time in water with a heavy sword around my waist. I dropped like a stone. I hit the riverbed and said loud in my head, *OK, I get it. I'll go where you want me to.* I didn't know if that message went anywhere but I hoped that it went somewhere soon. I had about twenty seconds of air left in me.

In fact, I had forty seconds' worth. Just as I thought my lungs were going to erupt blowing my head clean off, I was released and scrambled to the surface gasping and spluttering. I waded to the bank and asked the air, 'Now what?'

What was a telekinetic game of hot and cold. Every time I went in a direction that my unseen force didn't want me to go I froze up, usually falling over. I then had to change direction until I found the way it wanted me to go. This went on for quite a while. I was walking deep into the yew forest. Not good. I racked my brains trying to remember if I had ever heard a story about someone accidentally wandering into the Yewlands and making it out alive. I hadn't, 'cause I suspected it had never happened. Finally I decided I wasn't going to play this stupid game any more if it just meant I was prolonging my ultimate demise, so I sat down and refused to move. That's when my possessor actually took control of my walking. Unkind invisible hands manipulated individual bones in my body forcing one foot in front of the other, and pressing so much strain on my knees and hips that I finally screamed and agreed to continue my guided walk on my own steam.

Eventually the powers that drove me only had to give my wrist a tweak to keep me in the right direction. All the while I kept a look out for Brendan and Nora. I hadn't seen what had happened to them. They might have fallen in the water like Araf but if they were in here I worried most about Nora. She was unprepared for this – but then again, so was I. I decided to worry about myself for a while.

After what seemed like hours I came to a point where my spirit guide would only let me walk into a tree. Ahead was a yew that to me looked exactly like the zillions of ones I had been forced to walk past. I took a deep breath and said to myself *this is it*. After all I had been through, I was going to be killed alone in the forest by a tree. I pondered the philosophical implications of this. If a man falls over in a forest without making any noise is he really dead? I thought about that for a nanosecond and decided the answer was – yes. I felt a Fergalish smile light my face and wished my old cuz was here with me to share the joke.

I placed my hand on the bark and said, 'What do you want?'

You would think a tree that was older than most dinosaur fossils would be beyond shocking, but I think I puzzled this one. A voice came into my head that was surprisingly pleasant.

You never know with trees. Some of them just reach into your brain and take what they want to know. Others can't do that and wait for you to speak or at least think purposefully. With the reputation the yews had and the psychic push and pull I had just been through, I was expecting an unpleasant experience. Instead, my mind was filled with a voice (or a feeling of a voice) that was neither male nor female – or maybe it was both.

'What do I want?'

'Yeah, what do you what? You just pushed and pulled me like a hundred miles and now here I am so what the hell do you want?'

'It is we that should be asking that question of you,' the tree said, using 'we' like it was the 'royal we'.

'Yeah,' I said, 'well, I asked first.'

That was the last thing I got to say for a while. If I can presume to know anything about yew tree behaviour I would have to guess that he/she got tired of this banter and just decided to go straight to the source. Pain and deafening white noise erupted from inside my head. I dropped to my knees, presumably screaming but I couldn't hear anything over the internal commotion. I started to reach for my head but then stopped 'cause I was afraid that I wouldn't find any top to my skull. I had a mental image of my brain being exposed and tree branches spinning around in my grey matter like it was soup.

'You are terrified,' the tree said, *'yet you jest.'*

'You discovered my secret,' I said through gritted teeth.

'I do not understand you. Explain.'

'Get it over with.'

I remembered seeing an old gory horror movie where people's heads exploded and their insides splattered all over the room. I was now sure I was seconds away from decorating the yew forest in the same way. When I didn't answer the tree, the pressure got worse, something I would have thought was impossible. I remembered the look on Spideog's face when he realised he would have to go back to the Yewlands to be re-judged. The yews had subsequently found him again worthy but at the time he was sure he was going to die. The pain I experienced was so intense that I knew that if I somehow survived, I would choose death rather than go through this again.

'You wish I should begin the judgement?' the androgynous voice of the tree shouted in my head.

'Whatever.'

The bush turned the egg beater in my head up to the frappe setting.

'Once again,' the tree said, *'you are speaking in contrast to your true feelings.'*

'OK, you want my true feelings? I don't want to be here. I didn't mean to come into the Yewlands, I'm not prepared for a judgement and I don't want to die. And while I'm at it could you loosen the vice on my head?'

Surprisingly he/she did and as soon as I could think properly I said, 'I was unconscious when I entered the Yewlands. Has any of your kind seen my companions?'

'We are yew. We are not here to answer your questions.'

'But the woman that was with me, she is unprepared for judgement. Her son was with me too but at least he was trained by Master Spideog.'

'You speak of the archer?'

'Yes, his name is Brendan. Have you seen him?'

'*The archer you call Brendan spoke of Spideog's death. Is this true?*'

'It is,' I said, 'I witnessed it.'

'*Let us see,*' the tree said and the pain returned with a vengeance. My brain, like a crappy video movie, fast-forwarded my memories. Stopping, then zooming ahead until once again I was forced to watch Spideog fall. Then the pain in my head subsided, only to be replaced by an ache in my chest.

'*He was killed by your knife,*' said the voice of the tree in my head, but only the male voice. In my defence the female voice said, '*But not by his hand.*'

What followed was a debate in a language (or maybe even a different plane) that I couldn't begin to fathom. As best I could figure out it was a domestic squabble. Where before the voices of the tree were speaking as one, now the male and female were backing and forthing. As it got faster and seemingly more heated I wondered what would happen if they didn't come to a conclusion. Can a tree get a divorce from itself? I wondered if there were yew trees all over the forest where the male and female parts hadn't spoken to each other for centuries.

Finally the squabble ended. '*We shall judge you now.*'

'What happened to the others?'

'*You will be judged.*'

'I don't want to be judged, I'm not ready to be judged. I want to know what happened to my friends.'

'*If you will not be judged then you must eat of the fruit.*'

A bough laden with red berries drifted before my face as I felt the bones in my arm and hand reach for the poisonous fruit.

'Who died and made you god?'

The push on my arm stopped as the male voice said with a sneer, '*We are before the gods. We have been makers of gods.*'

'I hope you didn't make Lugh.'

'*What do you know of Lugh?*' the tree demanded but didn't wait for an answer. Once again the pain dropped me to my knees as my encounters with the Oracle of Mount Cas were replayed for me and the timber sticking into my brain.

When it was done I felt the female tree ask, *'Why would Macha take the child?'*

'I don't know.'

'You will be judged,' they both said.

'I'm not ready.'

'No matter,' the yew replied, *'we must know what you know.'*

This wasn't like the memories that flash before your eyes when you think you are going to die. I've been that close to death enough times since arriving at The Land to know what that is like. No, this remembering was like re-experiencing my life over again. Not just the sights and sounds and smells but also the emotions. The warmth of my father's embrace, the sting of bullying at school, the pain of constantly moving home and the abandonment of friends. The loneliness of being the new kid. The excitement of that first kiss, puberty – oh gods, not again. The attack in my living room that changed my life for ever. The terror of Cialtie. The discovery of my mother – her first approving smile. The other smile – Fergal's smile and then no … Fergal's death. I knelt, paralysed, re-living my life and all the way through, stabbing like knives and caressing like velvet, were my emotions. My loves, my hates, my losses. Essa, Araf, Tuan, Spideog, Frank, Jesse, Brendan, Ruuuuuby.

When it ended I was in shock. Like when I killed my first person (an event I just replayed seconds ago) I was unable to think. I was unable to … be. I was emotionally spent, not even able to weep.

'What can we give you?' the tree spoke into my throbbing head.

I hardly heard the question. I fell prostrate on the ground. 'I don't ever want to go through that again,' I moaned.

'Very well,' the tree replied, *'from this day forth, you, Conor of Duir, have safe passage through Ioho.'*

I rolled over on my back and looked up at the branches and needles blocking out the sky. I tried to imagine ever coming here again and knew I never would. At least not alone. 'And any of my travelling companions?'

'And all that travel with you,' the tree said without hesitation.

I rolled over and propped myself up on all fours. Then, making sure I didn't touch the tree, I tried to stand. I was wobbly but intact. I felt the tug of the yew and placed my hands once again on its rough bark.

'You have given us much to contemplate, Prince of Hazel and Oak. We would like to give you a gift but you are unworthy of a wand or bow.' The female voice then spoke. *'We have seen that you often fight with banta. Accept this with our blessing. May it serve you well.'* The familiar sound that I now know is moisture being sucked from wood, followed by a crack, preceded a large branch falling from the tree. I picked up the staff and cracked off the smaller branches that were withering even as I looked at it. It wouldn't take much work at all to make this into a proper banta stick. I guess I was supposed to say thank you but instead I placed my hand again on the trunk and asked, 'Where are my companions?' But the tree ignored me. I could feel a deep internal conversation that made me feel like I was a long-forgotten annoyance.

I tried to remember which direction I had come but couldn't. That was a lifetime ago. I tried touching another tree to at least get directions, but it seemed that free passage also meant screw you. I was ignored. I wondered what would happen if I decided to carve my initials in one of these trees – would it ignore me then? I almost took out the Lawnmower and put that thought to the test but decided against it. I had just survived a yew judging unprepared – pushing my luck might be foolish. I closed my eyes, spun around and then started walking in the direction I was facing. It was as good a way to go as any.

Even though every cell in my body told me to be quiet, I shouted out, 'BRENDAN, NORA,' but eventually stopped. Not only because it felt so wrong to be making noise in here, but also because

I'm sure if they heard me they would be too afraid to answer. Getting out of this forest was the only plan of action I could think of.

The day stretched on. The heat seemed to somehow radiate down from the closed green canopy. The air smelled of moss and didn't move. I had a mental image of filling a balloon with this air and when I got out, watching it sink. Late in the day I heard water and then made it to the river. I began to walk back the way I had come. I must have been upriver from where the boat was beached, either that or somebody had stolen it, 'cause I didn't once see it on my travels. All the while the yews ignored me. It was a strange feeling. Almost like being in a forest back in the Real World.

The sun was low with twilight threatening when I reached the sentinel yews at the entrance of the Yewlands. I had a choice of walking around deep into the forest or climbing the root-covered boulder on the riverside. As much as that tree scared me, I decided to test my freedom of the Yewlands and scrabbled up onto the arthritic roots of that ancient tree. The yew knew I was there. I could feel him/her but I wasn't stopped or interfered with. At the top of the boulder I was rewarded with the sight of Araf and Nora sitting next to a small fire. I shouted to them and received an enthusiastic wave back.

I had so many questions for them but I never got to ask them. As I climbed down I was startled by what I thought was a large yellow insect. It buzzed past my ear and as I watched it fly by it looped in mid-air and came back at me. As it came towards my face I raised my hand to swat it. At first I thought it was a bee or wasp that had stung me but when I looked at the back of my hand I saw it was another gold amulet. I withdrew it from the flesh of my hand; it was shaped like a small tornado. I recognised it immediately. It was almost identical to the one my mother had once given me, except hers didn't have a pin on the end. It was a *rothlú* amulet, and as soon as I recognised it it kicked in. After that, everything was pain.

Chapter Twelve
The Hermit of Thunder Bay

Pain. Imagine each cell in your body being removed then scrubbed with a wire brush before it was popped back into place. That's the feeling you get from a *rothlú* spell. I never thought I would be nostalgic about pain, but I remembered the last time I had this all-over body ache – my cousin was stealing my shoes. This time there was no tug on my foot to wake me. I opened my eyes the tiniest of cracks. I had no idea where I was but if it was daytime and out of doors, then the light was certainly going to be painful. Luckily when I opened my eyes I was greeted with gloom and deep shadows. I decided to give moving a try and discovered it wasn't a good idea. I dropped my head back onto whatever I was on and slipped back into unconsciousness.

It was just as gloomy when I awoke again but this time, moving was only excruciating as opposed to being beyond the threshold of consciousness. I seemed to be lying on a pile of fresh straw in what I first thought was a dungeon. I crawled over to the only source of light. It was a candle infused with sparkling gold dust, Leprechaun-made – so I knew at least I wouldn't be without light for a couple of years. Next to the candle was a shot glass with something that smelled mighty powerful. All of my instincts told me to leave it alone, but when I thought about it (which was difficult with the fife and drum band playing inside my head) I figured that if whoever got me here wanted me dead, I'd already be in the ground. I held my nose and knocked it back. My toes actually curled and my head tilted to a forty-five-degree angle. A full sweat broke out on my forehead and, even though there was no one there, I said the immortal words, 'Haba yazza.' When my vision cleared and the impulse to vomit passed, I felt much better.

I was in a cave. I guessed that was better than a dungeon. I grabbed the candle and, careful not to let it blow out, I explored the perimeter looking for an exit. After two trips around, I sat down, confused. There was no way out. I went around again – this time slowly looking for a hidden door or a crack or anything but there was nothing. I must have been dropped in from above, but the walls were so smooth there was no way of climbing or seeing what was up there. That's when a memory hit me that filled me with panic. What if there is no way out? I remembered my father warning me that a *rothlú* spell could transport someone to the edge of a cliff. What if it stuck me in the middle of a cave that has no exit? What if I'm doomed to sit and thirst to death in a dark cave?

In all of my days and through all of my troubles I never had an actual panic attack. I was building to a good one but then thought, no, not a dark cave – a cave with a candle in it, a clean bed and a shot of hooch. Somebody brought me here, somebody wants me here. I relaxed, sat on my straw bed and thought. I had been stabbed twice with gold amulet darts. One knocked me out and the other brought me here. Somebody wanted me to drift into the Yewlands and whoever it was wanted me here. But who? I never heard of anybody using amulet darts but now that I thought on it – it was a pretty cool idea. And the *rothlú* that had got me in my hand honed in on me like one of Dahy's knives. All of this information didn't help me figure out who my captor was. Part of me, the same part that previously started to panic, feared that it was Cialtie but somehow this didn't seem like his style.

With nothing better to do, I picked up the candle and climbed onto the rock in the centre of the cave. I was holding the candle up, hoping to see if there was a way out from above when I lost my footing. It was a tiny stumble, I didn't fall but I jostled the flame enough to blow it out.

You just can't imagine how dark cave-dark is, until you're forced to endure it. The black seemed so opaque it felt like I could cut it. I dropped the candle and then carefully climbed down. Then on all fours I crawled until I found my pile of straw and sat. I sat staring into the sense-depriving darkness and started hallucinating shades of blackness. Imagine seeing wind – that was the kind of tricks my brain was playing with that total absence of light. I finally had to close my eyes. Strangely the darkness behind my eyelids was much more bearable.

I dozed again and in my dream, a small hand took my own hand in hers and led me out of the cave. Even though we were outside and I could feel the breeze and sunshine on my face I still couldn't see.

'Is this what it's like for you, Ruby?'

She didn't say anything but I sensed her nodding her head yes. She led me down a grassy hill and asked very politely of a tree if I could have a stick. Together we walked with our sticks sweeping before us as we listened and sensed and smelled our way through a day that – even though I couldn't see – felt glorious.

'See,' she said, 'It's not so bad.'

Light. Blinding light entered the dream, bleaching out the mental image of Ruby and the pastoral scene. Painful blinding light burned into my eyes. I had to cover my face with my arm.

Where the dream ended and the reality began is open for debate. The blinding light focused itself into a doorway of light and in that doorway formed the shape of a man. It wasn't until I pushed myself up into a sitting position and felt the straw underneath my hands that I knew for certain that this was real.

The silhouette in the doorway said, 'Come,' then turned and walked away.

The Lawnmower was still around my waist, so I drew it and walked towards the light.

My captor sat on a cave shelf looking out over a vista of endless sea. If I hadn't heard the voice I would have thought that he was a she. Long brown hair fell to the middle of his back. His clothes were animal skins – not the nicely tailored stuff my Mom often wears, but home-made pelts that wouldn't have looked out of place in a B grade caveman vs. dinosaur movie. He didn't turn around.

'Put away your sword, Prince of Hazel and Oak,' he said in a croaky voice that made me think he didn't use it very often.

'First I want some answers,' I said.

In reply, he threw a speck of gold out in front of him. It hovered in the air and then like a bullet zoomed in and hit me in the hand. I dropped the Lawnmower with a clang. When I tried to pick it up, I found that my right hand was numb and I couldn't move my fingers.

When I reached for the sword with my left hand, he said, 'Do you really wish to lose the use of that hand as well?'

He had turned around, and in his hand was another tiny amulet ready to make it so I would need assistance if I ever wanted to zip up my fly. The long hair down his back was matched by an even longer beard. Even though he looked like a children's picture book version of a comic troll, his eyes told me that he meant business. I let go of the sword and stood. He turned back to his view.

'What have you done to my hand?'

'Sensation in your hand will return in a few moments. I have no desire to harm you, Conor. Come sit next to me and enjoy the vista.'

I've learned the hard way since arriving in The Land that when you're outgunned and outmanoeuvred the best thing to do is just say OK. So I said, 'OK,' and sat. We dangled our legs over the ledge and looked out at a crystal blue sea edged by green rolling hills more manicured than any golf course. On a dock were two simple wooden sailboats. The place was postcard beautiful.

'Where are we?' I asked, trying to sound more conversational and less confrontational.

'This is Ba Toirniúil.'

Ba Toirniúil means Thunder Bay. I had heard of this place. This is where immortals come when they no longer wish to live. This is where you go when you want to sail away into old age.

'Whose boats are they?' I asked.

When he didn't answer, I figured this was going to be one of those I-ask-the-questions-around-here type situations but then he said, 'I make them for whomever needs them.'

'Wait a minute … are you the Hermit of Thunder Bay?'

He kept looking out to sea but I could see a small smile. 'I suppose I am a hermit and I do live here in Thunder Bay. You have heard of me?'

'I heard one of my guards say that his companion looked like the Hermit of Thunder Bay when he hadn't shaved.'

He thought about this for a long while before he said, 'So I'm famous in Duir for not shaving?'

'Apparently so,' I said.

After another long pause he whispered, almost to himself, 'I suppose it is better than being entirely forgotten.'

I didn't like the tone in his voice and decided that this line of conversation might bring us to morose musings that I wanted to avoid. So I said, 'Should I call you Hermy? Or do you have a real name?'

He actually looked at me then. It's unsettling when a guy as crazy looking as this one gives you a look like *you're* the crazy one. 'Hermy? Why would you call me Hermy?'

'Everyone needs a name.'

The long pause kicked in again. I was starting to realise that chats with Hermy were about waiting a lot. Eventually he said, 'A name is not something I require. One only needs a name if one is going to converse. I have not spoken to anyone but you, Conor of Duir, since … well, since long before you were born.'

'But you're talking to me now.'

Wait … 'Yes, it appears I am.'

'Were you the one who knocked me out so I would drift into the Yewlands?'

… 'Yes.'

'And did you throw that homing *rothlú* that brought me here?'

… 'Yes.'

'Why?' He didn't answer, or was taking his usual sweet time so I pressed him. 'Why, Hermy?'

'My mother instructed me.'

'Your mother?' I said looking around. 'I thought the idea of being a hermit is that you live alone. You're a hermit who lives with his mother?'

Hermy laughed at that. It was a sweet little chuckle, like he had only just remembered how to do it. 'No, my mother is long dead.'

'Oh, sorry.'

'You should be. Your family holds the guilt of her murder.'

That reply made my stomach do a little flip-flop. Had he brought a son of Duir here to avenge his mother's death? I looked down at the hundred foot drop and scooted over – out of shoving range.

'Someone in my family killed your mother?'

Hermy nodded once.

'Let me guess – Cialtie?'

Showing no emotion, Hermy nodded again.

Cialtie murdered his mother and this long-dead mother is leaving him instructions. I rattled that riddle around in my noggin and in less than the time it took for Hermy to say, 'Hello,' I came up with the answer.

'You're Ona's son?'

… 'I am,' he said.

'So why did Ona want me to enter the Yewlands?'

In reply he stood and walked over to a corner of his cave, picked up a long banta stick and handed it to me before re-sitting.

The wood was smooth and sticky, with the smell of fresh bees-wax polish. 'Is this the branch the yew gave me?'

… 'It is.'

'You finished it for me?'

… 'I did.'

'Thanks,' I said. 'Why does … did your mother want me to have this?'

… 'You of all people, Son of the One-Handed Prince, should know that Ona's will comes without explanation.'

'I'm no longer the Son of the One-Handed Prince,' I said quickly.

… 'My point exactly,' he said, standing. 'Excuse my manners but it has been very long since I have had a guest. Would you like tea?'

'Thank you,' I said and watched him start a small fire with a fire coin then fill a kettle from a rain barrel.

'If you haven't talked to anybody in so long, how did you know I was the Son of the One-Handed Prince?'

My host placed a frying pan on the fire next to the kettle and then reached into a jar and pulled out a dripping handful of some seaweedy type stuff and threw it sizzling into the pan. 'Would you like some …' he stood frozen, looking up to the ceiling, then finally said, 'I do not think I ever heard a word for what this is.'

I looked at whatever it was steaming in the pan and decided that it was probably better that it remained unnamed.

'I have heard about your many exploits, Conor, from the beeches. Beech trees do love to gossip.'

'I've heard that. So what did Ona say about me, exactly?'

I had to wait until Hermy finished making tea out of some sort of moss. When he handed it to me I was relieved to find that my fingers worked fine. It tasted exactly like tea made from moss.

'She never mentioned you specifically.'

'Wait, I thought you said Ona told you that I was to get a yew staff?'

... 'No, Ona knew someone was to receive a yew staff – I just guessed it was you.'

'You sent me into the Yewlands on a guess?'

In reply he shrugged.

'And what if the yews had killed me?'

'That would have been – unfortunate.'

'Yeah, especially for me.'

He nodded in agreement like it was the first time it occurred to him. He stirred the dinner and then slid a portion into each of two wooden bowls. 'Would you like some ...'

'Shall we call it gloop?'

He sighed in that exasperated way that made me realise he was getting to know me. 'If we must.'

After tasting it, I decided that gloop was the perfect name for this stuff. It's rare to get a dull meal in The Land but Hermy succeeded in cooking one.

'Do you know what happened to my friends?'

'The archer and the woman both survived their judgement. If that is what you wish to know. The archer exited the Yewlands not long after you. He held wood suitable for a bow.'

I hadn't realised how much subconscious tension I had been holding in my shoulders until they relaxed with that news. 'I must get to them – they will be worried about me.'

'There is no need for them to worry, Conor. I will not harm you.'

'They don't know that.'

113

'That your disappearance may cause your companions to fret is the least of your worries.'

'So tell me, oh great bearded one who seems to know everything, if my friends are the least of my worries what is the worst of my worries?'

If Hermy noticed my annoyance it didn't make him hurry up with his reply but when he did, he sure got my attention.

'I would say your biggest worry should be – the blind child.'

'What do you know about Ruby?'

This time the pregnant pause before his answer was unacceptable. I didn't care if this guy had gadgets on him that could make me as limp as a Salvador Dali painting, I grabbed him by the arm and spun him to face me. 'Tell me.'

'Ruby,' he said, 'is that her name?'

'What do you know?'

'I, Conor, only know what my mother has written.'

'And what did your mother say?'

'Ona never spoke of these things, all of her prophecies were written.'

I stood. 'Don't screw with me, Hermy. What did your mother write?'

I had to take deep breaths while waiting for him to answer; otherwise, I think I would have stabbed him.

'She said, "The blind child will need help from the bearer of the yew staff."'

It took me a moment to realise he was talking about me. 'Where is she?'

'… According to the poplar trees your grandmother, Lugh and Cialtie are holding her in Castle Onn in the Gorselands.'

'I have to get to Duir and put a rescue party together.' I paced around the room looking for an exit. 'How do I get out of here?'

Without looking at me, Hermy made a gesture with his right hand and another one of those damn flying amulets flew out and

114

boomeranged into my neck. This time my whole body went limp and I crumpled to the ground, not even able to move my eyeballs. The hermit rolled me over on my back. His long beard swept over my face but I couldn't feel it. He placed my new yew staff in my hand and said, 'Ona did not write about a rescue party. She only mentioned you. I'm sorry if the paralysing amulet is uncomfortable but in the long run it speeds up the recovery from the *rothlú*. You will thank me later.'

He pulled a chain from round his neck and then from the hundreds of amulets hanging from it, he picked a tiny gold twin tornado. He looped it onto a chain and hung it around my neck. 'If you find her, this will bring you home.' Then he pulled a single twister from his collection, placed it in my palm and closed my fingers around it.

'I have been thinking,' he said, 'and I do not like the name Hermy. If I must have a name then let it be the one I owned when I lived in Castle Duir. Call me Eth.' Then he held my closed fist next to his mouth and incanted, '*Rothlú.*'

Chapter Thirteen

Captain Jesse

Eth? Eth? I knew that name and I had almost figured out where I had heard it when my brain was disassembled and scattered halfway across the land. By the time it got reassembled, that thought and any other was replaced by pain and unconsciousness.

Eth was right about one thing: this *rothlú* spell didn't seem to hurt as much as usual. When I finally came to I had specific pains in my legs, wrists and neck but not the usual all-over pain that comes from being magically disappeared and reappeared somewhere else. It wasn't until I attempted to sit up that I realised why I had pains in my wrists, neck and legs. I was hog-tied. I didn't like waking up in bondage the first time it happened. Now that it seemed to be occurring with regularity, I really, really didn't like it.

I was in a tent. Not an opulent dwelling that took a dozen servants to hump around and erect, like Cialtie had. No, this was a thin silken thing, designed to be light and small to carry. I rolled over – not easy with my legs tied bent and attached to a cord around my neck. I quickly learned that my binder knew what he was doing. I tried a couple of times to test my bonds but soon realised that every time I struggled, the rope tightened around my neck. So I decided to think rather than squirm.

Through the flap of the tent I saw a campfire. The smoke coming from the fire rose to a screen dome where it disappeared. This was a fire that belonged to someone who didn't want anyone else to know he or she was here. Outside, the sound of approaching horses had my captors on their feet. I could see the shoes and dark leggings – my captors were Brownies.

I couldn't quite hear all the conversation but my guard's diction was as good as his knotsmanship. 'Yes sir, I found him just lying unconscious in the middle of the field,' he said but then added a coda to that sentence that sent a chill down my spine. He finished by saying, 'Your Highness.'

On no, I thought, and began to struggle even if it was going to strangle me. The last time I had seen the Brownie King I had delivered to him the body of his dead son. He promised that the next time he saw me he would kill me. I rolled over and pushed up against the side of the tent almost knocking it over. I heard the footsteps as they entered but the noose around my neck was now so tight I could no longer turn my head. I heard a voice exclaim, 'You!' Then I heard the unmistakable sound of a knife being pulled from its sheath. I was wheezing, gasping for breath as the rope cut into my neck but that was the least of my problems. I closed my eyes and waited for the pain of the knife entering my back.

The knife cut through the rope in a spot that released everything. My legs dropped straight and my hands were freed. I immediately worked on loosening the rope around my neck and rolled on my back gasping for breath. My vision was blurry; I had been seconds away from passing out. I was expecting a view of Bwika, the hulking King of the Brownies, but as my vision cleared I was rewarded by the smiling face of his son Codna.

'Conor?' he said in a voice that changed an octave in the middle of a word. 'What are you doing here?'

'Choking,' I replied.

I tried sitting up as the prince motioned for the guard to leave us alone. Then he closed the tent flap, plopped down next to me and clumsily wrapped his arms around me. 'I'm so glad to see you,' he said.

I was a bit surprised by the attack hug but I returned it. 'Hey Jesse,' I said, using the nickname I had given him the first time we had met. 'How you doing?'

Jesse looked over his shoulder to make sure no one was listening and then whispered, 'Awful.'

I lowered my tone with him. 'Is your dad outside?'

He looked confused. 'No.'

'Oh, I heard the guard "yes sir"-ing and saying "Your Highness."'

Jesse looked embarrassed and then smiled, 'He was talking about me. This is my troop. I'm the captain.'

'You are?'

'After I stood up to my father in the throne room,' Jesse said. 'Remember? It was over giving you your horse back.'

'Oh I remember,' I replied.

'Well, after that, Dad said I had *bivka*.'

'I have no idea what bivka is but you were pretty awesome that day.'

Jesse blushed. I almost expected him to say, 'Aw shucks.'

'When I came back with The Turlow's horse, you know, the one you gave me, everybody assumed I stole it. Dad was so impressed with my transformation, he gave me a small troop to lead. They were the bottom of the barrel but I didn't know that. I had watched Demne,' Jesse stopped at the mention of his dead brother and swallowed hard. 'You know Frank?'

I nodded. Of course I remembered Frank.

'Well I had watched a lot of his training in the Torkc Guards and I just did the same drills his combat master had put him through. My men loved it. Last month we had war games in the Alderlands and my troop won. Dad promoted me to commander.'

'Congratulations,' I said, slapping him on the arm. 'That's wonderful.'

Jesse rubbed his arm where I had hit him. 'No it's not. I'm just pretending to be a leader. I go watch other commanders and just do what they do. Well, I change it so no one will notice, but I really have no idea what I'm doing. I just put on a gruff voice and make sure nobody sees me ...' He turned and looked away, covering his face.

'Hey, guy, it's OK.'

'But it's terrifying, Conor. I think any minute everybody is going to figure out that I'm faking it.'

I had to cover my mouth to stop from laughing. 'Oh Jesse, we're all faking it. Before the battle at the Hall of Knowledge last winter I figured out that bravery was just pretending not to be scared. You're not doing anything every other commander hasn't done. You learn by watching what others do, then you change it to suit you. It sounds to me like you're pretty good at it.'

'Really?' he said, wiping his nose. 'You're not just saying that?'

'If I had a Brownie troop that needed commanding – you would be the guy I would pick.'

'Wow, really?' he said, unconsciously sitting up straighter.

I nodded.

'I'm so glad to see you, Conor. Say, what are you doing out here alone anyway?'

So I told him the whole story about the raid on Yew House on Mount Cas and how my grandmother and Lugh had kidnapped Ruby. Maybe I shouldn't have. He was technically the enemy, but then I remembered what I had said to him so long ago in the Brownielands. 'Others can make us enemies but no one can unmake us friends.' Then I told him how the Hermit of Thunder Bay had puppeteered me into the situation I was in now.

'You went into battle with Lugh? Weren't you scared?'

'I pretended not to be.'

Jesse nodded and smiled like a schoolboy remembering a lesson.

'So I have to get to Castle Onn – the hermit told me that's where they are holding Ruby. Do you know where it is?'

'I've never been there,' Jesse said, 'but that's where I'm going.'

Jesse went on to explain that his father had sent him to represent the Brownies at a meeting called by Cialtie. Apparently the new Turlow was going to attend, and there were rumours that Lugh was again abroad in The Land and that he would be there. Cialtie had promised he would reveal a secret weapon or something that would ensure that Duir would soon be liberated.

'Liberated from its gold you mean,' I said sarcastically.

Jesse laughed. 'That's what my father thinks.'

'Jesse, do you really think that if you win this war Cialtie will just hand over Castle Duir to the Brownies?'

'My father does.'

'Yeah, but do you?'

Jesse thought for a time. It's never an easy thing for a son to judge his father. Finally he looked up and said, 'No, I do not.'

'Can you tell your father that?'

'I could, but he wouldn't listen. What should I do, Conor?'

'Aw, Jesse, I have no idea. He's not only your father, he's also your king. You kinda have to do what he says.'

'Even if he's wrong?'

I shrugged. A wilful father I had experience with, but a wilful *and stupid* father – would be awful.

'The more pressing problem,' I said, 'is what are you going to do with me?'

'What do you mean?'

'Well, I'm your prisoner, aren't I?'

Jesse thought for a second. 'I suppose you are,' he said, then giggled. 'Maybe I should take your shoes.'

I started laughing too until Jesse shushed me and said, 'Wait here.'

Jesse's voice when addressing his scout was so different to the childlike tone he used with me. I couldn't quite make out what was being said until the scout said, 'Right away, sir'. Then I heard him gallop off.

Jesse came back into the tent with water and an apple. I drank deeply then devoured the apple.

'OK,' Jesse said, 'I quizzed my scout and he hadn't recognised you, so I told him you were one of Cialtie's scouts that had been waylaid. I told him not to mention it to anyone for fear of embarrassing Cialtie. Then I sent everyone back to the main troop.' He threw clothes at me. 'Here, quickly, put these on.'

This wasn't the meek weepy Jesse I knew – this was Captain Prince Codna of the Alderlands. His voice shocked me, so I just did what he said. I was bigger than the average Brownie but luckily Brownie clothes are pretty stretchy. Jesse held out a hooded cloak and I put it on. It was tight but if I didn't move around too much it was OK. Jesse walked behind me and tied a triangular cloth across my face like a cowboy train robber's bandana, and then he fixed a translucent piece of black muslin across my eyes. Finally he walked in front of me and lifted the hood over my head.

'This is the uniform of the Brownies Shadowguard. Castle Onn is a half day's ride. You can get to the outskirts of the castle if you run fast.'

We didn't have a lot of time. Our plans were much more hurried than I liked.

'Are you sure you want to do this?' I asked. 'If this plan falls apart then you are going to be in a whole heap of trouble.'

'I can't defy my father, but I can't let Cialtie kidnap a young girl.'

I placed my hand on Jesse's shoulders. As I looked at him it was like looking into an illusion. I saw the young sweet kid I had always known at the same time as I saw the steely commander. 'You're a brave man, Captain Codna.'

'As long as that's what people believe.' He tried to smile but just missed it.

I turned to leave.

'Oh, and Conor – you can't wear those shoes.'

I was never a runner before I got to The Land. I always figured that if the creator of the universe wanted human beings to jog he wouldn't have allowed us to invent the Ferrari. But there was no sports car handy so I was hoofing it as fast as I could, hoping I could get to the place where Jesse and I had agreed to meet before his troop got there. He said he would try to delay them as much as possible but still they were on horseback and I was running. And I wasn't in my Nikes. If I didn't know better, I would have accused that Brownie of orchestrating this whole thing just so he could finally get his hands on my sneakers.

So I was trying to keep up a decent speed in these stupid Brownie slippers. They had stretchy sides so the fact that they were too small wasn't too bad but the leather soles were so thin, I might as well have been barefoot. Every time I stepped on a sharp rock or a pointy twig, I shouted, '*Slek*,' which is a very rude Brownie curse word that Jesse's late brother Frank had taught me. I thought it only appropriate. I tried to separate my mind and body the way the Fili had taught me but every time I stubbed my toe, my mind and body came together and my mind told me that I was running too much. This Brownie outfit didn't help either. I tried to remember if I had ever seen an Olympic marathon runner wearing woollen leggings and came up with nothing. Gosh, I wonder why not?

Through my discomfort, I remembered Dad telling me about the mantra that inspired him to win the boat race against his brother. He told me he kept saying, 'Rowing beats Cialtie,' over and over again in his head. I started saying that but then changed my chant to, 'Running saves Ruby.'

My new yew banta staff was heavy in my hand. I said to myself, *I wish this damn stick was lighter* – and it was. That broke my concentration and I thought out loud, 'I wish this stick was heavier.' Even though I had asked for it I was unprepared for the sudden weight in my right hand. I tipped over at full speed and crashed painfully onto the ground. I sat up and when the cartoon tweeting birds that were flying around my head finally disappeared I said, 'Cool,' and then 'Ow,' but maybe not in that order. I started back at a jog and as I picked up speed I willed my stick to go light again and thought, *I need to look into the stuff this stick can do but not now. Now – running saves Ruby. Running saves Ruby. Running …*

My mindless-running-chanting universe was disturbed by a feeling of vulnerability. I looked around and found I was no longer in a forest. Jesse had told me that before you get to Castle Onn there is an expanse of treeless fields that borders the Hollylands. We had agreed to meet at the treeline. I looked behind me and saw that I had run past that. I circled back, hoping no one had seen me, and finally came to rest under a cherry tree. It was too early in the season for fruit and the tree constantly apologised for that, regardless of how many times I told him it was all right. I was sweating from head to toe and desperately wanted to peel off some of these hot clothes just for a second but was afraid that if I did, that would be the moment when Jesse and the Brownies arrived.

With the tree still pestering me if there was anything he could do, I asked if he minded if I climbed. Delighted that he could be of any service the cherry gladly agreed. I picked up my yew staff from the ground. It was regular yew weight again and I mentally asked it to lose its weight. As it grew lighter I flippantly asked the wood to become lighter than air. The stick shot up and out of my fingers then fell to the ground. I stared at it thinking then smiling. I picked it up again and this time held on tight with both hands.

Lighter than air, I said in my head and I instantly shot twenty feet in to the air until I let go screaming. I hit the ground hard and then was hit in the kidneys by my falling stick. After determining that none of my bones was broken I said, 'Wow,' and tried again. This time when I spoke to the wood I said, *just a little bit lighter than air*. The stick rose and I felt the pull on my outstretched arms. *A tiny bit lighter*, I said as my full weight was slowly pulled off the ground. I found I could regulate this anti-gravity effect. I could only go up and down but I figured if I gave myself enough time I could also get it to hover. But time I didn't have, so I just used my new-found floating stick to propel me to the top of the cherry tree where under the cover of leaves I stripped off some of the sticky wool and let the breeze cool me down while I scratched.

The cherry tree told me of Jesse's Brownie troop's approach. It was something I asked him to do and the tree was delighted he could be of further assistance. Cherries are helpful to the point of annoyance. They are also not very inquisitive. The tree seemed to not notice that I flew into its top branches. I re-donned my damp, smelly Brownie-wear, covered my face and eyes with the Brownie ninja gear and waited until Jesse and his charges were almost below me. I then instructed my staff to go light-ish and jumped.

The effect was just as I had hoped. It looked like a slow motion scene from a bad action movie. I arrived from that dizzying height on my feet and then placed my hands on my hips. Jesse had told me that Shadowguards never speak. Good thing 'cause I almost said, 'Ta da!'

Jesse's troop was stunned and impressed. After their initial shock they gave a Brownie salute that I returned. The most shocked of the entire group was Jesse. I could tell he was dying to ask me how I had just jumped out of a four-storey-high tree but finally he just said, 'Now that my Shadowguard is here, it is time to meet with Cialtie and Lord Lugh.'

Chapter Fourteen

Ivy Lodge

The Ivy Lodge half lived up to its name. It was more of a castle than a lodge, but as for the ivy – it sure had a lot of that. From the outside it looked fine, majestic even, like the main building of some venerable old university. But once you got inside it was terrifyingly apparent that this place was going to come crashing down any second. It seemed that the ivy was the only thing holding it up.

The origins of Ivy Lodge lived in that timeline between history and legend. Apparently Mom and Dad weren't the first to take a Choosing simultaneously. It had been done before, a long time ago. Supposedly these two lovers from an ancient time had a love so strong they couldn't be apart from each other – even for an instant. Against all advice they performed the Rite of Choosing hand-in-hand. For their daring and effort they each received a major rune. The woman was given Gort – the man Tinne. They became the King and Queen of Holly and Ivy. Together they built Ivy Lodge in the new Hollylands far to the north. When the castle was completed they held a midwinter celebration that was ill-attended due to distance and bad weather. After that they never held another party, they never left the castle grounds or each other's side. They received visitors with courtesy but never warmth. They had no children. Then one day, reports came back that the castle was deserted. The holly trees and the ivy, no longer tied to runes, spread across The Land and King Holly and Queen Ivy were never seen again.

The Hollylands we had just passed through were as wild as the inside of the Lodge. It felt cold up here, even though it was approaching high summer. The cool air still didn't stop a trickle of sweat from sliding down my back, but that had less to do with the temperature than the anticipation of waltzing into a lion's den.

Inside the Lodge was crawling with Banshees, which removed all doubt, if there was any, that this was Cialtie's party. I drew some pretty serious stares with my hoodie, bandana-ed face and gauze-covered eyes but I must have been intimidating enough to stop anyone from saying, 'Who are you supposed to be?'

We were ushered into a small room that contained a couple of chairs and a table with a pitcher of water and a bowl of apples. Cialtie obviously wasn't maxing out his hospitality budget. Saying that, as soon as Jesse and I were alone I lifted my bandana and wolfed down an apple. Considering where I was, I wondered if this was to be my last meal. I laughed at that thought and then thought some more and realised it wasn't funny.

'Are you all right?' I whispered to Jesse.

Without looking at me he replied, 'I'm pretending to be fine.'

I smiled under my mask and tried to do the same.

After half an hour we were instructed by our Banshee party-planner that the meeting was about to begin. We were escorted through corridors where periodic cracks in the walls allowed vein-like ivy to push in and attach pale green leaves to the stonework. At the entrance to the main hall, a Banshee honour guard informed us that I could only enter if I unmasked and disarmed.

'I am Prince Codna, Emissary and son of King Bwika of the Alderlands, this is my Shadowguard. We both enter unmolested or I return to my father now.'

Wow, Jesse really had this faking brave stuff down.

126

The guard didn't protest. When we got inside it was obvious from all of the bodyguards present that he had gotten a similar response from everybody. Bad guys, it seems, like their henchmen.

I was very glad of my mask and eye gauze. Even though I was expecting to see my uncle, I'm pretty sure my heart-pounding terror combined with my overwhelming desire to attack him would have shown on my face. He was flanked by two Banshees: one a male archer and the other a sorceress wearing a thin leather belt that held her wand against her hip.

To his left were Grandma and her boyfriend Lugh. In a normal family, a grandson would be delighted to see his grandmother but normal my family was not. I hadn't expected to see her but I was hoping Ruby would be with them. She had to be nearby – the question was how to find her.

To Cialtie's right was a group of three Banshees, all dressed up in Banshee finery.

There were no chairs. We took our place standing in an empty space between two pillars.

'Mother, Father,' Cialtie said addressing Macha and Lugh, 'may I introduce Prince Codna of the Brownielands.'

Jesse bowed formally. 'Lord Lugh, it is an honour to finally see you. I am, as are all of the Brownie clan, at your service.' He straightened up and then bowed again to my grandmother. 'Lady Macha, The Land rejoices at the news of your reappearance. I am your humble servant.'

As Jesse instructed me, I only slightly bowed my head. I was supposed to act like I wasn't there.

Then Cialtie gestured to his right. 'And may I introduce you to the newly ascended Turlow.'

The new Banshee chief looked small and uncomfortable between his two beefy bodyguards. He bowed and mumbled, 'My lord and lady.'

'Our generals have already had several meetings about our upcoming siege of Castle Duir,' Cialtie said.

Had they? I wanted to turn to Jesse and ask him but remembered I wasn't supposed to be there.

'Both Banshees and Brownies have expressed doubts about the success of such an attack, especially after your defeat at the Hall of Knowledge.'

I noticed Cialtie said 'Your defeat' like he had nothing to do with it. If I was the new Turlow or Jesse I would have pointed out that attacking the Hazellands was Cialtie's idea, but these guys were too green to stand up to my uncle.

'Your hesitations are not without merit, my friends, but worry no longer. As I have promised, we will soon have a new ally, one that will ensure our victory as foretold by Ona.'

Once again I was glad for the mask that covered my face. A new ally? I was expecting a new weapon, maybe, but an ally? Who's left? I thought for a second that maybe it was the Mertain. They were plenty angry at me and Graysea for stealing the dragon blood but Red was furious with Cialtie and the Banshees, he wouldn't allow his brother to fall in with this bunch. That only left the Elves. Dad told me it was hopeless trying to enlist the Elves. He said that when a conflict comes, they disappear into the forest. But if Cialtie could coopt them, then potentially that would mean the trees would be on my uncle's side. At that moment I couldn't imagine what the trees could do to help but I had been surprised by enough plants in The Land to know that making enemies of a tree is a bad idea.

'Following the predictions of Ona has proved a folly for you before, Lord Cialtie,' Jesse said. 'What makes this time different?'

Wow, that snapped me out of my reverie. I take back what I said about Jesse being too green. Cialtie gave the Brownie prince a look that almost made me duck. If my uncle could shoot daggers from his eyes, then Jesse would have been a pegboard. Bringing up Cialtie's unsuccessful tenure as Lord of Duir was either stupid or brave. I previously would have said that Jesse was being stupid but his recent behaviour was changing my opinion of the shoe thief.

After an interminable length of time Cialtie bowed his head as if to say, 'Fair enough,' and composed himself enough to answer. 'It is true that Ona's predictions are often obtuse but tonight you will see for yourself the fruit of our research.' He turned to the Banshee sorceress and said, 'Taline, is all prepared?'

'Yes my lord,' the witch answered.

'Then begin.'

Taline let loose a modulating scream that made all of the non-Banshees in the room wince. From the corners of the chamber servants appeared carrying bowls. Five bowls in all were placed on the floor in a cross pattern. After the servants left, Taline walked to the centre of the receptacles. For a split second I thought I saw a woman walking with her but decided it was a trick of the gauze mask I was wearing. She began to speak in a Banshee dialect I did not understand. Periodically I almost caught a word that sounded like something my father had tried to make me learn as a child. She reached into the bowl in front of her and took out a small glob of sap. Then I heard her use the Ogham word, 'Iodhadh.' My heart pounded in my chest. She was using Shadowmagic and the sap she was using was yew.

I remembered overhearing my mother and Fand speculating about the kind of raw Shadowmagic power that might be attained using yew sap. They had both smiled at the thought of it then stopped themselves as if talking like that was too frightening a prospect.

The Banshee sorceress fanned her hands over the bowls to her right and left – pale Shadowflames sparked to life. Like Mom's Shadowflames, these gave off neither heat nor light but unlike Mom's Shadowmagic, these seemed to suck the light from the room.

All around there were candelabras and chandeliers. None of the candles had gone out but it was noticeably darker in there – and colder. Maybe it just seemed colder because of the shiver that was running down my spine as I started to realise what I was witnessing.

When Taline closed her hand around the sap and placed her fist into the Shadowfire and incanted, 'Duir' – I was then sure she was doing something I thought only my mother and Fand could do. This was a Shadowcasting.

The Banshee sorceress rolled her head and warbled as if in a trance then opened her hand and dropped a translucent rune onto the floor. Emblazoned on its surface was the major rune of Duir. While continuing to moan and writhe she picked more sap from the bowl and began the long process of creating a shadow of all the major runes in Tir na Nog. 'Fearn, Saille, Nuin, Tinne, Quert, Muhn, Ur, Nion, Gort, Getal, Straif, Ruis, Ailm, Onn, Eadth, Iodhadh, Beith, Luis', and finally my mother's rune – 'Cull.'

When the formation of the Shadowrunes was complete, the sorceress then placed them in a grid on the floor in front of her and ignited them with Shadowflame. Then began the process of sorting the runes into the proper order for casting. This took longer than when Mom did it. The Banshee didn't really know what she was doing. She looked like some old biddy wondering where to put the next piece in her jigsaw puzzle. That scared me most of all. It felt like I was watching a monkey spinning dials in a nuclear power plant.

All the while she moaned and rocked. The Shadowfire travelled up her hands and then engulfed both of her arms to the shoulder. She tore off her cloak and threw it into the corner where it continued to burn with a pale blue Shadowfire. I was tempted to go over and stamp it out. I wondered if that would even work.

This was taking a long time. I looked around the room. The Turlow and his guards, who had never seen anything like this before, looked on with a mixture of repulsion and anticipation. Jesse was successfully standing expressionless but I knew he was terrified. Lugh and Grandma held maniacal expressions but maybe that was just the way I will always see them now. Cialtie seemed to be getting impatient and then proved it by shouting, 'When will you be ready?'

The sorceress held up a finger as if to say, 'Wait a minute,' but then her loss of concentration allowed the Shadowfire to rocket up her arms and engulf her whole body. She screamed for just a second as if she was being burned. Shadowfire doesn't burn but I imagine if I instantly became covered with that stuff that I'd freak out a lot worse than her. She composed herself and using the palms of her hands she pushed the Shadowfire away from her face and let the rest of her body burn. She may not have been a competent Shadowwitch but no one could accuse her of being undramatic.

At the edges of the Shadowflame that surrounded her I began to see bits of a form: a leg, a hand. Just as I had decided that it must be a trick of the light, I saw the translucent face of a woman whisper into the sorceress's ear. She obviously heard it because she stopped, listened and then changed the pattern of her Shadowcasting runes. The runes were now forming the shape of a star. It was very different from the periodic-table-like pattern my mother used. The ghostlike face continued to appear and instruct the sorceress until finally she rocked her head back and breathed deeply. Then from the bowl of yew sap she took a glob and prepared to make another rune. As she held it over the Shadowfire and incanted, the face that had only appeared at the edges of the fire began to take form. No longer a reflection of the fire, the face grew more substantial. She still was not real, still translucent, but she was no longer a trick of the Shadowlight. A whole woman appeared before us. I had seen visions in Shadowfire before but this wasn't like that. This was a real rooting-tooting, I'm-about-to-pee-myself ghost.

The ghost, although insubstantial, had some power. She ran her hands over the sorceress and extinguished the Shadowfire on her head and shoulders, until only her hands once again were afire. Then she spoke into the witch's ear. This time I almost heard something. The Banshee turned to Cialtie and said, 'Now.'

Lugh and Macha smiled and left. As we waited, the ghost continued to instruct the sorceress. I shot a quick glance to Jesse and then regretted it. His eyes mirrored the wrongness that we were both feeling about whatever was happening in this place but he, unlike me, had no mask to hide it from Cialtie. But the wrongness had just begun.

I heard her before I saw Lugh roughly drag her in to the room. Little Ruby, not the obstreperous and defiant self-confident woman-child I had known but a scared and frightened blind girl who was alone and mistreated far from home. It took all of my will not to run to her. I remembered the last time I had to stand by and watch someone I love being mistreated by Cialtie. That time I had waited too long and Fergal died. This time I swore to myself I would not let that happen again. But what could I do?

My hand reached slowly up to my neck. If I had to I could rush Ruby and activate the twin *rothlú* amulet that the hermit had placed around my neck. I might make it, but if I did that would leave Jesse with questions he couldn't answer. Questions that would get him killed. I had to wait and watch.

Lugh pushed Ruby to the centre of the flaming Shadowfire bowls. She had lost her sunglasses. Her hair covered half her face and was knotted and wild. Her visionless eyes darted frantically around the room. I so desperately wanted to shout to her to let her know that I was here and she was not alone.

Lugh drew a dagger from his belt and placed it at Ruby's throat. I grabbed the *rothlú* amulet and yanked it. The silver chain broke and clattered loudly to the floor in the pin-dropping quiet chamber. I wondered if I could get to Ruby before Lugh cut. Just when I decided that I had to risk it, Jesse spoke.

'Are you planning to kill that child?'

At first I didn't even know it was Jesse, the voice was so forceful.

Macha answered. 'Ona's prophecy calls for the blood of the blind child.'

'What does it say – exactly?' Jesse almost shouted. 'Does it demand her death?'

My grandmother was obviously not used to being spoken to like this. She replied with only an indignant glare.

Jesse, bless him, was undaunted. He spoke like the prince that he was. Only he and I knew just how badly he was shaking under his cloak. 'If the spell calls for blood, take some blood, but I will not stand by and watch an unnecessary murder of the child.'

I didn't know if it was the right thing to do or not, but I took that to be an order from my prince and stepped forward towards Lugh with my staff held ready to strike. This also got me that bit closer to Ruby if things got really sticky.

During all of this, the ghost impatiently circled around the centre of the room.

'How dare you reproach me,' Lugh said and lifted his hand in a gesture that I knew all too well. I braced myself for the inevitable gale that was about to smash me into the next state.

'Father,' Cialtie shouted. It was maybe the first time I had ever been glad to hear that voice. 'The Brownie is right. There is no need to kill the child. She still may be of use to us.'

Lugh still didn't take the knife away from Ruby's throat. 'Once we have the Shadowwitch we won't need this child.'

'You are probably right, Father, but why chance it? You of all people should know how swiftly winds can change.'

'Very well,' Lugh said and removed the dagger from Ruby's neck. I relaxed then and stepped back into the room. That's when

133

Lugh grabbed the girl's hand and in a flash ran the edge of the blade across Ruby's palm. Ruby screamed and tried to pull away but Lugh held her wrist firm. Blood dripped from her hand as she stopped squirming and fainted dead away. The Banshee sorceress picked up a bowl and let the blood drip into it. The blood continued to drip as Lugh held Ruby's pale lifeless body by her hair. I had to get her out of here. The sorceress held up a finger indicating that she had enough blood. One of the servants was called and Lugh handed Ruby over like she was a rag doll left after play.

'Make sure her wound is dressed,' a voice said, saying what I would have said if I could. It was the new Turlow. The Banshee servant bowed her head yes. I had assumed this Turlow was just a Cialtie lackey; maybe there was hope for him.

Lugh and Macha backed into their original positions as the ghost sat cross-legged across from the Banshee witch. Who was this ghost? Lugh said something about a Shadowwitch? I was pondering this when the Banshee finally opened her hand and revealed the last rune. It was less substantial than the others and was clearer than the blueish Shadowrunes that were scattered around the floor. It looked like it was made of the same stuff as the ghost. Then, proving that it was, the ghost picked it up. That's when I came very close to giving myself away. An audible gasp left my bandana-covered mouth. Luckily only Jesse seemed to notice. He gave me a hard disapproving stare. The reason for my surprise was the rune. It was identical to the one my mother made when she undertook the Rite of Choosing using Shadowmagic as opposed to real magic. Mom for the first time ever used tree sap to fuel the changing as opposed to gold. The rune she received for her efforts was transparent and contained a rune that no one had ever seen before. No one knew its meaning and there had never been anything like it – until now.

The ghost held this new Shadowrune on the palms of her hands. Taline pushed all of the remaining runes into a pile underneath the hands and ignited them with Shadowflame. The ghost threw back her head in a silent scream – could the Shadowfire be burning her? Taline then poured Ruby's blood from the bowl into the cupped hands and onto the rune. Smoke immediately poured up from the hands but then dissipated – there was no scent. Then the changes began in the ghost. First there was red. The major arteries began to form like those see-through pages in a biology book. Then the major organs darkened at the same time as the skeleton. Finally flesh began to appear as the sound of a faraway whine grew into a full-blown scream of agony.

When it was done a naked woman lay still, kneeling with her head in her lap like she was praying. Black hair fell in front of her face. My grandmother stepped forward and took the cloak off her back and laid it over the former ghost's shoulders. Then she shushed the Banshee sorceress away and knelt across from the prostrate woman. She reached over, pushed back her hair and then placed her hands on each side of the woman's face and lifted it to hers. I was amazed that the woman's black eyes were open. My grandmother leaned in and stared directly into the woman's eyes and said, 'Welcome back, Maeve.'

Chapter Fifteen

Maeve

Maeve – the first Shadowwitch, the inventor of Shadowmagic, the mad Druid who had decimated half of her people's rowan forest in a maniacal quest for power. The leader who swore an oath to overthrow the House of Duir. The Fili Queen who attempted to harness a power so strong that it destroyed her and her army. She was back, and so was her army.

Outside, hundreds of soldiers suddenly appeared, naked and screaming. Cialtie, it seemed, had anticipated this. Banshees were ready, passing out cloaks and boots. Then they led the dazed Fili into the Lodge where they found their old yew bows hanging. Even though the bows were all almost identical, the proper owner walked straight up to his own weapon and picked it out like it was a son or daughter.

Maeve and her Fili army were back and in league with Cialtie, the Banshees and the Brownies. Cialtie was right. This was the ally that ensured his victory.

I took off my masks when it was just me and Jesse in his tent. 'I have to find Ruby and get back to Duir,' I said, 'but I don't know how to do it without getting you into trouble. Any ideas?'

But Jesse wasn't ready for a chat about planning. He was still way too freaked out. 'Did you see what they did?' he asked, wide-eyed and pale.

'I sure did.'

'Whatever happened in there … it can't be … it can't be right.'

'No, it was very wrong and I'm freaked out too.'

Jesse continued to look off into nothing. I tried to snap him out of it. 'Hey,' I said playfully punching him on the arm, 'you were awesome in there.'

'I was?'

'Hell yes. The way you stood up to Lugh. That was, like, the bravest thing I've ever seen.'

'What?' he said, finally looking at me. 'Really? Gosh I almost forgot I did that. I did do that, didn't I?'

'You sure did.'

Jesse smiled. 'I was terrified.'

'Well, you pretended not to be very well. It was – princely.'

He looked like he'd been slapped. 'Gosh, I think that's the nicest thing anyone has ever said to me.'

Jesse then burst into tears and gave me a hug. That may not be princely behaviour in anybody else's book but it was just fine in mine.

A Banshee guard outside the tent announced himself and asked loudly if he could speak with Prince Codna. I only had time to turn away and throw up my hood before he entered the tent. Jesse nodded to the messenger and wiped his eyes.

'I have been sent to ask if you or any of the Brownies have seen the girl,' the Banshee said, standing to attention.

'What girl?' Jesse asked.

'The blind girl, Your Highness. She has powers of which we were previously unaware. She has killed two guards and escaped.'

I almost turned then. Surely this was some kind of joke.

'I find that hard to believe,' Jesse said.

'It is true, sir. She is gone and all that is left of two of my most trusted guards are their clothes.'

'This is indeed very strange,' he said in his faux-prince voice. 'I shall assign some Brownies to help you with the search.'

The guard saluted and left.

Jesse picked up my bandana and eye gauze mask and handed them to me. 'Go find her, Conor, and get her back home.'

'But what about you? Won't it be suspicious if your Shadowguard disappears?'

'Don't worry about me. I'm sure I can find a new Shadowguard.'

I put on my mask and stood. Before I left Jesse took my hand and said, 'I remember what you once said, Conor. No one can unmake us friends.'

Outside the tent was a disorganised mess. Soldiers were running all over the place looking into tents and under bushes. If Ruby was wandering around out here I had no chance of finding her first. Saying that, how could she have escaped? The messenger said she had killed two guards. Now that certainly wasn't true. Maybe she had help. Maybe Mom or Araf had organised a breakout.

I decided to risk going in to the Lodge to see if I could have a look at where she had been held. I had to risk talking to a couple of Banshee guards. I was worried that maybe speaking would give away that I was a fake Shadowguard, but I didn't seem to arouse any suspicion.

Ruby's holding cell made me want to cry. There was just a straw mat and a bucket for her to use as a toilet. On the floor was a half-eaten apple. How could anybody do this to a young girl? By the door, a pile of soldier's uniforms lay on top of two pairs of shoes. I picked up one of the cloaks and dust fell from the inside of the sleeves.

OK, I said to myself, *let's assume she hasn't been rescued, or worse kidnapped by somebody else – let's assume she really did escape on her own. Where could she have gone?* I imagined I was a young girl grop-ing along these stone walls. I followed a wall out of the room and into the corridor. The roof was broken here and the wall was covered with pale ivy. I got down on my hands and knees and discovered that some of the stems were broken. Could Ruby have done that as she was feeling along the wall? Further along I found what almost looked like an ivy bush. I looked inside and found an opening in the wall behind it. Vines had grown up from below in what must have been an old dumb waiter shaft. There was still a rope hanging down. At the bottom of the shaft was daylight. There was no way I could fit in there, but Ruby could. As I was poking my head back in, I saw a clump of matted hair hanging from a thorny vine. It was black, just like Ruby's. 'Aren't you a clever girl,' I said to myself.

I ran outside and around the Lodge until I found where that shaft let out. There was a half-ruined stone outbuilding that prob-ably had been some sort of cooking place or maybe a laundry. In the dirt I found the imprint of a very Worldly sneaker print. She had definitely been there. I rubbed out her footprint and looked into the holly forest beyond.

A Banshee saw me climbing from the outbuilding. 'Found anything?'

'No,' I replied. 'Have you searched the holly forest yet?'

'Twice,' he said. 'She's not out there.'

'Maybe she climbed a tree.'

'Not those trees, mate. Anytime you get near them they scratch the hell out of you.'

To prove his words he held out his arm. It was covered with deep scratches. He continued around the castle searching in a way a person does when he knows there's no point but has to keep going because his superior officer ordered him to.

I looked at the holly forest before me. *You gotta be out there somewhere, my little gem.* The hollies here weren't like trees, they were more like gigantic bushes. Most were about two storeys high; palm-sized leaves covered them from top to bottom and those leaves were hard and spiked on all sides. There was no way to get to the trunk of these trees without some serious hacking, or permission. I walked up to the nearest plant. I had never spoken to a holly before. I tentatively reached towards it. My last experience with talking to a strange oak made me think twice before bounding up and hugging a tree. I pinched a leaf between my index finger and thumb and gave it a dainty shake like the kind you'd get from a germ-phobic posh lady.

'Hello there, Mr Holly,' I said as politely as I could. I braced myself for an attack but could only hear, no not hear, feel – I could feel a tiny voice, but it was just out of reach like I was trying to listen to a conversation through a hotel wall. I got the impression that if I were able to reach through the leaves and touch some wood that I might be able to converse with this plant. I remembered the welted-up scratches on the soldier's arm but if these trees could help me find Ruby that would be a small price. I scrunched up my eyes and pushed my hand past the wall of leaves and felt around for a branch. The moment I touched it the leaves closed around my arm and spiked leaves penetrated my skin. The pain was excruciating but I was prepared for it and didn't try to pull away. It was the pulling away that had scratched that soldier up so much. Mr Holly's voice was strong in my mind now and the first thing I realised was that it was Ms Holly.

'*Who be you?*' she asked as I grimaced in pain.

The question led me to surmise that hollies couldn't just reach into my head and take out any information like some of the other trees in The Land. I didn't answer. I wanted to keep my identity a secret. I had no idea if Hollies gossiped or not.

She was in my brain enough to ask, '*You are Faerie?*'

'Yes ma'am.'

'*I want you to tell me,*' she demanded.

'I am Faerie,' I said. 'I'm looking for a young girl.'

'What do you want with this child?'

'I want to help her, she's lost.'

'Others today have said this to us but in their blood they harboured malice.'

I looked down at my wrist, beads of blood oozed out of a ring of tiny pinpricks caused by the sharp leaves.

'You can read blood?'

'Your blood (actually it felt more like she said sap) reveals to us the truth in what you say.'

'Then know this, ma'am,' I said. 'This young girl is lost and alone. She has been mistreated by these people. I'm here to take her home to her family. Do you know where she is?'

The tree didn't speak for a while. I got a faint impression that she was talking to someone else.

'The girl is with us. She is very afraid and says she can no longer see.'

'Will you lead me to her?'

She released my wrist but I remained in contact with the branch. *'Walk north touching my sisters. We will lead you to her.'*

At did as I was told. While trying to look casual, I touched the leaves of every holly I passed. In my head I received instant messages that subtly changed my direction until I found a large tree that somehow I knew she was under. I looked around; I could hear distant shouting but no one was about.

I pinched a leaf between my fingers and asked, 'Is the girl here?'

The tree replied by saying, *'Give me your blood.'*

I tried to reach through the wall of leaves like I did before but the tree instructed me just to prick my thumb on one of the leaf's spines.

As soon as I did the tree asked, *'Do you mean to harm this child?'*

My heart began to race in my chest. I had found her. 'No ma'am,' I said. 'I've come to rescue her.'

'How do you propose to do that? The child cannot travel: she is hurt and exhausted.'

'I have an amulet that will return us home to her father and grandmother.'

I felt the tree believe me and then heard the creaking sound of living wood moving. A gap opened in the dome of leaves that covered the holly from top to bottom and I entered. I thought she wasn't there at first. I looked all around the base of the trunk and didn't find her. Then I looked up. She was about six feet above me, asleep, cradled in a basket of branches provided by the holly.

I felt tears come to my eyes. I placed my hand on the trunk and said, 'Thank you.'

It was tight in there but the holly pushed apart branches as I climbed. She was still asleep when I reached her. She was pale, dirty and her hair was a tangled mess but still I thought she was the most beautiful thing I had ever seen. I gently pushed her hair away from her face. She opened her eyes and – screamed. She screamed one of those world famous Ruby migraine-inducing screams. I placed my hand across her mouth; I don't know how but the sound was still amazingly loud.

'Shhhhh, Ruby, it's me,' I shout-whispered.

She couldn't hear me over the internal sound she was making with her scream so she bit me. I quickly pulled my palm back and fell backwards about five feet and got stuck upside-down in the branches. Ruby then started banging on my ankle with something really hard.

'Ruby,' I shouted, not caring who heard me; every living creature within a twenty-five-mile radius must have heard that scream. 'Ruby, damn it, stop. It's me, Conor.'

'Conor, Conor O'Neil?'

'Yes, now shut up.'

The holly tried to help me untangle myself but only succeeded in dropping me another five feet onto my head. Ruby climbed down. When I took her in my arms she broke down into uncontrollable quaking sobs.

'Shhhh, it's all right,' I said, but it wasn't.

Outside the tree I heard soldiers shouting, 'In there. That one.' *'There are men surrounding me,'* the holly pulsed into my brain.

I reached to my neck for the *rothlú* charm and then panicked when it wasn't there. I then remembered I had taken it off inside the Lodge. I frantically searched for the pocket I knew was somewhere in this borrowed set of clothes.

Outside I heard a voice say. 'Hack it down.'

The tree's voice in my head barked, *'Quickly, Faerie.'*

I found the amulet at the same time as I saw a sword slice through the holly's wall of leaves. At the same time I felt the tree's pain and terror.

I didn't have time to thank or apologise to the tree. I only had time to say, 'This is gonna hurt, Ruby,' and then I said, *'Rothlú.'*

I can't tell you how disappointed I was when I felt wet grass pressing against the side of my face. I really thought I was going to wake up between clean sheets in my nice warm bed in Castle Duir. Instead, I was once again face down in a field somewhere. This had been my third *rothlú* spell (or was it four? I didn't even know any more) in two days. Brains were not meant to be scrambled on a regular basis. I tried to think where I was and how I got there. It was definitely a *rothlú* so it must be important, but at that moment I couldn't think and all I wanted to do was go back to sleep in the dirt or if that wasn't possible, then die. At least I wouldn't hurt any more.

Then a scream brought me back to the present. At the sound of Ruby's screech my brain cells finally organised themselves enough so I remembered what I was doing. I was saving Ruby. The hairy hermit told me that the *rothlú* would get me home but it obviously hadn't – I was face down in grass and Ruby was once again in trouble. Forcing myself to ignore the all-over body pain, I jumped to my feet. Ruby stopped screaming and began jumping. She wrapped her arms around my legs.

I pushed her back. 'What's wrong? Are you all right? Where are we?'

Ruby continued to jump. 'You're awake!'

I placed my hands on her shoulder, and tried to make her hold still. It didn't work and it hurt. I felt like I had just been worked over in an alley by a loan shark.

'Ruby, why are you screaming?'

She looked at me like I'd just asked a stupid question. 'You wouldn't wake up so I did one of my waking the dead screams. And it worked.'

'So you're OK?'

'Yes, yes,' she said, grabbing my hand and pulling me.

I took a few steps and then had to stop. I turned away and thought I was going to be sick. She grabbed my hand again.

'Come on, come on, you have to meet someone. She is sooooooo nice.'

I quickly straightened up and finally had a look around. I let Ruby lead me to her new friend as a smile crossed my face. I reached out and placed my hands on that venerable old bark and said, 'Hello, Mother Oak.'

Chapter Sixteen
The Worry Stone

The moment I touched her I received that blessed loving calm that comes every time I'm with Mother Oak, and through her I could also feel the joy and unconditional love coming from Ruby, who was touching the oak's trunk as well. But the calm didn't last. I was surprised and then scared by what I could only describe as panic rising up in Mother Oak. I tried to pull my hand away but was frozen to the spot just like when I was attacked by the oak outside of Castle Duir. I groaned and dropped to my knees as the tree's will probed my mind for information.

'Why are you being so mean to him?' I heard Ruby yell and it stopped.

I fell backwards hard on my butt and caught my breath. Ruby continued to talk to her and I listened to that one side of the conversation.

'Yes … I guess so … Promise … OK.'

Ruby walked over to me and said, 'She said she was surprised and did a bad thing. She wants to talk to you and promises to be nice.'

I didn't get up right away. I really had been sucker punched by the old woman. An attack from Mother Oak was the last thing I expected and after *rothlú*-ing around for a couple of days, I just wanted to curl up and drool for a while. But this was Mother Oak. I had to at least find out what made her act that way. I didn't even stand, I just scooted backwards and sat against her trunk and tentatively placed my hands on her bark.

Back was the old Mother Oak. *'Oh my, I am so sorry Conor. I try never to intrude on anyone's private thoughts but I saw something at the fore of your mind and it scared me so I just had to learn more. I am afraid I forgot myself. Please forgive me.'*

She really was terribly sorry. There was no hiding emotion when you are talking to the Grand Lady of Glen Duir. Of course she was forgiven and I stood, hugged her once and then climbed a little, allowing her to build a place for me to sit in her branches.

As I settled in, I also felt through Mother Oak the emotional presence of Ruby. 'Is everything all right?'

'Yes dear,' the tree reassured.

'I'm fine, Ruby,' I said. 'It was just a misunderstanding.'

'I was wondering, my child, if I may have a chat with Conor on my own for a moment.'

'Oh, like grown-up stuff.'

I felt Mother Oak smile. *'Yes. One thing I certainly am is grown-up.'*

'OK,' Ruby said and then she was out of my head.

'Again I am sorry for my rudeness before, but I saw in your mind that Maeve is alive. Can this truly be so? The child spoke of horrible things that Banshees did to her and she spoke of ghosts.'

'All true, I'm afraid. Cialtie has somehow brought Maeve and her Fili army back.'

'Oh, my, my. I had hoped that the past would stay past. I do not know if I can sprout through another season if such turmoil again grows in The Land.'

The old oak creaked and I could almost feel the weight of her boughs pressing down on my shoulders.

'Don't worry ma'am. My mom and dad will figure out something,' I said, hoping it was true. 'I have to go now and warn everyone.'

'*Yes, yes of course, Conor,*' the tree said as if I roused her from deep thought. '*And you must get that dear girl back to her father and grandmother. Ask her to come back to me.*'

'Hey Ruby,' I shouted. 'Mother Oak wants to speak to you and then we have to go.'

I climbed down and was going to leave them alone but the tree asked me to stay. Ruby wrapped her arms around the trunk. The two of them didn't speak for a while – they just felt. Love flowed between them like a two-way street.

'*You have been through so much my little sprout. But you are with Conor now and he will take good care of you. Can I tell you a secret?*'

Ruby nodded her head. 'Yes.'

'*Conor is the finest young man I have ever met.*'

'Really?' I said.

'*Shush, I was speaking to Ruby. Goodbye you two. Take care of each other. I'm afraid there are going to be dark times ahead. Just remember that I have been in this glen for oh so very a long time and the one thing I know is – after winter there has always been spring.*'

I had never walked back to the castle from Glen Duir but I knew it was going to take more than a day. 'You up for a long hike?'

Ruby took my hand and said, 'Sure.'

Mother Oak had given her a stick that she had trimmed and she set off sweeping it before her.

'Don't you feel bad after that *rothlú* spell that brought us here?'

'My tummy was a little funny when I first got here but I'm OK now.'

'Well, I feel like crap.'

'You said a dirty word.'

'Sorry.'

'I won't tell.'

'Thanks.'

We trudged along for the rest of the day. Ruby hummed some song, most of the time while I grunted along. The sun got lower and Ruby started to get tired. There was no point in stopping. We had no food and no way to make a fire so I gave her a piggyback. She quickly fell asleep. It's amazing how rapidly the young girl on my back began to feel like a proverbial eight-hundred-pound gorilla. As the sun was setting I had to quit.

'I'm cold.'

I gave her my Brownie cloak. 'I'm afraid I don't have a fire coin, Ruby.'

'That's OK,' she said. 'Go ask a tree for two sticks.'

'Why?'

'To rub together.'

'Oh,' I laughed. 'I'm afraid rubbing sticks together will only get us splinters. I have to rest, Ruby. Just for an hour.'

I lay down and she snuggled up on my chest.

'Will that Lugh man find us here?'

I don't even remember if I stayed awake long enough to answer. The next thing I do remember, Ruby was prying open one of my eyelids and frantically whispering, 'Wake up. Someone's coming.'

The two of us ran out of the clearing and hid behind some oaks, making sure not to touch them. It was a small party of riders. In front, one of the riders hung over his saddle with his head down. In his hand he was dangling a vial that glowed with a yellow light. He was a scout and was obviously following our trail. I thought about climbing the tree in front of us but I was too afraid of getting comatised like the last time I talked to a strange oak. Running was no good either. The forest wasn't thick enough to slow down a rider. I had nowhere to run and nowhere to hide. I drew the Lawnmower and waited. I still could only make out their silhouettes. The scout spotted where we had bedded down, and then looked directly to the tree we were hiding behind.

I stepped out and said, 'Who goes there?'

The scout dismounted and pushed back his hood. Hair cascaded over the scout's shoulders like a cheesy shampoo commercial. It was only when she placed the light next to her face that everything instantly became all right again in The Land.

'Conor,' she yipped. She ran and crashed into me, giving me a bone-crunching hug.

'Hi, Essa. Miss me?'

A fire was built and food was brought. Essa sent a message back to Castle Duir that we had been found and Tuan was flying in to pick us up air-ambulance style.

Ruby started jabbering on about her abduction like it was some sort of fun adventure. I'm sure that if I had experienced a similar trauma at her age I would have become a curled-up snivelling wreck, but Ruby was obviously made of sterner stuff.

As she was recounting her story I remembered something. A Banshee had said she had killed two guards.

'Ruby, how did you escape? Weren't you being guarded?'

Ruby crinkled up her nose at the thought of it. 'The guards were mean. One of them saw me rubbing my worry stone and he told me to give it to him. I said no because Grandma had given it to me, so he grabbed it. Then I was alone. I just crawled along the wall until I found that way out.'

'Ruby, what's a worry stone?'

She reached into her pocket and pulled out a smooth pebble-sized piece of green marble with a dent in it. She held it in her hand and rubbed her thumb on the indentation. 'I found it on the floor as I was crawling out.'

'Can I see it?' Essa asked. 'I promise to give it back.'

As Ruby handed it over, a thought formed in my mind. I reached out to stop Essa from touching the stone but I was too slow.

When Essa touched the pebble, she didn't scream. It was more like she had all of the wind knocked out of her. She dropped her head down and then after catching her breath, she looked at the back of her hands. They were spidery, wrinkled and covered with spots. When she looked up, the firelight showed the eighty-year-old woman who I had first seen at the police station in the Real World.

'Oh, not again!' Essa said in her old woman voice.

'What's happening?' Ruby asked.

'Your worry stone, Ruby, it's from Ireland; when Essa touched it she became the age she would be in the Real World.'

'Damn it, damn it, damn it.'

'She said a naughty word.'

'Yes, Ruby, I think she did.'

I was expecting Ruby to love the ride home on dragon-back but I could tell it scared her. She held on white-knuckled and shook almost the whole way. Of course, that didn't stop her, when she got back, from bragging about how fun it was.

The return of the prodigal son was nothing compared to Ruby's return. I don't think I had ever seen anybody so happy to see anybody as the residents of Castle Duir were with the rearrival of Ruby. Most of the people there had never seen her, but the gloom that had been hanging over the place since her kidnap broke with an exuberance that was almost like a festival. While Ruby got all the attention I just stood by and said, 'Don't worry about me. I'm fine.'

Brendan unaged, like, ten years instantly when he saw her. I came close to trying to separate them, he was hugging his daughter so hard, but Ruby didn't seem to mind. Nora, who had been mad at me ever since I left her granddaughter alone in the Forest of Duir, kissed my cheek and said, 'I have no words to tell you how grateful I am.'

'Aw shucks, ma'am,' I said. 'It was nothin'.'

Graysea was very glad to see me. I got smothered with kisses and then she insisted on finning-up and giving me a thorough mermaid medical work-up. I told her I was fine, just tired, and asked her to have a look at Ruby's hand. She healed the cut in seconds.

'I like her better than Essa,' Ruby said after her treatment.

'You have seen Essa already?' Graysea asked curtly.

'Well, yeah,' I said, 'she was the one who found us in the forest. I wouldn't worry about her, she's … well, she's not looking her best.'

Essa was still on her way back to Castle Duir. Tuan had offered her some dragon blood in the forest but I told her I had a plan and it might be a good idea if she stayed like that. She agreed, but wouldn't take a dragon lift back to Duir. I think her exact words were, 'I'll hit the next person who treats me like an old woman.'

Essa was summed up best by Ruby who said, 'She's scary.'

After a night's sleep that I had to insist upon, I sat down with Mom, Dad, Nieve, Fand and Dahy. I felt like I was reporting to the Spanish Inquisition. I told them the whole story of what had happened on my way to the Yewlands. When I got to Hermy, Dad interrupted.

'What did you say his name was?'

'Sorry, I made up Hermy. Let me think. Oh yeah, just as I was *rothlú*-ing away he said his name was Eth.'

Dad was on his feet. 'Eth? What else did he say?'

'He said he was Ona's son.'

Dad covered his mouth with his left hand. I can tell when he's emotional because he never uses his right hand – the one that was missing for so long. As I watched him and waited for him to speak, it came to me where I had heard that name before. Eth was Dad's best friend. He was the one who was with Dad on the day of the boat race. When Dad woke up in the infirmary he had blamed Eth for the loss of his hand and Eth left – never to be seen again.

'I have to go to Thunder Bay at once.'

'Hold on, Dad,' I said. 'There is other stuff I have to tell you and I think there is somewhere I have to go first.'

Mom gave Dad one of those one-second looks that conveyed an entire paragraph of information. It instantly said, 'I know you're upset, but calm down, we have to think about this.' It also said, 'I love you.' It's amazing what women can do with just a look and a tiny finger movement.

I continued recanting my adventure. When I got to Cialtie and his witch's Shadowcasting, it was my mother's turn to get upset. When I told her about how Ruby's blood was used to darken the shadow of her rune she reached to her neck and pulled her rune from under her top. It was dark red, almost black.

'It suddenly went dark two days ago,' Mom said.

'Yeah, that would be about right.'

And then I upset everybody by telling them that Maeve was back. Of all people, it was Fand who was still calm enough to make light of my story. She said, 'Conor, you are many things but you are never dull.'

'And I'm not even done yet. The reason Ruby was able to escape from the Ivy Lodge was because she killed her two guards.'

I'm not sure who said 'What?' but I'm pretty sure it was everybody.

I reached into my pocket and took out Ruby's marble worry stone. Mom went to reach for it but I stopped her. 'Don't touch it, Mom, that little thing will kill you.'

'What is it?'

'It's a stone from a place on the west coast of Ireland called Connemara. They call it Connemara marble. Nora said she bought it on a trip over there. She says that she was aware of major ley-lines while she was in Connemara. Ages ago, Spideog showed me a stone axe that he had brought back from the Real World but it was only a wooden handle. He said the stone vanished in the portal during his journey back to The Land.'

'That is correct,' Mom said. 'Stone will not pass between the worlds.'

'Well, this did,' I said picking up the worry stone. 'And I'm pretty sure if anyone in The Land touches it, it's exactly like when they touch the ground in the Real World. They become their actual Real World age.'

'That is an interesting theory,' Dahy said.

'It's more than a theory, Master D,' I said as I walked to the door. I opened it and the eighty-year-old Essa came in.

'Oh my dear,' Fand said. 'Did you …'

'Yes, I touched the damn rock,' Essa said, already tired of having to explain her looks.

'Why haven't you spoken to Tuan and changed back?'

''Cause Essa is going to help me with something. We're going to go on a trip.'

'A trip,' Dad said. 'To where?'

'I thought we'd go and get some more of this stuff.'

Chapter Seventeen

Connemara

'Tell me again why we didn't bring horses?' Essa said as she looked around at the nothingness in all directions.

Essa, Brendan and I had arrived at the Fairy Fingers about ten minutes earlier. Mom, Nieve and Fand had communed with Nora, who was becoming a bit of an insta-sorceress, and they searched for ley-lines on the west coast of Ireland. It was not surprising to learn that for travelling back and forth between the Real World and Tir na Nog, Ireland was ley-line central. The problem was there were so many magic spots in the Emerald Isle that it was hard to find the right one. Especially when the most recent map Mom had of Ireland looked like it was printed on woolly mammoth skin. It was concluded that a stone circle called the Fairy Fingers would be the nearest place to Connemara. Fand said Cullen, or should I say Cucullen, built it to mark his favourite portal spot. She added, 'He was always building crap like that.' I loved how Fand incorporated 'crap' into her daily language ever since I taught it to her.

The Fairy Fingers had a sign pointing to it from the road but no other signs around gave us any help as to what direction civilisation lay. Assuming that the time of day was the same here as in The Land (a big assumption) we decided to walk in the opposite direction to the sun and trudge west. That way if we didn't find any people, at least the sea would stop us from walking for ever.

'Because,' I said answering Essa, 'people in the modern Real World don't ride horses. It would draw attention to us.'

Sometimes I think the gods just spend all of their time messing with my life 'cause at that moment we heard the unmistakable clip-clop of horses' hooves followed by two riders cantering up the middle of the road behind us. Essa gave me one of her most reproachful stares. I turned to Brendan for support.

'Tell her that's just a fluke. People don't ride horses around here.'

'As much as I enjoy watching Conor make a fool out of himself, he's right,' Brendan said, 'people don't ride horses any more.'

Apparently the gods don't just screw with me, they mess with Brendan as well 'cause immediately after saying that, four more riders cantered up behind us. Brendan and I just stared at each other open-mouthed as Essa shook her head.

'Are you certain that you two are from here?' Essa asked.

'We're not from here,' Brendan said, 'we're from a different part of the Real World but still – this isn't the middle of nowhere – this is Ireland. I'm certain they have the internal combustion engine here.'

'Could Mom have sent us back in time?'

'If I had to choose between Deirdre sending us back in time or you two being idiots ...' Essa stared at us and then said, 'Do I really have to finish that sentence?'

Several more groups of horses rode past. I really started to think that we were in the past until I saw one of the riders wearing a pair of Nikes. One thing I'm certain of is that Nikes were definitely around at the same time as cars. The question is – where were the cars and why was everybody riding?

A pony and cart came up behind us with an old man holding the reins. 'Get out of the way, you idiots,' he shouted.

He had plenty of room but we moved further over to the side of the road.

As he went, by I asked, 'Why is everybody on horseback?'

'Because they're not so stupid as to be walking like you.'

Obviously this was not the runner up in the Connemara Miss Congeniality contest. Brendan and I smiled at each other and let him past but Essa said, 'Excuse me, can we get a lift in your cart?'

His reply would have made a sailor blush.

'He said a dirty word,' Brendan said, doing an imitation of his daughter.

'I believe you are right, Detective Fallon.'

Brendan and I thought it was funny. Old lady Essa, though, seemed to have outgrown her sense of humour. She reached into her pocket, took out a gold sphere and then blew on it in the direction of the cart. The old man keeled over in his seat and the horse veered off towards the side of the road and stopped. Brendan and my smiles vanished as we ran to the old guy. He was out cold.

'What did you do to him?' Brendan asked.

Essa slowly sauntered up to the old guy and placed her hands on both sides of his head. 'He will be fine. He's just asleep. Throw him in the back.'

Brendan and I looked at each other.

'You can either throw him in the back and cover him with some of that burlap or we can stand around staring at each other until someone comes along and starts asking questions.'

When Essa talks like that there really is no other choice than to do what she says. I picked up the old guy under his shoulders and Brendan got his feet.

As we were carrying him, Brendan said, 'In all of my time as a cop I always wondered how so many nice people ended up leading a life of crime. I'm starting to understand now.'

Essa took the reins and Brendan and I sat on the back of the cart with our legs dangling over the end. It was painfully slow.

Riders continually passed us. One shouted, 'Nice pony.' To which I replied, 'Nice horsey.' We eventually passed houses with cars outside but still we didn't see anyone driving. I wanted to ask why everybody was on horses but when you cart-jack an octogenarian it's best to keep a low profile.

After what seemed like days, with every person who rode by looking at us like we were under a microscope, we came to a large plastic road sign that read, 'ROAD CLOSED FOR PONY FESTIVAL.'

It was getting to be around lunchtime and the town was hopping. In all directions there were ponies and horses in stables, attached to ponycarts and with riders. Stalls were set up selling saddles, bridles and all sorts of horsey things. An old-fashioned blacksmith was firing up a forge and performing a horse-shoeing demonstration. And underfoot everywhere was horse crap. All of the festival goers were wearing rubber wellington boots – I on the other hand still had on those flimsy Brownies slippers. I had a look around town to see if there was a proper shoe store but it didn't look like this was a place where I could get a new pair of Nikes.

'You know what?' Brendan said with a smile worthy of Fergal. 'I'd really like a Guinness.'

'A what?' Essa said.

'I'll show you,' Brendan said, pointing to a pub.

Essa parked the cart and the sleeping old man as far back in the parking lot as she could.

The pub smelled of horse manure, decades of stale beer and peat fire smoke. I instantly felt like I could spend some serious time in there. Essa and I found a low table and Brendan went up to the bar to ask where he could change his dollars into local currency. Standing next to him a tall American offered to swap him enough for a few pints and sandwiches. The American, wearing a new tweed flat cap, even helped him carry the food over to the table.

'So y'awl from Scranton too?' the tall American asked in a Dixie accent. He didn't wait for an answer and sat down without an invite.

'Santa's Car,' he said, hoisting his pint for a toast. 'I learned that today.'

'Sláinte Mhaith?' I said.

'Yeah, that's it. A local told me it was Gaelic for "Here's mud in your eye".'

'I'm not sure if that's the literal translation.'

'No? No matter, I've got so much Guinness in me I won't remember tomorrow. I'm Alexander Hawthorn-Twait. Now don't get all excited about the fancy name. My granddaddy was a Texas horse thief who went straight and gave himself a fancy title. I'm just a normal millionaire grandson of a horse thief. Friends call me Al. So where'd yooaall say you were from?'

'I'm a Scrantonian too,' I said.

'And how about you ma'am?

'I am from Munn.'

The American lit up. 'Well my, my, I'd never have thought I'd find me someone from my neck of the woods out here in the middle of nowhere. But I don't know a Munn, Kentucky?'

Essa was speaking English using one of my Aunt Nieve's magic spells. The result was that she sounded to the listener like she was speaking in the accent that they were most familiar with. I didn't hear it because to me it sounded as if Essa was speaking ancient Gaelic.

Before Essa could say anything I reached over, patted her hand and said, 'Essa has a habit of mimicking people's accents. Don't you dear?' I turned back to our guest and secretly twirled my finger around my ear.

'Oh, OK,' he said, 'well, you tell your mother I think that's charming.'

'I am not his mother,' Essa said.

Brendan actually spit out his mouthful of Guinness.

'I beg your pardon.'

Brendan continued to laugh and like a yawn I caught it too. We both giggled like schoolboys as Essa got angrier.

'What's so funny?' Al asked, confused.

'Brendan pointed to me and said, 'She's his girlfriend.'

'I am not.'

Maybe it was the Guinness we had drunk, or the look on Essa's face, or maybe just the niceness of being back in the Real World again but Brendan and I lost it. We were laughing so hard we couldn't speak.

Al looked uncomfortable. 'I think you boys are pulling my leg.'

Essa heard that and actually looked under the table and Brendan laughed so hard he fell off his chair.

'You folks are very strange.' Al stood up to leave.

I wanted to say something, apologise; I knew we were being rude but I just couldn't get any words out. Al stomped off and Brendan and I continued like that until Essa's deadly stares calmed us down.

I raised a toast, 'To Santa's Car.'

Essa finally took a sip of her Guinness. When she placed her glass back on the table she sported a white Guinness moustache.

'Well, watcha think?' Brendan asked.

'Can I have something that isn't black?'

Brendan figured that we had made too much of a spectacle of ourselves in the pub to then ask questions about where we could get marble, so he left us to nurse our pints and went to ask around town. Essa and I sat in silence. Al went back to drinking at the bar, periodically giving us strange looks.

Finally Essa said, 'I would really like to get back to The Land soon so I can no longer be mistaken for your grandmother.'

'You do make a lovely grandma.'

'Would hitting you in here draw attention to us?' she said.

'Yes.'

'You're lucky then.'

We didn't have enough money to buy anything else so we took tiny sips of our drinks and politely declined every time a barmaid came by and asked us if we wanted anything else. I got the distinct impression that we weren't spending enough money in there.

I got up to use *the loo*. While I was in there I heard a commotion in the pub. As soon as I opened the men's room door I saw a chair flying through the air and heard Essa screaming, 'Get your hands off of me.'

A policeman shouted, 'She's got something in her hand. She's got a gun!'

Everyone was on their feet. I saw Essa's hand being held over her head as her golden ball was prised out of her fingers. There were three cops around her. I knew I couldn't help her in this crowded pub so, while everyone was looking at her being cuffed, I dropped my chin and began to walk out the door. On the bar I spotted Al's new tweed cap. I swiped it and put it on low so it covered my eyes.

Outside an ambulance was trying to revive the old man. He was still asleep. I could tell that 'cause he was snoring and it was loud. The snoring must have been what made someone look underneath the burlap.

I wandered around town, periodically stopping to admire a pony or peruse a saddle stall. Basically I just tried to look anonymous while keeping an eye out for Brendan. Luckily I spotted him as he was making his way back into the pub. I spun him around and told him to keep walking and act normal.

'What's the matter with you, O'Neil?'

'Essa's been arrested.'

'What?'

'Yeah, three of your guys got her in the pub while I was in the men's room. Somebody found the old guy in the back of the cart. He got taken away in an ambulance.'

'I would have thought Essa would blow the place up before she allowed herself to be arrested.'

'She was about to but they wrestled that gold ball thing out of her hand before she could do anything. Now she's just a crazy eighty-year-old woman with an attitude problem.'

Brendan thought for a moment and despite our situation, smiled. 'I bet she said some naughty words too.'

'Yeah, I imagine she did,' I said matching his smile.

'So what now, another jail break?'

'I've never tried one without any magic backup,' I said.

'We have to reunite Essa with her magic ball,' Brendan said. 'Not only is it our only weapon – it's how we get back to Tir na Nog.'

That hadn't occurred to me. 'Oh yeah. Any ideas?'

'Well, it's risky, but I could see if the local police will extend a little professional courtesy.'

The police station was in the next town over. Brendan had exchanged all of his money so we had enough for a cab but the one cab driver in town was busy 'fleecing rich Yanks', so we took the bus.

The police station was attached to a veterinary practice. Brendan initially told me to wait outside while he went in but I refused. I didn't want to be waiting outside for hours wondering what the hell had gone wrong. My initial idea was to steal a sheep and then mistakenly take it in to the cop station instead of the vet's. That way I would be inside to see what happened. That drew one of those looks from Brendan that stifles all further discussion. Finally we came up with the simpler plan of me going in first and reporting a lost wallet. Sure, it made more sense, but it just didn't have the panache of my sheep idea.

I suspect that in this tiny Irish town a lost wallet would have been the highlight of the day, but on this particular one they had a bona fide crazy criminal locked up in their cell. (Well, it wasn't a cell, it was just a windowless office, but for now it was a cell.) The garda (what they call cops there) hardly listened to me and handed me a pen and a lost property form. While I was dawdling over my paperwork, Brendan came in.

Actually what I should say is Detective Fallon of the Scranton Fraternal Order of Police stormed in. He didn't pause to introduce himself. He strode up to the counter, flashed his badge and ID and said, 'I want to speak to your superior officer.'

The old policeman was taken aback. 'Ah, he's unavailable at this time.'

A younger cop came from the back.

'Where is he?' Brendan demanded.

'I think he's castrating a cat.'

Well, that would explain the police station being next to a veterinarian's office, I thought.

'I can get him,' the younger cop said. 'Who should I say wants him?'

Brendan flashed his badge and ID again but the young cop insisted on looking at it carefully.

'Detective Brendan Fallon of the Scranton, Pennsylvania PD. Is that correct?'

'Yes,' Brendan replied brusquely.

'I'll be back in a moment,' the young cop said.

'Would this be concerning the woman we arrested today?' the older cop asked.

'I would prefer to speak to your superior,' Brendan said.

'I'm not sure you do,' he said, but before Brendan could ask him why, the young cop appeared in the doorway with his hands behind his back. He stepped up to Brendan and then brought out what I thought was a gun. He pulled a trigger and two darts attached to wires exploded out of the front of the thing. The darts hit Brendan in the chest and he started dancing around like a puppet on a string.

The taser stopped humming and Brendan slid to the ground.

'What the hell are you doing?' the old cop shouted.

The young cop pulled the electric darts out of Brendan's chest, 'Jeez, did you see that? This thing really works.'

'I can see that it works,' the old guy said. 'But what the hell did you do it for?'

The young cop rolled Brendan onto his side and reached for his handcuffs. 'This fella's a fugitive. Remember I was telling you about that America's Most Wanted programme I watch on the teli? This guy is wanted by the FBI. He blew up a police station and kidnapped a G-man, or a young girl ... I can't remember, but this is him.'

Brendan was coming to as the cop secured the cuffs. I backed out of the room and mumbled, 'I'll come back when you're less ... busy.' I pulled my stolen cap over my eyes and left. The two cops hardly noticed me.

I got outside and said the only thing I could think of. 'Oh crap.'

Chapter Eighteen

Connemara Maeve

I got a room in Mrs McDunna's Bed and Breakfast. It was not as cheap as I would have liked, but then again, I didn't have any money so she wasn't going to get paid anyway. I spent my first night hidden in my room in case the cops figured out that I was the third member of the international crime syndicate they were arresting.

Mrs McDunna's Irish breakfast was gorgeous. Since the next prospect I had of eating again was this time the next day, I ate an entire loaf of her home-made soda bread. It was lovely but sat in my stomach like a rock. She asked me what I was going to do that day. I panicked and said I was going to buy a pony. So half an hour later I left to pretend to buy one.

The town was nice, but it only took an hour to see every nook and cranny of it. I cased out the police/vet office. There was a door in the back. I snuck up and tried it but it was locked. I knew I should have taken classes in burglary when I was growing up.

By late afternoon I was starving. As I was passing a tea shop with a couple of tables outside, I saw an old lady get up to leave. I quickly dropped into her empty chair and ate the sandwich crusts she had left behind. I checked the tea pot and poured a lukewarm half cup of black tea into her old cup and washed down my salvaged scraps.

'You seem to have gotten younger since sitting here.'

I looked up and a pretty young waitress was staring at me with her arms crossed.

'And I changed sex as well.' I put down my cup. 'This is really amazing tea.'

She was trying to be stern but that got her. She laughed and uncrossed her arms. 'So what's your story?'

'I lost my wallet,' I said. 'I'm waiting for money from my bank but they seem to be sending it via camel train.'

'So you've no money?'

'Not until tomorrow at the earliest,' I lied.

'Well, we're closing up here.'

'Oh, of course,' I said, standing.

She sighed and shook her head. 'Sit,' she said, taking away the old woman's plates. 'I'll bring you a proper cup of tea.'

She did, as well as some scones that stopped me from wanting to eat my shoes.

I waited for her as she locked the front door. 'Thanks for that,' I said.

'Don't mention it. I've always been a soft touch for vagabonds.'

'Well, on behalf of vagabonds and deadbeats everywhere, I salute you.'

She stood stock still and then just stared at me. Her scrutiny was intense. I felt like I was being scanned by a tree. 'What is your name?'

'Conor.'

'What aren't you telling me, Conor?'

That question made the scones do a little flip in my tummy. 'I haven't really told you anything.'

'No,' she said elongating the o like she was figuring something out. 'You haven't, have you? I think you should take me to dinner.'

'Actually, I did tell you one thing. I have no money, remember?'

'OK, I'll take you to dinner and you can pay me back when your money shows up.'

Part of me wanted to turn her down. She had a look about her that reminded me of a CIA interrogator in a spy movie. But the part of me that eats said, 'Great idea.'

'So is this a traditional Irish dish?' I said, pointing to my chicken vindaloo.

'Yes – curry is very Irish, right after cockles, mussels and stew.'

I took a big sip of beer to calm the fire on my tongue. 'Well, thank you … You know, I don't even know your name.'

'It's Maeve, and I should be thanking you. You're paying for this – eventually.'

'Maeve, oh my. That's a name with some history behind it. Is it a family name?'

'No. My ma always said she named me that because I was born a troublemaker.'

'Are you still a troublemaker?'

'What do you think?'

'Well, you do seem to have a penchant for having dinner with strange men.'

'Strange,' she said, rewearing that X-ray look of hers. 'Yes, "strange" is the right word when explaining you. Where are you from?'

'Scranton.'

She stared again. 'Where are you reeeeely from?'

'Scraaaaaaanton.'

'I can tell when you're lying.'

'I'd show you my driver's licence …'

'But you lost your wallet. Convenient.'

'OK,' I said, 'how about this. I live in the mystical Land of Tir na Nog, on top of a gold mine, and I'm here on a secret mission to get magical stones to stop the impending attack of my evil uncle and your namesake Queen Maeve.'

My confession didn't make my date smile as fast as I thought it would but finally the corners of her mouth turned upwards. 'And what do you do in this magical land?'

'Oh, I'm a prince, of course. I'm surprised you had to ask.'

'I see. So, Prince Conor, if you live on a gold mine why are you so broke?'

'Oh I have gold with me; I just can't find any place to change it into money.'

'Can I see your gold?'

'I don't carry it around. It's … well, it's heavy.'

She finally broke in to a full-blown laugh. 'You know I almost felt like I believed you, but you went too far with the prince thing.'

'You don't think I'm princely?' I said with mock indignation.

'I'm afraid not.'

'Good, all that bowing and yes Your Highness stuff really annoys me.'

'I can imagine how trying that must be.'

I offered to walk Maeve home but she said since she paid for the date she got to walk *me* home. Outside my B&B she asked, 'Is there a princess in your world?'

There was something about this woman that made me want to tell her the truth. 'Yes, but she's eighty years old, and I'm also kinda seeing a mermaid.'

She smiled and kissed me on the cheek. 'You can find me at the tea shop when your money arrives.' As she walked away she said over her shoulder, 'Good night, Prince Conor.'

I had had a wonderful night and that was the problem. I felt guilty. I shouldn't have been out having fun while my friends were in jail and I was no closer to figuring out how to help them or get back to The Land. I spent half the night staring at the ceiling trying to figure out what to do and awoke no closer to a solution.

After another soda-bread-filled breakfast, I spent most of the next day watching the comings and goings of the vet office/police station. My only hope was that these people were stupid enough to leave this place unguarded so I could just walk in and break out my pals. But I guess that the rule – prisoners must be guarded – had made it even to the west coast of Ireland.

Since I didn't have any money to pay her back, I had meant to stay away from Maeve's tea house but by about four in the afternoon loneliness and, if I'm honest, hunger forced me to swallow my pride and see her. I confessed that I still had no money. When I started to go she commanded me to sit and brought me sandwiches and tea.

'I'll add it to your bill.'

She then invited me to a pub that night to meet her friends. When I said no she said, 'Tonight is my treat.' I said I'd try and went back to the B&B.

I had no intention of going. Along with feeling guilty for taking advantage of the poor girl, I also thought meeting a bunch of people seemed like a bad idea. After all, I was spending my days casing out a police station trying to plan a jail break. I'm pretty sure that when you are about to commit a huge felony, one should keep a low profile. But the bored lonely guy talked the rational soon-to-be felon out of it and I showed up at the pub. It was busy in there. At the corner of the bar were a water jug and some glasses so I helped myself to a glass of water so I wouldn't look too out of place. There were lots of young people around but Maeve wasn't there. I guess I had waited too long to make up my mind. I was about to leave when she walked in.

'Oh, I hope you haven't been waiting all this time.' She was a bit flushed like she had been running.

'No, I just got here.'

'Oh good, sorry I'm late. My father had a guest over for dinner and I had to eat with them.'

'I'm sorry to pull you away.'

'Don't be. The guy was such a drip. You'd think an FBI man would be interesting, wouldn't you?'

I started choking on my water but managed to calm down quickly enough to ask, 'Your father's guest is an American FBI agent?'

'Yes, can you imagine?'

'And what does your father do?'

'He's a policeman.'

It took all of my will to keep a calm exterior. 'And do you remember the FBI man's name?'

'I'm not sure I do. I didn't like him much … It was an Italian name.'

'Was it Agent Murano?'

'Yes. How did you know that?'

'Ah … I … think I met him today. You know, walking around town.'

'Is he here because of you?'

My heart pounded in my chest. I looked around to see where the nearest exit was. 'Me?'

'Yes. Do you think the FBI is here to investigate your lost wallet?' She laughed and asked me what I would like to drink.

'I … actually, Maeve, I have been waiting a long time and I don't feel very well. I really have to go.'

I knew I wouldn't be able to sustain small talk so I unceremoniously left. As I was walking away I heard her shout after me, 'Conor,' but I kept going. I needed to think.

Back in the B&B I really didn't feel well. This was a serious mess. I wondered how the hell I could get out of it. I went through all sorts of scenarios, including putting my finger in my pocket and pretending I had a gun. I finally settled on watching tomorrow until there was only one person in the station and then attacking with a banta stick. This worried me. We were in the real world and hitting people with sticks could kill them, but I had to get Essa and Brendan out of there before they were moved to a bigger city – or worse, extradited back to the USA. With a plan, of sorts, I placed my head on the pillow and managed sleep. I used to complain how my nights were dreamless in the Real World but it didn't bother me this night.

I heard the bedroom door as it closed. By then it was too late. I opened my eyes to the sight of an Irish policeman aiming a taser at my forehead.

'My daughter told me you were staying here.'

'Honest, sir,' I said, staring cross-eyed at the needles of the taser, 'I didn't even kiss her.'

He backed up and sat in a chair. I sat up in bed.

'Where did you come from?'

'Scranton, Pennsylvania.'

The policeman looked casually at the weapon in his hand. 'I had never actually seen one of these things fire before your friend got it in the chest the other day. He said it was very painful.'

'I really am from Scranton.'

'I didn't ask you where you were from, I asked where you came from. My chief and your FBI have already checked and Detective Fallon didn't enter Ireland on his passport. So how did you get here and where did you come from?'

I dropped back into the bed and spread my arms wide. 'Shoot,' I said.

'Come again?'

'Shoot me. If I tell you the truth you won't believe me. In fact, if I tell my story around here you'll probably think I was making fun of you. So shoot me and get it over with.'

'Before I shoot you, Mr O'Neil … You are Conor O'Neil, yes?'

'Yeah,' I said. Denying it at this point would have been stupid.

'I may believe more than you think. Have you noticed what language we are speaking?'

I hadn't, not really. Because my father is a tyrannical linguist, it's normal for me to just drop into the language that is being spoken to me. Connemara is a gaeltacht, which means that a lot of people around here speak modern Irish. I had impressed a few of the locals by simply chatting to them in their language. But as I thought back on the nice chat me and the armed policeman were having, I realised we weren't speaking Irish, we were talking in ancient Gaelic. 'Where did you learn this language?'

'My parents taught it to me. I also have read all of your father's published work on pronunciation. I've always wondered where he got his insight. But I am not here to answer your questions. You are here to answer mine. How did you get here and from where?'

'Could I pee first?'

Chapter Nineteen

Mícheál

'How about I shoot you with this, you'll definitely pee yourself then.'

'OK, OK, I came from Tir na Nog. Detective Fallon, Essa and I arrived two days ago by way of ley-lines that intersect at the Fairy Fingers.'

The cop lowered his gun. 'Mick O'Hara said the last thing he remembered was passing the Fairy Fingers.'

'Is that the old guy we stole the cart from?'

'It is.'

'Yeah, sorry about that. Is he OK?'

The policeman laughed. 'He's fine. I don't recommend apologising to him in person. Not unless you want your ears ripped off.'

'I really could use that pee now.'

'One more question and maybe I'll let you relieve yourself. Are you from the House of Luis?'

OK, speaking ancient Gaelic is one thing but using Ogham made it almost unnecessary for me to walk to the bathroom for that pee. 'What do you know of Luis?'

The cop looked me hard in the eyes; it felt like the look a poker opponent has when he is deciding to bluff or not. 'I want to know if I'm speaking to a Fili.'

'What do you know of the Fili?'

'Are you Fili?' he said raising his taser again.

'No.'

He stood and walked menacingly towards me. 'What is your house?'

'Duir,' I said with a pride that surprised me.

'Well, I wouldn't want it be said that the first Faerie I met wet himself.' The policeman pocketed his gun and gestured towards the door. I got up and threw on a pair of trousers. As I reached the door he said, 'If you try to escape I'll find you, and if that happens I'll have to hand you over to Special Agent Murano. We wouldn't want that, would we?'

There was a window in the bathroom and I could have escaped that way if I wanted to, but he was right. Where would I go? The only plan I had come up with was to either single-handedly attack a police station or wait at the Fairy Fingers until someone came from The Land to see what happened to us. Now that I was busted by this guy I couldn't do the former and I didn't have time to wait around for the latter. Besides, this cop intrigued me. Where did he learn all of this stuff? And maybe, just maybe, he was an ally. When he said 'we' was that just a manner of speech or did he mean 'we'? If he was an ally, I could really use one right now.

The cop was in the hallway when I returned. 'You have a name?'

'Mícheál.'

'So what now, Officer Mícheál?'

'Well now, I've persuaded Mrs McDunna to cook me breakfast. Would you care to join me?'

We talked quietly but it didn't matter. I'm sure there were very few people around that could decipher a language that no one had spoken for several millennia.

'Why haven't you turned me over to the FBI?' was my first question.

'Partly because Murano is an idiot.'

'He's a sadistic idiot,' I added.

'That does not surprise me. My daughter took an instant dislike to him. She is usually a very good judge of character.'

'She likes me.'

That drew a stern look. 'Don't push it, O'Neil.'

'Sorry.'

'Now, tell me what you are doing here.'

'If I do,' I said, 'and you don't like what you hear, are you going to arrest me?'

'That depends whether I like what I hear or not.'

'My father is the Lord of Duir.'

'Your father is Finn?'

I was shocked again at his knowledge of The Land. I needed to be careful what I said to this guy. 'No, that was my grandfather but he is dead. My father, the one that the FBI and everyone in Scranton thinks I killed, is the new King of Duir.'

Mícheál took all of this in his stride. He wasn't incredulous at all. In fact, he increasingly looked eager for more news. 'This still doesn't explain why you are here.'

'The Land is at war. I came here to get something that will help us in the upcoming battle.'

'What?'

'Before I answer, can I ask you a question?'

'I suppose you deserve some questions answered.' He nodded yes.

'Why did you call your daughter Maeve?'

'When she was born she cried all the time for the first month of her life, it was maddening. There was nothing we could do to appease her. Every hour of the day when she wasn't eating or sleeping she was shrieking. My wife said if she was going to be this much trouble we might as well name her after the biggest trouble-maker of all.'

I thought back to the conversation I had had with Nora and said, 'You're a Druid, aren't you?'

Mícheál snickered at that. 'Druids are misguided hippies who go barefoot and wear woolly robes.'

'But you're not that kind of Druid, are you?'

His false smile vanished. 'No.'

'You know where your ancestors came from and you know why they had to leave.'

'I have been told that we were banished because we followed a sorceress that had the same name as my daughter.'

Here was the moment of truth – this was the moment where I had to decide whose side he was on. It wasn't a hard decision; without his help I was sunk. 'Queen Maeve is back and if you don't help us she will destroy every tree in Tir na Nog to fuel her lust for power.'

The garda sat back in his chair and placed his hand to his cheek like he had been slapped. Finally he said, 'Many of us thought this day would come and we have debated what to do.'

'There are more of you?'

'Yes.'

'What I need to know, Mícheál, is what will *you* do?'

It didn't take long for him to decide. He leaned in and said, 'What do you need?'

I told him about the marble. He suggested I stay out of sight all day in case Murano were to accidentally spot me.

'I've been here too long,' Mícheál, said standing. 'Meet me after dark outside the tea shop. I'll take you to The Grove.'

Before he left I grabbed his arm and said, 'You couldn't lend me some money could ya, I'd kill for a toothbrush.'

Maeve was the one to show up after dark at the tea shop. She was riding a motorscooter.

'Da says you lost your marbles.'

'In a manner of speaking.'

'He also says you're never going to pay me back for that dinner.'

'That, I'm afraid, is true.'

'I sure can pick 'em. Hop on.'

We drove to an old barn on the outskirts of town. Inside were about fifty men and women. The Grove turned out to be not a place but the collective noun for a group of Druids. Imagine a room full of bearded men and wild-haired women in hooded robes, and then throw out that image. The Grove was made up of normal-looking butcher, banker, baker types. The only thing they had in common was a story handed down from mother to son and father to daughter for scores of generations. A story that said their ancestors were expelled from The Land of Immortals. There must now in the Real World have been over a hundred thousand descendants of the original Fili; this group were the last ones, the only ones to keep the faith. The only ones to have never broken the chain.

My arrival silenced what seemed to have been a heated debate.

Maeve was the first to break the silence. 'Are you really a prince?'

'I'm afraid I am.'

Someone in the crowd said, 'A Prince of Oak?'

'Hazel and Oak, yes.'

A young man dressed in motorcycle leathers came to the fore, 'My name is Cullum. How do we know you are what you say?'

'It's a fair question, Cullum. I can offer no proof until after you help me. If at the Fairy Fingers I and my companions vanish in a puff of smoke, then you will know what I have told you is true. If nothing happens then you will know you have been made a fool of by an idiot. What have you got to lose?'

'If I help you break your friends out of jail, I have a lot to lose.'

I started to answer but the policeman held up a hand and stopped me.

'But I am willing to help because I believe he is what he claims to be. We have been waiting for an event like this for … for ever. Can we now pass it by for lack of faith?'

Cullum spoke again. 'Mícheál tells us you are at war again with Maeve.'

'This is true.'

'Some among us harbour a hope of someday returning to Tir na Nog. Maybe our best bet is to allow Maeve to win.'

'Maybe you're right. I don't know Queen Maeve, but I know her daughter Fand, who is my friend, and I know my uncle Cialtie. I know this war is not ours but has been thrust upon us by others. And I know that we are right.'

'Can you take us back with you?' Cullum asked.

'No, he cannot!' another voice shouted out. 'He is not The One!'

What followed was pandemonium as they all started arguing in a dialect that I couldn't quite grasp. 'Hey, hey,' I shouted, quieting them down. 'There is no use arguing. Essa is our sorceress, only she could answer that.'

'Time is short,' Mícheál said. 'Conor's companions are to be transported to Dublin tomorrow.'

That was the first time I had heard that news and it shocked me.

'I have already had the Mulhern boys, who work at the quarry, bring bags of marble offcuts to the Fairy Fingers. I won't go against the wishes of The Grove, but I for one think we should help Conor and his friends. When our ancestors came to this place they found a simple time. Still, they didn't subjugate, they were men and women of peace and teaching. I believe Conor when he says that he and his are not the instigators of this war. Maeve and her war was what got us into this mess – I feel it in my bones that backing Maeve again is not the way to get us out.'

I was asked to wait outside while they deliberated. Maeve said, 'I vote with Conor,' and came outside to keep me company.

'Could you do me a favour?' I asked.

'If I can.'

'Could you make sure Mrs McDunna gets paid, and those boys who got the marble from the quarry.'

Maeve placed her hands on her hips. 'You want me to pay all of your bills on the money I make serving cups of tea? Not forgetting that you owe me money too.'

'I don't want you to pay it with your salary – I was hoping you could pay it with this.' I pulled a bar of metal the size of a chocolate bar out of my backpack and handed it to her. She was so surprised by the weight, she almost dropped it.

'Is this gold?'

'Yup.'

'And what, you found this at the end of a rainbow?'

'Don't be silly – but I did get it from a Leprechaun.'

'What am I supposed to do with it?'

'Change it for money.'

'Where?'

'I don't know. If I had figured that out, I wouldn't have been hitting you up for meals this whole time.'

She shook her head no and handed it back to me.

'Take it, please,' I said. 'I really do live on a mountain of the stuff.'

A woman came out and said a decision had been made. Inside the Druids were standing almost at attention. Cullum and Mícheál stepped forward together.

'We have decided to help,' Cullum said.

The plan was a simple one. Mícheál was to start his shift at midnight. When the other cop left, I'd come in, we'd let Essa and Brendan out and then Essa would knock out Mícheál so he wouldn't get into trouble.

I waited outside until the other cop, the one that tasered Brendan the other day, left and then I just walked in the front door. It was easy – too easy. I was just inside the station and walking up to the counter when I heard the door open behind me and a familiar, if not pleasant, voice said, 'Conor O'Neil.'

I turned to see Special Agent Andrew Murano wearing one of those grins. You know like when a power-hungry fast-food manager catches a teen employee stealing a chicken nugget.

'Oh, crap.'

'An American I met over here told me a young Scrantonian stole his cap. I was almost back to my room when I saw a cap-wearing young man skulking around in the dark.'

'Well, aren't you quite the detective,' I said, more casually than I felt. This was not good.

'Officer,' Agent Andy said in his over-practised FBI voice, 'arrest that man, he's in cahoots with the other two.'

I turned and looked Mícheál in the eye. For a moment we communicated wordlessly and he seemed to be saying, 'Do it.' So I slugged him. Not hard but I made contact. I even threw in a grunt to make it sound more vicious than it was. The cop went down behind the counter with a loud moan. I picked up a stapler and brandished it towards the G-man. Murano instinctively reached for his gun but he didn't have one. The Irish wouldn't let him bring one into the country. Mícheál moaned loudly, which made me glance at him. He was pointing to something under the counter. I quickly reached to where he was indicating as Murano was saying something predictable like, 'Give it up' or 'There's nowhere to run', but he stopped mid-sentence when I levelled the taser at his chest.

I could see he was trying to be cool but underneath he was soiling his underwear. 'You don't even know how to use that thing,' he said.

'I bet I do.'

'I'll catch you eventually, O'Neil. There is no place for you to go.'

I dropped my weapon for a second. 'Nowhere to go? You were there last time. Surely you remember me stepping through the portal to Faerieland?'

'I don't remember anything after you attacked me.'

'Oh come on, Agent Andy. I can understand you telling that to your superiors back at the Bureau. I've told people about Faeries and Leprechauns and they tend to look at you funny after you do – but this is me. Surely you remember your car getting trashed by the dragon?'

The FBI man looked very uncomfortable. 'I told you, I only remember you attacking me.'

'Aw Andy, it's one thing to lie to your boss but you're just lying to yourself. Now be a nice G-man and lie down on your stomach with your hands behind your back.'

'No.'

'Andy, I've been told this taser thing hurts. Let me just tie you up nicely and we'll be on our way.'

'You'll have to shoot me first.'

Anybody else I would have argued with, but as far as Agent Andy was concerned – I didn't have to be told twice. The electrodes hit his chest and he danced around like an astronaut walking on the sun. I know it's wrong to enjoy seeing a fellow human being suffer, but – you can't be right all of the time.

Chapter Twenty

Eth

Brendan and Essa were simultaneously happy to see me and furious at me for leaving them to stew in jail for so long. We locked the FBI man in a closet. Essa used the same sleeping spell on him that she used on the old cart driver. Mícheál made us tie him up and put him to sleep too, so as to allay suspicion.

'Thank you Conor, Prince of Hazel and Oak,' Mícheál said before Essa knocked him out.

'I should be the one thanking you, Mícheál, Son of Rowan.'

The title obviously pleased him. 'Eh, this is nothing; what you have done for me is far greater.'

'And what have I done for you?'

'You've shown me that I and my parents and their parents and their parents' parents weren't deluded superstitious fools.'

Essa took out her gold ball and began to incant.

'Can I ask one favour?'

'Sure, Mícheál, anything.'

'Will you return and let us know who won?'

'I will – if I survive – that's a promise.'

We stole the cop car. After assaulting a garda and an FBI agent, what's another felony among friends? A dozen of the Druids were waiting for us at the Fairy Fingers.

'We want to come with you,' Cullum said speaking for the group.

'I've spoken to Essa about that and she doesn't have the power to do it. I'll speak to my mother and Fand, the Queen of the Fili, and let you know if it is possible when I come back.'

Cullum obviously didn't like that answer but he accepted it. The crowd began to murmur and then step backwards as a humming amber circle appeared in the air in front of Essa.

'Are you really coming back?' Maeve asked.

'I promised your father I would.'

'All is ready,' Essa announced.

'Good,' Maeve said. 'I'll buy you dinner.'

'By then you'll be able to afford it.'

There were six bags of broken marble. We took two bags each. Before I went through Maeve kissed me hard on the lips and then we walked into the portal.

We arrived back in the Hall of Spells. Essa walked up to me and dropped one of the bags full of rocks directly on my foot. 'Who was she?'

While hopping on one foot, I tried to mumble out a reply but she stormed off saying, 'I'm too old for this.' Then she shouted, 'Where is the dragon?'

A guard strode up to me and bowed. Now, as I have said many times, I don't like the bowing and Your Highnessing but right then I welcomed it.

'Oh boy,' I said to him, 'I could just kill a cup of tea.'

'Your father has instructed me to bring you to the Oak Room as soon as you arrive.'

'Tell you what, get me a cup of tea first and you will have the gratitude of the Prince of Oak.'

'Your father ordered me to bring you – right away.'

I guess the gratitude of a king out-trumps a prince.

Dad opened his arms to greet me. I ducked underneath and dove for the bowl of fruit on the table.

'Hungry?'

I swallowed down a mouthful of apple before I spoke. 'Being broke in the Real World is a drag.'

'Oh yes, son – that it is. Why do you think I taught languages to students who didn't care? In the Real World, if you don't work you don't eat. Are you OK? Did you get the marble?'

My answers were unintelligible with my mouth full. Dad, instead of trying to fight me, walked to the door and ordered me a meal.

'Now could we talk a bit before dinner arrives?'

I slowed down on the fruit and said, 'Yeah, sorry. I'm fine and yes we have six big bags of broken marble.'

'Good. The first thing we have to do is make sure it works. You'll need to find a volunteer willing to insta-age who won't turn to dust.'

'Forget Essa, people in the Real World thought she was my grandmother.'

'I imagine she didn't like that.'

'It doesn't take much imagination.'

'I'm putting you in charge of charting and laying the marble,' Dad said.

'Charting?'

'Of course.' Dad walked over to a table that had a map of the castle and its grounds. There were grids on all of the approaching slopes. 'Record and number every piece of marble and log its placement.'

'Why? Why don't we just sprinkle the stuff around? It'll take ten minutes.'

'Conor, these aren't just rocks, they're land mines. When this war is over we have to find every one and lock them away. In three hundred years, when you are Lord of Duir, you don't want to step on one of these things while you're walking the dog.'

'When I'm Lord of Duir I'm gonna get somebody else to walk my dog.'

Dad gave me his 'this is serious time, not joke time' look.

'OK, OK, I see your point. I'll start in the morning, unless it is morning. What time is it anyway?'

My dinner arrived and Dad sat with me while I filled him in on my adventures in Ireland.

'It's a lovely place, isn't it?' he said.

'Yeah, I wish I could have relaxed more,' I said. 'As usual I was too busy trying to stay out of jail. You know what else? I missed trees.'

'The older guys in The Land talk about going to Ireland in their youth and it being nothing but trees.'

'What happened to them all?'

'Modern man and their houses and their war ships. What is one tree when you have so many? When everyone thinks like that – well, then in time the land becomes as bald as an old admiral's head.' Dad thought for a while. Finally he said, 'It is the fate of Tir na Nog if Maeve is allowed to succeed.'

I finished my meal and could hardly keep my eyes open.

'Three more things, son.'

I did my best impression of a bored adolescent.

'There's a council meeting an hour after dawn tomorrow – be there.'

'OK,' I said with a moan.

'Secondly, you must take your Choosing.'

'Fine.'

'Seriously, there is a war coming. If something happens to me …'

'I said fine. Dad, I hate it when you talk like this.'

'I don't care what you hate. I'm a king and you are a prince. If I die without you holding a Duir Rune then Cialtie has a "legitimate" claim to the Oak Throne.'

'OK, after I get a couple of hours' sleep, I'll go to your crack-of-dawn meeting, then I'll mine the castle – and *then* I'll take my Choosing.'

'It's not that easy – you must prepare.'

'All right, all right,' I said stumbling to my feet. 'I'll do anything you want. Just let me go to bed.'

Dad smiled and kissed me on the forehead. 'Goodnight, my son.'

As I got to the door I made the mistake of saying, 'You said "three things"?'

'Yeah.' Dad sighed. 'You gotta tell your mermaid girlfriend that she can't just barge into my office any time she wants.'

'Firstly, she's not my girlfriend.'

Dad gave me a 'you're kidding me right?' look.

'OK, well she's … OK, I don't know what she is. But what do you mean "barge" into your office?'

'Every day, sometimes twice a day, she barges in and asks if there is any news about you. It's exasperating.'

I started laughing. 'Didn't you point out that you are, like – the king?'

'I did – several times. She doesn't take a hint. Even when the hint is "Don't come in here again." She says, "Even a king must be worried about his son."'

'Don't you have guards?'

'Yes! She gets past them too. She's amazing and annoying. Maybe I should stick her on my brother. She'd probably drive him so crazy he'd hang himself. Please tell her to stop.'

'I'll try.'

'There is no try, only do or not do,' Dad said joining his laughter with mine. 'Do … please.'

I was so tired I don't even remember walking back to my room. I think I actually started dreaming as I walked. When I first came to The Land, my dreams were so clear. I had never dreamt in the Real World, so when I awoke I actually had premonitions of what was to come but now as I got used to dreaming my dreams were getting like everyone else's. Just the crazy jumbled up fast-forward video of recent events. I dreamt of Ireland and The Grove of Druid. I dreamt of stealing hats from rich Americans, of dining with Maeve and tasering FBI men, but my favourite image was the one right before I woke up. Graysea talking so much that Cialtie was holding his head and screaming.

Graysea was waiting outside my door when I got up. She did the usual smother-with-kisses greeting and then came with me to breakfast. I filled her in on all of my exploits in the Real World. I left out any mention of Maeve; I still didn't have enough strength for that.

I excused myself but Graysea continued to follow me.

'I'm going to a high council meeting, Graysea, I don't think you can come.'

'Don't be silly. Your father loves me.'

'Well … be that as it may. This is a war council and I don't think you should be there.'

'If this is about a war then I'm more needed than ever.'

I reminded myself to apologise for laughing at Dad. This mermaid was not for turning.

I was late as usual. Dahy was talking about wall fortifications. I had obviously missed something as everybody gave me that look again. Everyone was there. Mom, Dad, Dahy, Nieve, Brendan, Gerard, Araf, Tuan, Fand, and even Lorcan the Leprechaun had been dragged out of his mine and made to don a general's cap again.

Essa was back to her beautiful young-looking self. I mouthed, 'You look great', but she only dagger-stared at Graysea. Dad took one look at Graysea and then at me. I shrugged, which said, *I couldn't stop her*. He nodded, which said, *I told you so*.

The big shock was the thin guy sitting next to Dad. His hair and face looked newly cut and shaved and he wore clothes a bit too big for him. He caught me looking at him and wiggled a few fingers at me for a wave.

'Hermy?' I said. 'I mean Eth?'

Dahy, who hates being interrupted, said, 'If you had been here at the beginning of this meeting, Prince Conor, then you would have been party to introductions.'

Dad came to my rescue. 'I had the prince up late last night; his tardiness is partly my fault. Yes, Conor, while you were away Tuan graciously offered me a lift to Thunder Bay. I reunited with my old friend Eth and he agreed to return with me.'

Eth looked as though he was going to speak. We waited and when he didn't Dahy continued with his assessment of arrow resupply on the parapets. Dahy was mid-sentence when Eth finally spoke. 'This is an exciting time for me.'

Eth sounded anything but excited. He spoke without emotion – or much volume. I'm pretty sure most people in the room didn't even hear what he said.

'It is good to be among people again. Overwhelming … but good … I think.'

Everyone leaned in and strained to hear what the hermit had to say.

'For the first time since the Race of the Twins of Macha, I have no idea what is in store for all of us.'

We all waited, not knowing if this was just another pregnant pause or if he was done.

Finally I asked, 'Your mother said nothing about this upcoming war?'

'There are only two prophecies left.'

We all waited. I was just about to say, 'And they are?' when Fand piped up.

'Eth is correct. I have studied the book of Ona's prophecies that Macha stole when she kidnapped Ruby. Every event has come to pass except two. One we know. It reads: "The elder son will die at the hand of the Lord of Duir." Cialtie has told Conor that this is the reason he wants the Oak Throne. If he is the king then there will be no king to kill him.'

Everyone looked to Dad, who betrayed no emotion.

'The other foresight seems to be about the upcoming war. It says: "Trees are the salvation of the Faeries." Fand looked to Eth. 'Are they the two prophecies of which you speak?'

'Essentially, yes.'

'Do you know what the latter means? Which trees and how can they help us?'

Eth opened his mouth but it took ages for anything to come out. 'As I am sure you are aware, my mother's pronouncements are all too often only transparent after the event. I do not know what that means. But when these two events come to pass then the era of my mother's visions will be at an end. Then maybe all of our lives will be our own again.'

Dad placed his hand on his old friend's shoulder. Eth looked close to tears. Cialtie's life wasn't the only one that had been ruined by Ona. I wonder if in her visions she saw what a curse her gift was to be for her son.

Dahy went back to droning on about armoury supplies. I was just wondering how I could position my head so as to nod off without anybody noticing when Graysea interrupted: 'There is going to be a war?'

Everyone silently moaned but only Essa had the courage to say what we all thought, 'That is what we have been speaking about for the last hour.' She uncharacteristically didn't add, 'You stupid trout.'

We all waited for Graysea to slink down in her seat, but the Mertain girl was not the slinking kind. 'If we are going to be at war, then why are we talking about weapons when the first thing we should be doing is preparing the infirmary. This castle is woefully unprepared for a rash of casualties. Many more Fili- and Imp-healers must be recruited now, and as for supplies ... I don't even know where to begin.'

Dad looked at Mom and then to Fand, they both nodded. I smiled at Dad.

'Thank you, Graysea,' Dad said, 'for pointing out our inadequacies. Would you care to assume supervision of the infirmary?'

'Yes, my lord. I will draw up an inventory and report to you as soon as it's done.'

'I'm sure there is someone else you can report to.'

'No,' she chirped, 'I like reporting to you.'

Dahy stood to resume his droning on but Dad mercifully stopped him. 'Master Dahy, I'm sure we can do the rest without everyone here. You all have a thousand things to do. Dismissed.'

Outside the room I was about to tell Graysea that I had to get to work when she said, 'I'd love to chat, Conor, but I'm too busy to just hang about.'

Looks like Dad found the answer to the Graysea problem. Just keep her busy.

I called Dahy's platoon together and asked all the soldiers younger than twenty-five to help me. We took over the Hall of

Spells and laid out all of the pieces of marble. One soldier, who had been overeager to help, had lied about his age. He touched a piece of marble and instantly became a wrinkled old man. It was a stupid thing for him to do but at least no one got hurt and it saved me from having to find a volunteer to see if the marble worked. I sent him to Graysea's infirmary where I had heard she already had a supply of dragon blood on ice. I'm sure Tuan appreciated not being stuck with a needle every time somebody needed a face lift.

I got a bunch of paper from Nieve. Paper, being made from trees, is a rare commodity in The Land. We laid out all of the pieces of marble on the paper and then drew outlines of them with charcoal. Then we numbered the pieces and their outlines. When this was over I wanted every one of those rocks back. I got Ruby to help. She was great at outlining – she said it was like being back in school. I met Dad later that evening and showed him what I had done. He said I should write down instructions on the last piece of paper.

When I asked why, he said, 'In case we're not around later to tell anybody what this is.' That was sobering.

Chapter Twenty-One

Master Eirnin

There wasn't enough marble to lay land mines around the perimeter of the entire castle so we decided to lay most of the marble in the North Glen. This was the same place that Maeve had assembled her army during the last Fili war. It was there she cast the Shadowmagic spell that went wrong and vanquished her and her army. Mom and her sorceress pals had a feeling Maeve would try to repeat the same spell – this time getting it right. Dad didn't want to give her a chance to do it from the same place.

What was left of the marble we decided to use to mine both sides of the road up to the main gate and the stable entrance. They were the weakest parts of the outer wall. This would force an aggressor to attack the main gate almost in single file. As far as the south and west battlements – well, they were up to us.

The next morning Dad called a general assembly in the court-yard to warn everyone to stay out of the glen and not stray from the main road up to the castle. My team and I spent the entire day pushing marble pieces into the ground and lightly covering them with grass cuttings. It would have only taken a couple of hours but we had to carefully log where every piece was placed for later mine removal. Finally, Dahy posted soldiers to warn anyone that this was a bad place to take a stroll with your grandmother.

I wasn't the only busy one around. Daily groups of Imps, Faeries and Pookas arrived at the castle to swell the ranks of the army, help build fortifications, smith swords and axes, make arrows and bows, cook food in makeshift kitchens, and prepare the infirmary. Essa and Dahy were drilling the soldiers and when they weren't, they were neck deep in the logistics of preparing for a siege. Nieve, Mom and Fand were like the three witches in *Macbeth*; they spent most of their time working on magical defences in their Shadowmagic laboratory, a lab that really did have a bubbling cauldron in the corner.

Everybody was pulling double duty. Lorcan was preparing the new recruits by night and spending the days inspecting the outer walls. He was worried that the mortar in the east wall, the one that had been rebuilt after the Battle of the Twins of Macha, hadn't had long enough to set. The three witches made up some sort of Shadowmagic goo that Lorcan's workmen and women were using to repoint the stonework.

Brendan took archery practice. Without any formal announcement Detective Fallon took Spideog's place and became the Duir Master-at-Arms. When he wasn't eating, sleeping or quality-timing with Ruby, he was in the armoury.

Araf tutored the soldiers in hand-to-hand combat. We all hoped it wouldn't come to that. At night he skirted around the castle and uprooted all the flowers that he had planted and repotted them safe in a greenhouse inside the east wall.

Graysea was really in her element. I don't think anyone had ever thought her smart enough to put her in a position of authority – what a mistake that was. She shouldered her new responsibility with the tenacity of a shark. She enlisted healers, knocked down walls and had a team of weavers working day and night making bandages. She turned the little room of healing into a full-blown hospital that included a salt-water swimming pool in the corner. Any time I stopped by to have a quick word she always told me she was too busy to talk. She looked awfully flustered but happy.

Pooka hawks came back with twice daily reports of Brownie and Banshee armies mustering for a march. No one other than me had seen Maeve and her Fili army. At one meeting Lorcan asked if I was sure I saw her but Mom had only to show her blood-blackened rune and all doubts were put to rest.

Dad wanted me to start preparing for The Choosing but since I was the only person who could walk among the yew without being judged or forced to eat poison berries, I was drafted to enter the Yewlands to ask the oldest of the trees if they knew what Ona meant when she said, 'Trees are the salvation of the Faeries.' Nora volunteered herself to join me.

'You wanna get judged again?' I joked.

'Oh, I have no intention of chatting with a yew ever again,' Nora said. 'It's just I have been cooped up in this castle worrying about my granddaughter ... I've got this young body – I need to ride. I need to stretch my legs.'

Since we didn't need to get to the yews at any specific time we decided that we would try to get there in a day. We left before dawn. (That was my idea, would you believe?) I don't know if it was Nora's new body or that she was unburdened from the worry of her granddaughter's safety, but Nora was lightning in the saddle. I remembered thinking last time that she was a pretty good equestrian – this trip she was on fire. Her horse Blackberry seemed to obey her every whim and kept Acorn galloping a lot faster and longer than he or I liked. The sun was still pretty high in the sky when we got to the River Lugar boathouse.

I had left the royal barge in the Yewlands. I thought we were going to have to row but then found a small boat with a gold rudder. This time I had bothered to learn the incantation and we sailed towards the Yewlands oar-free.

Nora took a seat in the back of the skiff and laid her head back, closed her eyes and held her face to the sun.

'Is this the tonic you were looking for?'

She didn't open her eyes but smiled as a breeze took her hair. 'It's nice to be out of that castle.'

'Aw come on, it's a nice castle.'

'That it is, Prince Conor. No offence to your little house, it's me that needed out. I now see why you young people are moving all the time. Your bodies (and now mine) just don't know how to sit still.'

'So you're not a fan of your new young frame?'

Nora laughed – a good laugh, not like the stilted things she uttered when her granddaughter was in peril. 'Oh, I wouldn't say that, Conor. I wouldn't say that.'

We travelled in silence. As Nora sunned herself, I worked on my new yew staff. I carefully carved a notch all around the diameter about three quarters of the way up and then around that tied a leather loop. My thinking was that if I ever needed to lighten the staff so much as to lift me in the air, I could secure my grip with the strap. I had visions of me being thirty feet in the air and then accidentally letting go of the stick. I knew that would hurt without ever needing to experience it. I was tempted to give my new adaptation a try but decided I'd probably just end up in the water.

I pulled over at Gerard's hut just before the entrance to the Yewlands and dropped Nora off.

'Sure you don't want to have a meal before you go in there?' Nora asked.

'No, but brew up some willow tea for when I get back. Yews give me a headache. I shouldn't be long.'

And I wasn't. I found the royal barge where I had left it and beached my little boat alongside. I got out and tried to speak to some trees – tried being the operative word. Just because I had the freedom of the Yewlands didn't mean that they would speak with

194

me. I went from tree to tree and got nothing until I took out a knife and threatened one tree that I was going to carve 'Conor & Essa & Graysea' inside a heart on its bark. That did the trick and I felt that familiar bone-crunching feeling as the tree made me drop the knife and fall to my knees.

'Hey, hey,' I said, 'I was just trying to get your attention.'

The male and female twin voice of the yew echoed in my head. '*Freedom of the Yewlands does not allow you to disturb our solemnity.*'

'I didn't mean to disturb you. I just have a question.'

'*We are not hazels, we are not here to bestow knowledge.*'

The tree made me stand and then spun me around. Just before it pushed me away I said, 'I know who has been killing yews.'

The tree acted faster than I expected. '*Who?*' it said with a voice so loud in my head I was glad I asked Nora to have that willow tea ready.

'Maeve.'

'*Maeve is gone.*'

'She's back. She's been around in a Shadowghost form but now she and her army are back. I suspect she was the one that has been killing trees. In her ghost form she would have been hard to detect.'

'*Where is she?*'

'I don't know but I do know that she will soon attack Duir. My mother thinks that with yew sap she might succeed where before she failed.'

'*Do you have more news?*'

'No, but I have a question.'

'*Ask.*'

So I told the tree about Ona's prediction about trees being the salvation of the Faeries. I waited as I felt the trees confer in the entire forest. The reply didn't take long.

'*The yews have no knowledge of what you ask.*'

'Who would?' I asked, but I had been released, and the yew once again ignored me. I wanted to ask again but then I laughed as I imagined the yew saying '*What part of "no knowledge" do you not understand?*'

I tied my little boat to the barge and then incanted the Ogham Dad had taught me and sailed back upstream to Nora.

Nora not only had tea ready but also soup and bread. We didn't have time for me to sit and eat so I carried the food into the barge and let Nora navigate for a while.

'What did the yew say?' she asked when we had gotten under way.

'They don't know.'

'Are you OK?'

'Yes, I'm just sore.'

'I have more tea in a flask if you're interested.' Nora poured me some more willow tea. 'I remember how I felt after tangling with a yew,' the young grandmother said.

'Oh yeah, I forgot. You got judged by a yew without any preparation and you came away worthy.'

'You sound surprised?'

'No offence Nora, but that's not usually how it works. Did the yews give you anything?'

Nora sat like Mona Lisa for a while and said, 'That would be telling.'

Nora rode back to Castle Duir like the wind and I followed like a leaf caught in her vortex. We got home just after midnight. I was shattered but Nora was exhilarated. She offered to stable and brush Acorn for me and I didn't say no.

The next day Dad ruined a good lie-in.

'I always thought being a prince meant that I could sleep late and do anything I wanted.'

'That's what "commoners" think when they dream about being royal,' Dad said. 'You know what royal people dream about?'

I didn't answer – it was too early for riddles.

'They dream about being commoners.'

We ate in silence. Well, Dad was silent; I produced a continuous low growl hoping that he would leave and let me go back to bed. He just sat there smiling like he had a surprise for me. Finally I cracked.

'What?'

'I don't think I'd have a breakfast that big if I were you.'

There are few things that can make me stop chewing but a sentence like that from my father is one of them. 'Why?'

'It's just that I've heard rumours that the first day at The Hive can be pretty rough.'

'The Hive?'

'Yes, you'll be spending the next couple of days with Master Eirnin.'

I tried to remember where I had seen the name Eirnin and then picked up the jar of honey on the table and read the name. 'You're sending me to the royal beekeeper?'

'You know how the US Secret Service not only guards the president but they also are in charge of catching money forgers?'

'No.'

'Well,' Dad went on, 'they are. Many people around here have more than one job.'

'Oh, can I be Court Jester?'

'You don't need any help from me to be a fool, son. As I was saying … Master Eirnin is not only the royal beekeeper, he is also in charge of preparing candidates for The Choosing.'

'Dad, there's a war coming. There are a million things that I should be doing.'

'Like sleeping late?'

'That is such a Dad thing to say.'

'I agree there are a million things you should be doing but the first thing on that list is The Choosing. You know why it's important. This is not open for discussion.'

'How old do I have to be before I am no longer bossed around by my dad?'

'You are old enough now that you no longer have to do what a father tells you to do.'

He stood and walked towards the door but before he went through he stopped and said, 'But you will never be too old to do the bidding of your King. Be in the stable in ten ... and I wouldn't wear your good Nikes if I were you.'

I didn't like the smile on his face. It was the same look that he had when he invited Essa and Graysea on the Mount Cas trip. I didn't have to worry about not wearing my Nikes, Jesse had mine. When this all calmed down and I went back to Ireland like I promised, I was going to get to some big city and swap a bar of gold for a couple of pairs of cool shoes.

Master Eirnin was waiting for me in the stables. He was an Imp, unsurprisingly. He didn't look very tall but he was on horseback so it was hard to tell. His cloth robe was stained and bulged in the middle. He looked jolly. 'You're late,' he said.

'Funny, that's what everyone says.'

This produced no response other than, 'Come.' He turned and walked his mount out of the stables. I hurried to find Acorn.

Master Eirnin came back and asked, 'What are you doing?'

'I'm saddling my horse.'

'Prince Conor, if I had wanted you to saddle your horse I would have said, "Saddle your horse." Now come.'

'On foot?'

He turned again. This time he took a coil of rope from his saddlebag. 'Would you prefer I tie this around your neck like a dog?'

'No sir.'

'Come.'

So I jogged next to the Master Beekeeper. He was not jolly.

'What did you have for breakfast?'

'What?'

The Imp pulled his reins to the right and reared his horse. It stopped directly in my way and I hit the horse and almost fell over. 'When I say come, I want you to come. When I ask you a question I expect an answer. Not another question. This is my final warning.'

He was wearing a floppy cap and I wondered if there was literally a bee in the beekeeper's bonnet. He started again and said, 'Come.'

I came.

'What did you have for breakfast?'

'I had tea, apple slices, eh … If I had known there was going to be a test …'

Snap; the crack of a whip made it to my ears a nanosecond before my mind registered the searing pain on my back.

'Hey!'

'Focus, prince. I asked about your breakfast. Not about what you think.'

'That doesn't mean …' I looked up and he was raising the whip again so I said quickly, 'OK, apple, tea, two eggs, oatmeal and bread.'

'And what did you have the previous morning?'

'Well, I really didn't have a normal breakfast …'

Crack. This time I lost my footing and went down. The whip cracked on my upper arm and it stung like I had been stabbed. 'What the hell are you doing?'

Master Eirnin walked his horse back and loomed over me. 'You only have two days to prepare, young prince. There is very little time to teach you.'

'Teach me what? That you're a sadist? I got that.'

'I am attempting to teach you to focus, Conor. If you fail to concentrate with me you will experience pain. If you lose your concentration in the Chamber of Runes – you will die.'

Chapter Twenty-Two
The Hive

I jogged behind Master Eirnin as he asked me all manner of mundane questions. Many of which I had no answer for, like 'Name the lineage of your mother's line back five generations.' I knew Mom and her father Liam but after that, nothing. That didn't stop the lash. Eirnin was a whip now, ask questions later kind of Imp.

Eirnin lived in a large conical brick house called The Hive. It did indeed contain a hive. Bumblebees half the size of my fist flew in and out of the many vents in the walls. These bees knew who was boss. They swerved for Master Eirnin but they acted like I wasn't even there. During my next two days at The Hive, I spent most of my time ducking insects big enough to carry off puppies. It was a shock when one bounced off your face as you turned but it was worse if one stung you. Luckily it only happened twice: once when I stepped on one in my bare feet and another time when I accidentally caught one under my armpit. Both times I felt like Julius Caesar just after he turned his back on Brutus. The one under my armpit actually hurt the most but the one on my foot made walking a chore. All this, though, was ahead of me as the beekeeper led me into the training room.

The air was stiflingly thick with the overpowering smell of honey. In the middle of the room was what looked like a long narrow Olympic-sized swimming pool. Instead of water, the pool seemed to be filled with a white mould. Eirnin picked up a rake and skimmed the mould from the top of the pool. Then with his bare hand he scraped the mould off the rake into a bucket and walked outside. By now I knew that if I didn't follow him, it hurt. Outside he dumped the mould on top of a compost heap.

'Oh, I get it,' I said back inside as he handed me the rake. 'This is one of those kung fu master things where after I do your cleaning, I learn something. This is like a metaphor – as I clean your mould, you mould my mind?'

Eirnin was immune to my charms. As he walked away he shook his head and said, 'If you were not Oisin's son I would be tempted to release you now and let you die.'

Underneath the mould was honey. I spent the entire morning skimming the mould off and piling it in the garden. It wasn't as disgusting as it sounds. The mould was pretty innocuous and the fresh air was a relief after spending time in the thick air of the training room. By lunch I was staring at a brick trench filled with golden honey. Eirnin returned and inspected my work. He inspected every edge to make sure no mould remained and found none.

'Come,' he said.

I was tempted to say, 'Aren't you going to give me a gold star?' but then remembered the lash and stepped lively into his wake.

On the other side of The Hive the master had set out a table with bread, dried fruit and meats and, of course, honey.

'Was yesterday's lunch as lavish as this?' he asked.

'Yesterday, I had a salad with …'

'Relax, young prince,' he said with a wave of his hand, 'that was not a test. I am only making conversation. Rest your mind for a bit, Conor; you will need all of your mental strength for this afternoon.'

Eirnin piled some special dark honey from a jar onto a slab of bread. After breathing honey fumes all morning I really was in no mood to eat the stuff but the Marquis de Beekeeper was a hard man to deny. He said it would make my brain work better and, since around here slow brains mean skin welts, I ate.

After lunch I followed the master back into the training room.

'Remove your clothing.'

'You speak English?'

Eirnin removed his whip from his belt and I started, reluctantly and nervously, to take off my clothes. When I got down to my underwear he said, 'That will be enough. I will answer your last query, Conor, for I know this must be confusing but after that you do my bidding or feel the lash.'

'Yes sir.'

'In order to implement your training I have met many times with your father about your upbringing. I have also endured your Aunt Nieve's hot gold ear and tongue treatment so I may speak to you in the language of your schooling.'

'Gosh. Well, that explains why you're so cranky.' I instantly regretted saying that and expected my all too exposed flesh to get a whuppin' but he ignored me – with maybe just the tiniest of smiles. There is no long-term defence against my charm.

Eirnin pointed to the pool of honey. 'Get in.'

'In there?'

This time the whip cracked and I jumped in before it hit me. Jumping into a pool of honey is not like jumping into a pool of water. I hit the surface expecting to go through but it was almost as bone-jarring as if I had hit concrete. The entire surface wobbled as I bounced back up. Then I started to sink but at an angle. That meant my feet wouldn't be under me when my head went below water … I mean honey. I tried to move my legs but – I was in honey. I looked to Master Eirnin – he was nowhere to be seen. My panic increased proportionally with every inch I sank. I was seconds away from screaming when I thought *maybe this too is a test. Surely he won't let me drown?* I mastered my panic as the honey reached level with my chin. My face fully submerged and I was thinking *maybe I could panic now* when I felt rope hit my hands. Eirnin hoisted me out and I hung there until my feet were directly below me.

'Why did you not call for me?'

'I thought it was a test.'

'Next time you are about to drown, feel free to call out.'

He slowly lowered me so I could stand, shoulder-deep in the honey.

'Now what?'

'Now you walk.'

And I did. For the rest of the day I did walking laps in a swimming pool filled with honey. What was it like? It was like walking in a pool of honey. It was hot, sticky and unbelievably slow going. As it got close to nightfall, the beekeeper had me walking sideways and then backwards. After rinsing in a nearby ice-cold spring, I was sent off to bed. I went back to my room and asked Aein to bring me some supper but I didn't eat it. My head hit the pillow and I went out like a used match.

The last place I wanted to go the next day was back to The Hive but a prince has to do what a king tells him to. Eirnin didn't even speak to me when I arrived. He just pointed to the pool and I slowly dropped into the honey so as to not lose my footing. This day began with mundane questions. He asked me to name all of my school teachers. Hesitation was met with the crack of a lash. Most of these didn't actually make contact but the memory of the pain from the ones that did made the sound as effective as the real thing. Let's just say, I hope nobody actually eats that honey. Dad showed up late in the morning wearing a smirk and drilled me on German, French and Greek verb conjugation. It was just like when I was a kid and I could see how much he was enjoying my torment.

Essa's dad showed up with lunch.

'I imagine,' Gerard said, 'you would like something that did not have honey on it.'

'Amen to that, Mr Winemaker. What brings you to Duir?'

'Oh I don't know, Conor, maybe the impending war.'

'Oh yeah. You know, I had almost forgotten about that with all of this hiking in honey stuff.'

'Then you are doing it right. I have been through Master Eirnin's tutelage. I know it feels pointless at the moment but what you are learning is to blend mind and body into one. You will be thankful when you step into the First Muirbhrúcht.'

'That's what I thought I would be doing here. I thought Eirnin would be telling what it would be like to walk The Choosing but he hasn't said a thing. I saw Dad and Mom do it and it looked awfully difficult. So what's it like?'

Gerard leaned back in his chair and laughed. 'Conor, my Choosing was long, long ago. You want to know what it was like? I'll tell you. It is like … walking in honey.'

'Really?'

'No, not really, but that is as close as you are going to get without actually entering the Hall of Choosing. Everyone says the First Muirbhrúcht is the hardest and in a way it is. You must be prepared for the shock of it. Like walking in honey, it will be like hitting a brick wall at first. You must slide into it. But unlike the pool here you will simultaneously be buffeted from all sides. Keeping your balance will require perfect concentration but your concentration will be tested by memories. Not actual memories – they will come during the Second Muirbhrúcht – but emotional memories. It is very disconcerting to have emotions without the underpinning memories. Many find it too much to bear. Fortunately you can quit after the First Muirbhrúcht and live.'

'But not after that?'

'That is correct. Once you enter the second archway only success allows you to survive.'

'But the Second Muirbhrúcht is easier?'

'That is what others say but I found it harder. Just remember: whatever the Chamber throws at you, you must keep walking, you must keep your balance and you must hold on to your rune.'

'What about the Third Muirbhrúcht?'

'Ah well,' the big man said. 'The third one is different for everyone. It is not difficult. In fact, it is the opposite, it is quite a relief. You see, if you make it that far – you receive a gift.'

'A gift?'

'Yes. Some receive an insight into their lives. A blacksmith may realise how better to forge steel, a dancer will leave The Choosing knowing a new step. Others get a glimpse of their future.'

'What did you get?'

'Oh my, I've never told anyone that.'

'Sorry, I didn't mean to pry.'

'No. I think I'd like to tell you, Conor.'

And he did. I felt honoured. When he was through I asked, 'You didn't bring any beer with you, by any chance?'

'There is far too much work ahead of you for beer drinking.' He stood to leave and then opened his arms to administer his famous rib-crushing hug. I stood and accepted it. As he lifted me off the ground he said, 'I'll have a cold one waiting for you in your chamber tonight when this is done.'

'Thanks, Gerard.'

As he walked away he stopped and said, 'Essa is very mad at you.'

'What did she say?'

'Nothing. That's how I know. I would look out if I were you.'

The rest of the day was more of the same with Master Eirnin making me walk while quizzing me and trying to make my concentration slip. Focusing had always been a problem for me at school. Maybe they should fill swimming pools with honey and give the teachers whips. OK, that's a bad idea but at this time in my life – with that life being on the line – the technique worked. I really did think I was ready.

Eirnin didn't, but he had no choice but to graduate me. 'Your father has told me that the Pooka hawk scouts have spotted Banshee troops marching towards Duir. You are needed at the castle.'

I got out of the pool and rinsed off. When I was clean and dressed I reported one last time to the Master Beekeeper.

'I listened to what Gerard told you at lunch, young prince. I have little to add. Your task is to keep focused and your goal is to reach past the Third Muirbhrúcht with your rune still in your fist. That may sound simple but the Chamber makes even that simple task very difficult. I hope to see you again, Prince of Hazel and Oak.'

'Won't you be at my Choosing?'

'No, I have seen too many of my pupils fail. I can no longer watch Choosings.'

With that cheery statement ringing in my ears I limped back to the castle. My first stop was to see Graysea in the hope that she had enough time to unswell the bee stings on my foot and armpit. If I hadn't just walked in there myself, I would have sworn I was in a different place than Castle Duir. The Room of Healing was now a proper blinding white infirmary with fully stacked shelves of bandages, sheets and medicine bottles. Cots were lined up in rows like airplanes on an aircraft carrier. Graysea was taking an inventory of a pile of things on the far wall but dropped everything when she saw me limping.

'Are you injured?'

'No … well … yes. It's a bee sting.' I sat on a cot, took off my Brownie slipper and showed her my double-sized foot.

'That is a bee sting?'

'They were big bees. I also got stung under my arm.'

Graysea sat down behind me and pulled my shirt over my head. 'You smell like honey.' She was reaching around to feel where the sting was when, of course, Essa walked in. Graysea didn't see her and started her healing fish transformation. I was hit with the pain of the stings for a second and then experienced that wonderful relief that only mermaid healing can provide. I had to close my eyes. When I opened them – Essa was gone.

'Damn.'

'Does something else hurt?'

'Oh, no, Graysea, thank you, I feel much better now.'

She kissed me on the cheek. 'I have so much to do. I imagine you do too.'

'Yes. Sleep.'

She slapped me on the arm. 'You're so silly.'

This time I managed to eat my supper before passing out.

I awoke to find Dad standing over me with a steaming cup of tea. I sat up in bed and groaned. Every muscle in my body was sore.

'I'm going to go back to the Real World,' I said, 'and open a gym with a honey pool. It's a hell of an all-body work-out.'

'That's why I brought you willow tea. Normally I would have given you a couple of days to recover but we don't have that kind of time.'

'How far away is Cialtie's army?'

'They're not here yet but they are coming. It's nothing for you to worry about today. Today is the day of your Choosing.'

'Dad, I know you're gung ho about me doing this but really with Cialtie on the march and me feeling like five miles of bad road, can't my Choosing wait?'

'No. Cialtie on the march is the reason why we can't wait. If something happens to me, you have to be holding a Duir Rune or my brother has a "legitimate" claim to the Oak Throne.'

'That's not the way Ona's prediction goes ...'

Dad put up his hand to stop me. 'You of all people should know that Ona's predictions are a curse and certainly are nothing to act upon. I loved that old woman but I often wish she had never been born. Her damn predictions are almost as much to blame for my brother as he is. We fight Cialtie not because of anything Ona has said. We stop him because he must be stopped. Get dressed, Prince of Hazel and Oak.'

I walked down the long staircase by myself. When I arrived at the Chamber of Runes, I had to momentarily shield my eyes from the supernova-like glow coming from the thousands of Leprechaun candles that covered almost every surface. When my pupils had finally contracted to a suitable diameter, I saw that almost everybody was there.

Mom and Dad were flanked by Nieve, Fand, Dahy, Gerard. Brendan and Araf were standing holding up a ceremonial robe. I waved hi to everybody and then turned my back to let my mates help me don what I hoped was not going to be my funeral shroud.

'If you don't make it,' Brendan said in my ear, 'can I have your room?'

'Araf,' I said, 'shouldn't you be doing a Choosing too?'

'I thought I would see if you survive before I tried it,' the Imp replied.

These guys were my mates. Making jokes was exactly what I needed.

As I walked to Mom I stopped and quietly asked Gerard, 'Essa?'

He just shook his head.

Well, that cinched it. I had suspected that I had blown it with the princess and now that she hadn't shown up here, I was sure of it.

Mom placed a blank wooden rune in my hand and then tilted my head down with both of her hands and kissed me on the forehead. She didn't say anything, and that scared me too.

Dad lifted the rune in my right hand and placed a nugget of gold underneath it. He placed his hands on my shoulders. 'For once in your life – concentrate.'

I turned and faced the first archway. It looked perfectly clear just like any other hallway I had ever walked down. I turned, 'Are you sure this thing's plugged in?'

I got nothing – not even a snicker. So what else is new? I stepped into the First Muirbhrúcht.

Chapter Twenty-Three
The Choosing

There is an old expression in The Land: 'The First Muirbhrúcht is the hardest.' That's what people say in Tir na Nog when they start some mundane task like baking a cake or cleaning out a moat. It's like when Real Worlders say: 'Every journey begins with a first step.' Well, let me tell ya: the first Muirbhrúcht is not like baking a cake.

I had once seen Dad thoughtlessly run at a Muirbhrúcht and bounce back like a pinball off a bumper so I entered it slowly expecting the barrier to be a bit like jumping into Master Eirnin's honey pool. What I wasn't prepared for was the turbulence. I had seen people walk in the Chamber of Runes and you don't walk that slowly for nothing, but I expected the resistance to come from the front. In reality it came from all directions. Like the honey pool, the surrounding air – or whatever was in it – was hard to push against but forces pushed different parts of you in different directions – and they were fierce. I thought I was going to get my ears ripped off. Saying that, losing my ears wouldn't have been that bad a thing 'cause it sounded like my head was in a washing machine. That must be where they got the name from. *Muirbhrúcht* means tidal wave and it sounded like my head was under one.

I wasn't three steps in when I started laughing. At first I thought it was just the usual little nervous giggling bout I get when I'm in mortal danger or in an uncomfortable situation, like when Fergal and I thought we were going to be killed by Big Hair and his Banshee tribe – but when I tried to stop, I found that I couldn't and I didn't know why. No matter what horrible things I imagined: squashed puppies with their eyes bulging out, Essa snogging The Turlow, tofu burgers, I still couldn't stop laughing. The strange thing was, I wasn't laughing *at* anything. I just had an overwhelming need to laugh but nothing in my head said anything funny. I threw my head back and howled with laughter, for a nanosecond I stopped my forward momentum. Immediately the ear-ripping turbulence intensified by a factor of 100. Let me tell you, even though I was laughing there was nothing funny about that. I instinctively knew that the increased pressure was because I had stopped moving and pushed into the non-gooey ectoplasm that passed for air in there. I continued to move. The turbulence subsided and so did my giggles.

When the sorrow hit me I remembered what I had been told. The First Muirbhrúcht bombards the Chooser with emotions. Getting past these emotional attacks was not easy. In life when emotions hit it is almost always the result of a thought but here in the First Muirbhrúcht the emotions were pure feeling. No manner of cheery thought could dispel the soul-crushing sorrow. I am tempted to call it grief but it wasn't that. Grief is the cause of sorrow – this feeling had no cause. There was no poisonous thought I could divert or mask with levity. I simply wanted to die – to sit and stop everything because what was wrong with my life at that moment went beyond my mind. My entire being was simply agony and nothing anywhere, in any world, could fix it. Through all of this I kept my feet moving and my fingers wrapped around my rune. I don't know how. I'm sure I couldn't have withstood one second longer. Fortunately sorrow was replaced by rage and I welcomed it. Even though I could feel the veins in my temples popping and my jaw clamping down until I thought my face would snap – I welcomed the rage. I wanted to kill someone and that was a lot better than wanting to die. I toyed with putting a thought with the emotion and it wasn't hard to imagine my Uncle Cialtie. I thought of what he did to Fergal. How he killed his mother and how he lied to his own son and then shamed him before ultimately killing him. And then like a snowball tumbling down a hill gaining size as it went, I added Fergal's death to all of the other deaths he was responsible for: Frank, Spideog, everyone who died in the attack on the Hall of Knowledge, all who died in the Battle of the Twins of Macha, the genocide of the village of More, the destruction of the Hazellands. By the time my mind had conjured up all of those atrocities, I wasn't sure if the rage I felt came from The Choosing or from my own mind.

The last emotion was contentment. It was a little gift that the First Muirbhrúcht gave me right at the end. In some respects this was the most dangerous emotion of all. After all that went before, I felt like sitting down and just enjoying the feeling. I think I would have, but the habit of putting one foot in front of the other that had been whipped into me by Master Eirnin came in handy.

Then I popped out of the First Muirbhrúcht.

The silence was almost the best part. I wanted to turn around and shout 'I did it!', but I had been instructed not to turn except on the way out or if I wanted to give up. Apparently you can turn around after the First Muirbhrúcht and live – but Oisin didn't raise no quitter. I wanted to rest a while but I had been warned not to do that also. Apparently taking too long of a break saps your energy. I didn't have all that much zip to begin with, so I gritted my teeth and entered the Second Muirbhrúcht.

If the First Muirbhrúcht is the hardest then the second one is the prettiest. I was faintly aware of lights and colours sparkling in the air while in the First Muirbhrúcht – when I entered the second one, colour was all I saw. What, minutes before, had been crystal clear air was now alive with pulsating light. It was like the luminescent algae in the ocean that the Mertain call 'The Stream', except here it wasn't one colour, it was thousands.

The electric rainbow air made me hesitate but what made me stop in my tracks was the huge vision of my mother's face that loomed in front of me. Master Eirnin's training kicked in. I could almost feel the sting of his whip on my back and I automatically willed my feet to keep moving. Even though I was looking straight ahead, in the vision, I was looking *up* at my mother's face. This was the kind of paradox that usually happens in dreams but this was no dream. This was a memory, my memory. I not only saw the huge face looking down on me but I felt the loving arms that cradled the tiny me. I grew up with no memory of my mother but obviously they were in there. You might imagine that this would be emotionally overpowering but I reacted to this memory with the emotions of an infant. Babies are binary. They are either happy or sad, wet or dry, hungry or satiated. I was happy and it was such a simple happiness that I slowed. Immediately the pressure of the Muirbhrúcht forced the training back into my head and I continued forward.

The next memory was the other side of that coin – it was simple unhappiness. I was crying because she was crying. My mother was crying. I felt myself being taken from her arms. I tried to reach for her but I was so young my arms would not obey. When she was out of view I felt and tasted a salty tear hitting my face; when I looked up, Dad's face was as miserable as my mother's had been.

More childhood memories floated into view. Just like no one else can hear a tree talk, even though it's perfectly loud in your head, I'm sure no one else could see these visions but to me they played in the air like a Shadowcasting. These were memories that I had almost forgotten and they were captivating. The desire to just sit on the floor and watch, cross-legged, was overwhelming and if not for Master Eirnin I would have done just that and died.

I took back everything I ever said about the old beekeeper and his lash.

I remembered living in Ireland and then moving to England. I replayed a childhood event that always puzzled me. I saw myself maybe seven years old and coming home from school and telling Dad that a rider on a black horse had spoken to me. We were packed and in a hotel before midnight. Two days later we were on a boat to America.

I got to watch puberty and adolescence again which made me want to close my eyes and press fast-forward – and I found that I kind of could. I slowed things down when I came to Sally. Sally hadn't fared very well in my recent memories and it was nice to relive how wonderful we had been in the beginning. I had had girlfriends before her, but she was a real relationship. She taught me … no that's wrong … together we learned how to be close and how to trust. I was mad at her for her choices at the end but now I saw she didn't have the full picture – I never gave her a chance.

Nieve's spear flew at me again and I felt the tingling glow of my mother's protective force-field. And then I sped through the memories of my life since I discovered I was the Prince of Hazel and Oak: escaping from Cialtie, meeting my mother, meeting Fergal. I willed that scene to slow down and it did. My smile matched the ear-to-ear smile my cousin wore and I realised that the debilitating sorrow that I felt in the First Muirbhrúcht was the missing of Fergal. I re-saw that first sight I had of Essa with the light shining up on her face from that glowing ball. I swallowed hard as I walked, just as I had at her father's party.

I relived joining up with the Army of the Red Hand and how with Dad we stopped my uncle from destroying The Land. I remembered how proud I was of Dad and how I regained the feeling I had when I was a little kid – that he could do anything.

I got to travel back to the Hazellands with my mother again. How wonderful it was to get to actually know a mother that I had only ever fantasised about. That warm motherly love that I imagined and missed didn't even come close to the real thing.

Like an anchor against the madness, Araf was a solid presence all through the visions.

I had to laugh when I remembered how angry Brendan was when the cop was accidentally dragged to The Land. He came around fast. I don't know what I would have done if he hadn't been there to help me save my father.

I saw the bravery of Tuan, the treachery of The Turlow, the magnificence and terror of Red's transformation into a dragon. And then came Graysea. She really is the sweetest creature in any land. OK, she's a bit ditzy, but she is beautiful and talented and funny and would literally give anything to make me happy. But I realised that even though I am oh so fond of her, when I saw her she didn't make my heart skip like Essa. Maybe that was the gift of The Choosing. I knew now that I had to make Essa know that she is the only one for me.

After saving Dad with his dragon blood rebirth, all the most recent events sailed past. As I saw the scene of me entering the Chamber of Runes, I popped out. I took one deep breath and entered the Third Muirbhrúcht.

As Gerard warned me – this was a piece of cake. The resistance was still in the air but the pressure was gone. This was more like the honey pool than the previous two and I found myself sighing at the relief of it. A shower of sparks like from a grinding wheel issued from my closed fist but it didn't hurt and I hardly noticed it. I thought about what Gerard said had happened to him when he was here. Gerard had been hoping for some tip on how to make super wine but instead he received a vision of a young girl. He spent years looking for her but never found her until he had a child of his own. His gift from The Choosing was the promise of Essa.

I wouldn't mind a promise of Essa myself. I then had a panicky thought about seeing what our child would look like and then had another panic attack about receiving any vision of the future. Visions of the future were how The Land had gotten into this mess. Ona's predictions had ruined countless lives. I wasn't sure I wanted to know where the river of my life was to flow.

My gift was not a glimpse into my future. At least I think it wasn't. In front of me I saw the Druids I had met in Connemara, Ireland – the group calling themselves The Grove. They stood there waiting. The vision was as clear as it was completely unfathomable. I tried to ask them what they wanted but nothing would come out of my mouth. Then, at the last second, Ruby came up beside me and they all freaked.

The pressure of the air evaporated and I stumbled forward into the antechamber at the back of the Chamber of Runes. I had done it, I had walked my Choosing. In front of me was the oaken table – I opened my hand and let my new rune fall to the tabletop.

My rune didn't stay on the table for long. Before I even got a chance to look at it, an explosion shook the Chamber. I was thrown into the table, knocking it over as plaster and centuries of dust fell from the ceiling. I turned. This was supposed to be a proud moment, like a graduation. I had imagined my family and friends smiling and applauding – instead I saw them rushing out of the room. As she disappeared around the corner and up the staircase I saw that one of them was Essa – she had come. Another explosion rocked the room, the battle had begun.

I ran to join my comrades forgetting that Muirbhrúchts must be entered slowly and just like my father before me, I hit the backside of the barrier and bounced off it like it was a vertical trampoline. My body and head were thrown to the back wall and for a moment I saw stars. Then I pulled my wits about me, walked up to the archway, took a deep breath and began to slowly step in. I hesitated just in time to remember the rune. I picked it up, put it in my pocket and slid slowly past the barrier. Walking back through the Muirbhrúcht has all of the resistance without the mind games. It was still one of the most physically exhausting things I have ever done but at least my brains weren't being haunted by ghosts of Christmases past.

I dropped into a Fili mind chant. It was a version of the same chant Dad had used on the day he had lost his hand. His chant was 'Rowing beats Cialtie.' Mine was, 'Climbing stops Cialtie.'

'Climbing beats Cialtie. I worried about my friends but then pushed that thought from my mind and chanted. 'Climbing stops Cialtie.' I wondered what kind of weapon could have caused such a violent tremor this deep inside the castle … 'Climbing stops Cialtie.' I should have spent this time trying to figure out what my Choosing gift meant. What did the grove of Irish Druids have to do with me? But instead I chanted, 'Climbing stops Cialtie.' I was so lost in my mantra that I didn't even know I had made it through the Muirbhrúchts until I fell out into the Chamber on my hands and knees.

The Chamber was eerily silent. All around Leprechaun candles lay on their sides, burning where they had fallen. Several were scorching the base of the oak table and I crawled over and blew them out. It would be ironic to win a battle and lose the castle to a candle fire. I was completely drained. There was nothing I would have liked better than to have a beer and a nap but the time for leisure was not now and if my uncle got his way it would not be ever. I stood, took a deep breath and began the long sprint up the staircase to defend Duir.

Chapter Twenty-Four
War

The staircase back up from the Chamber of Runes has got to be the longest flight of stairs in any world. I had read reports of others, after walking The Choosing, being carried up those stairs on a stretcher. I initially tried to take them two at a time but after five minutes I was panting like a Himalayan mountain climber without oxygen.

Another explosion rocked the castle. I slipped and then bumped down half a dozen steps on my backside. Burning candles dropped on me from above, attempting to make me look like an illustration from a Jack Be Nimble rhyming book. I breathed a sigh of relief while I extinguished myself. If I had taken a full-blown tumble down these stairs … well, let's just say when you look up broken neck in a Tir na Nogian dictionary you see a picture of a guy lying at the bottom of *these* stairs.

Regardless of how tired I was, I got up and kept climbing. I really needed to get out of here before this castle shook again. Barring falling all the way down and breaking every bone in my body, I was worried that if this place got hit again there might be a cave-in and I would have to change my name to Rubble. It was now pitch dark in many places and there was no handrail. I really must institute a Castle Duir Department of Health and Safety.

My legs shook every time I put weight on them. Every step became a little mountain. Without realising it I was moving on all fours with my hands in front of me like a dog. *Climbing stops Cialtie … Climbing stops Cialtie …* The chant popped into my head instinctively.

It was so dark at the top of the stairs I banged my head into the door. I almost swooned when I stood but managed to fall forward, blinking into the light of the east wing corridor. I was expecting the guard to help me up but even he wasn't there. All hell really must be breaking loose if the Chamber guard had to leave his post.

I ran into the courtyard. All the activity was up on the battlements. I looked at the long flight of stairs up and knew that my legs wouldn't make it. I wished I could fly and then remembered that I almost could. I wrapped my fingers around my staff, slipped my other hand into the new leather strap and then willed my staff to lighten. I shot straight up into the air and found myself directly in the path of a huge boulder that had been propelled by a catapult. I panicked and commanded my staff to become heavy. It became so heavy so quickly that my hands went straight down, almost pulling my arms out of their sockets. Screaming I commanded my staff to lighten again and this time I really did dislocate my shoulder. The boulder at least missed me and sailed over my head into the section of the castle that I had just come from.

A guard spotted me writhing on the grass in pain. I recognised him. He was one of the guards that I had assigned to guard Brendan when he first came to The Land.

'Frick?' I asked.

'Frack,' he replied with a smile.

My arm was completely unusable. I told him that I had dislocated my shoulder and without asking, he picked me up and then slammed my upper arm into a wall. I blacked out. When I came to, the arm hurt like hell but it at least worked again.

'What is the situation?' I grunted.

'The Banshees have a catapult with an amazing range. They are alternately throwing boulders and some sort of explosive. Brendan has your mother and aunt conjuring up magic arrows. I cannot tarry any longer; I have been ordered to get gold from the infirmary.'

'I'll help.'

Frack ran ahead and I tried to keep up. He made it to the infirmary long before I did. Initially it looked like mayhem in there but I soon saw that my mermaid was coping with the injuries admirably. A guard told me that Graysea had just saved his best friend's life when he was sure he was a goner. It seemed that Graysea had cleared all of her critical patients from triage and was now working on the less injured. Frack was having trouble getting her attention; she kept telling him she was too busy to speak to anyone. I jumped in and pulled her away from an injured woman before she could fish up.

'Graysea, we need the gold my mother has stored here.'

She had that glow of a woman on a mission but I could also see the fatigue in her eyes.

'I don't have time …'

I didn't let go of her as she tried to go back to the injured woman. 'Listen. I need that gold. Brendan may have a way to stop other people from being injured by the catapult.'

That got her attention and she led me over to her store room and pointed to four small crates. I tried to lift one but my shoulder rebelled and I dropped the box screaming.

'Oh my, what has happened to you?'

'I dislocated it,' I said holding my shoulder.

Graysea slumped down next to me and placed her hand on my shoulder. I saw those gills slit open on her neck as I felt her fin press against my legs. I noticed the wince of pain on her face as my pain vanished. When she un-fished again she sighed, and I saw on her face the effort her healing was costing her.

221

'Thanks,' I said, and meant it. 'But you have to slow down, Graysea. This battle has only just begun. You can't heal everybody. You have to let the other healers do normal first aid. If you go all fishy on every injured person that comes in here – you won't make it.'

'But it's so hard to watch people suffer,' she said.

'I know but most will get better. You have to save yourself for the real life-threatening stuff. You're already exhausted.' I had a look around. Things here seem to be under control. 'Let the Imp-healers take over for a while – you should have a swim and recharge.'

An Imp came over to help us up. She said, 'Listen to him; we'll be fine for a while.'

Graysea reluctantly agreed and I led her over to her little swimming pool.

'I gotta go, thanks for the shoulder fix.' I kissed her and she flipped over the side of her pool. I watched as her face went under the water then a fin popped up like a dolphin.

I picked up two of the crates and tried to follow Frack but two crates of gold were one too many for me. A Leprechaun repair team ran past and I commandeered one of them to carry a crate. When their commander saw me struggling he decided that one crate was one too many for me and gave me another of his men. The two of them jogged behind me like they were carrying feather pillows.

I reached Brendan and his archery team just as the Banshees had launched another projectile.

'It's one of the bombs,' Brendan shouted.

The archers lifted their bows. The arrows were gold-tipped. Over in a corner I saw Mom and Nieve incanting over more arrowheads. Next to them were Leprechauns with a melting pot atop a blazing fire. The pot was streaked with overflowing molten gold.

It was way too frantic to ask what was going on so I just stood back and watched. The bomb that was shot from the catapult was as big as the boulder that had almost creamed me but it was rounder – more obviously manmade. Whoever did the aiming was having a good day 'cause it was coming right for us.

'Wait … wait,' Brendan was shouting. 'Wait for it to break its arc … Now!'

Brendan's archers were well trained. All but one arrow hit the bomb. I was expecting the arrows to make the thing blow up but when they hit they just bounced off. I turned to run but no one followed me; instead everyone just stared. That's when I noticed that the bomb wasn't falling. The arrows had hit just as it should have started on the downward trajectory of its arc, but instead the ball kept climbing.

I looked over to Brendan and said, 'What?'

He was smiling. 'The arrows make anything they hit lighter. It's one of your mom's spells. She said she got the idea from your yew staff.'

The bomb sailed well over the castle.

'So it's really my idea.'

'Yeah, right,' Brendan said. 'Deirdre and Nieve have arrows that can make stuff heavier too. If we alternate, then whoever is aiming that thing won't know what to do.'

'You learn this at cop school?'

'Nope, I'm making it up as I go along. I know it's hard to believe but in the police academy they didn't teach how to defend a castle from a siege.'

'Doesn't sound like a very good academy.'

'At the moment, Mr O'Neil, I would have to agree.'

A call went up and we all turned. The Banshees' catapult had let loose another one. This time it was a really big rock. Brendan ordered the heavy arrows and they fired as soon as the boulder was in range. The rock took a nosedive like a major league pitcher's slide and half buried itself in the muddy earth just past the treeline.

'You survived The Choosing, I see,' a familiar voice behind me said.

I turned to see Essa all decked out in her battle leathers. I felt guilty thinking how fantastic she looked but then realised that I think she looks great in everything she wears. 'You're speaking to me?'

'We're at war, Conor. There are thousands of people out there who are trying to kill you. You don't need to add me onto that list too.'

'Who says no good comes from war?'

'I'll get back to hating you when this is over,' she said.

'Right. What have you been doing?'

'I just came from a war council with Dahy and your father.'

'What's our next move?'

'Nothing really. Fortifications are good but we can't really plan anything until Cialtie shows his hand.'

'Any guesses?'

'Lots,' Essa said. 'Mostly it comes down to Maeve's Shadowmagic. Your mom and Fand are working on that.'

'So we just wait and play Scrabble until something happens?'

'Scrabble?'

'Oh, it's a game with wooden tiles with letters on them.'

'You play games with runes?'

'No ... well, I guess ...' I was saved a long explanation by the cry of a Pooka who was stationed on the wall to my left. He pointed to a dive-bombing hawk that was rocketing out of the sky. The bird extended its wings at the last second and landed on the Pooka's arm. He then gently placed the bird on the ground where it transformed into a naked woman. Another Pooka threw a robe over her as she cocked her head quickly over her shoulder just like a bird. The bird/scout tried to speak but failed on her first attempt.

Often Pookas, after a change, take a moment to get their heads back into non-animal mode. She dropped her head to compose herself; when she looked back up her jerky movements were gone.

'They are coming,' she said.

The Pooka/hawk informed us that a division of Banshee and Brownie foot soldiers were making their way through the oaks and seemed to be converging on the north face of the castle. Dahy sent troops to all of the other battlements and ordered scouts to check the other approaches to make sure that this was not some sort of diversion.

Dad stood next to me on the battlements as I waited for the first of our attackers to appear.

'We'll see now if your Irish stone minefield works.'

'I guess.'

He placed his hand on my shoulder. 'Gosh, I almost forgot. How was The Choosing? I'm so sorry we all had to leave you in there.'

'That's OK, Dad. War is pretty much as good an excuse as any.'

Dad didn't laugh like I had hoped he would. 'I guess,' he said turning away, 'but damn it, how much more of my life can my brother screw up? This has got to stop.' He paused and I could tell he was thinking about what it was going to take to stop my uncle. Then he shook his head as if to drive away the mood. 'So can you tell me what you saw in the Third Muirbhrúcht?'

'Well …'

'Hey,' Dad said quickly, 'you don't have to tell me.'

'No it's not that. It's just I don't really know what it meant.'

'Oh, that's not unusual, son. Ona once said that the visions of the Third Muirbhrúcht are like when you are trying to remember someone's name. You try and try but you can't remember it – so you give up. Then it comes to you.'

'I saw the Druids I had met in Ireland – the descendants of the banished Fili. They seemed to want something from me but I don't know what.'

'Well, maybe when this is all over we can go back together and find out. We'll probably need a holiday.'

It was nice pretending for that second that we were a normal father and son planning a summer holiday and not two soldiers about to spin the coin on our futures with the fortunes of war.

'I'd like that, Dad.'

A sentry shouted, 'Invaders north!'

We ran to the parapet as a row of Brownies stepped out of the treeline and set up long-range crossbows in the dirt. Unlike handheld crossbows, these were the mortars of the arrow-shooting family. The strings had to be set while the archer was sitting, using his feet to steady the bow. Two hands were needed to pull back the bow strings, then they were aimed using a monopod. These guys were well trained and successfully got off almost a shot a minute. The arrows were big and had some sort of enchantment in them. As they approached their target they split into twenty or so smaller arrows, producing in the sky the same effect as an entire platoon of synchronised archers.

Still, we were behind a stone wall and it was just a matter of ducking to avoid getting struck. However, we soon found out that the shafts of the arrows were covered in poisonous thorns. Dahy quickly set up an arrow-sweeping team but it meant you had to watch your step. These things were everywhere.

Brendan set his best archers to the task of taking out the crossbows but they were pretty far away. Until we could come up with a plan it looked like we would have to live with incoming fire for a while.

Under the cover of the arrow artillery, about two hundred Banshees and Brownies advanced out of the forest. They walked behind siege ladders that had shields attached to them.

When Dahy saw the small size of the force he said, 'Damn him.' There was no disguising the revulsion on his face. 'Cialtie is doing it again. How can he send so many to slaughter just to test our defences?'

As he had done on the attack of the Hall of Knowledge, Cialtie sent a small group on a suicide mission, just to see what kind of defences we had. I wanted to shout at them to go back but I knew it would do no good. I remembered what Cialtie did to the survivors of his last suicide wave. As they marched back to their own lines, Cialtie mowed them down like blades of grass.

Brendan's elite archery team aimed arrows at the feet of the advancing soldiers. They were remarkably accurate. Don't get me wrong, most of them missed, but they hit about one in ten. Not bad going considering the size of the targets. I didn't feel bad for the ones that got hit – they were, in fact, the lucky ones. They wouldn't have to walk into my minefield.

Often the shields would drop when someone went down and I saw with a heavy heart that most of the attackers were Brownies. I scoured the field to see if Jesse was in the group. What lies had Cialtie told the Brownies to make them do such a foolish thing? How stupid could King Bwika be if he thought that an alliance with my uncle would be good for his people?

As they came closer the ladder-bearers got smarter and hunkered down behind their shields. Brendan stopped firing and we just watched as they approached the line were I had buried the Connemara marble. Some of the advancing soldiers noticed the lack of arrow fire and boldly stuck their heads above their shields so as to see what was going on. They looked nervous. They knew something was going to happen. A good soldier always knows that whenever war gets easy – that's the time to worry.

I was worried.

Chapter Twenty-Five
Dumb Idea

They were behind their shield/ladders so I didn't see it happen. Half of the ladders just fell as if there had never been anyone carrying them. Almost all the rest of the shield/ladder teams had fatalities. The ones that survived were in shock after experiencing galloping old age.

A group of three newly made octogenarians dropped their shields and tried to hobble back to their own lines where they were reminded that retreat was not an option. Their own men filled them with arrows. The remaining men, some looking ancient, regrouped under a handful of shield/ladders. An archer shot one of them before Brendan could stop him. We did nothing as the old men found the base of the walls and set up their siege ladders. It was pathetic to watch the terrified and exhausted soldiers struggling up the ladders with swords drawn. No one lifted a bow or a blade to stop them.

A guy who looked like he was over a hundred crested the wall to my right, sword drawn. As I went to him he jabbed the blade at me, but I casually parried it to the right and grabbed his wrist with both of my hands. I shook the sword free of his grasp as he swung pathetic punches with his other hand. He was panting and out of breath as I pulled him from his ladder and onto the parapet.

John Lenahan

'It's OK,' I said to him, 'we won't hurt you.'

The fall to the ground had obviously pained him. I wondered if he had broken his hip or something. I felt awful, like I had started a fight in an old folks' home. When he finally rolled onto his back he had tears in his eyes. 'What happened to me?' he said.

When Cialtie realised that instead of fighting the attackers we were actually saving them, he ordered a resumption of the crossbow fire. In the end we saved about half who tried to scale the walls. A couple who were young and unaffected by the marble spell put up a fight but most, like any old man after climbing a fifty-foot ladder, appreciated the help.

Araf and I locked up our prisoners of war. I wondered if Tuan had enough blood in him to help all of the new Grey Ones that we would have after this thing was over. No, not this thing – this war. We were at war. I was at war – again – and it made me sick to my stomach. I watched in horror as people marched and died, as comrades took arrows and attackers fell screaming. I had been here before. I had been in battle and I knew that this was just the beginning. That it would get worse and worse until it was just me and someone else, toe to toe, swords drawn. Me and a stranger with whom I had no quarrel would be locked into the dance called kill or be killed. But the part I dreaded most was what would happen to me. What I would become when it was just me or him. That was the time when the primordial part of my brain would flood with those Neanderthal endorphins that would fool me into thinking I was enjoying this. Like some stupid junkie who thinks heroin is his friend, I would revel in the event. I had experienced that battle lust before and it had scared me, revolted me, but at the same time I had never felt so alive. I was afraid to experience that again. Right there and then I swore I wouldn't.

229

Dragon Tuan kept glancing over his shoulder and giving me that look.

'Keep your eyes on the road … or the air,' I shouted to him. 'I know what I'm doing.'

The Pooka turned his huge reptilian head back towards the open skies but not before he gave a smoky snort that I interpreted as, 'Do you?'

The brimstone smoke made me tear up. As I rubbed my eyes I wondered, *Do I know what I'm doing?* I hadn't told anybody other than Tuan about this escapade. My dragon pal had wanted nothing to do with it until I blackmailed him. I wasn't proud of myself but it did tickle me that probably the most powerful creature in all of The Land could be so easily manipulated by threatening to tell his mom he had an Imp girlfriend.

I definitely hadn't told my mom where I was going. I didn't even have to wonder what her response would be. Hey, I knew what everyone's opinion of what I was about to do would be. They'd all say I was crazy and I'd be lying if I said a pretty big part of me didn't agree with them.

I shivered in my dragon saddle. Tuan had warned me that I would need a coat but as usual I hadn't listened. It was so warm at ground level I couldn't imagine that we would be flying high enough so as to see my breath. What else was I unprepared for?

It was easy to imagine how badly Dad was going to flip out when he heard about this. Tuan wasn't even supposed to be in dragon form let alone flying over enemy lines. I think maybe that was one of the reasons Tuan had agreed to help me – he was miffed that Dad had grounded him. Dad had said that they would be expecting us to use Dragon Tuan as a weapon and he was sure they had an anti-dragon defence waiting. Dad ordered Tuan to stay at ground level for his own safety but my Pooka buddy thought that maybe he should have had a say in this decision. Saying that, if Cialtie did have anti-dragon cannons,

Tuan wanted to be out of range and that's why we were flying so high.

We were almost to the drop zone. I looked over the side of my magical mount and saw the tiny campfires below just beginning to be lit. They were pinpricks of light and I wondered if this is what the paratroopers on D-day felt like. But then I thought, *at least those guys jumped as a team – I am going in there all by myself with no real plan and no real parachute*. I came close to not going through with it, but then in my mind's eye I saw the bleeding and bloated corpses of my friends and family. Before I could chicken out I just pulled my feet out of the stirrups and slid off into the twilight sky.

I always thought that I would never have enough courage for skydiving, and now here I was jumping off a dragon without a parachute. I hoped my yew staff was up to the demands that I was about to put on it and, for that matter, I hoped I had enough command over the staff so as not to become a strain. I had tied some ropes around my waist and then attached them to the staff in case the G-forces were too much for my hands. After all, skydivers don't hang by their hands from parachutes.

As The Land began to get closer below me I decided it was time to order my yew staff to slow my descent. I was sure I told it to slow down just the tiniest bit, but as usual the stick read that as *slow down a lot* and I was almost cut in half by the force on my waist. I now see why skydivers use harnesses around their backsides and not rope tied around their waists. I instantly had the wind knocked out of me and worried I had ruptured some vital internal organ. I lost grip on the staff and went back into free-fall. When I finally got my senses back I was a lot closer to the ground than I wanted to be. I once again asked for a tiny slowdown and got it. I inched up the magical anti-gravity and, bit by bit, I was just about under control when I hit the ground. I rolled like a good paratrooper and then tried to stand. My midsection felt like I had just gone twelve rounds with a welterweight boxing champion but worse than that, I was exactly opposite to where I wanted to be.

The Brownies had bivouacked on the edge of the yew forest. Luckily I had fallen inside of the guarded perimeter which meant the sentries were looking the wrong way when I descended from the sky. However, I was on the wrong side of the camp. Since I had been given freedom of the Yewlands, I hoped I would touch down close enough to the forest so I could scamper into the yews if there was trouble. Only an idiot would follow me into Ioho but considering where I was, there would be no briar patch for this Brer Rabbit to escape into. I had worn a Brownie-like cloak, so I pulled the hood over my head and started walking for the centre of camp. There were a lot of Brownies here. It made me wonder if anybody was left in the Alderlands but it gave me confidence. If it had just been a small troop someone might have wondered who I was, but since almost the entire Brownie nation was here I didn't expect anyone to say, 'I never saw you at the Brownie prom.'

Now that I was in the thick of this huge camp I started to wonder *what was I thinking?* My plan seemed like a good idea back at Castle Duir when I was all fired up, but here I started to realise how thin and downright stupid it was – not to mention danger-ous. My idea was to find Jesse and then get him to let me in to see his father so I could talk some sense into him. Now I knew why I hadn't told anybody about this plan. I knew they would try to talk me out of it or forbid it, and now that I was here I realised that they were right. I repeat – what was I thinking?

I reached into my robe and fumbled for my ropes to attach to my yew staff. Tuan said he would fly around as a bat or something looking for a signal and would pick me up in the sky. I felt bad about chickening out on my noble quest but I remembered my Shakespeare: 'The better part of valour is discretion.' Dad had once told me that the great thing about Shakespeare is you can always find a quote to help you justify anything. I remembered saying, 'Don't you mean Shookspeare?' He looked at me confused. 'You know, 'cause he's dead.'

I let out a snorting laugh at the memory. Hey, if I don't laugh at my jokes – who will? I heard a whispering voice ask, 'Conor?'

Twilight was almost finished. Out of the darkness, Jesse walked up to me and pushed back my hood, then quickly pulled it back up again. Of all the things that could have given me away, it had to be my laugh.

'What are you doing here?' he hissed.

'It was such a lovely night for a stroll I …'

He grabbed my arm and dragged me over to a more secluded spot. 'If you are discovered here it will be your death – and now maybe mine too. You are here to spy? How many of you are there?'

'No,' I said louder than I meant to and then quietly added, 'no, I came to talk to you and your father.'

'Why?'

'I wanted to try to talk you out of attacking Duir.'

'And what magical rhetoric did you have in mind that would turn all of these soldiers into farmhands?' This was a much more forceful and confident Jesse than I had known from just last winter.

'I … I just was going to say that – you can't trust Cialtie.'

Jesse turned away, mad, then spun and planted his face inches from mine. 'Are you *that* stupid? You thought if you showed up and said "pretty please" we would all go home?'

'No,' I said, 'well, yes. I'm sorry Jesse, I saw so many Brownies die today – I just had to do something to stop it. As soon as I got here I realised what a dumb idea this was. I was just about to fly out when you heard me.'

The old childlike Jesse flickered in the Brownie's eyes. 'You can fly?'

'Well, up and down.'

'What good would that do?'

'Tuan's out there ready to pick me up.'

Jesse quickly backed up and looked to the sky. 'Your battle dragon is above us now?' He said that louder than he should have and others began to notice.

I tried to quiet him down. 'He's not a battle dragon and he's only here as a taxi service.'

'A what?'

'To give me a ride. This was … *is* a peace mission. I promise.'

Jesse calmed down. 'I believe you, Conor, but coming here was madness.'

'Well, I'm famous for my wit and good looks, not my smarts.'

Jesse forced a pained smile. 'If we win this war you don't think Cialtie will give the Brownies Duir?'

'You know he won't, Jesse.'

Jesse nodded.

'And what will your father do when he realises that Cialtie has tricked him?'

Jesse turned his back on me and then in the dark I heard him say with a sigh, 'He will declare war on the Banshees.'

'And how will that turn out?'

Jesse didn't answer so I answered for him. 'Win or lose, there can be no good in this.'

He turned back. The only light came from a distant campfire that flickered and danced on Jesse's face. It created an illusion – one second I saw the confident young commander that he had become and the next I saw the frightened young boy. His eyes gleamed with boyish water but the soldier refused to allow a tear to fall. 'What should I do, Conor?'

I never got to answer. Not that I had an answer. Torkc guards appeared like magic out of the darkness. I got broadsided by an uncharacteristically brawny Brownie and went down like a quarterback on a broken play. The wind was knocked out of me for the second time in half an hour. I was still seeing stars when I was dragged to my feet. Then somebody clocked me in the head with something and I saw galaxies.

I awoke sitting on a wooden floor with my hands tied to a wooden pillar in the middle of a very large and very nice tent. As my eyes focused I saw a dais and at the top was the Alder Throne. This was King Bwika's tent. It didn't surprise me that the old jerk made his subjects cart around his quarter-ton throne. Those who are insecure in their power never leave their trappings of power behind. My father, on the other hand, only sat on the Oak Throne when he absolutely had to.

To my left and right there were guards. 'Hey guys,' I said, 'I'm not planning on making any trouble. Would you mind untying me?'

I didn't even get a smirk for my effort. 'No prob, I'm fine like this really.'

But despite what I said, I wasn't fine. In fact, I was in deep do-do. Bwika had me dead to rights. He now had me as a bargaining chip, a hostage. My mom and dad would now be forced to decide what was more important to them – their kingdom or their son. They would choose the kingdom – at least I hoped they would. I couldn't blame them after raising a son as stupid as me. And what if Bwika told Cialtie? I'm pretty sure my uncle would send me home a piece at a time. I could see him sending Mom and Dad an ear-gram with his list of demands. After that, my nickname could be Van Gogh.

I heard a bunch of people enter the tent from behind. Jesse appeared in my peripheral vision flanked by three guards. He wasn't tied up or anything but he didn't look like he was free to go. I almost said hello to him but decided he was in enough trouble without me adding to it. When he caught my eye there was no smile.

We were left waiting like this for a long while before Bwika waddled in flanked by his snazzily dressed honour guard. I know I should have been worried about other things but I asked the guard nearest me, 'How do you get your shirts ironed so neatly way out here?'

Bwika stopped in front of his dais and said, 'Prince Codna, inform the prisoner that he is to speak only when spoken to.'

Jesse looked to his dad then to me and said, 'Prince Conor, you are to speak only when …'

'No,' shouted Bwika. 'Like this.' The king turned, strode up and backhanded me across the face.

The blow cracked something in my jaw and my vision went white around the edges. I thought I was definitely going to pass out and then wished I had. Every part of me from the neck up screamed in pain.

By the time I was seeing things without little birdies flying around, Bwika was sitting on his throne.

'Who else is with you, spy?' Bwika asked.

'I didn't come here to spy, Your Highness.'

Bwika whistled and the rope around my chest tightened. All of the air was forced out of my lungs and I thought I was going to suffocate. Another whistle came from the king and I once again could breathe.

'Don't think about lying again, Faerie. Did you come to corrupt my son?'

'I admire your son, Your Highness. I imagine he is incorruptible.'

'Don't bandy words with me, Faerie. Why are you here?'

'I came to warn you,' I said.

'About what?'

'I came to warn you about Cialtie – he is not to be trusted.'

The king said nothing.

'My uncle started this war so he can take Duir for himself. He needs to retake the Oak Throne in order to fulfil Ona's prophecies. He will never let you or the Brownies have it.'

Bwika stared at me for long enough to make me wonder if maybe I had gotten through to him. Then he laughed. That cocky laugh that reaffirmed what I always thought about the Brownie monarch – he was an idiot.

I hung my head and whispered to Mom and Dad like it was a prayer, 'I'm so sorry for the trouble I'm about to cost you.' I had been so stupid and now I had given my enemies the upper hand in this battle. What would Dad have to concede to get me back? If he didn't give up his kingdom he would have to give up part of his heart. I was so sorry I was about to put him through this.

'You are a spy, Faerie,' Bwika said, 'and I sentence you to death by the sword.'

Death? Oh, crap. I hadn't thought of that.

Chapter Twenty-Six
King Bwika

The king pointed to the chief of his honour guard, who drew his sword and came at me.

'Father,' Jesse said, 'you should listen to what Prince Conor has to say.'

Bwika was on his feet. 'In this room,' he shouted, 'I am addressed as Your Highness.'

I wouldn't have wanted to be Jesse at that moment but the king's outburst was enough to halt the progress of my decapitator.

'I have tried speaking to the king and it hasn't worked,' Jesse said. 'Now I am appealing to my father. Listen to Conor, Father, he makes sense.'

'You dare defy me in the room of the Alder Throne.'

'The room of the Alder Throne is back in the Alderlands, Father – where we should be. We don't belong here. Can you actually say you like it here?'

Bwika was turning red with rage. 'This land should be ours.'

'But do you like it here? Would you really rather live here than in the Alderlands?'

'The gold his father sits on belongs to us. They disrespect the Brownies – they have even stopped our stipend.'

'Now hold on,' I said, 'Duir only stopped your stipend of gold after you declared war on us.'

I shouldn't have spoken. Jesse had been getting through to him but then idiot Duir boy had to open his big mouth. Bwika exploded like a thermometer in a heat wave. I didn't even understand him for about a minute. There were some Brownie swear words in there, and my ancestors were mentioned, but he was so manic that a translation would have been impossible. Let's just say he was very, very angry. When Jesse tried to calm him down, Bwika barked something at his guards that made all of us look at each other to see if anyone understood it.

Bwika repeated himself. 'GAG HIM.'

The guard started to walk towards me.

'Not him – Codna.'

Jesse looked shocked and then hurt as the guard tied a handkerchief across his mouth. When Jesse tried to remove it the guard tied his hands behind his back as well. I looked to my Brownie friend. Despite what a brave soldier he had become, the wounded son had a tear sliding down his cheek.

'Now,' Bwika said, pointing to me, 'kill him.'

The honour guard, still shaken by the unrest in the room, hesitated, but not for as long as I would have liked. He hoiked up his sword and came at me. From his posture I had the awful feeling that he was going to attempt to split my head straight down the middle – not the way I had imagined I would go. My idea of a good death was in bed from old age. I took in a long breath, revelling in the enjoyment of just that simple act. Life slowed down for me as it always does when I'm in mortal peril. I was glad of it this time 'cause I couldn't think of any way out of this mess. I had time to compose my final words. I toyed with some sort of death curse or something noble like, 'I only regret that I have but one life to give for Duir.' That would play well but then I figured Dad would probably rumble me and everyone would think I was a jerk for plagiarising my final words. I decided on cheeky, my default for covering when I was actually scared out of my wits.

'Don't I even get a chance to duel one of you guys to the death?' I said, squeezing my eyes shut. And then ... nothing.

When I opened my eyes to see what was taking so long, everybody was looking at me. I glanced to the gagged Jesse and saw him nodding at me with wide eyes. I got the message – *Yes* – but *yes* what? I had been in so much terror that I hadn't even remembered what I said. My executioner looked at me waiting and then looked to Bwika.

'Kill him,' Bwika said.

'Wait, wait,' I said retracing my mental steps, 'I challenge you to a duel to the death.' Then as an unsure question I added, 'As is my right?' I looked to Jesse, who again nodded yes.

Bwika forced his bulk off his throne and then walked down the dais until he was inches away from my face. He was still awfully red. 'Who do you challenge?' he asked.

'Ah ... you ... Your Highness.'

Bwika straightened and then laughed. He walked past me and shouted, 'Bring him.'

News had obviously swept through the camp that I was here. Bwika ordered light, and a ring of torch-bearing Brownies stood in a semicircle making and lighting the fighting area. In the middle of the makeshift arena stood a hulking Brownie. Seriously, this guy was like an extra for a barbarian vs. caveman movie. I didn't know they actually made Brownies that big. He, of course, was topless except for strange leather shoulder pads and wore a short leather skirt. It was the kind of outfit that people couldn't help but make fun of but with this guy, if they did, they only did it once. He held a shiny, sharp blade. Stuck in the ground in front of him was a dull old sword. I pulled it out and ran my finger down it. You could shave a balloon with the edge on this thing without popping it.

'Sporting,' I said. 'Can I have my own sword?'

'The Sword of Duir,' Bwika said, 'is back with its rightful owner. Me.'

I started to say, 'What do you mean back, it was never yours.' But instead I said, 'It looks good on you. Why don't *you* use it then? I thought I was fighting you, not Steroid Boy here.'

I don't think Steroid Boy knew what steroids were but I could tell he didn't like the nickname.

'A king may choose his champion.'

'I'm a prince, you know, can I call home and get one too? Why don't you fight me, Your Highness? Tell you what, I'll fight you with my banta against your sword.'

Bwika smiled but it was forced.

'No, I imagine you're too slow even for a fight like that.'

Steroid Boy wasn't waiting for '1, 2, 3 start'. He raised his sword and came at me with the kind of ferocity that you usually get when someone insults one's king or mother. I parried the swing above my head and let his blade slide past my shoulder. His right side was wide open and I caught him on the arm with a counter-attack. My sword didn't even break his skin.

'Thanks so much for this sword. I might as well be fighting with a tent pole.'

Steroid Boy was fast and strong but luckily he had no finesse. Don't get me wrong, fast and strong were enough to get me very dead but if this guy had had any training, I would have been watching this scene from above while grooming my wings. I ducked and rolled and succeeded on coming up on the other side so I could look Bwika in the eyes.

'It's the weight, isn't it? You've gotten too fat even to fight against a guy with only a stick.'

I did another duck and dive. This time Steroid Boy's blade came so close to my nose I wasn't sure if I had been nicked or not. I really had to start paying attention to the fight, but I thought maybe I was getting through to the monarch.

'You know, maybe if you cut the cakes out of your diet you could lose a stone or two and you could get back to fighting weight.'

I parried a forearm swipe and tried to lock swords with my attacker – big mistake. He threw me off and onto my back like I was a schoolgirl – and I've known a few tough schoolgirls. I was winded and the big guy wasn't waiting for me to get up. I was just deciding which way to roll when Bwika shouted, 'Stop!'

Steroid Boy halted like he was on a leash. I slowly got to my feet, panting.

'Give him his stick,' the king ordered.

I threw away my useless sword.

Bwika stepped up and drew the Sword of Duir. 'I shall enjoy killing you with your own blade.'

'The Lawnmower would never hurt me.'

'The what?'

'The Lawnmower, that's the name of the sword you stole from me.'

'What is a lawnmower?'

'It's a machine in the Real World that keeps grass short.'

'What is wrong with sheep?' the king asked as my stick was thrown to me.

I caught my banta then immediately flipped it under my armpits and commanded it to lift me up and away from there. I didn't want or need this fight. I was doing the noble thing – running away. OK maybe I have a different definition of noble but I knew that this was a no-win situation. If I lost I died and if I won then somebody here would kill me for killing their king. Running away may not be dignified but it was smart. Bwika took a menacing step towards me and I again commanded my stick to lift me out of there – nothing. I pulled the staff out from under my arms and had a look.

'Hey, this isn't my banta stick.' Bwika took a couple of steps closer and I held the stick in front of me in a defensive position.

'That seems to be a fine alder wood banta stick – what is your problem?'

'My problem is that one of your henchmen is a thief.'

Bwika gave me a look that reminded me that calling a Brownie thief was not an insult. Then he ran at me swinging steel.

Like all big guys he surprised me with how fast he moved. He may have been old, stupid and overweight but you don't get to be King of the Brownies without knowing how to handle yourself in a fight. I used the stick to deflect his sword, being careful to give a little, so he wouldn't cut the wood. I remembered the stick vs. sword fight I had with Essa so long ago and wished I had paid more attention. He was backing me into a crowd of Brownies. I had a feeling that if I landed in with them it would hurt as much as the blade so I took a wide swipe at Bwika's head and rolled over so my back was Brownie-free.

I back-pedalled as Bwika swung. I succeeded in getting a few body hits in with my stick but they hardly seemed to faze the big guy. I knew I didn't have a chance up close with the Lawnmower. My only hope was that he would tire out as I kept losing ground. I blocked one forearm swipe too well and he took about half a foot off the top of my stick. It wasn't that bad though, he had cut it at an angle and I now had a pointy end to my weapon.

Then he made what could have been a fatal mistake. He tried one of those Zorro-like forehand/backhanded swipes and when he finished his whole body was wide open. I instinctively jabbed the sharp end of my stick towards his throat but pulled back just before contact. I could have done it then. I could have killed him but as I said, regicide was not the idea here. The idea was to get out alive. I locked eyes with Bwika hoping he would acknowledge that I just gave him his life but there was no such recognition on his face. The only thing on his face was growing rage. I used that and waited for his next attack. It was wild, I dodged it and while the sword was out of position I jammed the sharp end of my stick into the king's foot. Then I turned and ran.

The Brownies had grouped, not into a circle like with most fights but in a semi-circle. I made an assumption – one that my life depended on – that the reason they didn't want to place their backs to that part of the night was because that part creeped them out. And the creepiest place in all The Land is the yew forest. Bwika chased after me but I don't think he could have caught me even without the limp I had just given him. Other Brownies closed in. It was dark, I had no idea where the edge of the forest was, or even if it was the right kind of forest, but if trees didn't start looming soon I was done for.

A quick Brownie came from my right and tried to tackle me. With a move that would have made an All-American fullback proud, I straight-armed him. He hit the ground and enjoyed a dirt sandwich just as I saw the skeletal outlines of yews form out of the darkness.

A Brownie came at me from the left. I pointed ahead and shouted, 'Yews', and it worked. He pulled up so fast he lost his footing and ate a bit of earth himself. All the other Brownie soldiers stopped too. I found out later that the Brownies have a children's poem that teaches them about the dispositions of different trees. The first line goes, 'When you meet a yew – that's the end of you.'

All of the Brownie soldiers held back but I guess Bwika was no poetry fan. When I cleared the first tree I looked back and saw the beefy monarch loping at full speed, red-faced, sword outstretched and he was coming right for me.

'Bwika, NO!' I shouted but the king was not in his right mind. He got within two footfalls of the first yew and stopped like he was a bird hitting a window. I ran to the tree and placed my hands on the sinuous bark. 'Stop, leave him, he didn't mean to come here. He was chasing me. He didn't come here to be judged.'

I ran to Bwika and tried to pull him away. He groaned from the pain of my pull fighting against the yew tree's bone hold. When I tried a second time to move him the trees pushed me back by my sternum. It felt like I had been kicked in the chest.

To Bwika's credit he knew what was happening and he knew the danger he was in but he didn't whimper or beg – just the opposite. He tried to turn to me; when he found that impossible he shouted, 'I don't need help from you, Faerie.'

I ran around the tree so I could see the king's face. Once more I touched the yew. 'You said I have freedom of the Yewlands, King Bwika is with me.'

The tree broke his/her silence. '*This Brownie is not your companion, he was attempting to kill you. Your minds are open to us, Faerie – do not attempt to lie.*'

'He's not prepared for the Choosing, he didn't mean to enter the Yewlands. He shouldn't have to die because of an accident.'

'*Falling from a cliff is an accident,*' the tree said with its twin male and female voice, '*yet often there is death.*'

'But you can stop this,' I pleaded. Let him go.'

'*The Brownie has entered the Yewlands, he shall be judged.*'

'I told you, Faerie, I need no succour from you,' Bwika grunted. 'I'm not afraid of being judged by a damn tree.'

There was nothing I could do. I may have the freedom of the Yewlands but that sure doesn't mean I have any sway over them. I thought, *You're on your own, Brownie king, but if I were you I wouldn't start a trial by swearing at my judge.*

'When I want your advice I'll ask for it,' Bwika said. That's when I realised we were linked in mind through the tree. I should have let go. A yew trial should be a private thing but, like seeing a car wreck, I just couldn't look away.

Bwika's life flashed before my eyes. His was not a privileged royal upbringing. Unlike most princes he came from humble stock and rose through the Brownie military. Through sheer hard work, physical strength and cunning Bwika gained the highest of military positions in the Alderlands – Chief of the Torkc Guards. It was there he saw his chance and he sowed seeds of discontent into the king's son and finally influenced him into challenging his father to a duel. The prize – the throne. Bwika secretly coached both father and son and, as the fight's referee, poisoned both combatants' blades. When it was over the Brownielands had no king and no heir. Bwika ascended to the throne until a rune holder could be found. Two years later he came to Duir, took his Choosing and received the Alder Rune.

My anxiety lessened. If the Chamber of Runes found him worthy of a major rune then maybe so will the yews. But then I remembered something that Spideog had said to me, 'Many a Runelord had been found wanting by the yews.'

Next was the birth of his sons: two in quick succession by two different women. He banished both mothers as soon as they dared to even suggest a course of parenting different to the father. Both children were raised by a succession of nannies who were fired with regularity. Demne, the one I called Frank, was so desperate for his father's approval that he volunteered for a suicide mission to destroy the Tree of Knowledge. Bwika, in his hubris, let him do it and we all know how that ended. Jesse's upbringing was even more painful to watch. Every time I saw him through his father's eyes he was a cowering slip of a thing. Bwika only recently had come to show any interest in him, now that he had come into his own.

When the tree started to ask Bwika about this war and why he supported Cialtie and Maeve – the Yew Killer – I couldn't take it any more. I let go of the tree and dropped to my knees with the kind of emotional exhaustion that can make even opening your eyes seem like a chore.

When I did look up I saw Jesse. He alone had ventured close to the yew forest. He was watching his father looking up, kneeling, straining at the base of the yew.

'Don't come any closer, Jesse,' I warned.

'What are they doing to him?' he asked. There were tears in his eyes.

'He's being judged.'

'Will they kill him?'

I wanted to give him hope. He looked like he needed hope but I had been listening in and I knew Bwika's chances were not good. 'Maybe.'

A groaning defiant scream made me turn. Bwika was on his feet; his hands were shaking, reaching for the now low hanging yew berries. It was over. He had been judged and found unworthy. The tree was forcing him to eat its poisonous fruit.

Jesse screamed, 'No', and ran to his father. I screamed the same thing and ran to intercept him but was way too late. Jesse's hand touched his father's shoulder and then he too froze solid. Bwika stuffed a handful of berries into his face; the juice of them flowed down his chin like blood. He had one last effort of will in him and he used it to look at his son and smile, then he collapsed face first into the tree's trunk.

I ran to Jesse; he was immobile with his hand outstretched. Moments before, that hand had rested on the shoulder of his father. His eyes were swimming in the tears of a child. I came up behind him and reached around his waist trying to drag him back into the camp. I couldn't budge him an inch. I gave up and buried my face into his back.

'Jesse, do you know what you have done? You're going to be judged.'

Chapter Twenty-Seven

Prince Codna

The tree pulled Jesse's hands to its trunk. I ran around and touched the tree myself.

'He really is a friend of mine. I demand he be given the freedom of the Yewlands. I came to see him. He must not be judged.'

The yew didn't answer, he/she ignored me.

'HE IS MY FRIEND!'

A movie of Jesse's life entered my mind as I fell to my knees pleading for the tree to stop. His earliest memories were of nannies who, while outwardly raising him with iron discipline, secretly tried to give him some of the nurturing that every child needs. He was never as fast or as strong as his brother and his father set the tone for the way everyone looked at him. All considered him a weedy child, a sissy. Only his brother gave him the kind of love and defence that he needed. I saw that without his brother, Jesse may not have made it in that tough Brownie world. It made me sad that Frank was dead. Jesse finally, just in the last year, had started coming into himself. His confidence and stature both grew. Now his father began to take pride in him, but Jesse's newfound prowess was despite his father's influence not because of it.

The tree pushed me away as it spoke privately with its defendant. Out in the open field the Brownie soldiers were slowly moving closer. I motioned for them to stop and they did. I waited, my heart pounding, for any movement of the branches that bore the yew's poisonous berries. After what was probably only five minutes but seemed like hours, Jesse stood up, said, 'Thank you', and then stepped away from the tree.

'Are you OK?'

Jesse didn't reply for the longest time and then nodded yes.

'Jesse, you passed the judgement.'

'Yes,' he said still staring at the yew.

'Did you receive a gift?'

'I did,' he said.

'What did you get?'

'The yew asked me what I wanted,' he said, finally looking at me. 'I asked for the body of my father.'

I saw him start to stagger. I quickly ran to him and put my arms around his waist. He dropped his head on my shoulder and burst into tears. It didn't last long. He pushed me away, keeping his back to the rest of the Brownies, and composed himself.

'This is no way for a captain of the Torkc Guards to behave,' he said.

'Don't you mean – this is no way for the King of the Brownies to behave?'

He looked at me incredulously.

'Aren't you the next in line to the throne?' I asked.

'I … I guess I am … until a major rune is chosen.'

'Which I'm sure will be chosen by you.'

Jesse stood for a minute taking this all in, then a tiny smile crossed his face as he wiped the tears from his eyes. 'Then this is definitely no way for the King of the Brownies to behave.'

'I think, Your Highness, this is absolutely the right way for a king to behave.'

We carried Bwika out of the forest. Now I know what they mean by dead weight. When we had staggered clear of the yews,

Steroid Boy came towards us and drew on me. I dropped Bwika's legs to defend myself.

'Prince Conor is under my protection,' Jesse said.

'But Captain Codna,' Steroid Boy began.

'I think, soldier, the title you should be using is – Your Highness.'

Steroid Boy was obviously not the brightest bulb in the marquee. He looked to the dead king and then to the son. Finally he twigged. 'Yes, Your Highness.'

'Make yourself useful, big boy,' I said, 'relieve the king of the king.'

This confused Steroid Boy even further until he said, 'Oh, of course.' He picked up the late King Bwika. I was pleased to see that even he struggled a bit with the weight of him.

What looked like half of the Brownie nation was waiting for us in the field in front of the camp. Jesse walked up to one of the soldiers and took from him a torch. Then he placed his fingers in his mouth and produced a whistle that made me stick my finger in my ear hole to make sure it wasn't bleeding. The crowd started to part in the back as Jesse's horse cantered his way to his master. I smiled to see that the obedient steed was The Turlow's old horse that I had given him. Jesse handed me his torch and then performed an impressive running mount on the bareback horse. I returned the torch. From atop his mount and in the dramatic flickering light of the flame, King Codna addressed his people.

'King Bwika is dead. He died under the branches of the yews,' he shouted, then waited for the murmur to die down. 'My father was a great king …'

I waited and wondered if he was going to follow that statement with, 'But not a good father.'

Instead he said, 'But he was not infallible. He grew up in an age that believed the Alderlands were a place of banishment.

Understand, he loved the Brownielands, and Alder Keep, but he believed that our rightful home was there on top of Duir Hill.'

Jesse turned his horse and pointed to Duir, then turned back to his people. He looked more regal with every passing second.

'I do not know what happened in the first age. I have no magic that can show me what the Ancients did or did not do to our ancestors. But I do know one thing. If they envisioned the Alderlands to be an abyss, a prison we Brownies were supposed to escape from, then they were oh so very wrong. If the Ancients gave us the Alderlands as banishment then they were not as all-knowing as the great stories have said. Because as you all know, when they threw away the Alderlands they threw away Paradise.'

This was good stirring stuff but it was also a tiny bit heretical. I looked around to see what the reaction would be. I didn't have to wait long.

A voice from the back started it: 'Codna, Codna.' It didn't take long before the chant was taken up by everyone in the field. 'Codna, Codna, Codna, Codna.'

Jesse held up his hand and silenced the crowd. 'Prince Conor came here on a mission of peace. He came with information that makes me believe that Cialtie never had any intention of giving us Duir if we win this war.'

A loud murmur rumbled through the crowd. It raised the emotional temperature in the field. Jesse silenced it with two words.

'No matter … I for one miss my home. I don't like it here and I don't think that even all the gold in the mines of Duir are worth the lives of the good Brownies that we will lose in this quarrel. For what will we win? A home we don't like? And what will happen if we have all the wealth in the land? I'll tell you what would happen – there would be nothing left to steal. What fun would that be?'

A Fergalish smile overtook my face. Jesse looked to me for affirmation and I bowed my lowest bow.

'I want to go home,' King Codna shouted. 'Are you with me?'

There was no doubting the answer. The Brownies went wild.

When we got back to his tent and we were finally alone, Jesse asked, 'Was that all right?'

'All right?' I said, 'All right? What are you talking about? That was awesome.'

'Oh gods, Conor, how can I be king?'

'Just like that, Jesse,' I said. 'I've never seen anything more kingly in my life.'

He smiled and held his hand out for me to shake. It was still trembling.

'Screw that,' I said and gave him a big hug.

Jesse gave me back the Lawnmower and sent someone out to retrieve my yew staff. Outside, the Brownie camp was wasting no time packing up to go home. Jesse gave me a sitting harness that Brownies use to sit in trees and I tied that to my staff.

'Long live King Codna,' I said.

'Maybe I should call myself King Jesse,' then he crumpled his face and said, 'maybe not. Goodbye Conor, I shall always remember what you said, "No one can unmake us friends."'

'And now I hope no one can ever make us enemies again.' I bowed once more to the new king and commanded my yew staff to lift me into the night. When I had well cleared the treetops I fired one of my mother's Shadowmagic flares and waited comfortably in my new harness.

It only took a couple of minutes for Tuan to show up. He had been flying around as a bat waiting for me so he had lost his saddle. It took me three attempts at landing on his back before I held on long enough to get my balance and crawl into a decent riding position.

Tuan gave me evil looks all the way home. He's good at it in his dragon face. When we landed in the courtyard of Castle Duir, the dragon turned into Tuan again and instantly gave me an earful.

'What took you so long? I was flapping around in the dark for hours.'

'Sorry. Eh … could you put some clothes on?'

'I almost went into the Brownie camp all flames-a-flaming.'

'I'm really sorry but it got complicated. I'm glad you didn't fly in. Bwika's dead and the Brownies are going back to the Alderlands.'

'What? How did you do that?'

'I'll tell you when there is less of you to see. Will you get dressed please?'

For the sake of modesty, Tuan turned into his wolfhound and went in search of one of his several clothes stashes as I made my way to a bed. I always find this waking in bondage thing exhausting. I just wanted sleep.

An honour guard intercepted me before I even got under a roof and I was unceremoniously escorted to the War Room. I felt like a prisoner. 'You guys know I'm a prince, right?' They all said they did but that didn't stop them from insisting I go with them. I toyed with the idea of testing whether I was, in fact, free to go to my room but I just didn't have the strength for those kinds of games. Saying that, I was pretty sure I was in big trouble with my friends and family for escaping on Tuan-back – I wasn't sure I had the strength for this meeting either.

Behind me I heard Tuan. I turned to see him with his own soldiers. 'I would advise you to take your hand off my arm,' he said with a very animal-like growl, 'unless you want to be holding on to the arm of a bear.' The guard let go quickly.

Essa was in the hallway outside the meeting room. She ran at me and I immediately put my arms up to defend myself – this was Essa after all – but she wrapped her arms around my neck and said, 'Thank the gods you're all right.'

'Maybe I should go for a late night walk more often.'

Essa pushed back. 'You weren't walking. You were flying with Tuan.'

'Oh you know about that?'

'Everyone knows about that,' Essa said. 'Your mother performed an emergency Shadowcasting to find out where you were. The casting said you were in the Yewlands. Your father mobilised an entire platoon to figure out a way to get you.'

'Oh, so maybe they're a little mad at me?'

Essa's face went through four seasons of emotions. She laughed, then her eyes welled up, then she looked like she was going to hit me before she re-hugged me and said, 'I thought I would never see you again.'

'Hey, I ain't going anywhere,' I said, smoothing her hair. 'You're stuck with me for a long time.'

She looked up at me; her face was inches from mine. 'How long?'

'For ever,' I said. 'That is if my mother doesn't kill me in the next ten minutes.'

A cough from behind broke our embrace. It was Dahy. 'The king demands your presence.' He looked embarrassed at interrupting us.

'I thought you would be mad at me too.'

'I'm furious,' the old general said, 'but kissing a sweetheart in a time of war is an important thing.'

'Well, Dahy! I never realised what an old softie you are.'

'Careful, Conor,' he said as he motioned me through the door.

Everybody was there: Mom, Dad, Dahy, Lorcan, Nieve, Fand, Brendan, Nora, Gerard, Eth, two Runelords I didn't know and half a dozen other uniformed types and they all looked awfully mad at me. Dad had that look I had only seen a couple of times before. It was where he was so mad that he actually couldn't get the first syllables out of his mouth. Mom, whom I didn't have as much experience reading, had a face like I had *never* seen before.

I decided to head off what was coming. 'Bwika's dead,' I said calmly. 'Codna is king and the Brownies are no longer at war with us. They are on their way back to the Alderlands now.

If Dad found it difficult speaking before, he found it impossible now. It was a nice moment. Mom stepped up. 'Could you tell us this news again, Conor, and extrapolate a bit.'

So I did. I told them the whole tale leaving out only what I had used on Tuan to blackmail him into giving me a lift.

When I finished Dad said, 'You could have been taken hostage. You could have compromised us all.'

'I know it was stupid. I promise I won't do it again, but right now I need to put my head down. Can I go to bed now, Mommy and Daddy?'

I stood up and had one of those head rushes I get when I stand up too fast on the same day that I've been knocked unconscious. Essa jumped up and gave me a hand. We were almost at the door when Graysea burst in.

'You're safe,' she gushed, taking my arm away from Essa. She placed her hand on my neck and announced, 'He is exhausted. I am taking him straight to bed.'

Essa looked miffed and took my other arm. For a second I thought she was going to start pulling and I was going to be drawn and quartered by competing women.

Nieve behind me said, 'Now to our Shadow defences.'

Essa had to stay for that meeting. She let go of my arm and said to Graysea, 'Take good care of him.'

I thought that maybe I should stay too, but then I figured I had just cut the size of the attacking force by half – that was enough for a day. War would have to be planned without me.

Graysea walked me back to my room and lay down in my bed with me. When I started to protest she shushed me and then sprouted gills in her neck and a fin. I had bruises and rope burns and contusions that were so all over I hadn't even noticed how bad I felt until my mermaid doctor melted them all away.

'I thought I told you to stop doing that for everybody.'

'You were right; I was overextending myself in the infirmary. I am now only healing in the urgent cases. But you, dear sweet Conor,' she kissed me on the cheek as she got up and walked to the door, 'are not everybody. Sleep.'

Sleep came instantly. I had one of those strange movie dreams where I was a private detective. I was waiting in my 1920s deco-rated office when in came a beautiful client. It was Maeve, the girl from the tea shop in Connemara. She wore red lipstick and a low-cut red dress that had a slit that showed off her shapely right leg as she walked. She said she wanted to find her real mother and I agreed when she paid me in advance – with a pair of Nikes.

I put on the sneakers; they didn't go with my grey suit and fedora but hey, this was my dream. I wandered through countless speakeasies and police stations until, finally, I told Connemara Maeve I had found her mother. Together we drove up a long gated driveway of a Hollywood house that looked like it belonged to a movie star. The door opened and my Irish client came face to face with her mother – it was Maeve. The other Maeve, the outlawed

Queen of the Druids, the tree killer that almost destroyed all of The Land with her corruption of Shadowmagic – the Maeve that was brought back from some abyss by the spilled blood of Ruby. She looked at the Irish girl and said, 'Who are you?'

I turned to my glamorous client but she no longer wore makeup and was dressed in her modest tea-shop waitress's uniform. 'Tell her,' she said.

I opened my eyes with a start. On either side of my bed stood two burly soldiers in green-stained leather armour. At the foot of my bed a wild-haired woman, also in green leathers, stood staring at me with eyes that had almost no colour at all. I sat up in bed my heart pounding.

'I was just dreaming about you,' I said.

Chapter Twenty-Eight

Fand

'You were in the Hollylands when I regained form.'

How the hell did she know that? I thought. *I was hooded.*

Like Maeve was reading my mind she said, 'I sensed your presence from the hallway. Who are you?'

This was a freaky moment. I had been in a deep sleep and then woke up only to be confronted with the very scary long-lost legendary Shadowwitch and her two eyeless henchmen. Then the realisation hit me that this was one of those dreams within a dream and I relaxed.

'Buzz off lady; I got more sleeping to do.'

I was about to snuggle down under my covers again when Maeve kind of went see-through and walked towards me. She didn't stop at the bed. When she came to the footboard she just kept coming and walked right through it like it wasn't there. She stood translucent in the middle of my bed like she was waist deep in a swimming pool. Dream or no dream, I instinctively backed up; she didn't look like a healthy thing to touch. I pulled my legs back and then she solidified again. When she did, the bed around her just exploded. The sheets and the mattress ripped apart and the wood frame of the bed cracked in two, sending wood splintering across the room. I ended up on the floor at the Fili Queen's feet and said, 'OK, maybe this isn't a dream.'

'I ask again, Faerie, who are you?'

Considering she had trashed my bed by just touching it, I thought that maybe answering her was a good idea. 'I'm Conor, nice to meet you.'

'You are Conor, Son of Oisin?'

'That's me.'

'Where is your father?'

I didn't have to answer because at that moment, one of the west-wing guards burst into the room with his sword drawn. 'Stand away from the prince,' he said.

It wasn't until then that I noticed that Maeve's henchmen were unarmed. One of them faced the guard who repeated his command, 'Back away from the prince.'

The henchman reached towards the confused guard who must have been wondering, *What is this unarmed nut doing?* The guard finally reared back and swung. It was a long wide swing. He did it that way to allow the unarmed man time to get out of the way but he just stood there. A second before the guard's sword hit him, the Fili became ghost-like and the blade sliced through him like he wasn't there. The guard, who had been preparing for impact, fell forward, off balance, and exposed his back. Maeve's man reached his hand into the guard's side and then solidified. The guard screamed but only for a second. There was a crack of bones and a horrible squelching noise. I could only imagine that what had just happened to my bed was what was happening inside that poor guard's body. The guard went limp. It looked as if the Fili was holding him up, then as if to confirm that thought, he went spooky and the guard fell to the floor.

Another guard came through the door and the other Fili dispatched him in exactly the same manner. The floor was now covered with more blood than I had ever seen. And I have seen a lot of blood.

Maeve loomed over me. My feet slid on the bed sheet under my heels as I tried to push myself back into the wall. 'I tire of asking you questions twice, Faerie. Where is your father?'

'I am here.' Dad was standing at my door. Two of his honour guard entered the room before him.

'Don't attack,' I called from the floor, 'they can kill with a touch.'

Dad stepped into the room. 'What do you want, Maeve?'

The ghost queen smiled but not in anything resembling a heartwarming way. 'I want from you what I wanted from your father – Duir.'

'Duir is not mine to give. Tenure of the Oak Throne is chosen by the Chamber of Runes.'

Maeve threw her head back and laughed one of those laughs that only bad guys and bad actors can do. 'The clan of Duir builds a magic room that always magically seems to give the clan of Duir their magic Rune. Magically convenient, do you not think?'

'And you think you deserve the Oak Throne? Why?'

Maeve walked right up to Dad. His guard went to step in between them but Dad stopped him. When they were nose to nose Maeve flickered into her ghost form. It only took a second but in that time she reached into the chest of Dad's bodyguard. He gasped as she solidified and he screamed as her hand came out holding his beating heart.

'Power,' she said. 'Duir is mine because this time, you cannot stop me.'

She dropped the heart to the ground and then looked at her hand. It was covered with blood but then she flickered translucent, and the blood fell to the floor – her hand was clean. No one tried to attack or stop her. It was an impressive display of power and ruthlessness.

'You cannot stop us. I have an army with this power. And your son cannot stop me by corrupting the Brownie prince. We don't need the Brownies.' I was now on my feet. She looked at me and said, 'We will deal with Prince Codna in time.'

She reached into a pouch that hung from her waist and took out a piece of marble. 'And I will not be stopped by pieces of the Real World.' She threw the rock to Dad's other guard. I started to shout, 'Don't touch that!' but didn't have time. He instinctively caught the piece of Connemara marble and instantly was reduced to dust.

'What has happened to you?' Dad hissed. 'You are not even Hawathiee.'

'You are right, son of Finn. I am better than Hawathiee and I shall rule you all. But I am not without a heart.'

I found that statement hard to believe after what she had just done to our guard's heart.

'I shall give you until sunrise tomorrow to leave. After that …'

She didn't say anything else but she didn't have to. They went see-through and turned to leave. Maeve walked through the door but the bodyguards went through the wall. One of them bumped into my yew banta stick and was surprised that it blocked his way just as if he had been solid. The stick then fell to the ground and he stepped over it.

Dad shouted to the guards outside in the hall, 'Let them pass unmolested.'

After they left I tried to speak but I couldn't breathe. I ran out of the room and vomited in the hallway. Dad came out and held my shoulders. After everything in my stomach had come up I still retched. When I finally finished I stood shaking like I was standing outside in the snow. A guard held out his canteen and I rinsed out my mouth. The hallway was crowded by then. I looked to Dad and said, 'What are we going to do?'

An Imp-healer came running down the corridor calling my name. 'Prince Conor, come quick.'

I looked up confused, tired.

The woman slid to a stop in front of me and said, 'It's Matron Graysea.'

There was a circle of people in the infirmary around Graysea's lifeless form. Blood had pooled on one side of her kelp robe. A nurse was applying a pressure bandage to her injured side. I knelt down and asked if I could see the wound. It was not as bad as the ones I had seen in my room but it was the same thing. I could spot bits of broken ribs oozing out with the blood before the bandage was replaced.

'What happened?' I asked.

'That woman and those men walked through the walls into the infirmary then started pushing over tables. Graysea went to yell at them – you know like she does – and the woman slid her hand right through her side.'

'Get her in water,' I said.

Araf was already in the infirmary and he lifted her up as the nurse kept pressure on the wound. Araf went into the pool holding her in his arms. When he dipped her head under the water gills appeared on her neck and her feet melded into one fin.

'This is a good sign,' one of the Imp-healers said.

Still she didn't wake up.

'Conor, is she OK?' came a voice behind me. It was Essa.

I remembered all of the names Essa had called Graysea and I almost shouted, 'What do you care?' but before I lost it, I recognised that my anger was not with Essa. 'I don't know.'

She nodded. 'I hate to pull you and Araf away but the king wants you both at the war council.'

The Imp-healer said, 'Go. We will look after her. I will notify you of any change.'

'I'll be there presently,' Araf said as he stepped dripping out of the pool.

The war council was waiting for my report but when I sat I was too choked up to start. Dad broke the silence as someone brought me a cup of tea that soothed my stomach and steadied my nerves.

'Maeve was here,' Dad said. 'She has a power over her corporeal being. She is impervious to a sword, can walk through solid walls and can reach inside and … she can kill with a touch. Her soldiers can too.'

Everyone looked to me and I nodded in agreement.

'Are you saying,' Dahy asked, 'that she and her army are invincible?'

Dad looked to everyone in the room. They all wanted him to say it wasn't so but he couldn't. 'I am,' he said, 'I see no way to stop her.'

'My lord?' Lorcan said.

Dad's eyes stared at the table. His shoulders were hunched over like that statue of Atlas, except the world that was pressing down on Dad was invisible. Finally he looked up and pushed his shoulders back. 'We must evacuate Castle Duir.'

'Where will we all go?' Mom said with uncharacteristic panic in her voice.

'Faerie and Leprechaun are always welcome in the Heatherlands,' Araf said as he entered the room wearing a robe from the infirmary.

'And Cull,' Gerard said.

'And the Pinelands,' Tuan echoed.

Dad nodded, acknowledging his allies. 'Lorcan, we cannot give Maeve unfettered access to the gold. We can't leave her with that much power. Can you seal the mines?

Lorcan looked like he had been slapped. 'You mean destroy them?'

Dad nodded yes.

Lorcan looked around like he wanted someone to slap him on the back and say, 'Just kidding.' Finally he said, 'Yes, my lord.'

'No,' said a soft voice at the end of the table. Fand was looking straight at Dad. Her usual delicate expression was gone and in its place was the countenance of a determined queen. 'No. I will not run. I will not allow my mother to simply take Duir. I will not allow my mother to ruin more lives. After her last atrocity the Fili nation was almost destroyed. Most were killed and the rest banished with only a handful of us left to bear her shame. I have lived most of my life in shame. I will not watch her do it again. Tomorrow I will face her. Tomorrow I will stop her – or die.'

'And I will stand with you.' It was Nora.

'Mother, no,' Brendan said.

'Son, my father and his father and his father before that told of the folly of Queen Maeve. We were told that the reason we were banished from Paradise was because none of the Druids had the guts to stand up to her. I will not be banished again. Take Ruby and get far from here, but Maeve is entering Duir over my dead body.'

Ever since I had heard Dad say that there was no way to stop Maeve, something was tugging at the corner of my mind. Even while Fand and Nora were proposing to fight to the death, my concentration was being pulled by something. The recent events had been so traumatic I couldn't put my finger on it but some little part of my brain was telling me that I must remember. Then … pop … it came to me.

'We can fight them,' I said. Everyone looked. 'When one of Maeve's thugs left my room he knocked over my yew banta stick – while he was in ghost form. If we can convince the yews to give us enough wood – I think yew arrows will stop them. At least we can go down swinging.'

'Yew arrows will work?' Dad asked.

'I'm pretty sure. The soldier was surprised when he couldn't walk through it.'

'Son, I know you are tired but can you convince the yews to help us?'

'I can try – but with those trees it's anybody's guess.'

'Tuan,' Dad said, 'I realise I have been treating you like a glorified flying carpet, but will you help us?'

'Of course, Lord Oisin. But tell me – do you have a flying carpet?'

'So let me get this straight,' I said. 'Are we staying and fighting?'

I looked around the room. Fand was defiantly determined to stand up to her mother. Everyone else was looking to everyone else. Dad stood. 'Get the wood, son.'

'Bet you didn't expect to see me so soon,' I said to the yew. If the tree found my salutation amusing he/she hid it well. 'Maeve is back,' I said. 'She is about to attack Duir. I … we need yew wood to stop her. Will you help?'

'*We do not concern ourselves with the landly doings of the Hawathiee.*'

'Then concern yourself with the safety of your own. Maeve is a tree killer. She decimated the rowans when she was queen and I am certain she is responsible for the recent killings of the yew.'

'What proof do you have of that?' said an actual voice, not an inside-my-head tree voice. I turned and saw an elf leaning against the adjacent tree.

Elves in The Land dress like you would think an Elf would dress – dark green tights and a leather tunic tied tightly around the waist. They are always thin – not Brownie thin but I've never seen a fat one. And do they have pointy ears? I hear you ask. Don't be silly. Saying that, I hadn't met many Elves during my time in The Land, except for the one I talked to at Gerard's party; all the other sightings were fleeting glimpses in distant trees. Elves keep to themselves.

Just the other day I asked Dad what side the Elves would take in the upcoming war and he said exactly what Cialtie had said. 'At the first sign of trouble Elves climb their trees and hide.'

'Hi,' I said to the Elf. 'Were you eavesdropping?'

'What proof do you have that Maeve killed yews?'

'Maeve was brought back to life with yew sap. Whether she got it herself or got someone else to get it for her – she is responsible.'

'How do you know this?'

'I was there when she was … reborn.'

Another real voice, this time from the tree behind me said, 'Show us.'

I turned in time to see another Elf with his hand on a yew trunk before the painful yew brain scan began.

I fell to my knees as the scene of Maeve's rebirth played in my head. The vision was dark, just like it had been when I watched it through the gauze mask I was wearing. It was not only painful to watch because of what the yews were doing to my head, it was also hard to see Ruby again being treated so badly.

When the mind-video of Maeve solidifying had finished, a different voice asked, 'Why do you need yew wood?'

I didn't know who had spoken but when I looked up every yew within my vision had an Elf at its trunk.

'I can't believe I'm saying this, but – have a look at what happened to me first thing this morning.' I squeezed my eyes in anticipation of the pain. I watched again the horror movie that was my morning. It was just as bad the second time around.

'We must confer,' the yew said. I started to listen to the conversations that seemed to be happening all over the yew forest – male/

female yews and also Elves – but soon the noise and information got too much. I remembered what happened to me when a pine tree gave me information overload and backed my hand off the tree. I rolled onto the grass and placed my head down just for a second. I was asleep in a minute.

I was in that barn in Connemara, Ireland. The Druids – The Grove – were around me wearing robes. 'Awake,' they were chanting, 'awake.'

When I opened my eyes I was being shaken by an Elf saying the same thing. I sat up quickly, not knowing how long I had slept. 'Will you help us?'

The Elf turned his back on me and placed his palms skyward.

All trees make a sound when they are donating wood. It's an eerie sound as the tree sucks the moisture out of the wood before cracking off a branch. I had heard it many times when I had begged for firewood but I … in fact, no one … has ever heard an entire forest donating wood at the same time. The sound of cracks began to domino around the entire forest as every yew dropped branches to the ground. It sent chills down my back.

'Thank you,' I said to the Elf.

He shook his head, grabbed my wrist and pushed my palm onto the yew. 'Thank Ioho.'

I felt the contact not only with the tree I was touching but it almost felt like I was in contact with the entire forest, which I suppose I was. 'Duir thanks you.'

'Your request was just and your adversary is ours,' the trees spoke. *'May you succeed in your undertaking, Hawathiee.'*

'Prince Conor,' the Elf said, 'I am Bran. It is the way of the Elf to stay out of conflicts. When other Hawathiee ask us, "Whose side are you on?" it has been our custom to say, "We side with the trees." This time it seems that Duir and the trees are on the same side. We will help you.'

'Do you speak for all the Elves, Bran?'

The Elf thought about that for a bit. 'I speak *with* all the Elves.'

'Good enough for me. Let's get to work and get some ghost-proof arrows to Castle Duir.'

We bundled up the branches and Elves packed them on their backs and legged it to Castle Duir. I warned them about the marble mines and told them to go around to the west side where there was a small entrance. I was going to be back to the castle before them and promised to warn the guards of their approach.

Eth had given me some gold wire and a half a dozen *rothlú* charms. We bundled some of the bigger branches with that and then shouted, '*Rothlú.*' The bundles vanished – presumably to reappear at home. I asked Bran if he could coordinate from here and he said he could. For a pacifist Elf type he got military pretty quick. We hung bunches of yew wood off dragon Tuan until he gave me a look that I interpreted as, 'Put one more stick on my back and I'm making charcoal.' And we headed back to Duir.

I wasn't going to be there long, though. The Chamber of Runes had given me a gift and I had just figured it out.

Chapter Twenty-Nine
The Grove

'Does it always rain like this here?' Ruby asked me with a jiggly voice as we galloped down the road from the Fairy Fingers.

'This is Ireland,' I said as the horizontal rain dripped off my nose and onto her head, 'so to answer your question – yes.'

'That must be why it's so green here.'

I laughed. 'I never thought about it but I guess you're right. And how do you know it's green? Can you, like, smell it?'

'It's called the Emerald Island, bozo. I can read braille, you know?'

'Do you think if I got into one of those automobile contraptions without touching the ground, that I would still end up looking like your grandmother?' Essa shouted over her shoulder.

'What do you suggest, we steal one?' I shouted back.

'Yes.'

'Last time we were here you stole a horse and cart, and ended up in jail. Remember?'

'This time,' she said, 'I'll add a snoring cure to the spell.'

'The town's not far. If you're nice I'll see about getting you a towel.'

I kicked my horse and got a sense that she didn't like it. I hadn't brought Acorn in case things got hairy and I had to leave my mount behind. I didn't even know this horse's name so Ruby dubbed it Connie. Short for where we were going.

I looked behind to make sure that the young woman we had brought with us, Anula, was keeping up. She looked scared and unhappy but she kept the pace.

Tuan and I had made it back to Castle Duir from the Yewlands – just. Towards the end of the flight every wing stroke bobbed us up and down in a way that gave me the impression that if Tuan stopped flapping, we would drop like a stone. I asked him if he wanted me to dump the load of yew wood but I only got a dirty look in reply. When we finally arrived, Tuan near collapsed. I wanted to throw up but didn't have time.

I got Mom, Dad, Nora, and Brendan together and told them about the vision I had in the Chamber of Runes. Then I told them what I thought it meant.

'I won't take Ruby unless you want me to,' I said to Brendan and Nora, 'but if she comes it will make my mission a whole lot easier, and she can stay there until this war is over. They are good people – they're Druids – they will take care of her.'

I had never seen two people more torn. They wanted to have their girl by their side but they also wanted her safe. They wanted to go with her to the Real World but they knew if they didn't defend their newly adopted home that there would be no place for them to go back to. In the end they agreed. That's why Ruby, her babysitter Anula, Essa and I were hammering down an Irish back road in the pouring rain.

It was getting late in the day. I didn't dare go to the police station to see Mícheál in case one of his fellow officers recognised me. Now that the pony show was over, three galloping horses were conspicuous enough. I pulled my hood down over my eyes and prayed that Agent Murano wasn't still around.

I walked dripping into the tea shop just as Maeve was closing up. She didn't look all that surprised to see me. She just smiled and said, 'I have been thinking about you all day.' She hugged me and as she did she saw Ruby come through the door. I felt her stiffen and say, 'Oh my …' She pulled away from me. Her whole front was wet from my rain. She dropped to one knee. I'm not sure if it was to get onto Ruby's level or if she went weak at the knees.

'Is she … blind?' Maeve asked with a hushed reverence.

'Hey Lady,' Ruby said, 'I'm right here. You can ask me yourself, you know?'

Then Ruby turned to me and said, 'Is she another one of your idiot girlfriends?'

Mícheál organised a meeting of 'The Grove' outside town in the same barn as before. He said it wasn't hard to get everyone together; they had all been on high alert since the last time we Tir na Nogians showed up. Still, it was almost midnight before everyone arrived. I felt sorry for Essa. Anula, Ruby and I were young enough to walk around but poor Essa was stuck sitting on her horse for hours. If she had to, she could have gotten down, but becoming an old woman was something she was not willing to do again. 'Three times was quite enough,' she said. So while we sat around drinking cups of tea she sat high above us like some princess, which – when you think about it – she was.

Ruby's appearance had freaked out Maeve. When I asked her why, she clammed up, saying I had to speak to her father, but her reaction fortified my suspicion. I had interpreted my vision properly.

At the barn I kept Ruby hidden for optimal effect. When everyone was there, I was called into the main room. This time they were decked out in long-hooded Druidy-type robes but the effect was ruined when I noticed most of them wearing modern sneakers. I wanted to ask them where I could get a nice pair of Nikes around here but then reminded myself to concentrate. This was an important occasion and I wanted to begin with the solemnity that it deserved – but as usual instead my opening salutation was more Scranton Conor than the Prince of Hazel and Oak.

'Hi everybody. Ah … the last time I was here one of you asked if you could come back with us and then another said that I wasn't "The One". That would be "The One" with a capital O.'

'That is correct, Conor,' Mícheál said. 'Since you have been here there has been much debate among The Grove. We do believe you are from The Land but you do not fulfil what was foretold.'

'Yeah, I get it. I'm not "The One".' I stepped around the corner and led Ruby by the hand into the main room. 'How about her?'

You know that look when everyone yells 'Surprise!' and the birthday person jumps and then opens her mouth wide right before she almost faints? Well this was like that but in reverse. Everybody freaked and two people actually did go down – just like I had seen in the Chamber of Runes.

'Hey, hey, listen up everybody,' I said, 'I don't have much time. Would any of you like to take a trip to Tir na Nog? We got apples there you just wouldn't believe.'

It was an hour before dawn when I rode through the portal back into the Hall of Spells. Nieve and Nora were there waiting.

'You are very wet,' Nieve said.

'Really? I hadn't noticed,' I replied as I dismounted into a growing puddle.

'Is she safe?' Nora asked, like the nervous grandmother that she was.

'Yes, Nora. She is with Mícheál. He is a good man. He helped me the last time I was there. He wanted to come but he saw that looking after the Blind Child Who Was Foretold was more important.'

'Oh, I hope they don't spoil her.'

'I wouldn't worry about that, Grandma. Ruby has a way of bringing people who know her down to earth.'

Nora nodded and relaxed, but I was pretty sure I wouldn't get a smile out of her until she saw her little Gem again.

Just then, the first of the two dozen Irish Druids came through the glowing circle. Tea shop Maeve was one of the first and I introduced her to Nora so she could tell her about her father.

Initially a lot more of The Grove wanted to come after seeing the Blind Child but then I warned them that we were walking into a war – possibly an unwinnable war. Dropping everything and travelling to a mystical land is a tough decision. Jumping into possibly certain death is even harder. I was impressed that I got twenty-four.

Brendan tore himself away from arrow-making when he heard I was back. I assured him that his daughter was safe and in good hands and he brought me up to speed on the defences. 'We have made about three hundred yew arrows. They are not all actually straight and I wouldn't bet on my chances of a bull's-eye at any distance but at close range they'll work. We also have quite a few yew bantas and a couple dozen pointed sticks.'

'Pointed sticks? Is that in case of vampire, Fili?'

Brendan smiled and shook his head. 'Is there any occasion where you aren't a wise ass?'

I went to visit Graysea in the infirmary. She had finally come out of her underwater coma and had changed back and forth from fish to female a couple of times. With each change she lost more of her injury. She could probably have fixed up someone else with a similar wound without too much trouble but apparently healing herself was harder. She tried to get out of bed when I came in but the Imp-healer threatened to sit on her if she tried to get up one more time.

'She talks mean,' Graysea said quietly after the healer was out of earshot, 'but she really is nice underneath. She reminds me of matron back in the grotto.'

'I wish matron was here to help you,' I said. 'You still look a bit pale.'

Graysea turned way and pinched her cheeks then turned back with a forced smile. 'Better?'

'Much,' I said. Out of the corner of my eye I saw the Imp-healer motioning me with her head that I should leave.

'Conor, I must talk to you … but … I'm very tired. Can we talk soon?'

'Of course,' I said, kissing her on her forehead. 'We'll talk tomorrow. You get some rest.'

I walked away with the sound of my own voice echoing 'tomorrow' in my mind and wondered if for any of us there would be a tomorrow.

I slept for an hour. What a mistake that was. I had one of those dreams that was so crazy I woke up more exhausted than when I went to sleep. I was at a square dance. All of my comrades in arms were on one side of the room: Brendan, Nora, Araf, Nieve, Essa, Dahy, Mom and Dad. Lined up on the other side were: Cialtie, The new Turlow, Macha, Oracle Lugh, Maeve and Cialtie's Banshee sorceress. We started off with a frantic square dance that culminated with us once again facing each other across the room. Then the square dance caller cried, 'Do-si-do!' and we came towards each other again but this time Cialtie and his side all grew fangs and pulled daggers. I found myself sitting up awake with sweat streaming down my back and a scream just south of my larynx. It was still an hour before dawn. Believe it or not I got out of bed without any prompting. When the day may be your last – getting up at dawn isn't such a bad idea after all.

Dad was up on the parapet looking out at the night sky as it was losing its daily fight with the sun. I climbed up next to him and handed him an apple.

He took a bite and then shook his head. 'We shouldn't be here,' he said dreamily to the night.

'Where should we be?' I asked.

'We should be … we should be tucked up in a cosy bed and then when we finally wake up we should be having a huge cooked breakfast next to a roaring fire. Instead we're chomping an apple on a cold wall. You know Conor, my biggest worry shouldn't be war, my biggest worry should be whether or not there is enough wine in the castle cellars.'

'Didn't your mother warn you there would be days like these?'

Dad laughed. I was glad to see he still could. 'My mother is one of the people out there making this day the way it is.'

'Oh yeah, I forgot that.'

We stood some more in silence until I broke it. 'Gods, I hate waiting.'

'Really. I like waiting. I use the time to think. Not daydreaming, mind you, but really thinking.' He looked at me and it seemed he looked older – like he used to look – and I felt younger, like I was looking up. 'Didn't I ever teach you to use waiting time to think critically?'

'Every time we had to wait in line and I said I was bored, you made me conjugate Latin verbs. Now that I think of it, maybe that's why I hate waiting so much.'

'Ire,' Dad said.

'Ire, eo, is, it, imus, itis, eunt,' I instantly responded.

Dad had said the Latin verb *go* and I involuntarily responded by conjugating it – the English equivalent of saying: I go, you go, he goes she goes …

'It seemed our waiting time was not wasted.'

'Yeah, Dad. My Latin will come in handy when we get attacked by Julius Caesar.'

'Mihi vera placet quod tu es callidissimus, nate,' Dad said. Loosely translated that is: *I am very proud of you, my son*.

Since Latin was the language of the day, I replied, 'Et tu, pater.'

Mom came up on the wall and took one look at the two of us with our watered-up eyes and said, 'Aw, you two are just a bunch of softies.'

'He started it,' I said.

She hugged us both and watered up a bit herself. Dahy crested the stairs and said, 'Are you ready for today, Your Highness?'

Dad and I simultaneously replied, 'Born ready.'

'How about you, my love?' Dad asked.

'As long as I am with my boys I can do anything,' Mom said.

By this time the sky was lightening and the wall was filling up.

'Lorcan,' I called. 'You ready?'

'Lorcan the Leprechaun is ready, my lord,' he shouted in reply.

'Brendan?'

'Detective Fallon of the Scranton PD is ready and able, Mr O'Neil.'

'Nieve?'

'I am with you, nephew of Oak.'

'Gerard?'

'The beer is free when this is over.'

'Tuan?'

The Pooka lifted his chin and as he did his head transformed into the head of a wolfhound. He barked once.

'Araf?'

The Imp didn't reply – but he did nod.

Essa by this time was at my side and I quietly asked, 'You ready for this?'

'As long as I'm with you, Conor.'

We all turned as Fand came up the stairs. Nora was at her side. It struck me that she had yet to see her mother. I could only imagine the conflicting emotions that must have been going through her mind.

'Are you ready, Your Highness?' I said to her.

She looked to the sky that was now almost fully light and said in that quiet composed voice of hers, 'If the sun in the sky is willing to face this day – then so am I.'

'Well, that's everybody, Mr King,' I said to Dad.

Dad slapped me on the back and said, 'You will make a wonderful Lord of Duir someday.'

'Thanks, Dad, but I've been meaning to speak to you about …'

I didn't get to finish that thought for just then, directly below us, the Fili ghost army solidified one row at a time. Each row appeared chanting until the whole army culminated in a cacophony that halted with the appearance of Maeve. The Fili Queen looked down at her cupped hands and they erupted with Shadowfire. She then tossed the fire in the air where it sparked like a firework. Each of the sparks found the hidden Connemara marble in the field. Then Maeve threw her hands forward and all of the marble came out of the ground and splatted into the castle wall.

I turned to Fand and said, 'I'll say one thing for your mom – she knows how to make an entrance.'

As soon as I said it I felt bad. For Fand this was not the time for levity. But then a strange, almost spooky, smile infected just the tiniest corner of her mouth. She never took her eyes off of her mother but she said, 'Yes, Conor, she does.'

Chapter Thirty

The Shadowrune

Let me tell you, walking right up, practically unarmed, to an army of people who had the power to casually rip major organs out of your chest was one of the most terrifying things I have ever done. Intellectually I had decided that I would do it, but it wasn't until I started actually moving towards them that the terror gripped me. It took every fibre of my being to stop myself from wrapping my arms around Dad's leg screaming, 'Please don't make me go.' I was really scared and I know I wasn't the only one. If we made it out of this alive I promised myself I would buy everyone new underwear. If they were anything like me, they were going to need it.

'Hello Mother.'

'Hello Fand.'

I don't know what I was expecting. I had never walked up to a murdering queen and her bloodthirsty army before but I was expecting something different than English afternoon-tea etiquette.

Maeve raised her hand and lifted it towards her daughter. Dahy tensed up and looked like he was going to give one of those pointed sticks a try. Fand raised one finger and calmed everyone. Maeve continued forward and gently placed her hand on the side of her daughter's face. Fand closed her eyes. Then Maeve went into ghost form and her hand entered Fand's head. Fand's eyes shot open and the two queens stared at each other with a burning intensity. I placed my hand on the pointed stick secured in my belt. If Maeve's palm came out with Fand's brain on it I was going to kill her no matter what happened to me.

Her hand came out brainless.

'You have become a Shadowwitch, daughter.'

'I have,' Fand replied.

'Then come and join us.'

'No, Mother.'

Maeve looked confused. 'You would oppose me?'

'With my life,' Fand said.

'As will I,' Nora said.

Maeve turned sharply to Nora. 'Who dares interrupt a conversation between the Queen of the Fili and her daughter?'

'I am your daughter too,' Nora said. 'I am the daughter of the daughter of the daughter's daughter who had to pay the ultimate price for your arrogance. I am the Fili that was banished from this land when you chose power over harmony. We are the Fili,' she said, pointing to the two dozen very brave Druids from Connemara who were standing behind us in the field. 'We are the Druids who have endured disease and hunger and old age and death for your sins. So do not presume it is not in my right to talk in front of the queen – for I am Fili and as far as I'm concerned you forfeited your crown eons ago. My queen is Fand.'

Maeve was taken aback but her honour guard were incensed and made a move towards Nora for speaking in such a way to their queen. Fand stood between them and Maeve called them off. Let's just say it was tense out there.

'You are a Shadowwitch, you know the kind of power we wield. You cannot stop me.'

'I do not know the power you wield, Mother. I have learned Shadowmagic not for power but for peace. I learned Shadowmancy not to emulate you but to understand you and ultimately avoid your fate. I have no idea of the power you wield, for I have never killed a tree.'

Maeve baulked at her daughter. 'How can you be a Shadowwitch without sap?'

'Oh, I use sap.'

'How do you get it?'

'I ask for it. Have you become so brutal, Mother, so power mad that you have forgotten how just to say "please"?'

Maeve was at least listening but her entourage was getting anxious – I could feel it in the air. Before another word could be said, a call came from the battlements behind us. From out of the oak forest on horseback came Macha, Lugh, The Turlow and Cialtie. Behind them followed what looked like the entire Banshee nation in full battle armour. They filled every visible space.

Maeve looked to her daughter and said: 'It is too late for talk, you cannot stop us.'

'We can stop you, Mother, with this.' Fand took an arrow out of her belt and handed it to Maeve who received it on the face-up palms of both her hands.

'Don't be foolish, daughter, have you not seen what we can do?' Maeve then faded into her ghost form. The arrow remained on her hands. Her face was the picture of confusion. She grabbed the arrow with one translucent hand and then felt the sharp tip with the other. When it pricked her spirit-skin, fear crossed her face and she dropped the arrow.

'Go back from where you came, Mother.'

'But I thought, Fand, it was you who called me forth.'

'I did not call you.'

'Then who?' Maeve asked, truly confused. 'We were lost in a void and then we … were … We found ourselves on a shadow island. A Shadowwitch of great power must have called us. I thought it was you.'

'When did this happen?' Mom asked. She walked up to Maeve and the old queen stepped back.

Maeve placed her hand out as if she was sensing the air in front of my mother. 'You have power. I can feel it. What do you conceal?'

Mom reached to her neck and pulled out from under her tunic her Shadowrune. When it was made during the unorthodox Choosing in the Chamber of Runes it was so clear it looked to me almost like a hologram of a rune. Now it looked old and cracked as if it was made out of ancient dried blood. Maeve instinctively reached for it but Mom pulled it back.

'Where did you get that?' Maeve asked.

'Last summer I performed The Choosing with oak sap and the Chamber rewarded me with this.'

Maeve was really shocked. 'Even I would not dare to do such a thing. You *created* that day. From your Choosing an island … a shadow island *became*. We who last saw the sun on this field during our battle with Finn found ourselves alive once more – with form but not substance.'

'How did you get here?' Mom asked.

'We simply walked under the waves to the mainland. We need neither food nor air.'

'This rune was clear for almost a year,' Mom said, 'and then this summer, on the night you stole the blood of a child, it darkened.'

Maeve thought, then nodded. 'We have a bond, Shadowwitch. What is your name?'

'Deirdre.'

'Daughter of Liam of the Hall of Knowledge?'

'I am his daughter,' Mom said, 'but Liam and the Hall are no more. All was destroyed – by your allies.

'And the Tree of Knowledge?'

'What care you of a tree?' Fand spat.

'The Great Hazel is a very special tree.'

281

'They are all special, Mother. The day you forgot that is the day you forgot how to be Hawathiee. Do you even remember why you fight? Has power corrupted you so that you use it only to gain more? Is power enough reason to lose me? Is your power enough reason to condemn the Fili to suffer, to grow old and die?'

Cialtie and his Banshee sorceress rode closer. He shouted, 'Enough talk, Maeve.'

'Your comrade Cialtie,' I said, 'tried to destroy all of The Land and everything in it. Has he told you that?'

The old queen looked sharply to me in a way that made me regret speaking then she looked to her daughter for affirmation. Fand nodded yes.

'I do not wish to kill you, daughter.'

'I have lived too long with your name,' Fand said. 'If I fail to stop you today I will kill myself for the shame of being your progeny.'

I imagine that even if I were to stab Maeve with my pointy stick it wouldn't hurt her as much as did her daughter's words.

Macha on horseback stepped forward with Lugh at her side. 'Enough, Maeve! Let this begin.'

'Macha kidnapped a Fili child so as to bleed her for you,' Nora said, 'and when she was through she wanted to kill her. Is this the kind of future you want for The Land?'

'And you know Lugh,' Dad piped in. 'Do you really think he will let you rule? Do you think any of them will?'

Maeve looked to all of us. If I was a betting man I would have bet that we were getting through to her. She looked down thoughtfully at her hands and then as fast as any viper she lashed out. Her hand in ghost form shot into Mom's chest. Mom screamed and arched her whole body back in pain and terror.

We were all frozen with shock but that didn't last long. When we all stepped forward to intervene, Maeve hissed, 'One step closer and you shall see her heart.'

That's the kind of threat that can stop you in your tracks. Maeve reached her other hand into Mom's chest and when she pulled it out, her fist contained Mom's Shadowrune. You could see it through her translucent fingers. She pulled sharply and it broke free of the leather necklace it hung from.

'Your opinion, daughter, is something I have never valued. Your intellect and thoughts have not ever been worthy of my notice.' Maeve, still with her hand in my mother's chest, held the rune up to the sunlight. 'And now I see – too late – how wrong I have been. You have become a better Fili Queen than I could ever be. Goodbye, my daughter … try to forgive me.' She placed the rune between her back teeth and then bit down hard. The Shadowrune erupted with amber light that made us all cover our eyes. When we could see again, we saw Maeve and her Fili army fading into their ghost form and then they kept on fading. Before anyone could speak – they were gone.

We all stared at the place where they had been with a 'What the heck happened here' expression on our faces – everyone except Cialtie. I could come up with a lot of nasty names for my uncle but 'slow' isn't one of them. He was looking around like a dog deciding whether or not to steal a hot dog from a picnic table. He was reassessing his rapidly changing power base. So I did the same.

OK, we had gotten rid of Maeve and her ghost army – this was a very good thing – but Cialtie still had a kick-ass Banshee army. Just us against them was a battle that could go either way, especially if Cialtie and his gang decided to take us out before we could get back behind castle walls.

'Maeve,' I shouted.

Dahy jumped and said, 'Where?'

Despite the tenseness of the moment, that made me laugh. 'No, not that Maeve – Connemara Maeve.'

'Yes, Conor,' came the waitress's voice from behind me.

'I think you should slowly walk the rest of The Grove back to the castle.'

'OK,' she said, in a voice I could tell was trying to be braver than she felt.

'Have your people stay where they are, Oisin,' Cialtie said, 'or my archers will fell them where they stand.'

'We are here under the protection of a parley, brother. Even you would not break that faith.'

'With all of the things you have accused me of,' Cialtie said, 'breaking a parley seems insignificant. Anyway, your parley was with Maeve, not me.'

'Uh oh,' I thought, but apparently I said it out loud. I got unanimous dirty looks from everyone on my side and a sickeningly sweet smile from my uncle.

'I have archers trained on this position,' Dahy said.

'Arrows do not worry a Lord of Wind,' Lugh said and then to demonstrate he flicked his hand and a wind tussled all of our hair.

I stifled a fart joke. This was definitely the wrong time for that.

'I see we have a new Turlow,' Dad said, bowing one of those little bows a king gives to another king. 'Now that you have lost your ghost army and the Brownies, are you sure you want to continue this conflict without allies? I will hold no ill will if you withdraw now.'

You got to hand it to Dad for a gutsy move but the new Turlow didn't look like he had enough backbone to dump Cialtie with the guy sitting right next to him.

'We Banshee have nothing to fear from the Faerie.'

'The day I lose my fear is the day I think I would be most afraid,' Dad said.

'Hey, Turlow,' I said. 'You know it's not just Faeries around here. We got Imps and Pooka, and Fili. There's even a mermaid back in there. And oh, I bet these guys will surprise you.' I pointed to the treeline and from every visible oak an Elf dropped down on a rope. The Elves, I learned, could climb oaks without the trees making them relive every horrible minute of their lives. I waved and they shot back up like their ropes were some kind of slow acting bungee. 'Those guys are, like, invisible when they are in the trees. I'd worry about getting out of here through that forest.'

'You have persuaded the Elves to enter this conflict?' The Turlow said, amazed.

'Yup,' I said, 'and I definitely would stay out of the Yewlands for a while if I were you. Boy, are those trees mad.'

'This matters not,' Cialtie said. 'We are not leaving. We are taking Castle Duir and you have made it easy for us to do it. My army is on the field, brother, your archers are useless and there are less than three score of you. Lay down your arms and I will be merciful.'

This wasn't good. As I looked to Cialtie and The Turlow and Lugh and Macha all glaring down on us from horseback like we were ants under a magnifying glass, the elation of Maeve's heart-ripping ghost army vanishing was starting to wane. We really were in a bad spot here. The Irish Druids weren't even armed. It was really just, me, Mom, Dad, Dahy, Essa and Araf. Brendan was up on the battlements with archers who were useless because of Lugh. We were so truly stuffed that even I couldn't come up with a smile, but amazingly and uncharacteristically – Dad did.

A tiny smile that was just noticeable enough to unnerve his opponent and hearten me appeared on the corners of his mouth. 'Are you sure, brother, you want to start this now?'

Cialtie's mouth turned at the corners as well. For as opposite as these two men were, the mirrored smile reminded me that they were still siblings. 'This day, my little brother, is long overdue.'

Dad nodded one of those slow thoughtful nods and took a deep breath. The scene reminded me of a showdown at the end of an old black and white western movie. 'Then I would like to introduce you to someone.'

Cialtie's smile vanished as he looked around for some kind of trick.

'This is Nora Fallon,' Dad said, pointing to his left.

Cialtie's smile returned. I half expected him to say, 'So what?'

Dad then addressed Macha. 'Mother, this is the grandmother of the little girl you kidnapped. Lugh, you may remember her son Brendan. Before we begin, she has something to say to all of you.'

Dad looked to Nora and nodded. She held her hands out in front of her, took a deep breath and shouted the immortal magic word, 'YEEEEHAAAA!'

Chapter Thirty-One
Nora

While I was begging the yews for arrows and then flitting to the Real World, Dad, Dahy and the rest of the war council were coming up with a plan – a plan they forgot to tell me about. I thought the idea was fight Maeve and die, but Dad formulated a strategy in case Fand succeeded in convincing her mother to give up the ghost. I guess that's why they pay him the big bucks.

Nora never did tell me what gift she received from the yews but she obviously told Dad. When the yews asked me what gift I desired, I didn't know what to say but Nora knew exactly what she wanted. She wanted the same power as the woman who had stolen her grandchild. She wanted power that could trump Macha's power. The yews gave Nora power over horses. They gave her power that superseded Macha's horsemanship. When Nora held out her arms and yeehaa-ed, Cialtie, Lugh, The Turlow and especially Macha were thrown from their rearing horses. All of them as you would imagine were shocked but Macha – the queen of all things equestrian – was absolutely dumbfounded. I'm pretty sure it had been a thousand years since a horse had disobeyed her.

Dahy had always taught us, 'When you're in a brawl, punch the biggest guy first.' Now that Maeve was gone, the new biggest guy was Lugh. With him still on the chessboard we had no archery cover and without arrows, we were sunk.

Lugh went off the back of his horse just like the others but unlike his companions he didn't hit the ground. As instinctively as you and I would reach out to grab a banister when we stumbled on a flight of stairs, Lugh conjured up a wind that caught him and sat him down on the ground feet first.

Dahy stepped up and threw a dagger directly at his head. The mountain oracle flicked his hand and Dahy's knife was blown off to the right. But this was a Dahy blade and it swung back on its target. I held my breath as it came at him from behind but just as the blade was about to stab the self-proclaimed god in the back of the neck, Lugh threw up his hand again. It was like he had eyes in the back of his head. The knife, though, wouldn't give up. Dahy must have incanted some serious knife homing voodoo into the thing 'cause it kept coming back like a stupid growling puppy that didn't know when to give up. Finally Lugh grew annoyed at swatting away at the knife like it was a persistent mosquito. With an increasingly aggravated look on his face, he finally held his hand in front of the approaching blade. The knife's homing magic was neutralised by the wind coming from his hand and the blade hovered just before the oracle's face.

'I think, Dahy,' Lugh said, 'I think I am going to kill you with your own blade.' Lugh reached through the wind tunnel he had created and grabbed the handle of the hovering knife. That was the last anybody saw of him. Dahy had made the handle of the knife out of Connemara marble. The moment the oracle touched it, he got old real fast and the dust he instantly became blew away in the last breeze he ever made. Then lots of things happened all at once.

The first thing was the arrows. As soon as Brendan saw Lugh dust it, he let the arrows fly. Since I had no idea what the game plan was, I decided to make sure I got the Connemara Druids back to the safety of the castle walls. From above it might have looked like I was running away but the reason these people were here was me. I didn't want perforated Irishmen and Irishwomen on my conscience.

A huge Banshee battle scream rose from the army. I had to cover my ears but as I looked to the Irish Druids they were all pointing and smiling. I looked back and saw the Banshees in full retreat. Then I heard more screaming – this time less Banshee-like. I looked to the north side of the castle and saw Jesse riding in front of the entire Brownie army as they charged at the now retreating Banshees.

The reason why Banshees are such good warriors is that they have that sixth sense that tells them when they are going to win. Conversely when they are going to lose, they know that too. King Jesse and the Brownies joining the side of the good guys was too much for them – they scampered.

A Banshee scream from Cialtie's sorceress made me turn. She was throwing sparks and fire from her fingertips but Nieve and Mom were repelling it until it backfired on the sorceress and she was blown off her feet. Dahy walked up to Macha who smiled seductively at him. He unceremoniously clocked her in the head with his banta stick.

Dad drew his sword and came for Cialtie. For a guy who had just lost two armies, a ghost army and a god, he didn't look as worried as he should have been. As Dad approached he just stood there with his hands at his sides. If it was me I think I would have stabbed him right then and there but Cialtie knew his brother. Dad placed the edge of the blade at Cialtie's chest. There was still so much noise around I didn't hear what Cialtie said. I watched his lips move and I saw the shock on my father's face. Then I saw him mouth '*Rothlú*', and he was gone.

Essa ran up and hugged me. 'Are you all right?'

'Yes,' I said incredulously. 'It looks like we all are. This is the strangest war I have ever been …' I didn't get to finish that statement due to the huge wet kiss that she planted on my lips. I guess now that the war between Duir and the Banshees was over, so was the war between Essa and me. In both conflicts – peace felt good.

Jesse galloped up to us and performed an impressive moving dismount from his horse Fluffy. I bowed my lowest bow and he did the same.

'King Codna,' I said.

'Prince Conor,' he replied and then ran and gave me a very un-royal-like hug.

'Thanks for coming back, Jesse.'

'It wasn't me – it was them,' Jesse said, pointing to his troops who were still chasing Banshees out of the field. 'With each step home, the angrier my people became. After a night at camp my commanders came to me and said they wanted Cialtie and his Banshees to pay for deceiving them.'

'Duir thanks you all,' I said, bowing again.

'Aw, any excuse to see my old friend Conor.'

What minutes before had been a battlefield began to resemble a family outdoor barbecue. Brendan came down and was snogging Nieve. I saw Dahy carrying Macha into the castle fireman style. I know it's not right for a grandson to think like this but after what she did to Ruby, I hoped they put her into that smelly dungeon that I was in the first time I got here.

Mom and Nora were on either side of Fand helping her back to the castle. Fand had been as strong as a steel girder during her spar with her mother but now that it was over she looked frail. Dad stood staring off into the distance. I came around his side and searched his eyes trying to figure out what he was looking at. He wasn't looking at anything. He was lost in thought.

'You OK, Dad?'

'Yes,' he said long and slow. Then he looked at me and smiled. 'Yes. Why shouldn't I be? We won. Or actually we averted a war, which is even better.'

'You are a victor in peace, Father.'

'A victor in peace,' Dad repeated. 'I like that. If only I could resolve all of my conflicts without bloodshed.'

I stepped over to where Dahy's blade was still sitting in the ground. The handle was roughly hewn out of marble and the blade was completely covered with gold. I picked it up. 'Good idea. Whose was it?'

'Dahy's,' Dad said. 'When it comes to killing bad guys – Dahy knows his business. Be careful with that. Actually, can I leave you with the job of making sure all of the Connemara marble is locked safely away?'

'Yes, Your Highness,' I said with a mocking bow.

Dad laughed. 'I give you one chore and you get stroppy.' When I straightened up he placed his hands on my shoulders and then brought me in for a hug. 'I'm so glad you're safe, son.'

'Me too … I don't mean I'm glad I'm safe, I mean I'm glad you're safe too.'

'I understood,' he said loosening his clinch. 'Oh, and I need the Lawnmower back for a little while.'

'OK,' I said, undoing the buckle on the belt that the Sword of Duir hung from. I handed it to Dad. 'You need it for some official kinging thing?'

'Yeah,' he said. 'Something like that.'

The Connemara Druids were all milling around in a bit of a daze. I asked them if they would help me move the marble inside and they all agreed – happy to have a job to do. In no time we had all the pieces of the Real World locked up in one of the dungeon vaults.

Later I had a meeting with Brendan and Nora. They wanted to go back to the Real World right away but Essa had sorceress stuff to do with Mom and Nieve. There had been protective snap spells placed all over the castle and they needed to be removed before one of us hurt ourselves. So we promised to go to the Real World in the morning to retrieve Ruby.

Araf found me right before sundown and said Graysea wanted to see me. He had a look on his face that made me worried.

'Is she OK?'

'She is fine, she … she wants to talk to you.'

'OK,' I said as he walked away. For as long as I have known that big guy I still have a hard time reading his thoughts.

I walked to the infirmary a bit slower than I could have. To be honest I was a little bit dreading seeing Graysea. Don't get me wrong, I still think she is one of the most beautiful and the sweetest women in all of The Land, but I was in love with Essa. From the moment I saw her – 'till the day I die – it's Essa and it was unfair to Graysea not to tell her that. It was just that it's never a good time to tell Graysea anything. She did that smothering me with kisses thing when she saw me and she had those lovely puppy dog eyes – it was just … hard to break her heart. And now that she was injured, I felt like I was kicking her when she was down. But I had to tell her.

I found her out of her tank and in a hospital bed. She looked so much better than the last time I had seen her. She had colour in her cheeks and her face lit up with a healthy smile when she saw me. She started to get out of bed but her Imp-healer grumbled, 'Graysea', and she meekly obeyed and sank back into her pillows.

'How is my Mertain wounded warrior?' I said kissing her on the cheek. She didn't answer and when I looked at her again her expression was disquieting. 'Graysea, are you OK?'

'Oh, yes,' she said, forcing a smile. I gave her a stern look and she said, 'No really, I'm fine, Conor. I found out that it takes me a lot longer to heal myself than others. My prison guard,' she said pointing to the Imp-healer, 'says I'll be up and around in a couple of days.'

I relaxed. 'That is very good to hear. So why the long face?'

'Well,' she said, looking down at her hands, 'you know I am very fond of you?'

Wait a minute, I thought, *that's what I was going to say.*

'You know I'm very fond of you,' she repeated, 'but I think that maybe we …'

'Hold on – are you breaking up with me?'

Graysea's angelic face started to crumble into tears. 'Oh, my poor sweet Conor. I don't know what to say. I just don't think it's fair of me to lead you on any more.'

'You are. You're breaking up with me. Why?' I said indignantly. I know it makes no sense. I should have been relieved. Hell, I had gone in there to break up with her but the male ego isn't a logical thing. 'Is there someone else?'

She once again concentrated on her hands and then nodded yes without looking up.

'Who?'

'I didn't mean for anything to happen.'

'Who?'

She lifted her gaze and pointed over my shoulder. I turned to see Araf duck back behind the doorframe like a naughty schoolboy.

'Araf! You're dumping me for Araf?'

'I'm sorry, Conor. I healed a small cut he had and then we started talking. It's just I need someone who talks to me.'

'And he does?'

'I'm so sorry, Conor.'

I looked back and the Imp was once again peeping around the corner. 'Araf,' I shouted and he ducked back around again. 'You come back here,' I said as I stormed towards the door.

'Don't hurt him,' Graysea called from her bed.

When I got to the doorway Araf was already halfway down the hall speeding like he was in an Olympic walking race. The sight of

Araf, the toughest guy I know, running away from me, added to Graysea saying, 'Don't hurt him', made me smile and that smile popped the stupid male ego bubble that was growing in my head. I ran after Araf and as I did I started laughing. He looked behind and started running. As I have mentioned before, for a big guy Araf can move awfully fast. I finally had to call to some guards to stop him, 'In the name of the prince.'

'Honest to the gods, Conor,' Araf said, panting, 'nothing has happened.'

I forced a stern countenance onto my face; it wasn't easy.

'We just started talking and then we talked some more. But nothing has happened. I haven't even kissed her.'

I just stared. It was fun watching Araf ramble.

'I'll leave Duir immediately.'

I had to grit my teeth to stop from cracking up. 'You haven't kissed her?' I asked.

'No … Your Highness.'

When he said that, I had to turn away. I'm pretty sure he thought I did it 'cause I was mad. When I composed myself I turned back and said, 'I think it's about time you did.'

'I beg your pardon?' Araf looked very confused. 'About time I did what?'

'Kiss her, you idiot.' I placed my hands on his broad shoulders as a Fergal-like ear to ear smile erupted on my face. 'You are two of my favouritest people in all of The Land. I couldn't be happier. I'm delighted for you both.'

He tried to say something but nothing came out.

'Now that's the Araf I know and love.'

He hugged me, almost breaking my back, and then ran off to the infirmary for that first kiss. With a sigh I remembered my first mermaid kiss – it's worth running for.

Speaking of kisses, now that she didn't want to kill me, I thought it might be a good moment to spend a little time with Essa but Mom and Nieve had her working late. I had a meal with the Connemara Druids but didn't have the strength to hang out with them. They were so enthusiastic. The older ones were getting that immortality buzz where they kept saying how they hadn't felt this good in ages and all the rest were going on and on about how good the apples were. I know I was just like them but I was really tired after all the almost dying stuff, so I snuck away to my room.

My head told me it was too early to go to bed but my body vetoed that thought as soon as I hit the mattress. It wasn't until I was horizontal that I realised just how stressful a couple of days I had had. I closed my eyes for a long peaceful sleep. But as so often happens in The Land – dreamland was not restful.

The entire night was a swordfight. I watched the Lawnmower face a thinner blade but the whole time I couldn't see who was fighting. It was just sword vs. sword. Even though there didn't seem to be anyone holding the blades the intensity was just the same as if it was a life and death battle. I squinted, trying to see who the fighters were. It wasn't until the earthquake hit that the fighters came in to focus and I saw where I was. The earthquake struck again and I opened my eyes.

The source of my dreamquake was Mom. She was shaking me with a voice and a facial expression that shot me instantly awake.

'What's wrong, Mom?' I asked but I didn't have to. My dream had told me all I needed to know.

'He's gone,' she said.

Chapter Thirty-Two
The Twins of Macha

The sunrise was beautiful from dragon-back but I hardly noticed. All I could think about was Dad. It was madness that he had gone off to fight Cialtie by himself. He had apparently slipped out not long after the non-battle. He wrote a note and gave it to a guard instructing him not to give it to Mom until morning. The note said what he intended to do, duel his brother, but it didn't say where. I knew. My dream filled in that missing piece.

This had to be a trap. What possessed Dad to just walk into a fight with his brother, I couldn't imagine. Cialtie couldn't be trusted – Dad of all people knows that.

My flight wasn't a long one but my mind was spinning back in time to cold winter mornings when I was a kid and Dad would make me cinnamon toast and hot chocolate. I remembered him biting into his toast, smiling and saying, 'They didn't have cinnamon when I was a boy.' I promised myself that when I went back to the Real World to get Ruby I would get Dad some cinnamon.

I frowned, remembering my behaviour as he forced me to learn dead languages. I felt goose bumps as I remembered him lifting the Sword of Duir high over the walls of Castle Duir. I started remembering the things he had said to me but I didn't recall them all. For instance, I didn't recollect him saying, 'Don't fly Dragon

Tuan over Cialtie or his army, I'm sure by now he has come up with some sort of anti-dragon weapon.' As usual Dad was right.

I don't know what hit us but Tuan folded his wings, dropped his head and went into a kamikaze nose dive. I kicked and shouted at him but he was out cold. I wrapped the reins around my yew staff and tried to slow the monster's fall. I could hear my yew staff threatening to crack but it was working. I was actually slowing our descent – still the ground was coming at us faster than I would have liked. Finally it was the reins that couldn't take the strain. They snapped and my stick kicked up and slammed into my chin. That is all I remember.

'You are awake, oh my, I was worried about you.'

I hadn't opened my eyes but the person who was talking to me didn't need to see me to know my brain was working again. *Mother Oak?* I thought.

'You have been in a fall, young Conor. I was worried you would never wake up.'

I tried to move and found that I couldn't. My first thought was that I had hurt my spine but as I opened my eyes I saw that I was tied to a tree – to Mother Oak. I was sitting on the ground with my back to her trunk. A rope, entwined with fine gold wire, went across my chest and under my armpits. It made it hard to breathe. I reached up to see if I could push the rope down and maybe shimmy out but pain shot through my body when I tried to move my left arm. Little white dots swam in front of my vision as I almost blacked out. My left arm was definitely broken and I think my left leg too. I tried to push down on the rope with my right hand but the rope seemed to know I was trying to escape and tightened until I couldn't breathe. I gave up and the rope actually cut me a little slack.

Can you get me out of this? I thought to Mother Oak.

'*Oh my poor sweet prince, if only I could.*'

My uncle tied me here didn't he?

'*Yes,*' came the tree's answer in my brain and I could feel the contempt she had for Cialtie. It was the first time I had ever felt anything but sweetness from the family tree.

Do you know where Tuan is?

'*The Pooka is on the other side of the glen where you crashed. I do not know his health but he is breathing.*'

That's good. Is my father here?

'*No, should Oisin be here?*'

He came to fight Cialtie.

'*Oh my, my, this is such an awful thing. The sons of Macha fighting.*' Then Mother Oak did what I can only describe as the tree equivalent of a sigh. '*But dear me, I would not be completely honest if I said I am surprised.*'

I tried to reach to my sock for my throwing knife but that was gone.

'*Your uncle took your knife, young one. He leaned you against my trunk and then simply threw the rope that holds you. It seemed to tie itself. I think it is Brownie-made.*'

Did you speak to him?

'*No, he knows better than to talk to me. I'd give him a piece of my mind, I would.*'

Despite my pain and my dire situation, I had to smile at the old tree's feistiness.

'*He is here,*' Mother Oak almost whispered in my head.

Who?

'Nephew,' came the slimy salutation that answered my question.

'Where is Tuan?'

Cialtie shook his head. 'What happened to, "Hello Uncle, it is good to see you again"? When the young forget their manners it is the beginning of the end of civilisation. But, if you must know, your Pooka flying horse woke up in considerable pain and I put him out of his misery.'

'What did you do to him?'

'Relax,' Cialtie said, 'I simply placed a sleeping coin under his head. I won't kill him unless I have to. It would be handy having a dragon for a pet.'

'Tuan will never be your pet.'

'OK,' Cialtie sighed. 'I'll kill him then – but not yet. There is a queue and you will be happy to know that you are in it. But first in the queue is your father. Where is he?'

'I was about to ask you that.'

'Oh, I see. I told your daddy that I was going to chop down Mother Tree here if he didn't face me. Let me guess, he didn't tell you he was coming and when you found what he was up to, you hopped on a dragon and beat him here?' Cialtie laughed. 'Oh, that's good. Is anyone else coming?'

I didn't answer.

'That's a maldar rope you're tied with. The Brownies use it for torture.' Cialtie whistled and the rope around my chest tightened. 'I can make you answer.'

The pressure on my chest made it hard to breathe. I replied, 'No', even though I was sure Mom was on her way.

'You are lying,' Cialtie said then he whistled again this time in a lower tone and the rope slackened. 'No matter. Any help leaving Duir on horseback will arrive long after this is done.'

'My father will kill you. You know that's what's going to happen. Ona predicted it. You of all people should know you can't thwart Ona's predictions.'

Cialtie turned on me with such fury that I was sure I had just moved up to the premier spot in his queue. 'Do not presume to lecture me on Ona's prophecies. This is the last prediction; there is none after this. You are right that Ona's predictions cannot be thwarted but there are none to follow this. This prediction can last for ever and all I have to do is rid The Land of the holders of the Duir Runes. With you and your father dead the Banshees will return, and since I will hold the only Duir Rune, the Runelords will be forced to accept me on the Oak Throne. The age of Ona's predictions will last for ever.'

'Let Conor go,' I heard Dad shout as he rode in to the field. 'He has nothing to do with this.'

'Hello brother.' Cialtie spun and drew his sword. 'He has everything to do with this. After I killed you, my plan was to track and kill Conor. It is so much more convenient that he is here. Now get down and let us commence.'

Dad dismounted and slowly drew the Lawnmower.

'I was foolish losing the Sword of Duir,' Cialtie said, 'I so wished to kill you with that blade. You wouldn't lend it to me now, would you?'

In reply Dad adopted an *en garde* position. If this was a fencing match he would have then saluted his opponent, but I had a feeling these guys were going to skip the niceties.

'Do you remember our last swordfight, brother?' Cialtie asked as he turned sideways and extended his sword with his left hand. Thanks to me it was the only one he had. His blade was thinner than the Lawnmower, just like in my dream.

'I do,' Dad said as he advanced on his brother. It wasn't a serious attack, just a preliminary thrust followed by Cialtie's backhanded parry. It was Dad's way of saying, 'Let's get this done.'

'I remember our father,' Cialtie paused and thought, 'or should I say your father, stopped the match before I killed you. Shame – imagine all of the trouble we could have avoided.'

'Is that why you killed him?' Dad said, attacking with a downward sweep that his brother easily deflected to the left.

'Are you still annoyed I killed your father? You just killed mine. I say we are even.' Cialtie threw himself at Dad with a ferocious attack that took him by surprise. He parried, back-pedalled and then stumbled but kept his footing. If I was Cialtie I would have followed it up with another attack but my uncle just stopped and laughed. Was he that confident or was it something else? Was he just past caring?

Dad again looked to me and said, 'Let the boy go.'

'No,' Cialtie replied as he wiped his nose with the stump of his right hand. Then he extended the hand-less arm to me. Around his wrist he wore a tight silver band. 'Even if he leaves here alive he is not leaving with his runehand. Isn't that the law in the Real World – an eye for an eye?'

Dad kinda lost it then. Dahy had always warned us about letting emotions cloud our fighting but I have always found that a little bit of old-fashioned rage can come in handy as long as you don't let your defences down. Dad came at his brother with a series of savage sweeping attacks alternating left and right. He even performed a full pirouette that brought with it 360 degrees of force. Cialtie went down blocking that one but quickly rolled. He was on one knee when Dad came at him with a sledge-hammer attack. Cialtie blocked it above his head and their pommels locked.

'Your fight is with me,' Dad grunted

'Everything is about you, isn't it?' Cialtie said. The strain of his defence showed in his voice.

That's when I saw Cialtie extend his arm. He turned his wrist back and forth. Since he had no hand, I at first didn't recognise the gesture but then it hit me. I shouted, 'Dad, watch out, he has a Banshee blade.'

A short blade shot out and hooked on the band that encircled Cialtie's stump. Dad took no time backing off and luckily wasn't there when the blade sliced through the space he had just occupied.

The sons of Macha, panting, once again faced off.

'If you had come to me earlier, Cialtie, we could have worked something out.'

'You don't get it, do you, brother?' Cialtie said. 'I am not fighting you – I am fighting Ona. I have been Ona's puppet since I was born. There is nothing you or anyone could have done. This now is the only chance I have at a life.'

'I feel sorry for you, brother, I really do, but I can't let you win.'

Dad called up to the tree. 'Mother Oak, can I have a banta stick?'

Above I heard the familiar sound of water being drawn from wood. A perfect fighting-stick-sized branch fell just behind Dad. He picked it up and quickly shaved off the dead small twigs that stuck out from the side.

Sword and sword vs. sword and stick – I remembered Dahy putting me through this muscle-aching drill. I also remembered thinking why do I need to learn that – when will this ever happen? As usual Master Dahy was right.

Cialtie didn't seem as confident as he had been before. Dad performed stuff right out of Dahy's drill book. Anything Cialtie tried was countered like Dad knew it was coming. But then Dad let his left hand drop. Cialtie came around with a full swing of his Banshee blade just as Dad brought the stick up to block. The blade stuck into the wood. Dad pulled the blade down and then kicked Cialtie in the wrist. The Banshee blade broke free from the silver cuff and then with another tug Dad snapped the gold wire that rode up my uncle's sleeve. Dad threw the stick, with the Banshee blade still attached, away and it was sword vs. sword again.

'When I took my Choosing,' Dad said, 'this is what I saw.'

'Fascinating,' Cialtie said. 'How did it end?'

Dad launched himself at his brother, shouting, 'Not well!'

I was forced to watch the sons of Macha do battle and with every thrust and parry I strained my muscles against my bonds. I watched as the man who made me sword-fight with him every week before he gave me my pocket money fought for his life. In my mind's eye I saw us sword-fighting in the backyard and sometimes in the living room and I watched him use the same techniques and tricks he taught me.

The good thing was that Dad was in great shape. Not just because of the dragon blood youth tonic but he had also been practising his swordsmanship. When he first became young again he would draw on me almost every time he saw me. When I finally impressed on him how annoying that was, he started sparring with the young castle guards who couldn't really complain about their king. Dad and Dahy still squared off periodically. The result was that Dad was a better swordsman than Cialtie and it was beginning to show. Cialtie was back-pedalling with every parry. Dad manoeuvred his opponent onto a downward slope. That was Dahy's rule number three – find the high ground.

Dad was now battling like a man possessed. Cialtie successfully turned and got the fight onto even ground and once again the swordsmen locked pommels.

'You never studied with Dahy, did you, brother?'

'I've always hated that pompous blowhard,' Cialtie said.

'I thought not,' Dad said, disengaging.

That's when Dad started an attack I was very familiar with. He came at his brother with a high downward swipe. Cialtie parried it off to his right – exactly as Dad expected. Then Dad did the move he always called, The Dahy. His sword kept going to the right. Cialtie fell for the fake. His eyes followed the blade when they should have been looking at the arm. Dad clocked him high in the cheek with his elbow and Cialtie went down. He raised his sword while lying on his back but Dad swatted it out of his hand.

If Cialtie was expecting mercy from his brother, he was mistaken. The time for mercy was over. Dad placed both hands on the hilt of the Lawnmower and came down on Cialtie like he was going to split him in half. Cialtie raised his right arm and the blade slammed into his stump and then notched into the silver cuff that encircled his wrist. Blood shot from his stump as Cialtie let out a painful grunt – then he whistled twice. The rope around my chest tightened with such a force that I screamed. Dad turned to look at me and that was all the distraction Cialtie needed. Life slowed down as I tried to warn Dad but the rope made it so I couldn't even catch a breath. When Dad's eyes turned back at his brother he saw him holding a knife. Before he could even react, Cialtie pushed the blade into Dad's chest.

I had been fighting the pressure on my ribs but when I saw that I shouted, 'NO!' As the air left my lungs the rope took up the slack and blackness crept into my peripheral vision. The last thing I heard, or should I say felt, was Mother Oak in my head saying, *'Oh no, not Oisin.'*

Chapter Thirty-Three
Mother Oak

For the second time today I came to from unconsciousness without opening my eyes. This time I didn't want to see what was out there. *Make it a dream*, I said to myself, *make it a dream. Let me open my eyes and see my father sitting on the edge of my bed brushing the hair out of my eyes.*

But the chest pain that came with every breath proved to me that this was real. I touched the rough bark at my back to see if Mother Oak was still there. She was and she was … she was crying.

I opened my eyes as leaves fell around me and saw Dad face down on the grass. His chest was tilted up at a strange angle because of the knife still sticking out of it. Another pain hit me in the chest and this pain had nothing to do with the Brownie rope. *Daddy.*

'Conor, be sharp,' Mother Oak shouted into my head. 'He comes.'

Cialtie staggered into my vision. His right sleeve was torn off and wrapped around his bleeding stump. He plopped down on the ground cross-legged in front of me like he was drunk. Then he leaned in and said, 'Tears for your father, good.'

'You bastard,' I said without looking at him – I couldn't.

'I've been a bastard since the day I was born, nephew, but I was genuine when I said your tears were good. He was a man worthy of tears.'

I looked up and saw tears in Cialtie's eyes. It's a rare thing to see a grown man cry but my uncle's crocodile tears didn't induce any sympathy in me. 'Go to hell,' I said to his face.

'Hell is where I have been,' he replied, standing. 'I have been in a living hell every day since I read Ona's prophecies. I have been marching to the rhythm of her maddening tin drum all of my life.'

'Oh shut up,' I shouted. 'I am so tired of your "this isn't my fault" speech. Save it for someone who doesn't know you.'

'I thought you at least would understand.'

'Oh I understand, Cialtie – I understand that you are an idiot as well as a sadistic bastard. You think because something is written it's done. Well, give me a pen and I'll write – Drop Dead. You did what you did. No one made you do anything. You killed your brother, my father – you. Your son ran to you and instead of hugging him – you chose to stab him – you. I was there. There was no one behind you. You killed Fergal – you. So go peddle your sob story somewhere else.'

'I had hoped to avoid this, nephew. I know you don't believe me but I don't want to kill you. I was saddened when I heard you took your Choosing. I was hoping just to take your runehand but now that you hold a Duir Rune I must kill you. Then I will finally be king, finally be safe.'

I laughed then, or at least I think it was a laugh. I was such a mess of emotions; if you were looking at me I don't know what you would have thought I was doing.

'I'm surprised you find that funny,' Cialtie said.

'You really are an idiot,' I said as I reached in to a small pocket on the side of my tunic. Cialtie raised his sword and stepped back but when he saw what was in my hand he stopped dead in his tracks.

You see, almost immediately after I completed my Choosing all hell broke loose and I never had the chance to talk to anybody about what happened. Since everyone assumed I would pick Duir and inherit the Oak Throne, nobody asked to see my new rune. I hadn't even told Dad. I was worried he was going to be disappointed, so I was waiting for a quiet moment alone to tell him but I never had the chance and now I never will.

I held up my new rune for Cialtie to see. On it was engraved the major symbol of – Cull. 'I'm not the new king – you are,' I said. 'I'm the new Lord of the Hazellands.' I thought of what Dad would have said to that. After the disappointment, he would have laughed at the thought of me being the new Dean of the Hall of Knowledge. I tried to laugh, too, but couldn't.

'You chose Cull?' Cialtie said, stepping forward for a closer look.

'Yes.'

'Then … then I am king.'

'Don't expect me to bow.'

'I'm safe. It is … it is over.'

I held out the rune. He sheathed his sword and came towards me to take it. I don't know what possessed me to do what I did. It might have been some sort of subliminal message from Mother Oak but I think it was just me remembering what she had said earlier about giving Cialtie '*a piece of my mind*'. All I know is that at that moment I needed Cialtie to talk with the family tree. As he reached for my rune I dropped it, grabbed my uncle's wrist and pushed it against Mother Oak's trunk. Both he and I stuck to the bark like we were steel touching an electromagnet.

I recognised the sensation instantly. It was identical to the attack of the oak tree at the perimeter of Castle Duir. The difference was that this time the attention was not directed at me. This time the guy in the hot seat was Cialtie.

The first thing I saw was the circular tree amulet. I had seen a template of it made in silver but I had never seen the one made of gold, the one that was used to obliterate a town. I had watched Cialtie place it on the stump of a tree he had just chopped down. In the centre he placed a small glass bottle, and stopped inside the bottle was a moth. Then he hopped on his horse and galloped out of there. Mother Oak's vision showed both of us what no one had ever seen – no one who lived, that is. Cialtie's amulet bomb went off and the destruction rippled out from the stump. The eerie thing about it was the sound – except for the crashing stones and the screaming people it was silent, even though it looked just like a shot from one of those ground-zero cameras at atomic blasts. It was hard to watch, no … not just hard, it was almost impossible. Admittedly these images were horrible but I was feeling them at a gut level that … I don't know how to describe it. It was so intense, I wasn't sure I could stand it. I screamed and then I heard Mother Oak in my head say, *'Oh I'm so sorry dear, that was not meant for you.'* Swiftly the overpowering intensity lifted. The vision was still forced on me and it was still tough to watch but I was saved the gut-churning emotional power – Cialtie was not.

The destruction of the village of More was followed by Cialtie's seduction of Mná, the Banshee sorceress who became Fergal's mother. I watched with nausea as Cialtie purred while he lied to the poor girl. He promised her he loved her – he promised her she would be his queen. Then I had to watch as her screams of labour were cut short by Cialtie beheading her.

Next came a string of murders: the cowardly attack on my grandfather's horse as he stepped through the portal to the Real World, Ona being smothered by a pillow, the killing of four striking Leprechaun miners as an example to the others.

Then I saw something that really surprised me. A Banshee carrying Dad's severed runehand through the Choosing. Cialtie had been too cowardly to attempt that himself so he promised the Banshee great riches for the attempt. When he succeeded in getting a Duir Rune he was rewarded only with death.

Hundreds of indecencies ranging from rudeness to inflicting debilitating pain flashed by, each one painting a portrait of a poisonous life. In the end Mother Oak did to Cialtie what the oak at Castle Duir had done to me. She showed him what his life could have been like if instead of killing Fergal he had accepted him. She showed a Cialtie walking along a beach with his boy. She showed him hugs and handmade presents and bedtime stories. She made him feel the joy of parenting, the swell of pride, the unconditional love. Then she showed him the truth. I heard Cialtie moan as he relived the stabbing of his son. I moaned with him as I again watched the blade enter Fergal's chest.

'You could have stopped all of this at any time,' Mother Oak said. *'Shame. Shame on you.'*

Mother Oak let us go. I almost blacked out from the emotional roller-coaster I had just been through. Then a sharp pain shot through my broken arm as the Brownie rope was ripped away from me and the tree. I was free. I tried to stand but found out, by falling, that my leg was definitely broken. I fell on my broken arm and once again my brain threatened unconsciousness. I looked across the field and saw the Sword of Duir lying about twenty-five feet away. I looked to Cialtie – he was down on his knees with his face buried in his hands. I started to crawl; it was agonisingly slow and painful. I didn't dare look behind me. I knew as soon as he saw what I was doing I was a goner. I finally got my hand on the pommel and turned to defend myself. I didn't need to.

What I saw was my uncle throwing the end of the Brownie rope up into Mother Oak where it attached to one of her higher boughs. Then he wrapped the other end around his neck and simply said, 'I'm sorry.' He whistled twice and the rope instantly halved in length, breaking his neck with an audible snap. I watched him twitch for a few seconds then slowly swing in the breeze.

Cialtie was wrong. The age of Ona wasn't meant to last for ever. It was meant to end today. Ona's final prediction finally came true. It was written that Cialtie would be killed by the Lord of Duir. The day Cialtie became king was the day he killed himself. We were finally free of Cialtie and Ona – but at what cost?

I crawled over to Dad and pushed him over onto his back. I pulled the knife out of his chest. It wasn't one of Dahy's knives – it was mine. 'Oh Dad, I'm so sorry,' I said as I dropped my head on his chest. A sob sent so much pain through my body I don't remember much after that.

I remember waking up still in the field and Mom was next to me. That was nice. She asked me what had happened and I told her in a dopey matter-of-fact way like it was some TV show I had seen years ago. It felt a lot like that time I killed that guy in the Fililands – my lights were on but nobody was home.

Next thing I remember I was under bedclothes in the infirmary. It was dark and I wondered where I was. A failed attempt to sit up made me realise that my arm and leg were encased in splints. I wondered what had happened to me. Did I fall out of a tree? I looked to my left and saw Tuan in the bed next to me. I was with Tuan, wasn't I? We crashed … Where were we going? Then the memory of the events in Glen Duir flooded back.

'Dad,' I said aloud.

Grief is a leash. I remembered this feeling after Fergal died. My thoughts would drift to the mundane things, the normal stuff of life: idle chat, food or laughter – then I would remember and the leash would stretch taut like a dog in the yard being pulled back by the neck – a crushing sadness and loss would snap me back into that place where my stomach would hurt and laughter was a foreign language. I knew from experience that the leash would grow longer each day but at that moment I found it hard to imagine life with idle anything.

The Imp-healer, the one that Graysea called the Prison Guard, shot up from her night duty desk and came over to me. She lifted up my head and held a shot glass of liquid to my lips. I didn't protest.

As I drifted off to what I hoped was dreamless sleep she brushed the hair from my eyes and said, 'I'm so sorry, Prince Conor.'

The next time I awoke it was daylight. I saw that Graysea was in the bed next to me. Her beautiful innocent face made me smile before the leash of grief snapped my mind back to reality. I gasped and she turned to me.

'Hi Conor, how are you feeling?' she asked.

Grief and pain are cousins to anger. A tiny demon in my brain wanted to yell at her and say, 'How do you think I feel, you stupid trout', but I remembered this from last time as well and I knew that misdirected anger only made things worse. I forced a comforting smile. 'Like I fell off a flying dragon.'

I sat up and saw that Tuan was in the bed to my right. 'How is the dragon?'

'He'll be OK,' she said. 'He broke a few more things than you, though. Your mom gave him something. He's going to be like that for a while.'

'As long as he's going to be OK. I don't think I could stand another …' I couldn't finish that sentence. My brave face was going to need some work. I turned away.

'Oh, you poor sweet thing,' Graysea said as she hopped over to my bed and hugged me. While I wept on her shoulder I was hardly aware of being transferred into another embrace. When I looked up bleary eyed, Essa was looking down at me.

'Oh Conor, I'm so sorry about your father,' she said.

We wept some more – she loved Oisin too.

There would be more tears later but when I finally got control of myself Araf was there with a pot of willow tea.

'Araf hasn't left your side since you were brought in here, except to get the tea,' Graysea said.

'Yeah,' I said, 'you mean he hasn't left *your* side.'

The two of them blushed.

Essa picked up the Cull Rune that was sitting on my bedside table. 'Your mother tells me that this is yours.'

'I'm afraid so,' I said. 'The Prince of Hazel and Oak is now Lord of the Hazellands.'

'I'm not sure what to say,' she said, and then laughed a little. 'Sorry.'

'No, no, I'm there with you, Essa. This is ridiculous.'

'It is not ridiculous, it is … just right,' Mom said.

'Hi Mom.'

'Hello son.'

We locked eyes and I knew what her look meant. 'Later,' it said clearer than any words. 'Later we will grieve but now I must be strong or else I won't be able to go on.'

I clenched my jaw and nodded to her and she nodded back.

'I always thought there was more hazel in you than oak,' she said.

Mom sat on the edge of Tuan's bed and placed her hands on both sides of his head. The Pooka blinked and then opened his eyes. He looked scared but Mom shushed him and told him everything was all right. The Prison Guard helped him sit up. It looked like it hurt – a lot.

When he was settled I said, 'How's it going, Councillor Tuan?'

Tuan tried to turn but it hurt too much. 'Is that you, Prince Conor?'

'It is.'

'No more dragon rides for you.'

'Fair enough,' I said.

Tuan started to cough and it looked like it hurt. The Imp-healer gave him something to drink that brought the colour back to his face, then she sat on the side of his bed and held his hand.

I stared at both of them. 'You and the Prison Guard?'

They both smiled at each other and Tuan shrugged.

I heard the tapping long before I saw the girl. Ruby came around the corner in high-speed mode, which meant she was thrashing her stick back and forth and people were diving out of her way.

'Where are you?'

'I'm here, Ruby.'

She came up to the side of the bed and then hopped on, making me gasp quite loudly.

'Careful, I broke my leg.'

'Oops, sorry. Why don't you get your mermaid girlfriend to fix it?'

'She won't let me,' Graysea said, pointing to the Prison Guard. 'And I'm not his girlfriend any more.'

'He dumped you for the princess, huh?'

'Ruby,' Brendan admonished as he rounded the corner.

'That was rude of me?' she asked from under her huge sunglasses.

Her dad said, 'Yes.'

'Sorry.'

'That's OK, Ruby.' Then Graysea leaned down and whispered, 'For the record, I dumped him.'

Ruby turned to me with a huge smile on her face and said, 'Ha ha.'

'Ruby,' her dad said again.

'Sorry,' the young girl said, but we all knew she wasn't.

'How was your stay in Connemara?'

She wrinkled her nose. 'It rained a lot and the food wasn't as good as here but Mícheál and his wife were nice. They taught me to play dominoes. But I'm glad to be back with Daddy and Grandma.'

'Well, I'm glad you're back. Shall we go for a pony ride when I get better?'

'No trees, though,' she said.

'No trees.'

Brendan picked her off my bed and she swiped her way out of the room.

'Sorry about Oisin,' Brendan said.

My chest was completely black and blue from the Brownie rope but it didn't hurt near as much as when people mentioned Dad. 'Thanks.'

'Who went to Ireland and got Ruby?'

'Nieve and I.'

'Did you get another Guinness?'

'Na. Considering I'm a wanted fugitive I decided against going to a pub and anyway, Nieve had to stay on a horse.'

'Fair enough.'

On cue Nieve came around the corner. She sat on the edge of my bed and took my hand in both of hers. Her eyes were awash with tears.

'You OK, Auntie?'

'I am not sure I know what *OK* means. I lost two of my brothers, I am the last of my generation and the only family I have left is you. OK is one of those strange words that you have brought from the Real World but if I understand it correctly – I am OK as long as I still have you.'

I couldn't actually make words right then but I vigorously nodded yes and we held each other for a time.

Over my aunt's shoulder I saw Dahy standing at the door. He looked … worried and old – not his usual confident and commanding presence. I waved and said, 'I'm OK, Dahy.'

'Good,' he said lowering his head again and left.

'So,' Brendan said when the leash of grief loosened a bit, 'what are you going to do now?'

'I don't know,' I said. 'I guess I have to build another dolman.'

Chapter Thirty-Four

A Wave

We buried Dad next to Fergal. Gerard sang a dirge and Mom spoke. She talked about meeting Dad at one of Gerard's parties. She admitted that she first fell in love with him when she saw him dance.

Oisin dancing? We were talking about the same guy? Dad dancing, now that's something I'd pay good money to see. But then, as would happen so often for so long, I was stabbed by the reality that never again would I get the chance to see Dad do anything.

I had been asked if I wanted to speak but I said no, I didn't think I could do it. Mom kept up her stoic face through the whole ceremony. Some may have thought she was being incredibly strong but to me she looked like a violin string about to snap.

When it was over, a bunch of burly Leprechauns lifted a capstone up onto two standing stones just like we had for Fergal. When it was done I picked up a pebble and threw it on top of Dad's dolman, and said, 'Goodbye Dad.'

I chose a pebble and handed it to Mom. She looked at it in her hand for a long time until tears dotted the small stone. 'I only just got him back,' she said. Then she threw the pebble onto her husband's monument and collapsed onto my shoulder weeping.

Fand and I got Mom into bed. The Fili Queen convinced her to take a dram of potcheen and she fell into her first proper sleep since the war ended.

'You could probably use a shot yourself,' I said to Fand. 'How are you holding up?'

'Grief, young Conor, is an emotion in which I am well versed. It is a wave that ebbs up and down – and like a wave over time, it diminishes in intensity until – calm. To answer your question, how would you say it? I'm doin' OK.' She smiled and placed her hand on my cheek. 'And you?'

'I wouldn't say I'm OK,' I said, turning away.

Fand placed her hand on my shoulder and said, 'Grief is a wound like any other. And like other wounds, healing takes time. We are fortunate here in The Land to have a surplus of time. Today, tomorrow seems far away but in some future tomorrow you will find peace. May I give you one piece of advice, Lord Conor?'

'Please,' I said.

'There is only one salve I know of that speeds the healing of this particular wound. That salve is forgiveness.'

I wanted to ask her what she meant but in that Fili ninja mystical way, she was almost out the door before I opened my mouth.

That night I had a strange triple date. Essa and I had dinner with Araf and Graysea, and Brendan and Nieve.

I told Nieve what Fand had said and asked her if she could forgive Cialtie.

'I think of Cialtie when he was my baby brother,' Nieve said. 'When I remember him like that it is easy to forgive him. I refuse to believe that my brother was born bad. I know how Ona's writings can push one into bad actions. I almost killed you, Conor, because of them.'

'Ah, water under the bridge, Auntie,' I said with a Fergalish smile.

She tried to return the smile but the weight of her thoughts thwarted her. 'My baby brothers fought and I have lost them both. My sorrow allows no room for hate.'

Brendan put his arm around her and she leant her head on his shoulder. The subject was changed by, of all people, Araf. 'Graysea and I are taking a trip to Mertain Island. I want to talk to the Mertain King about unbanishing Graysea.'

'Wow, that's a big trip. Don't you think you should learn to swim first?'

Graysea turned to Araf. 'You don't know how to swim?'

Araf hemmed and hawed but no actual words came out of his mouth. He did succeed in giving me a look that made me think I was going to get clubbed with a banta next time we were alone.

Believe it or not, I was up before the sun the next morning. I made a pot of tea and knocked on Macha's door. She answered faster than I expected. She was wearing a dressing gown.

'Did I wake you?' I asked.

'Sleep, Conor, has not been my companion as of late. What is this on the tray?'

I cleared my throat and said, 'Grandma, would you like to have tea with me this morning?'

I don't think she would have been more shocked if I had slapped her. 'Yes … Thank you, please come in.'

Her prison was a comfortable room in the east wing. The windows were barred and she had two guards at the door but it was a far cry from the dungeon I initially wished on her. She made space on a coffee table. When she asked me to sit I saw there was only one chair.

'I suppose they assumed I would not be having guests.'

I walked to the door and asked the guard if I could have his chair. He wanted to get me a fancier one but I assured him that his was OK. I returned and sat across from the woman who bore my father. She had poured two cups already and was tasting hers.

'This is lovely, what is it?'

'It's a Pooka blend. Queen Rhiannon sent it to me.'

She sipped some more and a faraway look washed over her face. 'I have never seen the Pookalands. I suppose now I never will. I cannot imagine I will ever be welcome anywhere again.'

I wanted to reassure her, tell her that she was being silly but I couldn't, she was probably right.

'I can't imagine anyone being kind to me ever again after what I have done. You, Conor, here, and with tea, is a shock.'

'Fand told me I should work on my forgiveness.'

'The apple has fallen far from the tree with that one.'

'Yeah, Fand is great. Saying that, her mother did a noble thing in the end.'

'You think killing one's self is noble?' Macha asked.

'I'm not sure about that but I do know that continuing the way she was going would have been wrong.'

'What is right and what is wrong is in the purview of the victors.'

'I've heard that before and I don't buy it. I think right and wrong is easier than that. I watched Maeve rip out a man's heart. Some things are just plain wrong.'

'Like kidnapping a young girl?'

My instinct was to reply, 'Yes', but I bit my tongue. 'I didn't come here to judge.'

'Why are you here, Conor?'

'I thought you might like to visit your sons' graves.'

I picked up a pebble and threw it on top of Fergal's dolman.

'Is that Cialtie's grave?' Macha asked.

'No, that's Cialtie's son's … your grandson. His name was Fergal.'

There was an awkward moment with neither of us knowing what to say. The uncomfortable silence was broken by a voice behind us.

'Hello Mother.'

Macha turned and was stunned to see her daughter holding a wooden box. Then she dropped her gaze and said, 'Nieve.'

Nieve stepped up to her mother and kissed her on the cheek. Macha tensed up like she was expecting a blow. There was history between these two women that existed long before recent events. 'I too, Mother,' Nieve said, 'am working on my forgiveness.'

Macha said nothing but her eyes filled up.

We walked over to a corner of the courtyard where a hole had been dug. Nieve opened the lid on her box and said, 'This is what is left of Cialtie.'

Cialtie's body had been cremated. Mom thought his ashes should be scattered, but after talking with Fand, Nieve argued that regardless of what we thought of him he did at one time sit on the Oak Throne and should be buried in Castle Duir. Mom acquiesced and we all agreed that maybe we should keep the grave unmarked until tempers cooled down.

Macha reached into the box and then placed a handful of the dust that was once her son into the grave. 'Goodbye, my Cialtie.'

Nieve poured in the rest of the remains and then left after I finished shovelling the dirt back into the hole.

As I walked my grandmother back to the castle, I threw a stone on top of Dad's dolman.

'Why do you do that?' Macha asked.

'It's what they do in Ireland. I do it just as a way of remembering.'

Macha picked up a pebble and said, 'Goodbye, my Oisin.'
Then she threw the stone and missed. She placed her hand in front
of her mouth trying to hide the flood of emotions but then
succumbed to them. She plopped down on the path cross-legged
like a little girl.

I didn't know what to do. I sat down across from her and took
her hand in mine. When she finally looked at me her face was
streaked with tears. I don't think I had ever seen a more wretched
face on a woman.

'I have been a failure as a mother.'

Again my immediate instinct was to say, 'No', but that would
have been a lie.

'I was a failure as a wife and a queen.' She placed her hand
tenderly on my cheek, 'And as a grandmother. I have wasted my
life loving the wrong men and now they are all dead because of
me.' Then she dropped her chin onto her chest and said in a voice
so low I almost didn't hear, 'Except Dahy, and he cannot even look
at me.'

'You know Dad said something to me that I am using at the
moment. He said, "No matter how dark things become, eventually they do get better."'

She looked me in the eyes and forced a smile. 'You are a good
boy, Conor. You and my daughter have been kind to me but I do
not believe there will be many more so forgiving … And who can
blame them.' She dropped her head again and said, 'The Pookas
think that when we die we are reborn. Maybe next time I can be
… good.'

'What are you talking about?'

'I would like you to find someone who could escort
me to Thunder Bay. I would like to sail off into the great
unknown.'

Helping someone kill themselves went against everything the
mortal me believed in, but here we were immortals and the only

option for death was sailing out to sea. To sail past the vitalising power that was The Land. I didn't know what to say. Luckily, I didn't have to say anything.

'I will take you, Macha,' Dahy said. He was standing off to our left. I suspect he had been watching us ever since I escorted Macha from her room.

Macha's head snapped towards the old master. She quickly stood and brushed her dress flat and wiped her eyes. 'That is very kind of you, Diddo,' she said.

The days passed like Fand warned me they would. Some were good and some were bad. Mom dragged me out for regal duties when some visiting Runelord appeared. It made my heart ache when I instinctively turned to smile with Dad only to find the Oak Throne empty.

Eventually the Runelords ordered a meet to discuss the House of Duir. It was decided that since no one held an Oak Rune that Castle Duir should be queened by Mom. It was not a unanimous vote. Some objected to someone from the House of Cull controlling the gold stipend but most of the Lords realised that without a rune the Leprechauns wouldn't follow anyone except their warrior queen. I was just glad nobody tried to foist the job on me.

After the meeting Mom and I were left alone in the Throne Room. She looked tired and I pointed to the Oak Throne and said, 'Well, my Queen, why don't you have a seat?'

Mom sat down on the dais steps and said, 'No, that is your father's chair. I'm only here stopping this place from crashing into chaos until someone chooses the Duir Rune. I suspect it won't be long. Master Eirnin told me that half of the un-runed Faeries in The Land have booked Choosing classes with him.'

'Rather them than me,' I said and sat next to her. 'Well, I think you're a great queen.' I raised an imaginary glass and toasted, 'May ye reign for ever.'

'Oh gods no, Conor,' she said placing her head on my shoulder and wrapping her arm around mine. 'I do not want this job for ever. I'm only doing this because Oisin would have wanted me to. If I had my choice I would lose myself in the Fililands. I would go someplace where I wasn't reminded of your father at every corner.'

'Dad always said, "Things do get better."'

'He also said he would never leave me and now he has left me twice.' She tried to smile with that line but failed. 'I hope someone chooses an Oak Rune soon – so I can maybe come and join you.'

'Me?' I said. 'Where am I going?'

She stood, placed her hands on her hips and put on her Queen Deirdre face. 'You, young man, have a kingdom to rule.'

I slouched on my step. 'Aw, Mom.'

Chapter Thirty-Five

Beginnings

You would think that since marriages around here have the potential to last centuries that the service would be longer than five minutes. Like some ceremony from America's old west, the Tir na Nogian wedding vows are practically, 'Take him? Take her? You're hitched.'

Not that I'm complaining. The faster the ceremony then the sooner we could start with the reception party. And since the reception was being thrown by the father of the bride and The Land's best party thrower, Gerard, then all of that 'Till death do us part,' stuff is something to get through quickly.

Yes, Essa and I got married. Hell, if attempted homicides, Banshee fiancés, Mermaids and even wars couldn't keep us apart then we figured – why fight it any more?

Gerard cracked open the wine that he had been saving since Essa was in the womb and we all had the most amazing vinous experience of our lives.

I wouldn't say it was a typical wedding. My best man, Araf, had a banta stick fight with my beautiful bride and beat her. Tuan got very drunk and started running and barking in his wolfhound mode. When he bit one of the guests, Graysea had to be called in to use her fish power to sober him up before he turned into a sloshed dragon and burned the place down. Jesse's Brownie entourage was caught stealing the Nikes that the Connemara Druids had bought me as a wedding present. I had the Brownies locked in a dungeon.

The only one missing was Dahy. He had escorted Macha to Thunder Bay a week earlier. I had hoped he would be back. When I mentioned it to Brendan he said something that sent a chill down my spine. He said he got the impression that Dahy was going to sail out to sea with her. Gods, I hoped not. I couldn't lose Dahy too.

Gerard caught me before the night ended and asked me if I wanted a beer.

'No thanks,' I said, 'I never thought I would say this but this wine is better than any beer.'

Gerard bowed a low bow and said, 'That is high praise indeed, Lord of the Hazellands.' Then he wrapped his huge arms around me and applied one of his anaconda-like hugs that lifted me off the ground and threatened to permanently damage my respiratory system. He released me but still held me at arm's length. 'I always wanted a son,' he said, his eyes getting misty, 'and you have just lost a father. No man can ever replace Oisin. Your father was a great man, Conor. But know this – I will always be here for you.'

This time it was my turn to mist up and attack *him* with a bear hug.

We let it be known the first order of business in the recovering Hazellands was to start a new junior school. Nora and Nieve shared the major teaching duties and half a dozen families took us up on the offer. Ruby now had classmates to boss around and hopefully that would stop her from getting me into trouble.

I convinced Lorcan to come and supervise the rebuilding of the Hall of Knowledge. If I was going to be in charge of creating a Tir na Nog university then I needed the very best builder/architect for the job. His one condition – I never call him Lorcan the Leprechaun again. I'll keep to that – until he's finished.

Tuan agreed to make his home in the Hazellands too. He is teaching Pooka studies and advanced critter morphing. Brendan is on a monthly commute between running the armoury in Duir and coming to the Hazellands to teach archery and spend time with Ruby. 'Even in Pixieland I can't avoid a long commute to work,' he complains.

Graysea teaches swimming and her first pupil was Araf. Every time I saw him walking back dripping from the pond I would hide so he wouldn't kill me.

Araf and Essa are really in their elements. Araf teaches agriculture and flower arranging as well as supervising The Field. Essa became professor of winemaking and banta-stick fighting.

Dahy had been gone for months when he showed up in the Hazellands. Weeks ago I had given him up as lost at sea.

'I thought you had sailed off and become a Grey One and more,' I said when he showed up in my temporary office in the ruins of the Hall of Knowledge.

'I will not lie to you, Conor, I came very close to doing just that but then I remembered your grandfather Liam and how he so loved this place and I had to help you restore it.'

Dahy wasn't a huggy kind of guy but I hugged him anyway. He even kind of returned it with a little pat on the back. 'Thanks Diddo, I need you.'

When I stepped back there was a scary look on the old master's face. 'Just because you are a Runelord now,' he said, 'doesn't mean you can call me Diddo.'

'Sorry, Master Dahy,' I quickly replied as I backed out of striking distance.

On the morning of the first day of the very first autumn term at the Hall of Knowledge University, Essa met me at the door and said, 'What the hell is that thing hanging around your neck?'

'It's a tie. It's what professors wear when they go to work in the Real World.'

'Well, I think it looks stupid,' she said.

'I always thought so too but today I need all of the psychological support I can get.'

'I have no idea what psychological means but I will always support you, my prince.' She kissed me and then hopped into the house and came back with a box tied with a bow.

'What's this?'

'I asked Nora what you are supposed to give as a gift to a first-day teacher.'

I undid the bow and smiled as I looked down at a beautiful shiny apple.

'Oh, and you get this too.' She kissed me, bade me good luck and pushed me out the door.

I walked into the central courtyard and stood before the new Tree of Knowledge. It was still young but it was lush and well over two storeys high. I placed my hand on the trunk and asked, 'Are you going to wish me luck too?'

Hazels are much too cool to actually converse with the Hawathiee but I could have sworn I felt an approving nod.

When I turned to leave I saw that Nieve had been watching me.

'You're not going to throw a spear at me, are you?'

My aunt walked towards me, took my face in her hands and kissed my forehead. 'No, I was going to do this.' She hooked her arm into mine and walked me to the new classrooms. It was fitting that Nieve was with me. The moment I first set eyes on her was the beginning of all the madness that I now just call life. 'Your father would be very proud, Conor.'

'My father, when he found out what I was teaching, would laugh his butt off.'

Nieve laughed with me. 'He probably would, but he still would have been very proud. I'm actually a little surprised you are teaching a course. I would have thought you would have been too busy.'

'Oh, I am too busy but I refuse to be relegated to ministerial paperwork and manuscript filing. I wanted to teach a course on joke-telling but no one would let me. Even when I pointed out I was the Lord of the Hazellands, they still wouldn't let me.'

We arrived at the classroom door. She brushed some lint off of my shoulder and then reached for my tie. 'What is this around your neck?'

'I'm not even going to explain it to you Auntie, 'cause I'm never going to wear one again. Do you want to come in and watch my first day as a professor?'

'No, Brendan and I are soon leaving for Castle Duir.'

'You know I would love to have you here, Nieve, but I'm glad you are helping Mom.'

She kissed me again, 'Are you all prepared?'

'Oh, if there is one thing Dad prepared me for – it's teaching this class.'

My students all stood and came to attention when I walked into the room. There was half a dozen: four Faeries, one female Imp and, I was glad to see, a nervous looking Banshee. They were all bright-eyed and young. They had taken this course in hopes of soon going on a Real World walk-about.

'Sit, sit,' I said, 'there is none of that bowing stuff in here. In here I am not Lord Anything.' I scratched my name on the blackboard behind me. 'I am Mister Conor O'Neil. You can call me by my first name – Mister.'

I looked for a reaction and got nothin'. Maybe it was a good thing I wasn't teaching joke-telling.

'Right, welcome to my class – Modern Real World Languages. I know you're not going to like it much but I'm going to teach you the way I learned. So,' I took a deep breath and when I spoke I surprised myself at just how much I sounded like my father. 'The language of the day is – Greek.'

Acknowledgements

It's hard writing a novel but these people made it a lot easier.

Yvonne Light, the uber-hyphenator.

Evo, Chris & Tee at the fabulous Podiobooks.com.

Scott and all at The Friday Project.

The amusing and inspiring commenters on the Hazel & Oak bulletin board at podiobooks (especially those that spotted my mistakes).

And everyone that emailed me at john@shadowmagic.co.uk – thank you so much. The kind words I have received about *Shadowmagic* make it a lot easier to sit down and put my fingers on the keyboard every day.

Shadowmagic

and

Shadowmagic:
Prince of Hazel and Oak

and

Shadowmagic:
Sons of Macha

are all available as free podcasts from
iTunes and www.podiobooks.com

and are read by the author